WAVES OF DEATH

Hornblower pulled off his cloak and left himself exposed to the spray that hurtled at him. He poised himself for a leap and sprang for the boom. As he landed on it a wave broke across it, sousing him to the skin, and he had to clutch desperately with fingers and toes to save himself from being washed off.

Suddenly he was riding an enormous tree trunk, clawing his way on all fours along the log, balancing in nightmare fashion on a pitching and rolling mount that could hurl him to his death at any moment. But he had no choice. There was more than his life at stake—there was England . . .

The Hornblower Saga

MR. MIDSHIPMAN HORNBLOWER
LIEUTENANT HORNBLOWER
HORNBLOWER AND THE HOTSPUR
HORNBLOWER AND THE ATROPOS
BEAT TO QUARTERS
SHIP OF THE LINE
FLYING COLORS
COMMODORE HORNBLOWER
LORD HORNBLOWER
ADMIRAL HORNBLOWER IN THE WEST
   INDIES
HORNBLOWER DURING THE CRISIS

   Also by C. S. Forester
THE HORNBLOWER COMPANION

NUMBER EIGHT IN THE

HORNBLOWER SAGA

The greatest naval adventures of all time!

COMMODORE HORNBLOWER

C.S. FORESTER

PINNACLE BOOKS • **LOS ANGELES**

COMMODORE HORNBLOWER

Copyright 1945, by the Curtis Publishing Company Copyright 1945, by C. S. Forester. Copyright renewed 1973 by Dorothy E. Forester

A Pinnacle Books edition, published by special arrangement with Little, Brown and Company.

ISBN: 0-523-40869-2

First printing, March 1975
Second printing, August 1975
Third printing, July 1976
Fourth printing, September 1978
Fifth printing, March 1980

Printed in the United States of America

PINNACLE BOOKS, INC.
2029 Century Park East
Los Angeles, California 90067

Chapter I

CAPTAIN SIR HORATIO HORNBLOWER sat in his bath, regarding with distaste his legs dangling over the end. They were thin and hairy, and recalled to his mind the legs of the spiders he had seen in Central America. It was hard to think about anything except his legs, seeing how they were forced upon his attention by their position under his nose as he sat in this ridiculous bath; they hung out at one end while his body protruded from the water at the other. It was only the middle portion of him, from his waist to above his knees, which was submerged, and that was bent almost double. Hornblower found it irritating to have to take a bath in this fashion, although he tried not to allow it to irritate him, and he strove desperately to dismiss from his mind recollections of thousands of more comfortable baths taken on the deck of a ship, under a wash-deck pump which threw over him unlimited quantities of stimulating seawater. He seized his soap and flannel, and began viciously to wash those parts of himself above the surface, and as he did so water slopped in quantities over the side onto the polished oak floor of his dressing room. That meant trouble for a housemaid, and in Hornblower's present mood he was glad to cause trouble.

He rose awkwardly to his feet in the bath, water flying in all directions, soaped and washed off the middle of himself, and yelled for Brown. Brown came in at once from the bedroom, although a good servant would have sensed his master's mood and delayed for a second or two so as to be sworn at. He hung a warm towel over Hornblower's shoulders, dexterously preventing the ends from dipping into the water as

1

Hornblower stepped out of the soapy mess and walked across the floor, leaving upon it a trail of drops and wet footprints. Hornblower towelled himself and stared gloomily through the door into the bedroom at the clothes which Brown had laid out for him.

"It's a lovely morning, sir," said Brown.

"God damn your eyes," said Hornblower.

He would have to put on that damned suit of buff and blue, the varnished boots and the gold fob; he had never worn that suit before, and he had hated it when the tailor tried it on him, hated it when his wife admired it, and he supposed he would go on hating it for the rest of his days and still have to wear it. His hatred was a double one, firstly a simple blind unreasoning hatred, and secondly a hatred for a suit which he was quite sure did not properly set off his looks, making him appear absurd instead of merely plain. He pulled the two-guinea linen shirt over his head, and then with infinite trouble dragged the tight buff trousers up over his legs. They fitted him like a skin, and it was only when they were fully on, and Brown had slipped behind him and hauled the waistband taut, that he realised that he had not yet put on his stockings. To take the trousers off again would be to admit a mistake, and he refused to do so, ripping out another oath at Brown's suggestion. Philosophically Brown knelt and rolled up the tight trouser legs, but they would not roll even as far as the knee, making it hopeless to try to put on the long stockings.

"Cut the tops off the damned things!" spluttered Hornblower.

Brown, kneeling on the floor, rolled a protesting eye up at him, but what he saw in Hornblower's face cut short anything he had in mind to say. In disciplined silence Brown obeyed orders, bringing the scissors from the dressing table. Snip, snip, snip! The tops of the stockings fell to the floor, and Hornblower put his feet into the mutilated ends and felt the first satisfaction of the day as Brown rolled down the trousers over them. The Fates might be against him, but he would show them that he still had a will of his own, by God. He crammed his feet into the varnished boots and refrained from swearing at their tightness—he remembered guiltily that he had been weak with the fashionable bootmaker and had not insisted on comfort, not with his wife standing by to see that the dictates of fashion were obeyed.

He stumped across to the dressing table and tied his neckcloth, and Brown buckled his stock. The ridiculous thing brushed his ears as he turned his head and his neck felt as if it were being stretched to double its length. He had never been more uncomfortable in his life; he would never draw an easy breath while wearing this damned choker which Brummell and the Prince Regent had made fashionable. He slipped on the flowered waistcoat—blue sprigged with pink—and then the broadcloth coat, buff, with big blue buttons; the inside of the pocket flaps and the reverse of the lapels and collar were of a matching blue. For twenty years Hornblower had worn nothing except uniform, and the image that the mirror reflected back to his jaundiced eyes was unnatural, grotesque, ridiculous. Uniform was comforting—no one could blame him if it did not suit him, because he had to wear it. But with civilian clothes he was presumed to display his own taste and choice—even though he was a married man—and people could laugh at him for what he wore. Brown attached the gold watch to the fob, and forced it into the pocket. It made an unsightly bulge there, over his belly, but Hornblower furiously put aside the idea of going without a watch so as to allow his clothes to fit better. He stuffed into his sleeve the linen handkerchief which Brown handed him after shaking scent onto it, and then he was ready.

"That's a beautiful suit, sir," said Brown.

"Beautiful rubbish!" said Hornblower.

3

He stumped back across the dressing room and knocked on the farther door.

"Come in," said his wife's voice.

Barbara was still sitting in her bath, her legs dangling over the edge just as his own had done.

"How handsome you look, dear," said Barbara. "It's a refreshing change to see you out of uniform."

Even Barbara, the nicest woman in the world, was not free of the besetting sin of womankind, approving of change merely because it was change; but Hornblower did not answer her as he had answered Brown.

"Thank you," he said, trying desperately to sound gracious as he said it.

"My towel, Hebe," said Barbara. The little Negro maid came gliding forward, and wrapped her up as she stepped out of the hip bath.

"Venus rises from the waves," said Hornblower gallantly. He was doing his best to fight down the feeling of awkwardness which possessed him when he saw his wife naked in the presence of another woman, even though Hebe was a mere servant, and coloured.

"I expect," said Barbara, standing while Hebe patted the towel to her skin to dry her, "the village has already heard of this strange habit of ours of taking baths every day. I can hardly imagine what they think of it."

Hornblower could imagine; he had been a village boy himself, once. Barbara threw off the towel and stood naked again for a moment as Hebe passed her silk shift over her head. Women, once the barriers were down, really had no sense of decency, and Barbara in that transparent shift was even more shocking than when she was naked. She sat at the dressing table and set to work to cream her face while Hebe brushed her hair; there were a myriad pots and jars on the dressing table and Barbara took ingredients from one after the other as though compounding a witches' brew.

"I'm glad to see," said Barbara, inspecting her re-

4

flection closely, "that the sun is shining. It is well to have a fine day for this morning's ceremony."

The thought of the ceremony had been in Hornblower's mind ever since he woke up; it could not be said that he disliked the prospect, but he was not comfortable about it. It would be the first landmark in a new way of life, and Hornblower felt a not unnatural distrust of his own reflections of his face in her mirror.

"Welcome to the new Squire of Smallbridge," she said, and smiled, turning towards him.

The smile transformed not only her expression but Hornblower's whole mental outlook as well. Barbara ceased to be the great lady, the earl's daughter with the bluest blood of the aristocracy in her veins, whose perfect poise and aplomb always afflicted Hornblower with the diffidence he detested; instead she became the woman who had stood unfrightened beside him upon the shot-torn decks of the *Lydia* in the Pacific, the woman who knew love in his arms, the beloved companion and the companionable lover. Hornblower's heart went out to her on the instant. He would have taken her in his arms and kissed her if it had not been that Hebe was in the room. But Barbara's eyes met his and read in them what was in his mind. She smiled another smile at him; they were in perfect accord with secrets shared between them and the world was a brighter place for both of them.

Barbara pulled on a pair of white silk stockings, and knotted above her knees the scarlet silk garters. Hebe stood ready with her gown, and Barbara dived into it. The gown flapped and billowed as Barbara made her way into it, and then at last she emerged, her arms waving as they pushed into the sleeves, and her hair tousled. No one could be a great lady in those conditions, and Hornblower loved her more dearly than ever. Hebe settled the gown about her mistress and hung a lace cape over her shoulders ready for the final adjustment of her hair. When the last pin had been inserted, the last curl fixed in place, the shoes eased upon her feet by a grovelling Hebe with a shoehorn, Barbara devoted her attention to settling on her head the vast hat with the roses and ribbons.

"And what is the time, my dear?" she asked.

"Nine o'clock," said Hornblower, hauling his watch with an effort from out of the tense fob-pocket in the front of his trousers.

"Excellent," said Barbara, reaching for the long white silk gloves which had come to her by devious smuggler's routes from Paris. "Hebe, Master Richard will be ready now. Tell nurse to bring him to me. And I think, dear, that your ribbon and star would be in the spirit of this morning's occasion."

"At my own front door?" protested Hornblower.

"I fear so," said Barbara. She wagged her head with its pyramid of roses, and this time it was not so much a smile that she bestowed upon him as a grin, and all Hornblower's objections to wearing his star evaporated on the spot. It was a tacit admission that she attached no more importance, as far as he and she were concerned, to the ceremony of welcoming him as the new Squire of Smallbridge than Hornblower himself. It was as if an augur winked.

In his bedroom Hornblower took the red ribbon of the Bath and the star from the drawer in his wardrobe, and Brown found for him the dogskin gloves which he tugged on as he walked down the stairs. A scared housemaid dropped him a curtsey; in the hall stood Wiggins the butler with Hornblower's tall beaver hat, and beside him John the footman in the new livery which Barbara had chosen. And here came Barbara with Richard in his nurse's arms. Richard's curls were pomaded into stiff decorum. The nurse set him down and twitched his petticoats and his lace collar into position, and Hornblower hastened to take one of his hands while Barbara took the other; Richard was not yet sufficiently accustomed to standing on his feet and was liable to go down on all fours

6

in a way which might not suit the dignity of his morning's ceremony. Wiggins and John threw open the door, and the three of them, Barbara and Hornblower with Richard between them, walked out to the head of the steps above the driveway, Hornblower remembering just in time to clap the tall hat on his head before crossing the threshold.

It seemed as if every inhabitant of Smallbridge were formed up below them. On one side was the parson with a herd of children; in front of the four tenant farmers in ill-fitting broadcloth with their labourers in their smocks, and on the other side a cluster of women in aprons and bonnets. Behind the children the ostler at the Coach and Horses stuck a fiddle under his chin and played a note; the parson waved a hand and the children burst into shrill piping:—

"See-ee the *conk*-ring he-ee-ee-ee-ero comes,
Sow-ow-ow-ow-ound the *trum*-pets, bee-ee-ee-eat the drums!"

Obviously this was meant for Hornblower, and he took off his hat and stood awkwardly; the tune meant nothing to his tone-deaf ear, but he could distinguish some of the words. The chorus came to a ragged end, and the parson took a step forward.

"Your ladyship," he began, "Sir Horatio. Welcome in the name of the village. Welcome, Sir Horatio, with all the glory you have won in the war against the Corsican tyrant. Welcome, your ladyship, wife of the hero before us, sister of the hero commanding our valiant army now in Spain, daughter of the highest nobility in the land! Welcome—"

"Man!" yelled Richard unexpectedly. "Da-da!"

The parson took the interruption without flinching; already well in his stride he continued to mouth out his fulsome sentences, telling of the joy the village of Smallbridge felt at finding itself in the ownership of a

7

famous sailor. Hornblower was distracted from the discourse by the necessity of holding on tight to Richard's hand—if Richard once got loose he evidently would go down on all fours and throw himself down the steps to make a closer acquaintance with the village children. Hornblower looked out over the lush green of the park; beyond it rose the massive curves of the Downs, and to one side the tower of Smallbridge church rose above the trees. On that side, too, an orchard was in full bloom, exquisitely lovely. Park and orchard and church were all his; he was the squire, a landed gentleman, owner of many acres, being welcomed by his tenantry. Behind him was his house, full of his servants; on his breast the ribbon and star of an order of chivalry; and in London Coutts & Company had in their vaults a store of golden guineas which were his as well. This was the climax of a man's ambition. Fame, wealth, security, love, a child—he had all that heart could desire. Hornblower, standing at the head of the steps while the parson droned on, was puzzled to find that he was still not happy. He was irritated with himself in consequence. He ought to be running over with pride and joy and happiness, and yet here he was contemplating the future with faint dismay; dismay at the thought of living on here, and positive distaste at the thought of spending the fashionable season in London, even though Barbara would be beside him all the time.

These disorderly thoughts of Hornblower's were suddenly broken into. Something had been said which should not have been said, and as the parson was the only person speaking, he must have said it, although he was still droning along in obvious ignorance of any blunder. Hornblower stole a glance at Barbara; her white teeth showed for a moment against her lower lip, clear proof of her vexation to anyone who knew her well. Otherwise she was exhibiting the stoical calm of the British upper classes. What was it that

8

had been said to upset her? Hornblower raked through his subconscious memory to recall the words the parson had been using, and which he had heard without attending. Yes, that was it. The stupid fool had spoken about Richard as though he were the child of both of them. It irritated Barbara unbearably to have her stepson taken to be her own child, and the more fond she grew of him the more it irritated her, curiously enough. But it was hard to blame the parson for his mistake; when a married pair arrives with a sixteen-months-old baby it is only natural to assume it to be their child.

Fortunately the parson went off at a tangent again; having given his attention to Barbara and Richard he now adverted to Hornblower's career.

"The man whose name is on every lip as the most daring, the most brilliant, and most successful of all the brilliant captains of whose services the British Navy can boast! The hero who as a young lieutenant boarded single-handed the deck of the *Castilla*—who as a young frigate captain in the lonely wastes of the Pacific in command of the fall *Lydia* fought and destroyed the huge *Natividad*—who carried the British flag to waters in which it had never before penetrated—who in command of a ship of the line flung himself upon the French squadron in Rosas Bay and achieved its destruction at the cost of his own captivity—and yet who, flung into the deepest dungeon by the tyrant Bonaparte, yet contrived to escape to wrench the cutter *Witch of Endor* from the ogre's grasp and sail home in her to the honour and the glory and the happiness which awaited him and which he so richly merited!"

"Hooray!" yelled the villagers.

The cheering came to an end and Hornblower suddenly realised that he had to speak in reply. He cursed himself for a fool for not having foreseen this obvious next step, and as he cursed himself the

9

silence grew longer and more awkward. Every eye was upon him.

"Ha—h'm," said Hornblower—he had still not been married long enough to Barbara to have completely mastered that old habit—while he groped wildly for something to say. He ought to have been ready for this, of course; he ought to have been preparing a speech instead of standing day-dreaming. "Ha—h'm. It is with pride that I look over this English countryside—"

He managed to say all that was necessary. The Corsican tyrant. The yeoman stock of England. The King and the Prince Regent. Lady Barbara. Richard. When he finished there was another awkward pause while people looked at each other, before one of the farmers stepped forward.

"Three cheers for 'er ladyship!"

Everyone cheered, to Richard's astonishment, expressed in a loud yell.

"Three cheers for Sir Horatio! One, two, three an' a tiger!"

There was nothing left to do now, except to withdraw gracefully into the house again and leave the tenantry to disperse. Thank God it was all over, anyway. John the footman stood at what he obviously thought was attention in the hall. Hornblower made a weary mental note to teach him to keep his elbows into his sides. If he were going to employ a footman he would make a good footman out of him. Here came the nurse, swooping down to find out how wet Richard had made himself. And here came the butler, hobbling along with a letter on a salver. Hornblower felt a rush of blood into his face as he saw the seal; that seal and that thick linen paper were used only by the Admiralty, as far as he knew. It was months, and it seemed like years, since he had last received any letter from the Admiralty. He snatched the letter from the salver, and only by the mercy of Providence

10

remembered to glance at Barbara in apology, before breaking the seal.

THE LORDS COMMISSIONERS OF THE ADMIRALTY,
WHITEHALL,
10th April, 1812.

Sir,

I am commanded by the Lords Commissioners to inform you that Their Lordships desire to employ you immediately as Commodore with a Captain under you on a service which Their Lordships consider worthy of an officer of your seniority and standing. You are hereby requested and required, therefore, to inform Their Lordships through me as speedily as possible as to whether or not you will accept this appointment, and in the event of your accepting it you are further requested and required to present yourself in person at this office without delay in order to receive verbally Their Lordships' instructions and also those of any other Minister of State whom it may be judged necessary you should address.

Your obed't servant,
E. NEPEAN, Sec^y to the Lords
Commissioners of the Admiralty.

Hornblower had to read the letter twice—the first time it conveyed no meaning to him at all. But at the second reading the glorious import of the letter burst in upon him. The first thing he was conscious of was that this life here in Smallbridge or in Bond Street need not continue. He was free of all that; he could take a bath under a wash-deck pump instead of in a damned hip bath with a kettleful of water in it; he could walk his own deck, breathe the sea air, take off these damned tight trousers and never put them on again; receive no deputations, speak to no damned tenants, never smell another pigsty or smack another horse's back. And that was only the first thing; the second was that he was being offered appointment as commodore—a commodore of the first class, too, with a captain under him, so that he would be like an admiral. He would have a broad pendant flying at the mainmast-head, compliments and honours—not that they mattered, but they would be outward signs of the trust reposed in him, of the promotion that was his. Louis at the Admiralty must have a good opinion of him, clearly, to appoint him commodore when he was hardly more than halfway up the captains' list. Of course, that phrase about "worthy of his seniority and standing" was merely formula, justifying the Admiralty in anticipation in putting him on half-pay should he decline; but—those last words, about consulting with Ministers of State, had enormous import. They meant that the mission to be entrusted to him would be one of responsibility, of international importance. Waves of excitement broke over him.

He hauled out his watch. Ten fifteen—the day was still young by civilian standards.

"Where's Brown?" he snapped at Wiggins.

Brown materialised miraculously in the background—not too miraculously, perhaps; the whole house must be aware of course that the master had received a letter from the Admiralty.

"Get out my best uniform and my sword. Have the horses put to in the chariot. You had better come with me, Brown—I shall want you to drive. Have my things for the night ready and yours too."

The servants scattered in all directions, for not merely must the weighty orders of the master be obeyed, but this was an affair of state and doubly important in consequence. So that as Hornblower came out of his preoccupation Barbara was standing there alone.

God, he had forgotten all about her in his excitement, and she was aware of it. She was drooping a little, and one corner of her mouth was down. Their

12

eyes met then, and that corner of her mouth went up for a moment, but then it went down again.

"It's the Admiralty," explained Hornblower lamely. "They'll appoint me commodore with a captain under me."

It was a pity that Hornblower could see her try to appear pleased.

"That's a high compliment," she said. "No more than you deserve, my dear, all the same. You must be pleased, and I am too."

"It will take me away from you," said Hornblower.

"Darling, I have had six months with you. Six months of the kind of happiness you have given me is more than any woman deserves. And you will come back to me."

"Of course I will," said Hornblower.

Chapter II

THIS was typical April weather. It had been miraculously sunny during the ceremony at the foot of the steps of Smallbridge House, but it had rained torrentially once already during the twenty-mile drive to London. Then the sun had reappeared, had warmed and dried them; but now as they crossed Wimbledon Common the sky was black again, and the first drops began to drive into their faces. Hornblower pulled his cloak about him and rebuttoned the collar. His cocked hat with its gold lace and button lay on his knees under the sheltering tent of the cloak; cocked hats worn for long in the rain accumulated pools of water in both crown and brim and were pulled out of shape.

Now it came, wind and rain, shrieking down from the west in unbelievable contrast to the delightful weather of only half an hour before. The near-side horse had the full brunt of it and was inclined to shirk its work in consequence. Brown laid the whiplash on its glistening haunch and it threw itself into the collar in a fresh spasm of energy. Brown was a good whip—he was good at everything. He had been the best captain's coxswain Hornblower had ever known, he had been a loyal subordinate during the escape from France, and he had made himself into the best manservant heart could desire. Now he sat here, tolerant of the driving rain, the slippery leather of the reins grasped in a big brown hand; hand and wrist and forearm acted like a spring to maintain that subtle pressure upon the horses' mouths—not enough pressure to interfere in the least with their work, but enough to give them confidence on the slippery road, and to have them under control in any emergency. They were pulling the chariot over the muddy macadam up the steep ascent of Wimbledon Common with a wholeheartedness they never displayed for Hornblower.

"Would you like to go to sea again, Brown?" asked Hornblower. The mere fact that he allowed himself to make this unnecessary speech was proof of how much Hornblower was lifted out of himself with excitement.

"I'd like it main well, sir," said Brown shortly.

Hornblower was left to guess what Brown really meant—whether his curtness was just the English way of concealing enthusiasm, or whether Brown was merely being in polite agreement with his master's mood.

The rain from Hornblower's wet hair was trickling down his neck now inside his collar. He ought to have brought a sou'-wester with him. He hunched himself together on the padded leather seat, resting his two hands on the hilt of the sword belted round his waist—the hundred-guinea sword given him by the Patriotic Fund. With the sword vertical his hands held the heavy wet cloak away from the cocked hat on

14

his knees. Another little rivulet coursed down inside his clothes and made him squirm. By the time the shower had passed he was thoroughly damp and uncomfortable, but here once more came the glorious sun. The raindrops in the gorse and the brambles shone like diamonds; the horses steamed; larks resumed their song far overhead, and Hornblower threw open his cloak and wiped his damp hair and neck with his handkerchief. Brown eased the horses to a walk at the crest of the hill to breathe them before the brisk descent.

"London, sir," he said.

And there it was. The rain had washed the smoke and dust out of the air so that even at that distance the gilt cross and ball over St. Paul's gleamed in the sunshine. The church spires, dwarfed by the dome, stood out with unnatural clarity. The very roof tops were distinct. Brown clicked his tongue at the horses and they broke once more into a trot, rattling the chariot down the steep descent into Wandsworth, and Hornblower pulled out his watch. It was no more than two o'clock, ample time to do business. Even though his shirt was damp inside his coat this was a far better day than he had anticipated when he sat in his bath that morning.

Brown drew the horses to a halt outside the Admiralty, and a ragged urchin appeared who guarded the wheel so that it did not muddy Hornblower's cloak and uniform as he climbed down from the chariot.

"At the Golden Cross, then, Brown," said Hornblower, fumbling for a copper for the urchin.

"Aye aye, sir," said Brown, wheeling the horses round.

Hornblower carefully put on his cocked hat, settled his coat more smoothly, and centred the buckle of his swordbelt. At Smallbridge House he was Sir Horatio, master of the house, lord of the manor, autocrat undisputed, but now he was just Captain Hornblower going in to see the Lords of the Admiralty. But Admi-

15

ral Louis was all cordiality. He left Hornblower waiting no more than three minutes in the anteroom—no longer than would be necessary to get rid of his visitor of the moment—and he shook hands with obvious pleasure at the sight of him; he rang the bell for a clerk to take Hornblower's wet cloak away, and with his own hands he pulled up a chair for him beside the vast fire which Louis maintained summer and winter since his return from the command of the East Indian Station.

"Lady Barbara is well, I trust?" he asked.

"Very well, thank you, sir," said Hornblower.

"And Master Hornblower?"

"Very well too, sir."

Hornblower was mastering his shyness rapidly. He sat farther back in his chair and welcomed the heat of the fire. That was a new portrait of Collingwood on the wall; it must have replaced the old one of Lord Barham. It was pleasant to note the red ribbon and the star and to look down at his own breast and to see that he wore the same decoration.

"And yet you left domestic bliss at the first moment you received our letter?"

"Of course, sir."

Hornblower realised that perhaps it might be more profitable not to be natural; it might be better to adopt a pose, to appear reluctant to take up his professional duties, or to make it look as if he were making a great personal sacrifice for his country, but for the life of him he could not do it. He was too pleased with his promotion, too full of curiosity regarding the mission the Admiralty had in mind for him. Louis' keen eyes were studying him closely, and he met their gaze frankly.

"What is it you plan for me, sir?" he asked; he would not even wait for Louis to make the first move.

"The Baltic," said Louis.

So that was it. The two words terminated a morning of wild speculation, tore up a wide cobweb of possibilities. It might have been anywhere in the world; Java or Jamaica, Cape Horn or the Cape of Good Hope, the Indian Ocean or the Mediterranean, anywhere within the twenty-five-thousand-mile circuit of the world where the British flag flew. And it was going to be the Baltic; Hornblower tried to sort out in his mind what he knew about the Baltic. He had not sailed in northern waters since he was a junior lieutenant.

"Admiral Keats is commanding there, isn't he?"

"At the moment, yes. But Saumarez is replacing him. His orders will be to give you the widest latitude of discretion."

That was a curious thing to say. It hinted at division of command, and that was inherently vicious. Better a bad commander-in-chief than a divided command. To tell a subordinate that his superior was under orders to grant him wide discretion was a dangerous thing to do, unless the subordinate was a man of superlative loyalty and commonsense. Hornblower gulped at that moment—he had honestly forgotten temporarily that he was the subordinate under consideration; maybe the Admiralty credited him with "superlative loyalty and commonsense."

Louis was eyeing him curiously.

"Don't you want to hear the size of your command?" he asked.

"Yes, of course," answered Hornblower, but he did not mind very much. The fact that he was going to command something was much more important than what he was going to command.

"You'll have the *Nonsuch*, seventy four," said Louis. "That will give you a ship of force should you need one. For the rest you'll have all the small stuff we can scrape together for you—*Lotus* and *Raven*, sloops; two bomb-ketches, *Moth* and *Harvey*; and the cutter *Clam*. That's all so far, but by the time you sail we might have some more ready for you. We want you to

17

be ready for all the inshore work that may come your way. There's likely to be plenty."

"I expect so," said Hornblower.

"Don't know whether you'll be fighting for the Russians or against them," mused Louis. "Same with the Swedes. God knows what's building up up there. But His Nibs'll tell you all about that."

Hornblower looked a question.

"Your revered brother-in-law, the most noble the Marquis Wellesley, K.P., His Britannic Majesty's Secretary of State for Foreign Affairs. We call him His Nibs for short. We'll walk across and see him in a minute. But there's something else important to settle. Who d'you want for captain in *Nonsuch?*"

Hornblower gasped at that. This was patronage on a grand scale. He had sometimes appointed midshipmen and surgeon's mates; a parson of shady record had once hungrily solicited him for nomination as chaplain in his ship, but to have a say in the appointment of a captain of a ship of the line was something infinitely more important than any of these. There were a hundred and twenty captains junior to Hornblower, men of most distinguished record, whose achievements were talked of with bated breath in the four quarters of the world, and who had won their way to that rank at the cost of their blood and by the performance of feats of skill and daring unparalleled in history. Certainly half of these, perhaps more, would jump at the suggestion of the command of a seventy four. Hornblower remembered his own joy at his appointment to *Sutherland* two years ago. Captains on half-pay, captains with shore appointments eating out their hearts with waiting for a sea command, it was in his power to change the whole life and career of one of these. Yet there was no hesitation about his decision. There might be more brilliant captains available, captains with more brains, but there was only one man that he wanted.

"I'll have Bush," he said, "if he's available."

"You can have him," said Louis, with a nod. "I was expecting you to ask for him. That wooden leg of his won't be too serious a handicap, you think."

"I don't think so," said Hornblower. It would have been irksome in the extreme to go to sea with any other captain than Bush.

"Very well, then," said Louis, looking round at the clock on the wall. "Let's walk across and see His Nibs, if you've no objection."

Chapter III

HORNBLOWER sat in his private sitting-room in the Golden Cross Inn. There was a fire burning, and on the table at which he sat there were no fewer than four wax candles lighted. All this luxury—the private sitting-room, the fire, the wax candles—gave Hornblower uneasy delight. He had been poor for so long, he had had to scrape and economise so carefully all his life, that recklessness with money gave him this queer dubious pleasure, this guilty joy. His bill tomorrow would contain an item of at least half a crown for light, and if he had been content with rush dips the charge would not have been more than twopence. The fire would be a shilling, too. And he could trust an innkeeper to make the maximum charges to a guest who obviously could afford them, a Knight of the Bath, with a servant, and a two-horse chariot. Tomorrow's bill would be nearer two guineas than one—Hornblower touched his breast pocket to reassure himself that his thick wad of one-pound notes was still there. He could afford to spend two guineas a day.

Reassured, he bent again to the notes which he had made during his interview with the Foreign

19

Secretary. They were in irregular order, jotted down as first one thing and then another had come into Wellesley's mind. It was quite clear that not even the Cabinet knew for certain whether the Russians were going to fight Bonaparte or not. No, that was the wrong way to put it. Nobody knew whether Bonaparte was going to fight the Russians or not. However much ill will the Czar bore towards the French—and obviously it was great—he would not fight unless he had to, unless Bonaparte deliberately attacked him. Certainly the Czar would make every possible concession rather than fight, at least at present while he was still trying to build up and reorganise his army.

"It's hard to think Boney will be mad enough to pick a quarrel," Wellesley had said, "when he can get practically all he wants without fighting."

But if there was going to be war it was desirable that England should have a striking force in the Baltic.

"If Boney chases Alexander out of Russia, I want you to be on hand to pick him up," said Wellesley. "We can always find a use for him."

Kings in exile were at least useful figureheads for any resistance that might still be maintained by countries which Bonaparte had overrun. Under her protecting wing England had the rulers of Sicily and Sardinia, the Netherlands and Portugal and Hesse, all of them helping to keep alive hope in the bosoms of their former subjects now ground beneath the tyrant's heel.

"So much depends on Sweden," was another remark of Wellesley's. "No one can guess what Bernadotte will do. Russia's conquest of Finland has irritated the Swedes, too. We try and point out to them that of the two Bonaparte's the worse menace to 'em. He's at the mouth of the Baltic, while Russia's only at the top. But it can't be comfortable for Sweden, having to choose between Russia and Bonaparte."

That was a pretty tangle, one way and the other—Sweden ruled by a Crown Prince who only three years before had been a French general, and some sort of connection by marriage with Bonaparte at that; Denmark and Norway in the tyrant's hands; Finland newly conquered by Russia, and the south shore of the Baltic swarming with Bonaparte's troops.

"He has army camps at Danzig and Stettin," Wellesley had said, "and South German troops echelonned all the way back to Berlin, to say nothing of the Prussians and the Austrians and the other allies."

With Europe at his feet Bonaparte was able to drag in his train the armies of his late enemies; if he were to make war upon Russia it seemed as though a substantial part of his army would be foreigners—Italians and South Germans, Prussians and Austrians, Dutchmen and Danes.

"There are even Spaniards and Portuguese, they tell me," said Wellesley. "I hope they have enjoyed the recent winter in Poland. You speak Spanish, I understand?"

Hornblower had said, "Yes."

"And French too?"

"Yes."

"Russian?"

"No."

"German?"

"No."

"Swedish? Polish? Lithuanian?"

"No."

"A pity. But most of the educated Russians speak French better than Russian, they tell me—although in that case, judging by the Russians I have met, they must be very ignorant of their own language. And we have a Swedish interpreter for you—you will have to arrange with the Admiralty how he will be rated in the ship's books—I believe that is the correct nautical expression."

It was typical of Wellesley to put in that little

21

sneer. He was an ex-Governor-General of India, and the present Foreign Secretary, a man of blue blood and of the height of fashion. In those few words he had been able to convey all his sublime ignorance and his consequent sublime contempt for matters nautical, as well as the man of fashion's feeling of lordly superiority over the uncouth sea-dog, even when the sea-dog in question happened to be his own brother-in-law. Hornblower had been a little nettled, and was still feeling sufficiently above himself to endeavour to irritate Wellesley in return.

"You are a master of all trades, Richard," he said, evenly.

It was just as well to remind the man of fashion that the sea-dog was closely enough related to be entitled to use the Christian name, and, in addition to that, it might annoy the Marquis to suggest he had anything to do with a trade.

"Not of yours, Hornblower, I'm afraid. Never could learn all those ports and starboards and back-your-lees and things of that sort. One has to learn those as a schoolboy, like *hic, haec, hoc*."

It was hard to prick the Marquis's sublime complacency; Hornblower turned away from that memory back to serious business. The Russians had a fair navy, as many as fourteen ships of the line, perhaps, at Reval and Kronstadt; Sweden nearly as many. The German and Pomeranian ports swarmed with French privateers, and an important part of Hornblower's duty would be to help protect British shipping from these wolves of the sea, for the Swedish trade was vital to England. From the Baltic came the naval stores that enabled England to rule the sea—the tar and the turpentine, the pine trees for masts, cordage and timber, rosin and oil. If Sweden were to ally herself with Bonaparte against Russia the Swedish contribution to the trade—far more than half—would be lost, and England would have to struggle along with the little that could be gleaned from Finland and Esthonia, convoyed through the Baltic in the teeth of the Swedish navy, and somehow got out through The Sound even though Bonaparte was master of Denmark. Russia would want those stores for her own navy, and she must be persuaded one way or another to part with enough to maintain the British navy at sea.

It was as well that England had not come to the rescue of Finland when Russia had attacked her; if she had there would be far less chance of Russia's going to war with Bonaparte. Diplomacy backed by force might perhaps protect Sweden from allying herself with Bonaparte, and might make the Baltic trade safe and might open the North German coastline to raids against Bonaparte's communications—under that sort of pressure, if by any miracle Bonaparte should sustain a reverse, even Prussia might be persuaded to change sides. That would be another of Hornblower's tasks, to help woo Sweden from her hereditary distrust of Russia, and to woo Prussia from her enforced alliance with France, while at the same time he must do nothing to imperil the Baltic trade. A false step could mean ruin.

Hornblower laid his notes down on the table and stared unseeing at the wall across the room. Fog and ice and shoals in the Baltic; the Russian navy and the Swedish navy and the French privateers; the Baltic trade and the Russian alliance and the attitude of Prussia; high politics and vital commerce—during the next few months the fate of Europe, the history of the world, would be balanced on a knife edge, and the responsibility would be his. Hornblower felt the quickening of his pulses, the tensing of his muscles, which he had known of old at the prospect of danger. Nearly a year had gone by since the last time he had experienced those symptoms, when he had entered the great cabin of the *Victory* to hear the verdict of the court-martial which might have condemned him to death. He felt he did not like this promise of peril,

23

this prospect of enormous responsibility; he had visualised nothing like this when he drove up earlier that day so gaily to receive his orders. It would be for this that he would be leaving Barbara's love and friendship, the life of a country squire, the tranquillity and peace of his newly won home.

Yet even while he sat there, almost despairing, almost disconsolate, the lure of the problems of the future began to make itself felt. He was being given a free hand by the Admiralty—he could not complain on that score. Reval froze in December; Kronstadt often in November. While the ice lasted he would have to base himself farther down the Baltic. Did Lübeck ever freeze? In any case it would be better to—Hornblower abruptly pushed his chair back from the table, quite unconscious of what he was doing. For him to think imaginatively while sitting still was quite impossible; he could do it for no longer than he could hold his breath; such a comparison was the more apt because if he was compelled to sit still when his brain was active he exhibited some of the characteristic symptoms of slow strangulation—his blood pressure mounted, and he thrashed about restlessly.

Tonight there was no question of having to sit still; having pushed back his chair he was able to pace up and down the room, from the table to the window and back again, a walk quite as long and perhaps more free from obstacles than he had known on many a quarterdeck. He had hardly begun when the sitting-room door opened quietly and Brown peered in through the crack, his attention attracted by the sound of the chair scraping on the floor. For Brown one glance was enough. The captain had begun to walk, which meant that he would not be going to bed for a very long time.

Brown was an intelligent man who used his brains on this job of looking after the captain. He closed the door again quietly, and waited a full ten minutes before entering the room. In ten minutes Hornblower had got well into the swing of his walk and his thoughts were pursuing a torrential course from which they could not easily be diverted. Brown was able to creep into the room without distracting his master—indeed, it would be very hard to say if Hornblower knew he entered or not. Brown, timing his moves accurately against the captain's crossing of the room, was able to reach the candles and snuff them—they had begun to gutter and to smell horribly—and then to reach the fireplace and put more coal on the fire, which had died down to red embers. Then he was able to make his way out of the room and settle down to a long wait; usually the captain was a considerate master who would not dream of keeping his servant up late merely eventually to put his master to bed. It was because Brown was aware of this that he did not resent the fact that tonight Hornblower had forgotten for once to tell him he might go to bed.

Up and down the room walked Hornblower, with a regular measured stride, turning with his foot two inches from the wainscoting under the window on one side, and on the other with his hip just brushing the end of the table as he turned. Russians and Swedes, convoys and privateers, Stockholm and Danzig, all these gave him plenty to think about. It would be cold in the Baltic, too, and he would have to make plans for conserving his crew's health in cold weather. And the first thing he must do, the moment his flotilla was assembled, must be to see that in every vessel there was an officer who could be relied upon to read and transmit signals correctly. Unless communications were good all discipline and organisation were wasted and he might as well not try to make any plans at all. Bomb-ketches had the disadvantage of—

At this point Hornblower was distracted by a knocking at the door.

"Come in," he rasped.

The door opened slowly, and revealed to his gaze both Brown and a scared innkeeper in a green baize apron.

"What is it?" snapped Hornblower. Now that he had halted in his quarterdeck walk he was suddenly aware that he was tired; much had happened since the Squire of Smallbridge had been welcomed by his tenants that morning, and the feeling in his legs told him that he must have been doing a fair amount of walking.

Brown and the innkeeper exchanged glances, and then the innkeeper took the plunge.

"It's like this, sir," he began, nervously. "His lordship is in number four just under this sitting-room, sir. His lordship's a man of hasty temper, sir, beggin' your pardon, sir. He says—beggin' your pardon again, sir— he says that two in the morning's late enough for anyone to walk up and down over his head. He says—"

"Two in the morning?" demanded Hornblower.

"It's nearer three, sir," interposed Brown, tactfully.

"Yes, sir, it struck the half-hour just when he rang for me the second time. He says if only you'd knock something over, or sing a song, it wouldn't be so bad. But just to hear you walking up and down, sir—his lordship says it makes him think about death and Judgment Day. It's too regular, like. I told him who you was, sir, the first time he rang. And now—"

Hornblower had come to the surface by now, fully emerged from the wave of thought that had engulfed him. He saw the nervous gesticulations of the innkeeper, caught between the devil of this unknown lordship downstairs and the deep sea of Captain Sir Horatio Hornblower upstairs, and he could not help smiling—in fact it was only with an effort that he prevented himself from laughing outright. He could visualise the whole ludicrous business, the irascible unknown peer down below, the innkeeper terrified of offending one or other of his two wealthy and influential guests, and as a crowning complication Brown

26

stubbornly refusing to allow until the last possible moment any intrusion upon his master's deliberations. Hornblower saw the obvious relief in the two men's faces when he smiled, and that really made him laugh this time. His temper had been short of late and Brown had expected an explosion, while the wretched innkeeper never expected anything else—innkeepers never looked for anything better than tantrums from the people fate compelled them to entertain. Hornblower remembered damning Brown's eyes without provocation only that very morning; Brown was not quite as clever as he might be, for this morning Hornblower had been fretting as an unemployed naval officer doomed to country life, while this evening he was a commodore with a flotilla awaiting him and nothing in the world could upset his temper— Brown had not allowed for that.

"My respects to his lordship," he said. "Tell him that the march of doom will cease from this moment. Brown, I shall go to bed."

The innkeeper fled in huge relief down the stairs, while Brown seized a candlestick—the candle in it was burned down to a stump—and let his master through into the bedroom. Hornblower peeled off his coat with the epaulettes of heavy bullion, and Brown caught it just in time to save it from falling to the floor. Shoes and shirt and trousers followed, and Hornblower pulled on the magnificent nightshirt which was laid out on the bed; a nightshirt of solid China silk, brocaded, with faggoting at the cuffs and neck, for which Barbara had sent a special order all the way to the East through her friends in the East India Company. The blanket-wrapped brick in the bed had cooled a good deal, but had diffused its warmth gratefully over much of the area; Hornblower snuggled down into its mild welcome.

"Good night, sir," said Brown, and darkness rushed into the room from out of the corners as he extinguished the candle. Tumultuous dreams rushed with them. Whether asleep or awake—next morning Hornblower could not decide which—his mind was turning over all through the rest of the night the endless implications of this coming campaign in the Baltic, where his life and his reputation and his self-respect would be once more at stake.

Chapter IV

H ORNBLOWER sat forward on the seat of the coach and peered out of the window.

"Wind's veering nor'ard a little," he said. "West by north now, I should say."

"Yes, dear," said Barbara patiently.

"I beg your pardon, dear," said Hornblower. "I interrupted you. You were telling me about my shirts."

"No. I had finished telling you about those, dear. What I was saying was that you must not let anyone unpack the flat sea-chest until the cold weather comes. Your sheepskin coat and your big fur cloak are in it, with plenty of camphor, and they'll be safe from moths just as they are. Have the chest put straight below when you go on board."

"Yes, dear."

The coach was clattering over the cobbles of Upper Deal. Barbara stirred a little and took Hornblower's hand in hers again.

"I don't like talking about furs," she said. "I hope— oh, I hope so much—that you'll be back before the cold weather comes."

"So do I, dear," said Hornblower, with perfect truth.

It was gloomy and dark inside the coach, but the light from the window shone on Barbara's face, illuminating it like a saint's in church. The mouth beneath the keen aquiline nose was set firm; there was nothing soft about the grey-blue eyes. No one could tell from Lady Barbara's expression the anxiety she felt; but she had slipped off her glove, and her hand was twining feverishly in Hornblower's.

"Come back to me, dear. Come back to me!" said Barbara softly.

"Of course I will," said Hornblower.

For all her patrician birth, for all her keen wit, for all her iron self-control, Barbara could say foolish things just like any blowsy wife of any ordinary seaman. It made Hornblower love her more dearly than ever that she should say pathetically "Come back to me" as if he had power over the French or Russian cannon-balls that would be aimed at him. Yet in that moment a horrible thought shot up in Hornblower's mind, like a bloated corpse rising to the surface from the ooze at the bottom of the sea. Lady Barbara had seen a husband off to war once before, and he had not returned. He had died under the surgeon's knife at Gibraltar after a splinter had torn open his groin in the battle of Rosas Bay. Was Barbara thinking of that dead husband now, at this moment? Hornblower shuddered a little at the thought, and Barbara, despite the close sympathy that always existed between them, misinterpreted the movement.

"My darling," she said, "my sweet."

She brought her other hand up and touched his cheek, and her lips sought his. He kissed her, fighting down the dreadful doubt that assailed him. He had contrived for months not to be jealous of the past—he was annoyed with himself for allowing it to happen at this time of all times, and his annoyance added to the devil's brew of emotions within him. The touch of her lips won him over; his heart came out to her, and he kissed her with all the passion of his love, while the coach lurched unstably over the cobbles, Barbara's monumental hat threatened to come adrift; she had to

29

withdraw from his arms to set it straight and to restore herself to her normal dignity. She was aware of, even if she had misinterpreted, the turmoil in Hornblower's soul, and she deliberately began a new line of conversation which would help them both to recover their composure ready for their imminent appearance in public again.

"I am pleased," she said, "whenever I think of the high compliment the government is paying you in giving you this new appointment."

"I am pleased that you are pleased, dear," said Hornblower.

"Hardly more than half-way up the captains' list, and yet they are giving you this command. You will be an admiral *in petto*."

She could have said nothing that could calm Hornblower more effectively. He grinned to himself at Barbara's mistake. She was trying to say that he would be an admiral on a small scale, in miniature, *en petit* as it would be phrased in French. But *en petit* meant nothing like *in petto*, all the same. *In petto* was Italian for "in the breast"; when the Pope appointed a cardinal *in petto* it meant that he intended to keep the appointment to himself for a time without making it public. It tickled Hornblower hugely to hear Barbara guilty of a solecism of that sort. And it made her human again in his eyes, of the same clay as his own. He warmed to her afresh, with tenderness and affection supplementing passion and love.

The coach came to a stop with a lurch and a squeaking of brakes, and the door opened. Hornblower jumped out and handed Barbara down before looking round him. It was blowing half a gale, west by north, undoubtedly. This morning it had been a strong breeze, southwesterly, so that it was both veering and strengthening. A little more northing in the wind and they would be weather-bound in The Downs until it backed again. The loss of an hour might mean the loss of days. Sky and sea were grey, and there were whitecaps a-plenty. The East India convoy was visible at anchor some way out—as far as they were concerned the wind had only to veer a trifle more for them to up-anchor and start down Channel. There was other shipping to the northward, and presumably the *Nonsuch* and the flotilla were there, but without a glass it was too far to tell ship from ship. The wind whipped round his ears and forced him to hold his hat on tightly. Across the cobbled street was the jetty with a dozen Deal luggers riding to it.

Brown stood waiting for orders while the coachman and footman were hauling the baggage out of the boot.

"I'll have a hoveller take me out to the ship, Brown," said Hornblower. "Make a bargain for me."

He could have had a signal sent from the castle to the *Nonsuch* for a boat, but that would consume precious time. Barbara was standing beside him holding onto her hat; the wind flapped her skirt round her like a flag. Her eyes were grey this morning—if sea and sky had been blue her eyes would have been blue too. And she was making herself smile at him.

"If you are going out to the ship in a lugger, dear," she said, "I could come too. The lugger could bring me back."

"You will be wet and cold," said Hornblower. "Close-hauled and with this wind it will be a rough passage."

"Do you think I mind?" said Barbara, and the thought of leaving her tore at his heart-strings again.

Brown was back again already, and with him a couple of Deal boatmen, handkerchiefs bound round their heads and earrings in their ears; their faces, burned by the wind and pickled by the salt, a solid brown like wood. They laid hold of Hornblower's sea-chests and began to carry them as if they were feathers toward the jetty; in nineteen years of war innumerable officers had had their chests carried down

31

to Deal jetty. Brown followed them, and Hornblower and Lady Barbara brought up the rear, Hornblower clutching tenaciously the leather portfolio containing his "most secret" orders.

"Morning, Captain." The captain of the lugger knuckled his forehead to Hornblower. "Morning, your ladyship. All the breeze anyone wants today. Still, you'll be able to weather the Goodwins, Captain, even with those unweatherly bombs of yours. Wind's fair for The Skaw once you're clear of The Downs."

So that was military secrecy in this England; this Deal hoveller knew just what force he had and whither he was bound—and tomorrow, as likely as not, he would have a rendezvous in mid-Channel with a French *chasse-marée*, exchanging tobacco for brandy and news for news. In three days Bonaparte in Paris would know that Hornblower had sailed for the Baltic—with a ship of the line and a flotilla.

"Easy with them cases!" roared the lugger captain suddenly. "Them bottles ain't made o' iron!"

They were lowering down into the lugger the rest of his baggage from the jetty; the additional cabin stores which Barbara had ordered for him and whose quality she had checked so carefully—a case of wine, a case of provisions, and the parcel of books which was her special present to him.

"Won't you take a seat in the cabin, your ladyship?" asked the lugger captain with queer untutored politeness. " 'Twill be a wet run out to *Nonsuch*."

Barbara caught Hornblower's eye and refused politely; Hornblower knew those stuffy, smelly cabins of old.

"A tarpaulin was fastened round Barbara's shoulders, and hung round her to the deck like a candle extinguisher. The wind was still pulling at her hat, and she put up her hand and with a single gesture snatched it from her head and drew it inside the tarpaulin. The brisk wind blew her hair instantly into

32

streamers, and she laughed, and with a shake of her head set her whole mane flying in the wind. Her cheeks flushed and her eyes sparkled, just as Hornblower could remember her in the old days when they rounded the Horn in *Lydia*. Hornblower wanted to kiss her.

"Cast off, there! Hands to the halliard!" roared the captain, coming aft and casually holding the tiller against his hip. The hands strained at the tackle, and the mainsail rose foot by foot; the lugger made a sternboard away from the jetty.

"Lively with that sheet, now Ge-arge!"

The captain hauled the tiller over, and the lugger checked herself, spun on her keel, and dashed forward, as handy as a horse in the hands of a skilful rider. As she came out from the lee of the jetty the wind took hold of her and laid her over, but the captain put down the tiller and Ge-arge hauled aft on the sheet until the sail was like a board, and the lugger, close-hauled—dramatically so to anyone unfamiliar with her type—plunged forward into the teeth of the gale, with the spray flying aft from her port bow in sheets. Even in the sheltered Downs there was enough of a sea running to make the lugger lively enough as she met it, pitch following roll as each wave passed under her from port bow to starboard quarter.

Hornblower suddenly realised that this was the moment when he should be seasick. He could not remember the start of any previous voyage when he had not been sick, and the motion of this lively little lugger should find him out if anything would. It was interesting that nothing of the sort was happening; Hornblower noticed with deep amazement that the horizon forward showed up above the boat's bow, and then disappeared as the lugger stood up on her stern, without his feeling any qualm at all. It was not so surprising that he had retained his sea legs; after twenty years at sea it was not easy to lose them, and he stood swaying easily with the boat's quick motion; he only lost his sea legs when he was really dizzy with seasickness, and that dread plague showed no signs of appearing. At the start of previous voyages he had always been worn-out with the fatigues of fitting out and commissioning, of course short of sleep and worn down with anxieties and worries and ready to be sick even without going to sea. As commodore he had had none of these worries; the Admiralty and the Foreign Office and the Treasury had heaped orders and advice upon him, but orders and responsibility were not nearly as harassing as the petty worries of finding a crew and dealing with dockyard authorities. He was perfectly at ease.

Barbara was having to hold on tightly, and now that she looked up at him she was obviously not quite as comfortable inside as she might be; she was filled with doubts if with nothing else. Hornblower felt both amusement and pride; it was pleasant to be newly at sea and yet not sick; and it was more pleasant still to be doing something better than Barbara, who was so good at everything. He was on the point of teasing her, of vaunting his own immunity, when commonsense and his tenderness for his wife saved him from such an incredible blunder. She would hate him if he did anything of the sort—he could remember with enormous clarity how much he hated the whole world when he was being seasick. He did his best for her.

"You're fortunate not to be sick, my dear," he said. "This motion is lively, but then you always had a good stomach."

She looked at him, with the wind whipping her tousled hair; she looked a trifle dubious, but Hornblower's words had heartened her. He made a very considerable sacrifice for her, one she would never know about.

"I envy you, dear," he said. "I'm feeling the gravest

doubts about myself, as I always do at the beginning of a voyage. But you are your usual happy self."

Surely no man could give a better proof of his love for his wife, that he should not only conceal his feeling of superiority but that he should even for her sake pretend to be seasick when he was not. Barbara was all concern at once.

"I am sorry, dearest," she said, her hand on his shoulder. "I hope so much you do not have to give way. It would be most inconvenient for you at this moment of taking up your command."

The stratagem was working; with something important to think about other than the condition of her stomach Barbara was forgetting her own qualms.

"I hope I shall last out," said Hornblower; he tried to grin a brave reluctant grin, and although he was no actor Barbara's wits were sufficiently dulled not to see through him. Hornblower's conscience pricked him when he saw that this stolid mock-heroism of his was making her fonder of him than ever. Her eyes were soft for him.

"Stand by to go about!" bellowed the captain of the lugger, and Hornblower looked up in surprise to see that they were close up under the stern of the *Nonsuch*. She had some canvas showing forward and her mizzen topsail backed so as to set her across the wind a trifle and give the lugger a lee on her starboard side. Hornblower flung back his boat cloak and stood clear so that he could be seen from the quarterdeck of the *Nonsuch;* for Bush's sake, if for no other reason, he did not want to come on board without due warning. Then he turned to Barbara.

"It's time to say good-bye, dear," he said.

Her face was without expression, like that of a marine under inspection.

"Good-bye, dearest," she said. Her lips were cold, and she did not incline towards him to offer them, but stood stiffly upright. It was like kissing a marble statue. Then she melted suddenly. "I'll cherish Richard, darling. Our child."

Barbara could have said nothing to endear her more to Hornblower. He crushed her hands in his.

The lugger came up into the wind, her canvas volleying, and then she shot into the two-decker's lee. Hornblower glanced up; there was a bosun's chair dangling ready to lower to the lugger.

"Belay that chair!" he yelled, and then to the captain, "Lay us alongside."

Hornblower had no intention of being swung up to the deck in a bosun's chair; it was too undignified a way of taking up his new command to be swung aboard legs dangling. The lugger surged beside the big ship; the painted ports were level with his shoulder, and beneath him boiled the green water confined between the two vessels. This was a nervous moment. If he were to miss his footing and fall into the sea so that he would have to be hauled in wet and dripping it would be far more undignified than any entrance in a bosun's chair. He let fall his cloak, pulled his hat firmly onto his head, and hitched his sword round out of his way. Then he leaped across the yard-wide gap, scrambling upwards the moment fingers and toes made contact. It was only the first three feet which were difficult; after that the tumble home of the *Nonsuch's* side made it easy. He was even able to pause to collect himself before making the final ascent to the entry port and to step down to the deck with all the dignity to be expected of a commodore.

Professionally speaking, this was the highest moment of his career up to now. As a captain he had grown accustomed to a captain's honours, the bosun's mates twittering on their pipes, the four sideboys and the marine sentries. But now he was a commodore taking up his command; there were six sideboys with their white gloves, there was the whole marine guard and the marine band, a long double lane of bosun's mates with their pipes, and at the end of the lane a crowd of officers in full dress. As he set his foot on the deck the drums beat a ruffle in competition with the bosun's calls, and then the fifes of the band struck up "Heart of oak are our ships, Jolly tars are our men . . ." With his hand at the salute Hornblower strode up the lane of bosun's mates and sideboys; all this was peculiarly exhilarating despite his efforts to tell himself that these outward signs of the dignity of his position were mere childish baubles. He had to check himself, or his face would have borne a stupid ecstatic grin; it was with difficulty that he forced himself to assume the stern composure a commodore should display. There was Bush at the end of the lane, saluting stiffly, and standing effortlessly despite his wooden leg, and it was so pleasant to see Bush that he had to fight down his grin all over again.

"Good morning, Captain Bush," he said, as gruffly as he knew how, and offering his hand with all he could manage of formal cordiality.

"Good morning, sir."

Bush brought down his hand from the salute and grasped Hornblower's, trying hard to act his part, as if there were no friendship in this handshake, but mere professional esteem. Hornblower noted that his hand was as hard as ever—promotion to captain's rank had not softened it. And try as he would Bush could not keep his face expressionless. The blue eyes were alight with pleasure, and the craggy features kept softening into a smile as they escaped from his control. It made it harder than ever for Hornblower to remain dignified.

Out of the tail of his eye Hornblower saw a seaman hauling briskly at the main signal halliards. A black ball was soaring up the mast, and as it reached the block a twitch of the seaman's wrist broke it out. It was the commodore's broad pendant, hoisted to distinguish the ship he was in, and as the pendant broke out a puff of smoke forward and a loud bang marked the first gun of the salute which welcomed it. This

37

was the highest, the greatest moment of all—thousands upon thousands of naval officers could serve all their lives and never have a distinguished pendant hoisted for them, never hear a single gun fired in their honour. Hornblower could not help smiling now. His last reserve was broken down; he met Bush's eye and he laughed outright, and Bush laughed with him. They were like a pair of schoolboys exulting over a successful bit of mischief. It was extraordinarily pleasant to be aware that Bush was not only pleased at serving with him again, but was also pleased just because Hornblower was pleased.

Bush glanced over the port-side rail, and Hornblower looked across with him. There was the rest of the squadron, the two ugly bomb-ketches, the two big ship-rigged sloops, and the graceful little cutter. There were puffs of smoke showing at the sides of each of them, blown to nothingness almost instantly by the wind, and then the boom of the shots as each ship saluted the pendant, firing gun for gun, taking the time from the commodore. Bush's eyes narrowed as he looked them over, observing whether everything was being done decently and in order, but his face lapsed into a grin again as soon as he was sure. The last shot of the salute was fired; eleven rounds from each ship. It was interesting to work out that the mere ceremony of hoisting his pendant had cost his country fifty pounds or so, at a time when she was fighting for her life against a tyrant who dominated all Europe. The twitter of the pipes brought the ceremony to an end; the ship's company took up their duties again, and the marines sloped arms and marched off, their boots sounding loud on the deck.

"A happy moment, Bush," said Hornblower.

"A happy moment indeed, sir."

There were presentations to be made; Bush brought forward the ship's officers one by one. At this first sight one face was like another, but Hornblower knew that in a short period of crowded living each individual would become distinct, his peculiarities known to the limit of boredom.

"We shall come to know each other better, I hope, gentlemen," said Hornblower, phrasing his thought politely.

A whip at the main yard-arm was bringing up his baggage from the lugger, with Brown standing by to supervise—he must have come on board by an unobtrusive route, through a gunport presumably. So the lugger and Barbara must still be alongside. Hornblower walked to the rail and peered over. True enough. And Barbara was standing just as he had left her, still, like a statue. But that must have been the last parcel swung up by the ship; Hornblower had hardly reached the side when the lugger cast off from the *Nonsuch's* chains, hoisted her big mainsail and wheeled away as effortlessly as a gull.

"Captain Bush," said Hornblower, "we shall get under weigh immediately, if you please. Make a signal to the flotilla to that effect."

Chapter V

I'LL put the pistols in this locker, sir," said Brown, completing the unpacking.

"Pistols?" said Hornblower.

Brown brought the case over to him; he had only mentioned them because he knew that Hornblower was not aware of the pistols' existence. It was a beautiful mahogany case, velvet-lined; the first thing to catch the eye inside was a white card. It bore some words in Barbara's handwriting: "To my dear husband. May he never need to use them, but if he must then may they serve him well, and at least may they remind him of his loving wife, who will pray every day for his safety, for his happiness, and for his success." Hornblower read the words twice before he put the card down to examine the pistols. They were beautiful weapons of bright steel inlaid with silver, double-barrelled, the butts of ebony, giving them a perfect balance in the hand. There were two copper tubes in the case to open next; they merely contained pistol bullets, each one cast flawlessly, a perfect sphere. The fact that the makers had gone to the trouble of casting special bullets and including them in the case recalled Hornblower's attention to the pistols. Inside the barrels were bright spiral lands; they were rifled pistols, then. The next copper box in the case contained a number of discs of thin leather impregnated with oil; these would be for wrapping up the bullet before inserting it into the barrel, so as to ensure a perfect fit. The brass rod and the little brass mallet would be for hammering the bullets home. The little brass cup must be a measure of the powder charge. It was small, but that was the way to ensure accuracy—a small powder charge, a heavy ball, and a true barrel. With these pistols he could rely on himself to hit a small bull's-eye at fifty yards, as long as he held true.

But there was one more copper box to open. It was full of little square bits of copper sheet, very thin indeed. He was puzzled at the sight of them; each bit of copper had a bulge in the centre, where the metal was especially thin, making the black contents just visible through it. It dawned slowly upon Hornblower that these must be the percussion caps he had heard vaguely about recently. To prove it he laid one on his desk and tapped it sharply with the brass mallet. There was a sharp crack, a puff of smoke from under the mallet, and when he lifted up the latter he could see that the cap was rent open, and the desk was marked with the stain of the explosion.

He looked at the pistols again. He must have been blind, not to have noticed the absence of flint and priming pan. The hammer rested on what appeared at first sight to be a simple block of metal, but this pivoted at a touch, revealing a shallow cavity below it clearly intended to receive a cap. At the base of the cavity was a small hole which must communicate with the breech end of the barrel. Put a charge in the pistol, put a cap in the cavity, and fix it firm with the metal block. Now snap the hammer down upon the block. The cap explodes; the flame passes through the hole into the charge, and the pistol is fired. No haphazard arrangement of flint and priming; rain or spray could never put these pistols out of action. Hornblower guessed there would not be a misfire once in a hundred shots. It was a wonderful present—it was very thoughtful indeed of Barbara to buy them for him. Heaven only knew what they must have cost; some skilled workman must have laboured for months over the rifling of those four barrels, and the copper caps—five hundred of them, every one hand-made—must have cost a pretty penny of themselves. But with those two pistols loaded he would have four men's lives in his hands; on a fine day with two flint-lock double-barrelled pistols he would expect one misfire, if not two, and if it were raining or there was spray flying it would be remarkable if he could fire a single shot. To Hornblower's mind the rifling was not as important as the percussion caps; in the usual shipboard scuffle when pistols were likely to be used accuracy was unimportant, for one generally pressed the muzzle against one's adversary's stomach before pulling the trigger.

Hornblower laid the pistols in their velvet nests and mused on. Dear Barbara. She was always thinking for him, trying to anticipate his wants, but something more than that as well. These pistols were an example of the way she tried to satisfy wants of his that he was not aware of. She had lifted her eyebrows when he had said that Gibbon would be all the reading material he would need on this commission, and she had bought and packed a score of other books for him; one of them, he could see from here, was this new poem in the Spenserian stanza, "Childe Harold" (whatever that might mean) by the mad peer Lord Byron. Everyone had been talking about it just before his departure; he must admit he was glad of the chance to read it, although he would never have dreamed of buying it for himself. Hornblower looked back over a life of Spartan self-denial with a twinge of queer regret that it should have ended, and then he got angrily out of his chair. In another moment he would be wishing he were not married to Barbara, and that was perfect nonsense.

He could tell, down here in his cabin, that the *Nonsuch* was still close-hauled to the strong northwesterly breeze; she was lying over to it so steadily that there was little roll in her motion, although she was pitching deeply as she met the short North Sea rollers. The telltale compass over his head showed that she was making good her course for The Skaw; and the whole cabin was resonant with the harping of the taut rigging transmitted through the timbers of the ship, while she creaked positively thunderously as she pitched, loud enough to make conversation difficult. There was one frame that made a noise like a pistol shot at one particular moment of each pitch, and he had already grown so used to the sound as to be able to anticipate it exactly, judging it by the ship's motion.

He had been puzzled for a space by a peculiar irregular thud over his head; in fact, he had been so piqued at his inability to account for it that he had put on his hat and gone up on the quarterdeck to find out what it was. There was nothing on sight on the deck which seemed likely to have made that rhythmical noise, no pump at work, nobody beating out oakum—even if it were conceivable that such a thing could be done on the quarterdeck of a ship of the line; there were only Bush and the officers of the watch, who immediately froze into inconspicuous immobility when the great man appeared on the companion. Heaven only knew what made that thumping; Hornblower began to wonder if his ears had deceived him and if the noise really came from a deck below. He had to make a pretence of having come on deck for a purpose—interesting to find that even a commodore, first class, still had to sink to such subterfuges—and he began to stride up and down the weather side of the quarterdeck, hands behind him, head bowed forward, in the old comfortable attitude. Enthusiasts had talked or written of pleasures innumerable, of gardens or women, wine or fishing; it was strange that no one had ever told of the pleasure of walking a quarterdeck.

But what was it that had made that slow thumping noise? He was forgetting why he had come upon deck. He darted covert glances from under his brows as he walked up and down and still saw nothing to account for it. The noise had not been audible since he came on deck, but still curiosity consumed him. He stood by the taffrail and looked back at the flotilla. The trim ship-rigged sloops were beating up against the strong breeze without difficulty, but the bomb-ketches were not so comfortable. The absence of a foremast, the huge triangular foresail, made it hard to keep them from yawing, even on a wind. Every now and then they would put their stumpy bowsprits down and take the sea in green over their bows.

He was not interested in bomb-ketches. He wanted to know what had been thumping the deck over his head when he was in his cabin, and then commonsense came to help him fight down his ridiculous self-consciousness. Why should not a commodore ask a simple question about a simple subject? Why in the world had he even hesitated for a moment? He swung round with determination.

"Captain Bush!" he called.

43

"Sir!" Bush came hastening aft to him, his wooden leg thumping the deck.

That was the noise! With every second step Bush took, his wooden leg with its leather button came down with a thump on the planking. Hornblower certainly could not ask the question he had just been forming in his mind.

"I hope I shall have the pleasure of your company at dinner this afternoon," said Hornblower, thinking rapidly.

"Thank you, sir. Yes, sir. Yes indeed," said Bush. He beamed with pleasure at the invitation so that Hornblower felt positively hypocritical as he made his way down into the cabin to supervise the last of his unpacking. Yet it was as well that he had been led by his own peculiar weaknesses to give that invitation instead of spending the evening, as he would otherwise have done, dreaming about Barbara, calling up in his mind the lovely drive through springtime England from Smallbridge to Deal, and making himself as miserable at sea as he had managed to make himself on land.

Bush would be able to tell him about the officers and men of the *Nonsuch,* who could be trusted and who must be watched, what was the material condition of the ship, if the stores were good or bad, and all the hundred other things he needed to know. And tomorrow, as soon as the weather moderated, he would signal for "All Captains," and so make the acquaintance of his other subordinates, and size them up, and perhaps begin to convey to them his own particular viewpoints and theories, so that when the time came for action there would be need for few signals and there would be common action directed speedily at a common objective.

Meanwhile, there was one more job to be done immediately; the present would be the best time, he supposed with a sigh, but he was conscious of a faint distaste for it even as he applied himself to it.

"Pass the word for Mr. Braun—for my clerk," he said to Brown, who was hanging up the last of the uniform coats behind the curtain against the bulkhead.

"Aye aye, sir," said Brown.

It was odd that his clerk and his coxswain should have names pronounced in identical fashion; it was that coincidence which had led him to add the unnecessary last three words to his order.

Mr. Braun was tall and spare, fair, youngish, and prematurely bald, and Hornblower did not like him, although typically he was more cordial to him than he would have been if he had liked him. He offered him the cabin chair while he himself sat back on the locker, and when he saw Mr. Braun's eyes resting curiously on the case of pistols—Barbara's gift—he condescended to discuss it with him as a conversational preliminary, pointing out the advantages of the percussion caps and the rifled barrels.

"Very good weapons indeed, sir," said Mr. Braun, replacing them in their velvet case.

He looked across the cabin at Hornblower, the dying light which came through the stern windows shining on his face and reflected in curious fashion from his pale green eyes.

"You speak good English," said Hornblower.

"Thank you, sir. My business before the war was largely with England. But I speak Russian and Swedish and Finnish and Polish and German and French just as well. Lithuanian a little. Esthonian a little, because it is so like Finnish."

"But Swedish is your native language, though?"

Mr. Braun shrugged his thin shoulders.

"My father spoke Swedish. My mother spoke German, sir. I spoke Finnish with my nurse, and French with one tutor and English with another. In my office we spoke Russian when we did not speak Polish."

"But I thought you were a Swede?"

Mr. Braun shrugged his shoulders again.

45

"A Swedish subject, sir, but I was born a Finn. I thought of myself as a Finn until three years ago."

So Mr. Braun was one more of these stateless individuals with whom all Europe seemed to be peopled nowadays—men and women without a country, Frenchmen, Germans, Austrians, Poles who had been uprooted by the chances of war and who dragged out a dreary existence in the hope that some day another chance of war would re-establish them.

"When Russia took advantage of her pact with Bonaparte," explained Mr. Braun, "to fall upon Finland, I was one of those who fought. What use was it? What could Finland do against all the might of Russia? I was one of the fortunate ones who escaped. My brothers are in Russian gaols at this very minute if they are alive, but I hope they are dead. Sweden was in revolution—there was no refuge for me there, even though it had been for Sweden that I was fighting. Germany, Denmark, Norway were in Bonaparte's hands, and Bonaparte would gladly have handed me back to oblige his new Russian ally. But I was in an English ship, one of those to which I sold timber, and so to England I came. One day I was the richest man in Finland, where there are few rich men, and the next I was the poorest man in England where there are many poor."

The pale green eyes reflected back the light again from the cabin window, and Hornblower realised anew that his clerk was a man of disquieting personality. It was not merely the fact that he was a refugee, and Hornblower, like everybody else, was surfeited with refugees and their tales of woe, although his conscience pricked him about them—the first ones had begun to arrive twenty years ago from France, and ever since then there had been an increasing tide from Poland and Italy and Germany. Braun's being a refugee was likely to prejudice Hornblower against him from the start, and actually had done so, as Hornblower admitted to himself with

46

his usual fussy sense of justice. But that was not the reason that Hornblower did not like them. There was less reason even than that—there was no reason at all.

It was irksome to Hornblower to think that for the rest of this commission he would have to work in close contact with this man. Yet the Admiralty orders in his desk enjoined upon him to pay the closest attention to the advice and information which he would receive from Braun, "a gentleman whose acquaintance with the Baltic countries is both extensive and intimate." Even this evening it was a great relief when Bush's knock at the cabin door, heralding his arrival for dinner, freed Hornblower from the man's presence. Braun slid unobtrusively out of the cabin with a bow to Bush; every line of his body indicated the pose—whether forced or natural Hornblower could not guess—of the man who has seen better days resignedly doing menial duties.

"How do you find your Swedish clerk, sir?" asked Bush.

"He's a Finn, not a Swede."

"A Finn? You don't say, sir! It'd be better not to let the men know that."

Bush's own honest face indicated a disquietude against which he struggled in vain.

"Of course," said Hornblower.

He tried to keep his face expressionless, to conceal that he had completely left out of account the superstition that prevailed about Finns at sea. In a sailor's mind every Finn was a warlock who could conjure up storms by lifting his finger, but Hornblower had quite failed to think of the shabby-genteel Mr. Braun as that kind of Finn, despite those unwholesome pale green eyes.

47

Chapter VI

Eight BELLS, sir."

Hornblower came back to consciousness not very willingly; he suspected he was being dragged away from delightful dreams, although he could not remember what they were.

"Still dark, sir," went on Brown remorselessly, "but a clear night. Wind steady at west by north, a strong breeze. The sloops an' the flotilla in sight to looard, an' we're hove-to, sir, under mizzen t's'l, main t'mast stays'l an' jib. An' here's your shirt, sir."

Hornblower swung his legs out of his cot and sleepily pulled off his nightshirt. He was minded at first just to put on those few clothes which would keep him warm on deck, but he had his dignity as commodore to remember, and he wanted to establish a reputation as a man who was never careless about any detail whatever. He had left orders to be called now, a quarter of an hour before it was really necessary, merely to be able to do so. So he put on uniform coat and trousers and boots, parted his hair carefully in the flickering light of the lantern Brown held, and put aside the thought of shaving. If he came on deck at four in the morning newly shaved everyone would guess that he had been in pains regarding his appearance. He clapped on his cocked hat, and struggled into the pea-jacket which Brown held for him. Outside his cabin door the sentry snapped to attention as the great man appeared. On the half-deck a group of high-spirited youngsters coming off watch subsided into awed and apprehensive silence at the sight of the commodore, which was a fit and proper thing to happen.

On the quarterdeck it was as raw and unfriendly as one might expect before dawn in the Kattegat on a spring morning. The bustle of calling the watch had just subsided; the figures which loomed up in the darkness and hurriedly moved over to the port side, leaving the starboard side clear for him, were unrecognisable. But the thump of Bush's wooden leg was unmistakable.

"Captain Bush!"

"Sir?"

"What time is sunrise this morning?"

"Er—about five thirty, sir."

"I don't want to know *about* what it will be. I asked 'What time is sunrise?' "

A second's silence while the crest-fallen Bush absorbed this rebuke, and then another voice answered.

"Five thirty four, sir."

That was that fresh-faced lad, Carlin, the second lieutenant of the ship. Hornblower would have given something to be sure whether Carlin really knew when sunrise was, or whether he was merely guessing, taking a chance that his commodore would not check his figures. As for Bush, it was bad luck on him that he should be rebuked publicly, but he should have known what time was sunrise, seeing that last night Hornblower had been making plans with him based on that very point. And it would do the discipline of the rest of the force no harm if it were known that the commodore spared no one, not even the captain of a ship of the line, his best friend.

Hornblower took a turn or two up and down the deck. Seven days out from The Downs, and no news. With the wind steady from the westward, there could be no news—nothing could have got out from the Baltic, or even from Gothenburg. He had not seen a sail yesterday after rounding The Skaw and coming up the Kattegat. His last news from Sweden was fifteen days old, then, and in fifteen days anything could happen. Sweden might have easily changed from unfriendly neutrality to open hostility. Before him lay the passage of The Sound, three miles wide at its narrowest point; on the starboard side would be Denmark, undoubtedly hostile under Bonaparte's domination whether she wanted to be or not. On the port side would be Sweden, and the main channel up The Sound lay under the guns of Helsingborg. If Sweden were England's enemy the guns of Denmark and Sweden—of Elsinore and of Helsingborg—might easily cripple the squadron as they ran the gauntlet. And retreat would always be perilous and difficult, if not entirely cut off. It might be as well to delay, to send in a boat to discover how Sweden stood at the present moment.

But on the other hand, to send in a boat would warn Sweden of his presence. If he dashed in now, the moment there was light enough to see the channel, he might get through scatheless, taking the defences by surprise even if Sweden were hostile. His vessels might be knocked about, but with the wind west by north, in an ideal quarter, even a crippled ship could struggle along until The Sound widened and they would be out of range. If Sweden's neutrality were still wobbling it would do no harm to let her see a British squadron handled with boldness and decision, nor for her to know that a British force was loose in the Baltic able to threaten her shores and ravage her shipping. Should Sweden turn hostile he could maintain himself one way or the other in the Baltic through the summer—and in the summer anything might happen—and with good fortune might fight his way out again in the autumn. There certainly were arguments in favour of temporising and delay and communicating with the shore, but there were more cogent arguments still in favour of prompt action.

The ship's bell struck one sharp note; hardly more than an hour before dawn, and already over there to leeward there was a hint of grey in the sky.

Hornblower opened his mouth to speak, and then checked himself. He had been about to issue a sharp order, consonant with the tenseness of the moment and with the accelerated beating of his pulse; but that was not the way he wanted to behave. While he had time to think and prepare himself he could still pose as a man of iron nerves.

"Captain Bush!" He managed to make himself drawl the words, and to give his orders with an air of complete indifference. "Signal all vessels to clear for action."

"Aye aye, sir."

Two red lights at the main yard-arm and a signal gun; that was the night signal for danger from the enemy which would send all hands to quarters. It took several seconds to bring a light for the lanterns; by the time the signal was acknowledged the *Nonsuch* was well on the way to being cleared for action—the watch below turned up, the decks sanded and the fire pumps manned, guns run out and bulkheads knocked down. It was still a pretty raw crew—Bush had been through purgatory trying to get his ship manned—but the job could have been worse done. Now the grey dawn had crept up over the eastern sky, and the rest of the squadron was just visible as vessels and not as solid nuclei in the gloom, but it was still not quite light enough to risk the passage. Hornblower turned to Bush and Hurst, the first lieutenant.

"If you please," he drawled, dragging out every word with all the nonchalance he could muster, "I will have the signal bent ready for hoisting, 'Proceed to leeward in the order of battle.'"

"Aye aye, sir."

Everything was done now. These last two minutes of waiting in inactivity, with nothing left to do, were especially trying. Hornblower was about to walk up and down, when he remembered that he must stand still to maintain his pose of indifference. The batteries on shore might have their furnaces alight, to heat shot

51

red hot; there was a possibility that in a few minutes the whole force of which he was so proud might be no more than a chain of blazing wrecks. Now it was time.

"Hoist," said Hornblower. "Captain Bush, I'll trouble you to square away and follow the squadron."

"Aye aye, sir," said Bush.

Bush's voice hinted at suppressed excitement; and it came to Hornblower, with a blinding flash of revelation, that his pose was ineffective with Bush. The latter had learned, during years of experience, that when Hornblower stood still instead of walking about, and when he drawled out his words as he was doing at present, then in Hornblower's opinion there was danger ahead. It was an intensely interesting discovery, but there was no time to think about it, not with the squadron going up The Sound.

Lotus was leading. Vickery, her commander, was the man Hornblower had picked out as the captain with the steadiest nerves who could be trusted to lead without flinching. Hornblower would have liked to lead, himself, but in this operation the rear would be the post of danger—the leading ships might well get through before the gunners on shore could get to their guns and find the range—and the *Nonsuch* as the most solidly built and best able to endure fire must come last so as to be able to succour and tow out of action any disabled ship. Hornblower watched *Lotus* set topsails and courses and square away. The cutter *Clam* followed—she was the feeblest of all; a single shot might sink her, and she must be given the best chance of getting through. Then the two ugly bomb-ketches, and then the other sloop, *Raven,* just ahead of *Nonsuch;* Hornblower was not sorry to have the opportunity to watch how her commander, Cole, would behave in action. *Nonsuch* followed, driving hard with the strong breeze on her starboard quarter. Hornblower watched Bush shaking the wind out of the mizzen topsail so as to keep exact station astern of the *Ra-*

ven. The big two-decker seemed a lumbering clumsy thing compared with the grace and elegance of the sloops.

That was Sweden in sight now, Cape Kullen, now on the port bow.

"A cast of the log, if you please, Mr. Hurst."

"Aye aye, sir."

Hornblower thought Hurst looked a little sidelong at him, unable to conceive why any sane man should want a cast of the log at a moment when the ship was about to risk everything; but Hornblower wanted to know how long the strain was likely to endure, and what was the use of being a commodore if one could not then indulge one's whims? A midshipman and a couple of quartermasters came running aft with log and glass; the speed of the ship was sufficient to make the quartermaster's arms vibrate as he held the reel above his head.

"Nigh on nine knots, sir," reported the midshipman to Hurst.

"Nigh on nine knots, sir," reported Hurst to Hornblower.

"Very good."

It would be a full eight hours, then, before they were beyond Saltholm and comparatively out of danger. There was the Danish coast on the starboard bow now, just visible in the half-light; the channel was narrowing fast. Hornblower could imagine sleepy sentries and lookouts peering from their posts at the hardly visible sails, and calling to their sergeants, and the sergeants coming sleepily to see for themselves and then hastening away to tell their lieutenants, and then the drums beating to arms and the gunners running to their pieces. On the Danish side they would make ready to fire, for there were the minions of Bonaparte, and any sail was likely to be an enemy. But on the Swedish side? What had Bernadotte decided during the last few days? Was Bonaparte's Marshal still neutral, or had he at last made up his

53

mind to throw the weight of Sweden on the side of his native land?

There were the low cliffs of Elsinore, and there were the steeples of Helsingborg in plain view to port, and the fortress above the town. *Lotus,* nearly a mile ahead, must be into the narrows. Hornblower levelled his glass at her; her yards were bracing round for the turn, and still no shot had been fired. *Clam* was turning next—please God the clumsy bomb-ketches did not misbehave. Ah! There it was. The heavy dull boom of a gun, and then the sullen roar of a salvo. Hornblower turned his glass to the Swedish coast. He could see no smoke there. Then to the Danish side. Smoke was evident, although the brisk wind was dispersing it fast. Under Bush's orders the helmsman was putting the wheel over a spoke or two, in readiness for the turn; Elsinore and Helsingborg were suddenly surprisingly near. Three miles wide was the channel, and Vickery in *Lotus* was carrying out his orders correctly and keeping well to the port side of the fairway, two miles from Denmark and only a mile from Sweden, with every vessel following exactly in his track. If the Swedish guns came into action and were well handled, they could deal the squadron some shrewd blows. Three jets of water from the surface of the sea on the starboard beam; although the eye could not see the ball that made them it was easy to imagine one could, as it skipped over the surface, but the last jet was a full cable's length from the side. The Swedish guns were still not firing; Hornblower wished he could tell whether it was because the Swedish gunners were taken by surprise or because they were under orders not to fire.

Elsinore was abaft the beam now, and the channel was opening wide. Hornblower shut his telescope with a snap, and a decided feeling of anticlimax. He could hardly imagine now what he had been worrying about. Calling up in his mind's eye the chart that he had so anxiously studied, he calculated that it would be an hour before they were in range of the shore again, where the fairway lay close in to the Swedish island of Hven—however that was pronounced in these barbarous northern tongues. This latter thought made him glance round. Braun was at his station on the quarterdeck, in attendance on the commodore, as he should be. With his hands on the rail he was gazing over at the Swedish shore; Hornblower could not see his face, but every line of the man's figure disclosed rapt attention. The poor devil of an exile was looking longingly on the shores on which he would never hope to set foot. The world was full of exiles, but Hornblower suddenly felt sorry for this one.

Here came the sun, peeping between two Swedish hills as they opened up the valley. It was full daylight, with every promise of a fine day. The minute warmth of the sun, as the shadow of the mizzen rigging ran across the quarterdeck, suddenly awoke in Hornblower the knowledge that he was stiff and chilled with having made himself stand still so long. He took a turn or two along the quarterdeck, restoring his circulation, and the fresh knowledge was borne in upon him that he wanted his breakfast. Glamorous visions of steaming cups of coffee danced momentarily in his mind's eye, and it was with a sense of acute disappointment that he remembered that, with the ship cleared for action and all fires out, there was no chance of hot food at all. So acute was the disappointment that he realised guiltily that his six months ashore had made him soft and self-indulgent; it was with positive distaste that he contemplated the prospect of breakfasting off biscuit and cold meat, and washing them down with ship's water which already had obviously been kept a long time in cask.

The thought reminded him of the men standing patiently at their guns. He wished Bush would remember about them, too. Hornblower could not possibly interfere in the details of the internal management of the ship—he would do more harm than good if he were to try—but he yearned to give the orders which were running through his mind. He tried for a moment to convey his wishes to Bush telepathically, but Bush seemed unreceptive, just as Hornblower expected. He walked over to the lee side as though to get a better view of the Swedish coast, stopping within two yards of Bush.

"Sweden still seems to be neutral," he said, casually.

"Yes, sir."

"We shall know better when we reach Hven—God knows how one's supposed to pronounce that. We must pass close under the gun's there; the fairway's that side."

"Yes, sir, I remember."

"But there's nearly an hour before we come to it. I shall have a bite of breakfast brought up to me here. Will you join me, Captain?"

"Thank you, sir. I shall be delighted."

An invitation of that sort from a commodore was as good as a command to a captain. But Bush was far too good an officer to dream of eating food when his men could not do so. Hornblower could see in his face his struggle against his nervous but impractical desire to have his crew at their guns every moment of his tense time; Bush after all was new to command ans found his responsibility heavy. But good sense won him over in the end.

"Mr. Hurst. Dismiss the watch below. Half an hour for them to get their breakfast."

That was exactly the order Hornblower had wanted him to give—but the pleasure at having brought it about did not in Hornblower's mind counterbalance the annoyance at having had to make a bit of casual conversation, and now there would have to be polite small talk over the breakfast. The tense silence of the ship at quarters changed to the bustle of dismissing the watch; Bush bawled orders for chairs and a table to be brought up to the quarterdeck, and fussed over having them set up just where the commodore would like them. A glance from Hornblower to Brown sufficed to spread the table with the delicacies suitable for the occasion which Brown could select from the stores Barbara had sent on board—the best hard bread money could buy; butter in a stone crock, not nearly rancid yet; strawberry jam; a heavily smoked ham; a smoked mutton ham from an Exmoor farm; Cheddar and Stilton cheese; potted char. Brown had had a brilliant idea, and squeezed some of the dwindling store of lemons for lemonade in order to disguise the flavour of the ship's water; he knew that Hornblower was quite incapable of drinking beer, even small beer, at breakfast time—and beer was the only alternative.

Bush ran an appreciative eye over the loaded table, and at Hornblower's invitation sat down with appetite. Bush had been poor, too, most of his life, with a host of indigent female relations dependent on his pay. He was not yet surfeited with luxury. But Hornblower's characteristic cross-grainedness had got the better of him; he had wanted coffee, and he could not have coffee, and so he wanted nothing at all. Even lemonade was a mere mockery; he ate resentfully. It seemed to him that Bush, spreading potted char liberally on a biscuit and eating with all the appetite one might expect of him after a night on deck, was doing so deliberately to annoy him. Bush cocked an eye at him across the table and thought better of his first idea of making an appreciative comment on the food. If his queer commodore chose to be in a bad mood it was best to leave him in it—Bush was better than a wife, thought Hornblower, his acute perceptions noting the gesture.

Hornblower pulled out his watch as a reminder to Bush of the next thing to be done.

"Call the watch below. Dismiss the watch on deck for breakfast," ordered Bush.

It was strange—dramatic, presumably, would be the right word—to be sitting here in this Baltic sunshine, breakfasting at leisure while no more than three miles away the hordes of the tyrant of Europe could only gaze at them impotently. Brown was offering cigars; Bush cut the end off his with the big sailor's clasp-knife which he brought out of a side pocket, and Brown brought the smouldering slow match from the tub beside the quarterdeck carronades to give them a light. Hornblower breathed in the smoke luxuriously and found it impossible to maintain his evil humour—not with the sun shining, his cigar drawing well, and the advanced guard of a million French soldiers three miles distant. The table was whipped away from between them and he stretched his legs. Even Bush did the same—at least, he sat farther back instead of perching on the edge of his chair; his wooden leg stuck out straight before him although the other one remained decorously bent. The *Nonsuch* was still thrashing along gloriously under plain sail, heeling a little to the wind with the green sea creaming joyously under her bows. Hornblower pulled at his cigar again in strange spiritual peace. After his recent discontent it was like the unbelievable cessation of toothache.

"Hven nearly within random shot, sir," reported the first lieutenant.

"Call all hands to quarters," ordered Bush, with a glance at Hornblower.

But Hornblower sat on tranquilly. He felt suddenly quite certain that the guns on Hven would not open fire, and he did not want to throw away ungratefully the cigar which had served him so well. Bush took a second glance at him and decided to sit still too. He hardly deigned to spare a glance for Hven as it came up under the lee bow and passed away under the lee quarter. Hornblower thought of Saltholm and Amager

58

lying ahead; that would be the time of greatest danger, for both islands were in Danish hands and the twelve-fathom channel passed between them and close to both of them. But there was plenty of time to finish this cigar. It was with sincere regret that he drew the last puff, rose slowly to his feet, and sauntered to the lee rail to pitch the end carefully overside.

The sudden swoop of his squadron in the grey dawn had taken the Elsinore garrison by surprise, but there could be no surprise for Saltholm and Amager. They could see his ships in this clear weather a dozen miles away, and the gunners would have ample time to make all preparations to receive them. He looked ahead down the line of vessels.

"Make a signal to *Moth*," he snapped over his shoulder: "'Keep better station.'"

If the line were to straggle it would be the longer exposed to fire. The land was in plain sight through his glass; it was lucky that Saltholm was low-lying so that its guns had only poor command. Copenhagen must be only just out of sight, below the horizon to starboard. Vickery was taking *Lotus* exactly down the course Hornblower had laid down for him in his orders. There was the smoke bursting out from Saltholm. There was the boom of the guns—a very irregular salvo. He could see no sign of damage to the ships ahead. *Lotus* was firing back; he doubted if her popgun nine-pounders could hit at that range, but the smoke might help to screen her. All Saltholm was covered with smoke now, and the boom of the guns across the water was in one continuous roll like a drum. They were still out of range of Amager at present; Vickery was wearing ship now for the turn. Bush very sensibly had leadsmen in the chains.

"By the mark seven!"

Seven fathoms was ample, with the tide making. Brown against green—those were the batteries on Saltholm, dimly visible in the smoke; young Carlin on the main deck was pointing out the target to the port-side twelve-pounders.

"By the deep six, and a half six!"

A sudden tremendous crash, as the port-side battery fired all together. The *Nonsuch* heaved with the recoil, and as she did so came the leadsman's cry:—

"And a half six!"

"Starboard your helm," said Bush. "Stand by, the starboard guns!"

Nonsuch poised herself for the turn; as far as Hornblower could tell, not a shot had yet been fired at her.

"By the mark five!"

They must be shaving the point of the shoal. There were the Amager batteries in plain sight; the starboard-side guns, with the additional elevation due to the heel of the ship, should be able to reach them. Both broadsides together, this time, an ear-splitting crash, and the smoke from the starboard guns billowed across the deck, bitter and irritant.

"And a half five!"

That was better. God, *Harvey* was hit. The bomb-ketch, two cable's lengths ahead of *Nonsuch*, changed in a moment from a fighting vessel to a wreck. Her towering mainmast, enormous for her size, had been cut through just above her deck; mast and shrouds, and the huge area of canvas she carried, were trailing over her quarter. Her stumpy mizzen topmast had gone as well, hanging down from the cap. *Raven*, as her orders dictated, swept past her, and *Harvey* lay helpless as *Nonsuch* hurtled down upon her.

"Back the main tops'l!" roared Bush.

"Stand by with the heaving line, there!" said Hurst.

"And a half five!" called for leadsman.

"Helm a-lee," said Bush, and then in the midst of the bustle the starboard broadside bellowed out again, as the guns bore on the Amager batteries, and the smoke swept across the decks. *Nonsuch* heaved over; her backed topsail caught the wind and checked her way as she recovered. She hovered with the battered *Harvey* close alongside. Hornblower could see Mound, her captain, directing the efforts of her crew from his station at the foot of her mizzenmast. Hornblower put his speaking-trumpet to his lips.

"Cut that wreckage away, smartly, now."

"Stand by for the line!" shouted Hurst.

The heaving line, well thrown, dropped across her mizzen shrouds, and Mound himself seized it; Hurst dashed below to superintend the passing across of the towline, which lay on the lower gun deck all ready to be passed out of an after gunport. A splintering crash forward told that one shot at least from Amager had struck home on *Nonsuch*. Axes were cutting furiously at the tangle of shrouds over the *Harvey's* side; a group of seamen were furiously hauling in the three-inch line from *Nonsuch* which had been bent on the heaving line. Another crash forward; Hornblower swung round to see that a couple of foremast shrouds had parted at the chains. With the *Nonsuch* lying nearly head to wind, neither port-side nor starboard-side guns bore to make reply, but Carlin had a couple of gun's crews hard at work with handspikes heaving the two foremost guns round—it would be as well to keep the batteries under fire so as not to allow them to indulge in mere target practice. Hornblower turned back; *Nonsuch's* stern was almost against *Harvey's* quarter, but some capable officer already had two spars out from the stern gallery to boom her off. The big cable itself was on its way over now; as Hornblower watched he saw *Harvey's* men reach and grasp it.

"We'll take you out stern first, Mr. Mound," yelled Hornblower through his speaking-trumpet—there was no time to waste while they took the cable forward. Mound waved acknowledgment.

"Quarter less five," came the voice of the leadsman; the leeway which the two vessels were making was carrying down on the Saltholm shoals.

On the heels of the cry came the bang-bang of the two guns which Carlin had brought to bear on the Amager batteries, and following that came the howl of shot passing overhead. There were holes in main and mizzen topsails—the enemy were trying to disable *Nonsuch*.

"Shall I square away, sir?" came Bush's voice at Hornblower's side.

Mound had taken a turn with the cable's end round the base of the *Harvey's* mizzenmast, which was stepped so far aft as to make a convenient point to tow from. He was waving his arms to show that all was secure, and his axemen were hacking at the last of the mainmast shrouds.

"Yes, Captain." Hornblower hesitated before dropping a word of advice on a matter which was strictly Bush's business. "Take the strain slowly, or you'll part the tow or pluck that mizzenmast clear out of her. Haul your headsails up to starboard, then get her slowly under way before you brace up your main tops'l."

"Aye aye, sir."

Bush showed no resentment at Hornblower's telling him what to do, for he knew very well that Hornblower's advice was something more valuable than gold could ever buy.

"And if I were doing it I'd keep the towline short—stern first with nothing to keep her under control, *Harvey*'ll tow better that way."

"Aye aye, sir."

Bush turned and began to bellow his orders. With the handling of the headsails the *Nonsuch* turned away from the wind, and instantly Carlin brought his guns into action again. The ship was wrapped in smoke and in the infernal din of the guns. Shots from Amager were still striking home or passing overhead, and in the next interval of comparative silence the voice of the leadsman made itself heard.

"And a half four!"

The sooner they were away from these shoals the better. Fore and mizzen topsails were filling slightly, and the headsails were drawing. The towline tightened, and as their ears recovered from the shock of the next broadside they became aware of a vast creaking as the cable and the bitts took the strain—on the *Nonsuch's* quarterdeck they could even hear *Harvey's* mizzenmast creaking with the strain. The ketch came round slowly, to the accompaniment of fierce bellowings at *Nonsuch's* helmsman, as the two-decker wavered at the pull across her stern. It was all satisfactory; Hornblower nodded to himself—if Bush were stealing glances at him (as he expected) and saw that nod it would do no harm.

"Hands to the braces!" bellowed Bush, echoing Hornblower's thoughts. With fore and mizzen topsails trimmed and drawing well, *Nonsuch* began to increase her speed, and the ketch followed her with as much docility as could be expected of a vessel with no rudder to keep her straight. Then she sheered off in ugly fashion to starboard before the tug of the line pulled her straight again to a *feu de joie* of creaks. Hornblower shook his head at the sight, and Bush held back his order to brace up the main topsail.

"Starboard your helm, Mr. Mound!" shouted Hornblower through his speaking-trumpet. Putting *Harvey's* rudder over might have some slight effect—the behaviour of every ship being towed was an individual problem. Speed was increasing, and that, too, might affect *Harvey's* behaviour for better or worse.

"By the mark five!"

That was better. And *Harvey* was behaving herself, too. She was yawing only very slightly now; either the increase in speed or the putting-over of the rudder was having its effect.

"That's well done, Captain Bush," said Hornblower pompously.

"Thank you, sir," said Bush, and promptly ordered the main topsail to be braced up.

63

"By the deep six!"

They were well off the Saltholm shoal, then, and Hornblower suddenly realised that the guns had not fired for some time, and he had heard nothing of any more firing from Amager. They were through the channel, then, out of range of the batteries, at a cost of only a single spar knocked away. There was no need to come within range of any other hostile gun—they could round Falsterbo well clear of the Swedish batteries.

"By the deep nine!"

Bush was looking at him with that expression of puzzled admiration which Hornblower had seen on his face before. Yet it had been easy enough. Anyone could have foreseen that it would be best to leave to the *Nonsuch* the duty of towing any cripples out of range, and, once that was granted, anyone would have the sense to have a cable roused out and led aft ready to undertake the duty instantly, with heaving lines and all the other gear to hand, and anyone would have posted *Nonsuch* last in the line, both to endure the worst of the enemy's fire and to be in position to run down to a cripple and start towing without delay. Anyone could have made those deductions—it was vaguely irritating that Bush should look like that.

"Make a general signal to heave-to," said Hornblower. "Captain Bush, stand by if you please to cast off the tow. I'll have *Harvey* jury-rigged before we round Falsterbo. Perhaps you'll be good enough to send a party on board to help with the work."

And with that he went off below. He had seen all he wanted both of Bush and of the world for the present. He was tired, drained of his energy. Later there would be time enough to sit at his desk and begin the weary business of: "Sir, I have the honour to report . . ." There would be dead and wounded to enumerate, too.

Chapter VII

HIS BRITANNIC MAJESTY'S seventy-four-gun ship *Nonsuch* was out of sight of land in the Baltic. She was under easy sail, running before that persistent westerly wind, and astern of her, like a couple of ugly ducklings following their portly mother, came the two bomb-ketches. Far out to starboard, only just in sight, was the *Lotus,* and far out to port was the *Raven.* Beyond the *Raven,* unseen from the *Nonsuch,* was the *Clam;* the four ships made a visual chain which could sweep the narrow neck of the Baltic, from Sweden to Rügen, from side to side. There was still no news; in spring, with the melting of the ice, the whole traffic of the Baltic was outwards, towards England and Europe, and with this westerly wind so long prevailing little was astir. The air was fresh and keen, despite the sunshine, and the sea was silver-grey under the dappled sky.

Hornblower gasped and shuddered as he took his bath under the wash-deck pump. For fifteen years he had served in tropical and Mediterranean waters; he had had lukewarm seawater pumped over him far more often than he could remember, and this Baltic water, chilled by the melting ice in the gulfs of Bothnia and Finland, and the snow water of the Vistula and the Oder, was still a shock to him. There was something stimulating about it, all the same, and he pranced grotesquely under the heavy jet, forgetful—as he always was while having his bath—of the proper dignity of the commodore. Half a dozen seamen, working in leisurely fashion under the direction of the ship's carpenter in replacing a shattered gunport, stole wondering glances at him. The two seamen at the

65

pump, and Brown standing by with towel and dressing gown, preserved a proper solemnity of aspect, close under his eyes as they were.

Suddenly the jet ceased; a skinny little midshipman was standing saluting his naked commodore. Despite the gravity of addressing so great a man the child was round-eyed with wonder at this fantastic behaviour on the part of an officer whose doings were a household word.

"What is it?" said Hornblower, water streaming off him. He could not return the salute.

"Mr. Montgomery sent me, sir. *Lotus* signals 'Sail to leeward,' sir."

"Very good."

Hornblower snatched the towel from Brown, but the message was too important for time to be wasted drying himself, and he ran up the companion still wet and naked with Brown following with his dressing gown. The officer of the watch touched his hat as Hornblower appeared on the quarterdeck—it was like some old fairy story, the way everybody rigidly ignored the commodore's lack of clothes.

"New signal from *Lotus*, sir. 'Chase has tacked. Chase is on the port tack, bearing east by north, half east.'"

Hornblower leaped to the compass; only the topsails of the *Lotus* were in sight from the deck as he took the bearing by eye. Whatever that sail was, he must intercept it and gather news. He looked up to see Bush hastening on deck, buttoning his coat.

"Captain Bush, I'll trouble you to alter course two points to starboard."

"Aye aye, sir."

"*Lotus* signalling again, sir. 'Chase is a ship. Probably British merchantman.'"

"Very good. Set all sail, Captain Bush, if you please."

"Aye aye, sir."

The pipes shrilled through the ship, and four

hundred men went pouring up the ratlines to loose the royals and set studding sails. Hornblower raised a professional eye to watch the operation, carried out under a storm of objurgation from the officer of the watch. The still clumsy crew was driven at top speed by the warrant officers through the evolution, and it was hardly completed before there was a yell from the masthead.

"Sail on the starboard bow!"

"Must be the ship *Lotus* can see, sir," said Bush. "Masthead, there! What can you see of the sail?"

"She's a ship, sir, close-hauled an' coming up fast. We're headin' to meet her."

"Hoist the colours, Mr. Hurst. If she was beating up for The Sound, sir, she would have tacked whether she saw *Lotus* or not."

"Yes," said Hornblower.

A shriek came from the masthead, where one of the midshipmen of the watch, an urchin who had not yet mastered his changing voice, had run up with a glass.

"British colours, sir!"

Hornblower remembered he was still wet and naked; at least, he was still wet in those parts of him which did not offer free play for the wind to dry him. He began to dab at these inner corners with the towel he still held, only to be interrupted again.

"There she is!" said Bush; the ship's upper sails were over the horizon, in view from the deck.

"Lay a course to pass her within hail, if you please," said Hornblower.

"Aye aye, sir. Starboard a point, quartermaster. Get those stu'ns'ls in again, Mr. Hurst."

The ship they were approaching held her course steadily; there was nothing suspicious about her, not even the fact that she had gone about immediately on sighting *Lotus*.

"Timber from the south Baltic, I expect, sir," said Bush, training his glass. "You can see the deck cargo now."

67

Like most ships bound out of the Baltic her decks were piled high with timber, like barricades along the bulwarks.

"Make the merchant ships' private signal if you please, Captain," said Hornblower.

He watched the reply run up the ship's halliards.

"A—T—numeral—five—seven, sir," read Hurst through his glass. "That's the correct reply for last winter, and she won't have received the new code yet."

"Signal her to heave-to," said Hornblower.

With no more delay than was to be expected of a merchant ship, unadept at reading signals, and with a small crew, the ship backed her main topsail and lay-to. The *Nonsuch* came hurtling down upon her.

"That's the yellow Q she's hoisting now, sir," said Hurst, suddenly. "The fever flag."

"Very good. Heave-to, Captain Bush, if you please."

"Aye aye, sir. I'll keep to wind'ard of her, too, if you've no objection, sir."

The *Nonsuch* laid her topsails to the mast and rounded-to, rocking in the gentle trough of the waves a pistol shot to windward. Hornblower took his speaking-trumpet.

"What ship's that?"

"*Maggie Jones* of London. Eleven days out from Memel!"

In addition to the man at the wheel there were only two figures visible on the poop deck of the *Maggie Jones;* one of them, wearing white duck trousers and a blue coat, was obviously the captain. It was he who was answering by speaking-trumpet.

"What's that yellow flag for?"

"Smallpox. Seven cases on board, and two dead. First case a week ago."

"Smallpox, by God!" muttered Bush. A frightful mental picture came up before his mind's eye, of what smallpox would do, let loose in his precious *Nonsuch,* with nine hundred men crammed into her restricted space.

"Why are you sailing without convoy?"

"None available at Memel. The rendezvous for the trade's off Langeland on the twenty fourth. We're beating up for the Belt now."

"What's the news?" Hornblower had waited patiently during all these interminable sentences before asking that question.

"The Russian embargo still holds, but we're sailing under licence."

"Sweden?"

"God knows, sir. Some say they've tightened up their embargo there."

A curious muffled howl came from below decks in the *Maggie Jones* at that moment, just audible in the *Nonsuch*.

"What's that noise?" asked Hornblower.

"One of the smallpox cases, sir. Delirious. They say the Czar's meeting Bernadotte next week for a conference somewhere in Finland."

"Any sign of war between France and Russia?"

"None that I could see in Memel."

That delirious patient must be very violent for his shrieks to reach Hornblower's ears at this distance against the wind. Hornblower heard them again. Was it possible for one man to make all that noise? It sounded more like a muffled chorus to Hornblower. Hornblower felt a sudden wave of suspicion surging up within him. The white-trousered figure on the *Maggie Jones's* poop was altogether too glib, too professional in his talk. A naval officer might possibly discuss the chances of war in the Baltic as coldly as this man was doing, but a merchant captain would put more feeling in his words. And more than one man was making that noise in her forecastle. The captain could easily have offered his information about the Czar's meeting with Bernadotte as a red herring to distract Hornblower's attention from the cries below deck. Something was wrong.

69

"Captain Bush," said Hornblower, "send a boat with a boarding party over to that ship."

"Sir!" protested Bush, wildly. "Sir—she has smallpox on board—sir! Aye aye, sir."

Bush's protests died an uneasy death at the look on Hornblower's face. Bush told himself that Hornblower knew as well as he did the frightful possibilities of the introduction of smallpox into *Nonsuch*. Hornblower knew the chances he was taking. And one more look at Hornblower's face told Bush that the decision had not been an easy one.

Hornblower put the trumpet to his lips again.

"I'm sending a boat to you," he shouted. It was hard at twenty yards' distance to detect any change in the manner of the man he was addressing, especially when hampered with a speaking-trumpet, but Hornblower thought he could see the captain start a little. Certainly there was a decided pause before he answered.

"As you wish, sir. I have warned you of smallpox. Could you send a surgeon and medicines?"

That was exactly what he should have said. But all the same, there was that suspicious pause before answering, as if the man had been taken by surprise and had searched round in his mind for the best reply to make. Bush was standing by, with misery in his face, hoping that Hornblower would countermand his order, but Hornblower made no sign. Under the orders of the boatswain the whaler rose to the pull of the tackles, was swayed outboard, and dropped into the sea. A midshipman and a boat's crew dropped down into her, sulkily. They would have gone cheerfully to board an armed enemy, but the thought of a loathsome disease unmanned them.

"Push off," ordered the officer of the watch, after a last glance at Hornblower. The whaler danced over the waves towards the *Maggie Jones,* and then Hornblower saw the captain dash his speaking-trumpet to the deck and look round wildly as though for some means of escape.

"Stay hove-to, or I'll sink you," roared Hornblower, and with a gesture of despair the captain stood still, dropping in defeat.

The whaler hooked onto the *Maggie Jones's* main chains and the midshipman let his party onto the decks with a rush. There was no sign of any opposition offered, but as the seamen ran aft there was the sudden pop of a pistol, and Hornblower saw the midshipman bending over the writhing, white-trousered body of the captain. He found himself taking an oath that he would break that midshipman, court-martial him, ruin him, and have him begging his bread in the gutter if he had wantonly killed the captain. Hornblower's hunger and thirst for news, for facts, for information, was so intense that the thought of the captain escaping him by death roused him to ferocious bitterness.

"Why the devil didn't I go myself?" he demanded of no one in particular. "Captain Bush, I'll be obliged if you'll have my barge called away."

"But the smallpox, sir—"

"Smallpox be damned. And there's none on board that ship."

The midshipman's voice came across the water to them.

"*Nonsuch* ahoy! She's a prize. Taken yesterday by a French privateer."

"Who's that captain I was speaking to?" demanded Hornblower.

"A renegade Englishman, sir. He shot himself as we came on board."

"Is he dead?"

"Not yet, sir."

"Mr. Hurst," said Bush, "send the surgeon over. I'll give him one minute to get his gear together. I want that renegade's life saved so that we can see how he looks at a yard-arm."

"Send him in my barge," said Hornblower, and then, through the speaking-trumpet, "send the prisoners and the ship's officers over to me."

"Aye aye, sir."

"And now I'll get some clothes on, by God," said Hornblower; he had only just realised that he had been standing naked on the quarterdeck for an hour or more—if he had obeyed his first impulse and gone over in his barge he would have boarded the *Maggie Jones* without a stitch on.

The captain and the two mates were ushered down into Hornblower's cabin, where he and Bush questioned them eagerly, the chart of the Baltic spread out before him.

"We heard that renegade tell you the truth, sir," said the captain. "We were ten days out from Memel bound for the Belt when he pounced on us yesterday—big ship-rigged privateer, ten guns a side, flush-decked. Name *Blanchefleur*, whatever way you say it. What the Frogs call a corvette. French colours. They put a prize crew on board under that renegade— Clarke's his name, sir—an' I think we were headed for Kiel when you caught us. They shut us up in the lazarette. God, how we yelled, hoping you'd hear us."

"We heard you," said Bush.

"How were things at Memel when you left?" demanded Hornblower.

The captain's face wrinkled; if he had been French he would have shrugged his shoulders.

"The same as ever. Russian ports are still closed to us, but they'll give anyone a licence to trade who asks for it. It's the same with the Swedes on the other side."

"What about war between Bonaparte and Russia?"

This time the tangle of doubt really made the captain shrug.

"Everyone's talking about it, but nothing definite yet. Soldiers everywhere. If Boney really fights 'em he'll find 'em as ready as Russians ever are."

"Do you think he will?"

"I wish you'd tell *me*, sir. I don't know. But it was true what Clarke told you, sir. The Czar and Bernadotte are meeting soon. Perhaps you can guess what that means. It means nothing to a plain man like me, sir. There have been so many of these meetings and conferences and congresses."

So there it was; Sweden and Russia were still in the equivocal position of being nominal enemies of England and nominal allies of Bonaparte, pretending to make war, pretending to be at peace, half belligerent, half neutral, in the strange manner which seemed to have become fashionable nowadays. It was all doubtful whether Bonaparte would take the tremendous step of waging war on Russia. No one could analyse Bonaparte's motives. One might think that he would do better for himself by turning all his vast resources towards finishing off the war in Spain and endeavouring to strike down England before attempting the conquest of the East; but on the other hand a swift decisive blow at Russia might free him from the menace of a powerful and doubtfully friendly nation at his back. Bonaparte had conquered so often; he had struck down every nation in Europe—except England—and it hardly seemed likely that Russia could withstand the impact of his massed forces. With Russia beaten he would have no enemies left on the mainland at all. There would only be England left to oppose him, singlehanded. It was comforting that England had not taken active measures in support of Finland when Russia attacked her, all the same. That made a working alliance with Russia far more practicable now.

"Now tell me more about this *Blanchefleur*," said Hornblower, bending over the chart.

"She nabbed us off Rügen, sir. Sassnitz bore so'west, eight miles. You see, sir—"

Hornblower listened to the explanation with attention. A twenty-gun corvette under a good French

73

captain was a serious menace loose in the Baltic. With the trade beginning to move on the melting of the ice it would be his first duty to capture her or drive her into port and blockade her. A ship of that force would be able to put up a good fight even against one of his sloops. He hoped he could entrap her, for she would be far too fast for *Nonsuch* to overhaul her in a stern chase. She was sending her prizes to Kiel, for there they could dispose of the prisoners, pick up a French crew, and start the hazardous voyage round Denmark to the west—Bonaparte needed naval stores, with ships of war building in every port from Hamburg to Trieste.

"Thank you, gentlemen," he said. "I'll not detain you longer. Captain Bush, we'll talk to the prisoners next."

But there was little to learn from the seamen of the captured prize crew, even though they were brought in separately for questioning. Four of them were Frenchmen; Hornblower conducted his own examination of them, with Bush looking on admiringly. Bush had already succeeded in forgetting all the little French he had so painfully learned during his enforced sojourn in France. Two were Danes, and two were Germans; Mr. Braun was called in to interpret while they were questioned. They were all experienced seamen, and as far as Hornblower could gather they had all been driven to take service in the *Blanchefleur* sooner than be conscripted into Bonaparte's navy or army. Even though they were faced with what might well be a lifetime in an English prison the Frenchmen refused any offer to serve in the British navy, but the others accepted immediately Braun put the suggestion to them. Bush rubbed his hands at acquiring four prime seamen in this fashion to help fill his chronically undermanned ships. They had picked up a little French in the *Blanchefleur*, and they would soon pick up enough English in the *Nonsuch* or the *Lotus;* certainly they would under the stimulus of a rope's end handled by an experienced petty officer.

"Take 'em away and read 'em in, Mr. Hurst," said Bush, rubbing his hands again. "Now, sir, shall we take a look at that damned renegade Englishman?"

Clarke was lying on the main deck of the *Nonsuch*, to which he had been hoisted from the boat by a tackle at the yard-arm, and the surgeon was still bending over him. He had tried to blow out his brains, but he had only succeeded in shattering his lower jaw. There was blood on his blue coat and on his white trousers, and his whole head was swathed in bandages, and he lay tossing in agony on the canvas sheet in which he had been hoisted. Hornblower peered down at him. The features he could see, chalk white so that the tan looked like a coat of dirt, were pinched and refined and weak, a thin nose and hollow cheeks, brown eyes like a woman's, with scanty sandy eyebrows above them. What little hair Hornblower could see was scanty and sandy too. Hornblower wondered what combination of circumstances could have led him into betraying his country and taking service with Bonaparte. Hatred of imprisonment, perhaps— Hornblower had known what it was to be a prisoner, in Ferrol and Rosas and in France. Yet that over-refined face did not seem to indicate the sort of personality that would fret itself to pieces in confinement. It might have been a woman, perhaps, who had driven him or led him to this, or he might be a deserter from the navy who had fled to escape punishment—it would be interesting to see if his back was scarred with the cat-o'-nine-tails. He might perhaps be an Irishman, one of those fanatics who in their desire to hurt England refused to see that the worst England had ever done to Ireland would be nothing compared with what Bonaparte would do to her if she were once in his power.

Whatever might be the case, he was a man of ability and quick wit. As soon as he had seen that *Lotus* had cut him off from escape to the mainland he had resolutely taken the only course that gave him any chance of safety. He had steered the *Maggie Jones* as innocently as kiss-your-hand up to *Nonsuch;* that suggestion of smallpox had been an ingenious one, and his conversation by speaking-trumpet had been very nearly natural.

"Is he going to live?" asked Bush of the surgeon.

"No, sir. The mandible is extensively comminuted on both sides—I mean his jaw is shattered, sir. There is some splintering of the maxilla as well, and his tongue—the whole glossopharyngeal region, in fact—is in rags. The hæmorrhage may prove fatal—in other words the man may bleed to death, although I do not think he will, now. But I do not think anything on earth can stop mortification—gangrene, in other words, sir—which in this area will prove immediately fatal. In any event the man will die of inanition, of hunger and thirst that is to say, even if we could keep him alive for a while by injections per rectum."

It was ghoulish to smile at the surgeon's pomposity, to make the inevitable light speech.

"It sounds as if nothing could save him, then."

It was a human life they were discussing.

"We must hang him, sir, before he dies," said Bush, turning to Hornblower. "We can convene a court-martial—"

"He cannot defend himself," replied Hornblower.

Bush spread his hands in a gesticulation which for him was vastly eloquent.

"What defence has he to offer, sir? We have all the evidence we need. The prisoners have supplied it apart from the obvious facts."

"He might be able to rebut the evidence, if he could speak," said Hornblower. It was an absurd thing to say. There could be no possible doubt of Clarke's guilt—his attempt at suicide proved it even if nothing else did; but Hornblower knew perfectly well that he was quite incapable of hanging a man who was physically unable to make any defence.

"He'll slip through our fingers if we wait, sir."

"Then let him."

"But the example to the men, sir—"

"No, no, no," flared Hornblower. "What sort of example would it be to the men to hang a dying man—a man who would not know what was being done to him, for that matter?"

It was horrible to see the faint play of expression in Bush's face. Bush was a kindly man, a good brother to his sisters and a good son to his mother, and yet there was that hint of the lust of cruelty, the desire for a hanging. No, that was not quite fair. What Bush lusted for was revenge—revenge on a traitor who had borne arms against their common country.

"It would teach the men not to desert, sir," said Bush, still feebly raising arguments. Hornblower knew—he had twenty years of experience—how every British captain was plagued by desertion, and spent half his waking hours wondering first how to find men and second how to retain them.

"It might," said Hornblower, "but I doubt it very much."

He could not imagine any good being done, and he certainly could picture the harm, if the men were forced to witness a helpless man, one who could not even stand on his feet, being noosed about the neck and swung up to the yard-arm.

Bush still hankered for blood. Even though he had no more to say, there was still a look in his face, there were still protests trembling on his lips.

"Thank you, Captain Bush," said Hornblower. "My mind is made up."

Bush did not know, and might never learn, that mere revenge, objectless, retaliatory, was always stale and unprofitable.

Chapter VIII

THE *Blanchefleur* would most likely still be hovering round the island of Rügen. Cape Arcona would be a profitable haunt—shipping coming down the Baltic from Russia and Finnish ports would make a landfall there, to be easily snapped up, hemmed in between the land and the two-fathom shoal of the Adlergrund. She would not know of the arrival of a British squadron, nor guess that the immediate recapture of the *Maggie Jones* had so quickly revealed her presence here.

"I think that is all perfectly plain, gentlemen?" said Hornblower, looking round his cabin at his assembled captains.

There was a murmur of assent. Vickery of the *Lotus* and Cole of the *Raven* were looking grimly expectant. Each of them was hoping that it would be his ship that would encounter the *Blanchefleur*—a successful single-ship action against a vessel of so nearly equal force would be the quickest way to be promoted captain from commander. Vickery was young and ardent—it was he who had commanded the boats at the cutting out of the *Sèvres*—and Cole was grey-headed and bent. Mound, captain of the *Harvey*, and Duncan, captain of the *Moth*, were both of them young lieutenants; Freeman of the cutter *Clam*, swarthy and with long black hair like a gypsy, was of a different type; it would be less surprising to hear he was captain of the smuggling craft than captain of a King's ship. It was Duncan who asked the next question.

"If you please, sir, is Swedish Pomerania neutral?"

"Whitehall would be glad to know the answer to

that question, Mr. Duncan," said Hornblower, with a grin. He wanted to appear stern and aloof, but it was not easy with these pleasant boys.

They grinned back at him; it was with a curious pang that Hornblower realised that his subordinates were already fond of him. He thought, guiltily, that if they only knew all the truth about him they might not like him so much.

"Any other questions, gentlemen? No? Then you can return to your ships and take your stations for the night."

At dawn when Hornblower came on deck there was a thin fog over the surface of the sea; with the dropping of the westerly wind the cold water flowing out from the melting ice packs of the Gulf of Finland had an opportunity of cooling the warm damp air and condensing its moisture into a cloud.

"It could be thicker, sir, but not much," grumbled Bush. The foremast was visible from the quarterdeck, but not the bowsprit. There was only a faint breeze from the north, and the *Nonsuch*, creeping along before it, was very silent, pitching hardly at all on the smooth sea, with a rattle of blocks and cordage.

"I took a cast with the deep-sea lead at six bells, sir," reported Montgomery. "Ninety one fathoms. Grey mud. That'll be the Arcona deep, sir."

"Very good, Mr. Montgomery," said Bush. Hornblower was nearly sure that Bush's curt manner to his lieutenants was modelled on the manner Hornblower used to employ towards him when he was first lieutenant.

"Nosing our way about with the lead," said Bush, disgustedly. "We might as well be a Dogger Bank trawler. And you remember what the prisoners said about the *Blanchefleur*, sir? They have pilots on board who know these waters like the palms of their hands."

Groping about in a fog in shoal waters was not the sort of exercise for which a big two-decker was designed, but the *Nonsuch* had a special value in this campaign. There were few ships this side of The Sound which could match her in force; under her protection the flotilla could cruise wherever necessary. Danes and Swedes and Russians and French had plenty of small craft, but when *Nonsuch* made her appearance they were powerless to hinder.

"If you please, sir," said Montgomery, touching his hat. "Isn't that gunfire which I can hear?"

Everybody listened, enwrapped in the clammy fog. The only noises to be heard were those of the ship, and the condensed fog dripping from the rigging to the deck. Then a flat-sounding thud came faintly to their ears.

"That's a gun, sir, or my name's not Sylvanus Montgomery!"

"From astern," said Hornblower.

"Beg your pardon, sir, but I thought it was on the port bow."

"Damn this fog," said Bush.

If the *Blanchefleur* once had warning of the presence of a British squadron in pursuit of her, and then got away, she would vanish like a needle in a haystack. Hornblower held up a wetted finger and glanced into the binnacle.

"Wind's north," he said. "Maybe nor' nor'east."

That was comforting. To leeward, the likely avenue of escape, lay Rügen and the coast of Swedish Pomerania, twenty miles away. If *Blanchefleur* did not slip through the net he had spread she would be hemmed in.

"Set the lead going, Mr. Montgomery," said Bush.

"Aye aye, sir."

"There's another gun!" said Hornblower. "On the port bow, sure enough."

A wild yell from the masthead.

"Sail ho! Sail right ahead!"

The mist was thinner in that direction. Perhaps as much as a quarter of a mile away could be seen the thinnest palest ghost of a ship creeping through the fog across the bows.

"Ship-rigged, flush-decked," said Bush. "That's the *Blanchefleur*, sure as a gun!"

She vanished as quickly as she had appeared, into a thicker bank of fog.

"Hard-a-starboard!" roared Bush. "Hands to the braces!"

Hornblower was at the binnacle, taking a hurried bearing.

"Steady as you go!" he ordered the helmsman. "Keep her at that!"

In this gentle breeze the heavily sparred privateer would be able to make better speed than a clumsy two-decker. All that could be hoped for would be to keep *Nonsuch* up to windward of her to head her off if she tried to break through the cordon.

"Call all hands," said Bush. "Beat to quarters."

The drums roared through the ship, and the hands came pouring up to their stations.

"Run out the guns," continued Bush. "One broadside into her, and she's ours."

The trucks roared as three hundred tons of metal were run out. At the breech of every gun there clustered an eager group; the linstocks smouldered sullenly.

"Masthead, there! Stay awake!" pealed Bush, and then more quietly to Hornblower, "He may double back and throw us off the scent."

There was always the possibility of the masthead being above this thin fog—the lookout in *Nonsuch* might catch a glimpse of the *Blanchefleur's* topmasts when nothing could be seen from the deck.

For several minutes there was no more sound save for the cry of the leadsman; *Nonsuch* rolled gently in the trough of the waves, but it was hard to realise in the mist of that she was making headway.

"By the mark twenty!" called the leadsman.

Before he had uttered the last word Hornblower

and Bush had turned to glance at each other; up to that moment their subconscious minds had been listening to the cries without their consciousness paying any attention. But "by the mark" meant that now there was at most twenty fathoms under them.

"Shoaling, sir," commented Bush.

Then the masthead lookout yelled again.

"Sail on the lee quarter, sir!"

Bush and Hornblower sprang to the rail, but in the clinging fog there was nothing to be seen.

"Masthead, there! What d'you see?"

"Nothin' now, sir. Just caught a glimpse of a ship's royals, sir. There they are again, sir. Two points—three points abaft the port beam."

"What's her course?"

"Same as ours, sir. She's gone again now."

"Shall we bear down on her, sir?" asked Bush.

"Not yet," said Hornblower.

"Stand to your guns on the portside!" ordered Bush.

Even a distant broadside might knock away a spar or two and leave the chase helpless.

"Tell the men not to fire without orders," said Hornblower. "That may be *Lotus*."

"So it may, by God," said Bush.

Lotus had been on *Nonsuch's* port beam in the cordon sweeping down towards Rügen. Someone had undoubtedly been firing—that must have been *Lotus*, and she would have turned in pursuit of the *Blanchefleur*, which could bring her into just the position where those royals had been seen; and the royals of two ship-rigged sloops, seen through mist, would resemble each other closely enough to deceive the eye even of an experienced seaman.

"Wind's freshening, sir," commented Hurst.

"That's so," said Bush. "Please God it clears this fog away."

Nonsuch was perceptibly leaning over to the freshening breeze. From forward came the cheerful music of the sea under the bows.

"By the deep eighteen!" called the leadsman.

Then twenty voices yelled together.

"There she is! Sail on the port beam! That's *Lotus!*"

The fog had cleared in this quarter, and there was *Lotus* under all sail, three cable's lengths away.

"Ask her where's the chase," snapped Bush.

"Sail—last—seen—ahead," read off the signal midshipman, glass to eye.

"Much use that is to us," Bush grumbled.

There were enough streaks of fog still remaining to obscure the whole circle of the horizon, even though there was a thin watery sunshine in the air, and a pale sun—silver instead of gold—visible to the eastward.

"There she is!" suddenly yelled someone at the masthead. "Hull down on the port quarter!"

"Stole away, by God!" said Hurst. "She must have put up her helm the moment she saw us."

The *Blanchefleur* was a good six miles away, with only her royals visible from the deck of the *Nonsuch*, heading downwind under all sail. A string of signal flags ran up *Lotus'* mast, and a gun from her called attention to the urgency of her signal.

"She's seen her too," said Bush.

"Wear ship, Captain Bush, if you please. Signal 'General chase.'"

Nonsuch came round on the other tack, amid the curses of the officers hurled at the men for their slowness. *Lotus* swung round with her bow pointing straight at *Blanchefleur*. With the coast of Pomerania ahead, *Nonsuch* to windward, and *Lotus* and *Raven* on either side, *Blanchefleur* was hemmed in.

"*Raven* must be nearly level with her over there, sir," said Bush, rubbing his hands. "And we'll pick the bombs up again soon, wherever they got to in the fog."

"By the deep fourteen!" chanted the leadsman.

Hornblower watched the man in the chains, whirling the lead with practised strength, dropping it in far ahead, reading off the depth as the ship passed

83

over the vertical line, and then hauling in ready for a fresh cast. It was tiring work, continuous severe exercise; moreover, the leadsman was bound to wet himself to the skin, hauling in a hundred feet of dripping line. Hornblower knew enough about life below decks to know that the man would have small chance of ever getting his clothes dry again; he could remember as a midshipman in Pellew's *Indefatigable* being at the lead that wild night when they went in and destroyed the *Droits de l'Homme* in the Biscay surf. He had been chilled to the bone that night, with fingers so numb as almost to be unable to feel the difference between the markers—the white calico and the leather with a hole in it and all the others. He probably could not heave the lead now if he tried, and he was quite sure he could not remember the arbitrary order of the markers. He hoped Bush would have the humanity and the commonsense to see that his leadsmen were relieved at proper intervals, and given special facilities for drying their clothes, but he could not interfere directly in the matter. Bush was personally responsible for the interior economy of the ship and would be quite rightly jealous of any interference; there were crumpled rose leaves in the bed even of a commodore.

"By the mark ten!" called the leadsman.

"*Raven* in sight beyond the chase, sir," reported a midshipman. "Heading to cut her off."

"Very good," said Hornblower.

"Rügen in sight, too, sir," said Bush. "That's Stubbenkammer, or whatever they call it—a white cliff, anyway."

Hornblower swung his glass round the horizon; fate was closing in on the *Blanchefleur*, unless she took refuge in the waters of Swedish Pomerania. And that was clearly what she was intending to do. Bush had the chart spread out before him and was taking bearings on the distant white streak of the Stubbenkammer. Hornblower studied the chart, looked over at the

84

distant ships, and back at the chart again. Stralsund was a fortress—it had stood more than one siege lately. If *Blanchefleur* got in there she would be safe if the Swedes saw fit to protect her. But the rest of the coast ahead was merely shoals and sand-banks; a couple of bays had water enough for coasting vessels—there were batteries marked in the chart to defend their entrances. Something might be attempted if *Blanchefleur* ran in one of those—she was probably of light enough draught—but it would be hopeless if she reached Stralsund.

"Signal *Lotus*," he said: "'Set course to cut chase off from Stralsund.'"

In the course of the interminable war every aid to navigation had disappeared. There was not a buoy left to mark the deep-water channel—the Bodden, the chart called it—up to Stralsund. Vickery in the *Lotus* would have to look lively with the lead as he found his way into it.

"By the mark seven!" called the leadsman; *Nonsuch* was in dangerously shoal water already; Bush was looking anxious.

"Shorten sail, if you please, Captain Bush."

There was no chance of *Nonsuch* overhauling *Blanchefleur*, and if they were going to run aground they might as well do so as gently as possible.

"Chase is hauling her wind, sir," said Hurst.

So she was; she was clearly giving up the attempt to reach Stralsund. That was thanks to Vickery, who had gone charging with gallant recklessness under full sail through the shoals to head her off.

"*Raven*'ll have a chance at her if she holds that course long!" said Bush in high excitement.

"Chase is going on the other tack!" said Hurst.

"And a half five!" called the leadsman.

Bush was biting his lips with anxiety; his precious ship was entangling herself among the shoals on a lee shore, and there was only thirty three feet of water under her now.

"Heave-to, Captain Bush," said Hornblower. There was no reason to run any further now until they could see what *Blanchefleur* intended. *Nonsuch* rounded-to and lay with her port bow breasting the gentle swell. The sun was pleasantly warm.

"What's happened to *Raven?*" exclaimed Bush.

The sloop's fore topmast, with yard and sail and everything, had broken clear off and was hanging down in a frightful tangle among her headsails.

"Aground, sir," said Hurst, glass to eye.

The force with which she had hit the sand had snapped her topmast clean off.

"She draws eight feet less than us, sir," said Bush, but all Hornblower's attention was directed again to *Blanchefleur*. Obviously she was finding her way up a channel to the shelter of Hiddensoe. On the chart there was a single sounding mark there, a laconic "2½" Fifteen feet of water, and a battery at the head of the long peninsula. *Blanchefleur* could reckon herself safe if the Swedes would defend her. On the horizon to windward Hornblower saw the queer topsails of the bomb-ketches; Duncan and Mound, after blundering about in the fog, must have caught sight of *Nonsuch* while on their way to the rendezvous off Cape Arcona.

"Send the boats to assist *Raven,* if you please, Captain Bush," said Hornblower.

"Aye aye, sir."

Hoisting longboat and cutter off their chocks and overside was an evolution calling for a couple of hundred hands. Pipes squealed and the bosun's cane stirred up the laggards. The sheaves squeaked in the blocks, bare feet stamped the decks, and even *Nonsuch's* massive bulk heeled a little with the transfer of weight. Hornblower betook himself to his telescope again.

Blanchefleur had found herself a curious anchorage. She lay between the main island of Rügen and the long narrow strip of Hiddensoe; the latter was more

86

of a sandspit than an island, a thread of sand dunes emerging from the yellow shallows. In fact *Blanchefleur's* spars were still in plain sight against the background of the low mud cliffs of Rügen; it was only her hull which was concealed by the dunes of Hiddensoe lying like a long curving breakwater in front of her. On one end of Hiddensoe was battery—Hornblower could see the silhouettes of the guns, black against the green of the grass-grown embrasures—which covered one entrance to the tiny roadstead; at the other end the breaking waves showed that there was not water enough even for a ship's longboat to pass. The squadron had succeeded in cutting off the privateer's escape into Stralsund, but it seemed as if she were just as safe where she was now, with miles of shoals all round her and a battery to protect her; any attempt to cut her out must be made by the ship's boats, rowing in plain view for miles through the shallows, then through a narrow channel under the guns of the battery, and finally bringing out the prize under the same guns and over the unknown shoals. That was not a tempting prospect; he could land marines on the seaward front of Hiddensoe and try to storm the battery by brute force, but the attempt would be inviting a bloody repulse if there were no surprise to cover the assaulting party. Besides, the battery's garrison would be Swedes, and he did not want to shed Swedish blood—Sweden was only a nominal enemy, but any vigorous action on his part might easily make her an active one. Hornblower remembered the paragraphs of his instructions which bore on this very point.

As if in echo to his thoughts the signal midshipman saluted with a new report.

"Signal from *Lotus*, sir."

Hornblower read the message written in crude capitals on the slate:—

"Flags of truce coming out from Stralsund. Have allowed them to pass."

"Acknowledge," said Hornblower.

What the devil did that mean? One flag of truce he could expect, but Vickery was reporting two at least. He swung his glass over to where Vickery had very sensibly anchored *Lotus*, right between *Blanchefleur's* refuge and any possible succour from Stralsund. There were one—two—three—small sails, heading straight for the *Nonsuch*, having just rounded *Lotus*. They were all of them of the queer Baltic rig, like Dutchmen with a foreign flavour—rounded bows and lee-boards and big gaff-mainsails. Close-hauled, with the white water creaming under their blunt bows and the spray flying in sheets even in this moderate breeze, they were clearly being sailed for all they were worth, as if it were a race.

"What in God's name?" said Bush, training his glass on them.

It might be a ruse to gain time. Hornblower looked round again at the spars of *Blanchefleur* above the sandspit. She had furled everything and was riding at anchor.

"White above yellow and blue, sir," said Bush, still watching the approaching boats. "That's Swedish colours under a flag of truce."

Hornblower turned his glass on the leader and confirmed Bush's decision.

"The next one, sir—" Bush laughed apologetically at his own innocence "—I know it's strange, sir, but it looks just like the British ens'n under a flag of truce."

It was hard to believe; and it was easy to make a mistake in identifying a small boat's flag at that distance. But Hornblower's glass seemed to show the same thing.

"What do you make of that second boat, Mr. Hurst?"

"British colours under white, sir," said Hurst without hesitation.

The third boat was some long way astern, and her colours were not so easy to make out.

"French, I think, sir," said Hurst, but the leading boat was approaching fast now.

It was a tall portly gentleman who was swung up onto the deck in the bosun's chair, clinging to his cocked hat. He wore a blue coat with gold buttons and epaulettes, and he hitched his sword and his stock into position before laying the hat—a fore-and-aft one with a white plume and a Swedish cockade—across his chest in a sweeping bow.

"Baron Basse," he said.

Hornblower bowed.

"Captain Sir Horatio Hornblower, commodore commanding this squadron."

Basse was a heavily jowled man with a big hook-nose and a cold grey eye; and it was obvious that he could only guess faintly at what Hornblower said.

"You fight?" he asked, with an effort.

"I am in pursuit of a privateer under French colours," said Hornblower, and then, realising the difficulty of making himself understood when he had to pick his words with diplomatic care, "Here, where's Mr. Braun?"

The interpreter came forward with a brief explanation of himself in Swedish, and Hornblower watched the interplay of glances between the two. They were clearly the deadliest political enemies, meeting here on the comparatively neutral ground of a British man-o'-war. Basse brought out a letter from his breast pocket and passed it to Braun, who glanced at it and handed it to Hornblower.

"That is a letter from the Governor-General of Swedish Pomerania," he explained, "saying that this gentleman, the Baron Basse, has his fulll confidence."

"I understand," said Hornblower.

Basse was already talking rapidly to Braun.

"He says," explained Braun, "that he wants to know what you will do."

"Tell him," said Hornblower, "that that depends on what the Swedes do. Ask him if Sweden is neutral."

89

Obviously the reply was not a simple "yes" or "no." Basse offered a lengthy explanation.

"He says that Sweden only wants to be at peace with all the world," said Braun.

"Tell him that that means neutrality, then, and neutrality has obligations as well as privileges. There is a ship of war under French colours there. She must be warned that her presence in Swedish waters can only be tolerated for a limited time, and I must be informed of what the time limit is."

Basse's heavy face showed considerable embarrassment at Braun's translation of Hornblower's demand. He worked his hands violently as he made his reply.

"He says he cannot violate the laws of international amity," said Braun.

"Say that that is exactly what he is doing. That ship cannot be allowed to use a Swedish port as a base of operations. She must be warned to leave, and if she will not, then she must be taken over and a guard put in her to make sure she does not slip away."

Basse positively wrung his hands as Braun spoke to him, but any reply he was going to make was cut short by Bush's salute to Hornblower.

"The French flag of truce is alongside, sir. Shall I allow them to send someone on board?"

"Oh yes," said Hornblower testily.

The new figure that came in through the entry port was even more decorative than Basse, although a much smaller man. Across his blue coat lay the watered red silk ribbon of the Legion of Honour, and its star glittered on his breast. He, too, swept off his hat in an elaborate bow.

"The Count Joseph Dumoulin," he said, speaking French, "Consul-General in Swedish Pomerania of His Imperial and Royal Majesty Napoleon, Emperor of the French, King of Italy, Protector of the Confederation of the Rhine, Mediator of the Swiss Republic."

"Captain Hornblower," said Hornblower. He was

suddenly excessively cautious, because his government had never recognised those resounding titles which Dumoulin had just reeled off. In the eyes of King George and his ministers, Napoleon, Emperor of the French, was merely General Bonaparte in his personal capacity, and Chief of the French Government in his official one. More than once British officers had found themselves in serious trouble for putting their names to documents—cartels and the like—which bore even incidental references to the Empire.

"Is there anyone who can speak French?" asked Dumoulin politely. "I regret bitterly my complete inability to speak English."

"You can address yourself to me, sir," said Hornblower, "and I should be glad of an explanation of your presence in this ship."

"You speak admirable French, sir," said Dumoulin. "Ah, of course I remember. You are the Captain Hornblower who made the sensational escape from France a year ago. It is a great pleasure to meet a gentleman of such renown."

He bowed again. It gave Hornblower a queer self-conscious pleasure to find that his reputation had preceded him even into this obscure corner of the Baltic, but it irritated him at the same time, as having nothing to do with the urgent matter in hand.

"Thank you," he said, "but I am still waiting for an explanation of why I have the honour of this visit."

"I am here to support *Monsieur le Baron* in his statement of the belligerent position of Swedish Pomerania."

Braun interpreted, and Basse's embarrassment perceptibly increased.

"Boat with English colours alongside, sir," interrupted Bush.

The man who came on board was immensely fat, and dressed in a sober black civilian suit.

"Hauptmann," he said, bending himself at the

waist; he spoke English with a thick German accent. "His Britannic Majesty's Consular Agent at Stralsund."

"What can I do for you, Mr. Hauptmann?" asked Hornblower, trying not to allow himself to grow bewildered.

"I have come," said Hauptmann—actually what he said was "I haf gome"—"to help explain to you the position here in Swedish Pomerania."

"I see no need for explanation," said Hornblower. "If Sweden is neutral, then that privateer must be either forced to leave or taken into custody. If Sweden is a belligerent, then my hands are free and I can take whatever steps I think proper."

He looked round at his audience. Braun began to translate into Swedish.

"What was it you said, Captain?" asked Dumoulin.

Desperately Hornblower plunged into a French translation, and the curse of Babel descended upon the *Nonsuch*. Everyone tried to speak at once; translation clashed with expostulation. Clearly, what Basse wanted was the best of both worlds, to make both France and England believe Sweden was friendly. What Dumoulin wanted was to make sure that *Blanchefleur* would be enabled to continue her depredations among British shipping. Hornblower looked at Hauptmann.

"Gome with me for a minute, please," said Hauptmann. He put his fat hand on Hornblower's shrinking arm and led him across the quarterdeck out of earshot.

"You are a young man," said Hauptmann, "and I know you naval officers. You are all headstrong. You must be guided by my advice. Do nothing in a hurry, sir. The international situation here is tense, very tense indeed. A false move may mean ruin. An insult to Sweden might mean war, actual war instead of pretended war. You must be careful what you do."

"I am always careful," snapped Hornblower, "but

do you expect me to allow that privateer to behave as if this were Brest or Toulon?"

Braun came over to them.

"Baron Basse asks me to say to you, sir, that Bonaparte has two hundred thousand men on the borders of Pomerania. He wants me to say that one cannot offend the master of an army that size."

"That bears out what I say, Captain," said Hauptmann.

Here came Dumoulin, and Basse after him—no one would trust any one of his colleagues to be alone with the British captain for a moment. Hornblower's tactical instinct came to his rescue; the best defensive is a vigorous local offensive. He turned on Hauptmann.

"May I ask, sir, how His Majesty maintains a consular agent in a port whose neutrality is in doubt?"

"It is necessary because of the need for licences to trade."

"Are you accredited to the Swedish government by His Majesty?"

"No, sir. I am accredited by His Bavarian Majesty."

"His *Bavarian* Majesty?"

"I am a subject of His Bavarian Majesty."

"Who happens to be at war with His Britannic Majesty," said Hornblower dryly. The whole tangle of Baltic politics, of hole-and-corner hostilities and neutralities, was utterly beyond unravelling. Hornblower listened to everyone's pleas and expostulations until he could bear it no longer; his impatience grew at length apparent to his anxious interviewers.

"I can form no conclusion at present, gentlemen," said Hornblower. "I must have time to think over the information you have given me. Baron Basse, as representative of a Governor-General, I fancy you are entitled to a seventeen-gun salute on leaving this ship?"

The salutes echoed over the yellow-green water as the officials went over the side. Seventeen guns for Baron Basse. Eleven for Dumoulin, the Consul-General. Hauptmann, as a mere Consular Agent, rated only five, the smallest salute noticed in naval ceremonial. Hornblower stood at the salute as Hauptmann went down into his boat, and then sprang into activity again.

"Signal for the captains of *Moth, Havey,* and *Clam* to come on board," he ordered, abruptly.

The bomb-vessels and the cutter were within easy signalling distance now; there were three hours of daylight left, and over there the spars of the French privateer still showed over the sand dunes of Hiddensoe as though to taunt him.

Chapter IX

H ORNBLOWER swung himself up over the side of the *Harvey,* where Lieutenant Mound stood at attention to welcome him with his two boatswain's mates twittering their pipes. The bang of a gun, coming unexpectedly and not a yard from him, made him jump. As the commodore was shifting his broad pendant from one ship to another (there it was breaking out at the lofty masthead of the *Harvey*) it was the correct moment for another salute, which they were firing off with one of the four six-pounders which *Harvey* carried aft.

"Belay that nonsense," said Hornblower.

Then he felt suddenly guilty. He had publicly described the navy's beloved ceremonial as nonsense—just as extraordinary, he had applied the term to a compliment which ought to have delighted him as it was only the second time he had received it. But discipline had not apparently suffered, although young Mound was grinning broadly as he gave the order to cease firing.

"Square away and let's get going, Mr. Mound," said Hornblower.

As the *Harvey* filled her sails and headed diagonally for the shore with *Moth* close astern, Hornblower looked round him. This was a new experience for him; in twenty years of service he had never seen action in a bomb-vessel. Above him towered the enormous mainmast (they had made a good job of replacing the spar shot away in The Sound) which had to make up in the amount of canvas it carried for the absence of a foremast. The mizzenmast, stepped far aft, was better proportioned to the diminutive vessel. The prodigious forestay necessary for the security of the mainmast was an iron chain, curiously incongruous amid the hempen rigging. The waist of the ketch was forward—that was the absurd but only way of describing her design—and there, on either side of her midline, were the two huge mortars which accounted for her quaint build. Hornblower knew that they were bedded upon a solid mass of oak against her kelson; under the direction of a gunner's mate four hands were laying out the immense thirteen-inch shells which the mortars fired. The bosun's mate with another party had passed a cable out from a starboard gunport, and, having carried it forward, were securing it to the anchor hanging at the cathead. That was the "spring"; Hornblower had often attached a spring to his cable as a practice evolution, but had never used one in action before. Close beside him in the port-side main chains a hand was heaving the lead; Hornblower thought to himself that nine tenths of the time he had spent in the Baltic the lead had been going, and presumably that would be the case for the rest of this commission.

"And a half three!" called the leadsman. These bomb-ketches drew less than nine feet.

Over there *Raven* was preparing to kedge off the shoal on which she was aground. Hornblower could see the cable, black against the water. She had already cleared away the raffle of her wrecked fore topmast. *Clam* was creeping out beyond her; Hornblower wondered if her gypsy-looking captain had fully grasped the complex instructions given him.

Mound was standing beside him, conning the ship. He was the only commissioned officer; a midshipman and two master's mates kept watches, and the two latter were standing wide-legged aft measuring with sextants the vertical angle subtended by *Blanchefleur's* spars. Hornblower could sense through the vessel an atmosphere of lightheartedness, only to be expected when the captain was but twenty years old. Discipline was bound to be easier in these small craft—Hornblower had often heard crabbed captains of vast seniority bewailing the fact.

"Quarter less three!" called the leadsman.

Seventeen feet of water.

"We are within range now, sir," said Mound.

"Those mortars of yours are more accurate when firing at less than extreme range, though, aren't they?"

"Yes, sir. And I would prefer to have a little to spare, too, in case they can shift anchorage."

"Leave yourself plenty of room to swing, though. We know nothing of these shoals."

"Aye aye, sir."

Mound swung round for a final glance at the tactical situation: at the spars of the *Blanchefleur* above the dunes where she was anchored far up the lagoon; the battery at the end of the spit; *Clam* taking up a position where she could see up the lagoon from a point just out of range of the battery; and *Lotus* waiting beyond the entrance to cut off escape in case by any miracle the *Blanchefleur* should be able to claw her way out to windward and make a fresh attempt to reach Stralsund. Mound kept on reaching for his trouser pockets and then hastily refraining from putting his hands in, when he remembered the commodore was beside him—an odd gesture, and he did it every few seconds.

"For God's sake, man," said Hornblower, "put your hands in your pockets and leave off fidgeting."

"Aye aye, sir," said Mound, a little startled. He plunged his hands in gratefully, and hunched his shoulders into a comfortable slouch, pleasantly relaxed. He took one more look round before calling to the midshipman standing by the cathead forward.

"Mr. Jones. Let go!"

The anchor cable roared out briefly as the crew of the ketch raced aloft to get in the canvas.

The *Harvey* swung slowly round until she rode bows upwind, pointing nearly straight at the invisible *Blanchefleur*. The *Moth*, Hornblower saw, anchored nearly abreast of her sister ship.

Mound moved with a deceptive appearance of leisureliness about the business of opening fire. He took a series of bearings to make sure that the anchor was holding. At a word from him a seaman tied a white rag to the spring where it lay on the deck as it passed forward to the captain, and Mound fished in his pocket, brought out a piece of chalk, and marked a scale on the deck beside the rag.

"Mr. Jones," he said, "take a turn on the capstan."

Four men at the capstan turned it easily. The white rag crept along the deck as the spring was wound in. The spring passed out through an after gunport and was attached to the anchor far forward; pulling in on it pulled the stern of the vessel round so that she lay at an angle to the wind, and the amount of the angle was roughly indicated by the movement of the white rag against the scale chalked on the deck.

"Carry on, Mr. Jones," said Mound, taking a rough bearing of the *Blanchefleur's* spars. The capstan clanked as the men at the bars spun it round.

"Steady!" called Mound, and they stopped.

"One more pawl," said Mound, sighting very carefully now for *Blanchefleur's* mainmast.

Clank! went the capstan as the men momentarily threw their weight on the bars.

"One more!"

Clank!

"I think that's right, sir," said Mound. The *Harvey's* centre line was pointing straight at *Blanchefleur.* "Of course the cables stretch and the anchor may drag a little, but it's easy enough to maintain a constant bearing by paying out or taking in on the spring."

"So I understand," said Hornblower.

He was familiar with the theory of the bomb-vessel; actually he was intensely interested in and excited at the prospect of the approaching demonstration. Ever since, at a desperate moment, he had tried to hit a small boat at long range with a six-pounder shot from the *Witch of Endor,* Hornblower had been conscious that naval gunnery was an art which should be improved if it were possible. At present it was chancy, literally hit-or-miss. Mortar fire from a bomb-vessel was the uttermost refinement of naval gunnery, brought to a high degree of perfection, although it was only a bastard offshot. The high trajectory and the low muzzle velocity of the projectile, and the avoidance of the disturbing factor of irregularities in the bore of the gun, made it possible to drop the shell with amazing accuracy.

"If you'll excuse me, sir," said Mound, "I'll go for-rard. I like to cut my fuses myself."

"I'll come with you," said Hornblower.

The two mortars were like big cauldrons in the eyes of the bomb-ketch.

"Eleven hundred yards," said Mound. "We'll try a pound and three quarters of powder, Mr. Jones."

"Aye aye, sir."

The powder was made up in cartridges of a pound, half a pound, and a quarter of a pound. The midshipman tore open one of each size, and poured the contents into the starboardside mortar, and pressed it home with an enormous wad of felt. Mound had a measuring rule in his hand, and was looking up at the sky in a calculating way. Then he bent over one of the big shells, and with a pair of scissors he cut the fuse with profound care.

"One and eleven sixteenths, sir," he said, apologetically. "Don't know why I decided on that. The fuse burns at different speeds according to the weather, and that seems right for now. Of course we don't want the shell to burst in the air, but if you have too long a fuse some Frog may get to it and put it out before it bursts."

"Naturally," said Hornblower.

The big shell was lifted up and placed in the muzzle of the mortar; a few inches down the bore narrowed abruptly, leaving a distinct step inside, on which the bold belt round the shell rested with reassuring solidity. The curve of the thirteen-inch shell, with the fuse protruding, was just level with the rim of the muzzle.

"Hoist the red swallow-tail," called Mound, raising his voice to reach the ears of the master's mate aft.

Hornblower turned and looked through his glass at *Clam*, anchored in the shallows a couple of miles away. It was under his personal supervision that this code of signals had been arranged, and he felt a keen anxiety that it should function correctly. Signals might easily be misunderstood. A red swallow-tail mounted to the *Clam's* peak.

"Signal acknowledged, sir," called the master's mate.

Mound took hold of the smouldering linstock, and applied it to the fuse of the shell. After a moment the fuse took fire, spluttering feebly.

"One, two, three, four, five," counted Mound, slowly, while the fuse still spluttered. Apparently he left himself a five-second margin in case the fuse burnt unsatisfactorily and had to be relit.

Then he pressed the linstock into the touch hole of the mortar, and it went off with a roar. Standing immediately behind the mortar. Hornblower could see the shell rise, its course marked by the spark of the burning fuse. Up and up it went, higher and higher, and then it disappeared as it began its downward flight at right angles now to the line of sight. They waited and they waited, and nothing more happened.

"Miss," said Mound. "Haul down the red swallow-tail."

"White pendant from *Clam*, sir," called the master's mate.

"That means 'Range too great,'" said Mound. "A pound and a half of powder this time, please, Mr. Jones."

Moth had two red swallow-tails hoisted, and two were hoisted in reply by *Clam*. Hornblower had foreseen the possibility of confusion, and had settled that signals to do with *Moth* should always be doubled. Then there would be no chance of *Harvey* making corrections for *Moth's* mistakes, or vice versa. *Moth's* mortar roared out, its report echoing over the water. From the *Harvey* they could see nothing of the flight of the shell.

"Double yellow flag from *Clam*, sir."

"That means *Moth's* shell dropped short," said Mound, "Hoist our red swallow-tail."

Again he fired the mortar, again the spark of the fuse soared towards the sky and disappeared, and again nothing more happened.

"White pendant from *Clam*, sir."

"Too long again?" said Mound, a little puzzled. "I hope they're not cross-eyed over there."

Moth fired again, and was rewarded by a double white pendant from *Clam*. This shell had passed over, when her preceding one had fallen short. It should be easy for *Moth* to find the target now. Mound was checking the bearing of the target.

"Still pointing straight at her," he grumbled. "Mr. Jones, take one half a quarter pound from that pound and a half."

Hornblower was trying to imagine what the captain of the *Blanchefleur* was doing at that moment on his own side of the sandspit. Probably until the very moment when the bomb-ketches opened fire he had felt secure, imagining that nothing except a direct assault on the battery could imperil him. But now shells must be dropping quite close to him, and he was unable to reply or defend himself in any active way. It would be hard for him to get under weigh; he had anchored his ship at the far end of the long narrow lagoon. The exit near him was shoal water too shallow even for a skiff—as the breakers showed—and with the wind as it was at present it was impossible for him to try to beat up the channel again closer to the battery. He must be regretting having dropped so far to leeward before anchoring; presumably he had done so to secure himself the better from the claws of a cutting-out attack. With boats or by kedging he might be able to haul his ship slowly up to the battery, near enough for its guns to be able to keep the bomb-ketches out of mortar range.

"Red swallow-tail at the dip, sir!" reported the master's mate excitedly.

That meant that the shell had fallen short but close.

"Put in two pinches more, Mr. Jones," said Mound.

Moth's mortar roared out again, but this time they saw the shell burst, apparently directly above the *Blanchefleur's* mastheads. They saw the big ball of smoke, and the sound of the explosion came faintly back to them on the wind. Mound shook his head gravely; either Duncan over there had not cut his fuse correctly or it had burnt away more rapidly than usual. Two blue flags at *Clam's* peak indicated that the fall of *Moth's* shot had been unobserved—the signalling system was still functioning correctly. Then Mound bent his gangling body over and applied the linstock to fuse and touch hole. The mortar roared; some freak of ballistics sent a fragment of blazing wad close over Hornblower's head, making him duck while

101

the smoke billowed round him, but as he looked up again he just caught sight of the spark of the fuse high up against the sky, poised at the top of its trajectory, before it disappeared from sight in its swift downward swoop. Hornblower, Mound, Jones, and the whole mortar's crew stood waiting tensely for the shell to end its flight. Then over the rim of the sand dune they saw a hint of white smoke, and the sound of the bursting shell came back to them directly afterwards.

"I think we've hit her, sir," said Mound, with elaborate carelessness.

"Black ball at *Clam's* masthead, sir!" shouted the master's mate.

That meant a hit. A thirteen-inch shell, soaring that immense distance into the air, had come plunging down onto *Blanchefleur's* decks and had exploded. Hornblower could not imagine what destruction it might cause.

"Both mortars together, now," snapped Mound, throwing aside all lackadaisical pose. "Jump to it, you men."

Two white pendants at the dip from *Clam* meant that *Moth's* next shot had fallen close but too far. Then both of *Harvey's* mortars roared—the little ketch dipped and plunged as the violence of the recoil forced her bow's down. Up went the black ball to *Clam's* masthead.

"Another hit!" exulted Mound.

Blanchefleur's topmasts, seen over the dunes, suddenly began to separate. She was turning round—her desperate crew was trying to tow her or kedge her back up the channel.

"Please God we wreck her before she gets away!" said Mound. "Why in hell doesn't *Moth* fire?"

Hornblower watched him closely; the temptation to fire his mortars the moment they were loaded, without waiting for *Moth* to take her turn, was powerful indeed, but to yield to it meant confusion for the observer over in *Clam* and eventual losing of all control. *Moth* fired, and two black balls at *Clam's* masthead showed that she, too, had scored a hit. But *Blanchefleur* had turned now; Hornblower could see the tiniest, smallest movement of her topmast against the upper edge of the dunes, only a yard or two at most. Mound fired his two mortars, and even while the shells were in the air his men leaped to the capstan and flung themselves on the bars. Clank—clank! Twice the pawl slipped over the ratchet as they hauled in on the spring and swung the ketch round to keep her mortars trained on the target. At that instant *Blanchefleur's* fore topmast fell from view. Only main and mizzen were in sight now.

"Another hit, by God!" shouted Hornblower, the words forced from him like a cork from a popgun. He was as excited as a schoolboy; he found he was jumping up and down on the deck. The foremast gone; he tried to picture the frightful destruction those shells must be causing, crashing down on the frail wooden decks. And there was smoke visible over the crest of the dunes too, more than could be accounted for by the bursting of the shells, and blacker. Probably she was on fire. Mizzenmast and mainmast came into line again—*Blanchefleur* was swinging across the channel. She must be out of control. Perhaps a shell had hit the cable out to the kedge, or wrecked the towing boats.

Moth fired again; and two red swallow-tails at the dip showed that her shells had fallen close and short—*Blanchefleur* must have swerved appreciably across the channel. Mound had noticed it, and was increasing the propelling charge in his mortars. That was smoke; undoubtedly it was smoke eddying from *Blanchefleur*. She must be on fire. And from the way she lay, stationary again—Hornblower could see that her topmasts made no movement at all to the sand dunes—she must have gone aground. Mound fired again, and they waited. There went the mizzen topmast, leaning over slowly, and then the main topmast disappeared as well. There was nothing to see now, except the smoke rising ever more thickly. Mound looked at Hornblower for orders.

"Better keep on firing," said Hornblower, thickly. Even if the crew were roasting alive in her it was his duty to see that *Blanchefleur* was utterly destroyed. The mortars roared out again, and the shells made their steep ascent, climbing upwards for ten full seconds before swooping down again. *Clam* signalled "Close and over." *Moth* fired again, and *Clam* signalled a hit for her; Hornblower's inner eye was seeing mental pictures of the shells plunging from the sky in among the crew of the *Blanchefleur* as they laboured amid the flames to save their ship, burning, dismasted, and aground. It took only the briefest interval of time for those pictures to form, for the moment the signal was seen in *Clam* Mound bent to fire the mortars, and yet the fuses had not taken fire when the sound of a violent explosion checked him. Hornblower whipped his glass to his eyes; an immense gust of smoke showed over the sand dunes, and in the smoke Hornblower thought he could make out flying specks—corpses or fragments of the ship, blown into the air by the explosion. The fire, or one of *Moth's* last shells, had reached *Blanchefleur's* magazines.

"Signal to *Clam*, Mr. Mound," said Hornblower: " 'What do you see of the enemy?' "

They waited for the answer.

" 'Enemy—totally—destroyed,' sir," read off the master's mate, and the crew gave a ragged cheer.

"Very good, Mr. Mound. I think we can leave these shallows now before daylight goes. Hang out the recall, if you please, with *Clam's* number and *Lotus'* number."

This watery northern sunshine was deceptive. It shone upon one but it gave one no heat at all. Hornblower shivered violently for a moment—he had been standing inactive, he told himself, upon the *Harvey's* deck for some hours, and he should have worn a greatcoat. Yet that was not the real explanation of the shudder, and he knew it. The excitement and interest had died away, leaving him gloomy and deflated. It had been a brutal and cold-blooded business, destroying a ship that had no chance of firing back at him. It would read well in a report, and brother-officers would tell each other of Hornblower's new achievement, destroying a big French privateer in the teeth of the Swedes and the French amid shoals innumerable. Only he would know of this feeling of inglorious anticlimax.

Chapter X

Bush wiped his mouth on his table napkin with his usual fussy attention to good manners.

"What do you think the Swedes'll say, sir?" he asked, greatly daring. The responsibility was none of his, and he knew by experience that Hornblower was likely to resent being reminded that Bush was thinking about it.

"They can say what they like," said Hornblower, "but nothing they can say can put *Blanchefleur* together again."

It was such a cordial reply compared with what Hornblower might have said that Bush wondered once more what it was which had wrought the change in Hornblower—whether his new mellowness was the consequence of success, of recognition, of promotion, or of marriage. Hornblower was inwardly debating that very question at that very moment as well, oddly enough, and he was inclined to attribute it to advancing years. For a few moments he subjected himself to his usual pitiless self-analysis, almost morbidly intense. He knew he had grown blandly tolerant of the fact that his hair was thinning, and turning grey over his temples—the first time he had seen a gleam of pink scalp as he combed his hair he had been utterly revolted, but by now he had at least grown accustomed to it. Then he looked down the double row of young faces at his table, and his heart warmed to them. Without a doubt, he was growing paternal, coming to like young people in a way new to him; he suddenly became aware, for that matter, that he was growing to like people young or old, and was losing—temporarily at least, said his cautious spirit—that urgent desire to get away by himself and torture himself.

He raised his glass.

"I give you a toast, gentlemen," he said, "to the three officers whose careful attention to duty and whose marked professional ability resulted in the destruction of a dangerous enemy."

Bush and Montgomery and the two midshipmen raised their glasses and drank with enthusiasm, while Mound and Duncan and Freeman looked down at the tablecloth with British modesty; Mound, taken unawares, was blushing like a girl and wriggling uncomfortably in his chair.

"Aren't you going to reply, Mr. Mound?" said Montgomery. "You're the senior."

"It was the commodore," said Mound, eyes still on the tablecloth. "It wasn't us. He did it all."

"That's right," agreed Freeman, shaking his gypsy locks.

It was time to change the subject, thought Hornblower, sensing the approach of an awkward gap in the conversation after this spell of mutual congratulation.

"A song, Mr. Freeman. We have all of us heard that you sing well. Let us hear you."

Hornblower did not add that it was from a Junior

Lord of the Admiralty that he had heard about Freeman's singing ability, and he concealed the fact that singing meant nothing to him. Other people had this strange desire to hear music, and it was well to gratify the odd whim.

There was nothing self-conscious about Freeman when it came to singing; he simply lifted his chin, opened his mouth, and sang:—

> "When first I looked in Chloe's eyes
> Sapphire seas and summer skies . . ."

An odd thing this music was. Freeman was clearly performing some interesting and difficult feat; he was giving decided pleasure to these others (Hornblower stole a glance at them) but all he was doing was to speak and to grunt in different fashions, and drag out the words in an arbitrary way—and such words. For the thousandth time in his life Hornblower gave up the struggle to imagine just what this music was which other people liked so much. He told himself, as he always did, that for him to make the attempt was like a blind man trying to imagine colour.

> "Chloe is my o—o—o—only love!"

Freeman finished his song, and everyone pounded on the table in genuine applause.

"A very good song, and very well sung," said Hornblower.

Montgomery was trying to catch his eye.

"Will you excuse me, sir?" he said. "I have the second dog-watch."

That sufficed to break up the party; the three lieutenants had to return to their own ships, Bush wanted to take a look round on deck, and the two midshipmen, with a proper appreciation of the insignificance of their species, hastened to offer their thanks for their entertainment and take their departure. That was quite the right sort of party, thought Hornblower, watching them go—good food, lively talk, and a quick ending. He stepped out onto the stern gallery, stooping carefully to avoid the low cove overhead. At six o'clock in the evening it was still broad daylight; the sun had not nearly set, but was shining into the gallery from right aft, and a faint streak beneath it showed where Bornholm lay just above the horizon.

The cutter, her mainsail pulled aft as flat as a board, passed close beneath him as she turned close-hauled under the stern with the three lieutenants in the sternsheets going back to their ships—the wind was northwesterly again. The young men were sky-larking together until one of them caught sight of the commodore up in the stern gallery, and then they promptly stiffened into correct attitudes. Hornblower smiled at himself for having grown fond of those boys, and he turned back into the cabin again to relieve them of the strain of being under his eye. Braun was waiting for him.

"I have read through the newspapers, sir," he said. *Lotus* had intercepted a Prussian fishing boat that afternoon, and had released her after confiscating her catch and taking these newspapers from her.

"Well?"

"This one is the *Königsberger Hartunsche Zeitung*, sir, published under French censorship, of course. This front page is taken up with the meeting at Dresden. Bonaparte is there with seven kings and twenty-one sovereign princes."

"Seven kings?"

"The Kings of Holland, Naples, Bavaria, Württemberg, Westphalia, Saxony, and Prussia, sir," read Braun. "The Grand Dukes of—"

"No need for the rest of the list," said Hornblower. He peered at the ragged sheets and found himself as usual thinking what a barbaric language German was. Bonaparte was clearly trying to frighten some-

108

one; it could not be England, who had faced Bonaparte's wrath without flinching for a dozen years. It might be his own subjects, all the vast mass of western Europe which he had conquered. But the obvious person for Bonaparte to try to cow was the Czar of Russia. There were plenty of good reasons why Russia should have grown restive under the bullying of her neighbour, and this supreme demonstration of Bonaparte's power was probably designed to frighten her into submission.

"Is there anything about troop movements?" asked Hornblower.

"Yes, sir. I was surprised at the freedom with which they were mentioned. The Imperial Guard is at Dresden. There's the First, the Second—" Braun turned the page—"and the Ninth Army Corps all mentioned. They are in Prussia—headquarters Danzig—and Warsaw."

"Nine army corps," reflected Hornblower. "Three hundred thousand men, I suppose."

"There's a paragraph here which speaks of Murat's reserve cavalry. It says 'there are forty thousand men, superbly mounted and equipped.' Bonaparte reviewed them."

An enormous mass of men was obviously accumulating on the frontier between Bonaparte's empire and Russia. Bonaparte would have the Prussian and Austrian armies under his orders too. Half a million men—six hundred thousand men—the imagination failed to grasp the figures. A vast tide of humanity was piling up here in eastern Europe. If Russia failed to be impressed by the threat, it was hard to believe that anything could survive the onrush of such a mass of men. The doom of Russia appeared to be sealed; she must either submit or be destroyed. No continental nation yet had successfully opposed Bonaparte, although every single one had felt the violence of his attack; only England still withstood him, and Spain still fought on although his armies had ravaged every village and every valley in the unhappy peninsula.

Doubt came back into Hornblower's mind. He could not see that Bonaparte would derive any benefit from the conquest of Russia proportionate to the effort needed, or even proportionate to the slight risk involved. Bonaparte ought to be able to find a far more profitable employment for the men and the money. Probably there would be no war. Russia would submit, and England would face a Europe every square mile of which would be in the tyrant's hands. And yet—

"This one is the *Warsaw Gazette*, sir," went on Braun. "A little more official from the French point of view even than the other one, although it's in the Polish language. Here is a long article about Russia. It speaks of 'the Cossack menace to Europe.' It calls Alexander 'the barbarian ruler of a barbarian people. . . . The successor of Genghis Khan.' It says that 'St. Petersburg is the focus of all the potential anarchy of Europe . . . a menace to the peace of the world . . . deliberately hostile to the benefits conferred upon the world by the French people.' "

"And that must be published with Bonaparte's consent," commented Hornblower, half to himself, but Braun was still deep in the article.

" 'The wanton ravisher of Finland,' " read Braun, more than half to himself. He raised his green eyes from the sheet. There was a gleam of hatred in them that startled Hornblower; it reminded him of what he was in a fair way to forget, that Braun was a penniless exile on account of Russia's attack on Finland. Braun had taken service with England, but that was at a time when Russia was at least England's nominal enemy. Hornblower made a mental note that it might be as well not to trust Braun with any confidential business regarding Russia; of her own free will Russia would never restore Finnish independence, and there was always the chance that

110

Bonaparte might do so—that he might restore what Bonaparte would call Finnish independence, for what that was worth. There were still people who might be deceived by Bonaparte's professions, despite his record of deceit and broken faith, of cruelty and robbery.

Braun would bear watching, thought Hornblower—that would be something more to bear in mind, as if he did not have enough worries or carry enough responsibility already. He could joke with Bush about the Swedes and the Russians, but secretly anxiety was gnawing at him. The Swedes might well be exasperated by the destruction of the *Blanchefleur* in Pomeranian waters. That might be the last straw; Bernadotte might at this very moment be contemplating whole-hearted alliance with Bonaparte and war with England. The prospect of the enmity of Sweden as well as that of France might easily break down Russia's resolution. England might find herself with the whole world in arms against her as a result of Hornblower's action. A fine climax that would be to his first independent command. Those cursed brothers of Barbara's would sneer in superior fashion at his failure.

Hornblower shook himself with an effort out of this nightmare, to find that Braun was obviously still in his. The hatred in his eyes, the intensity of his expression, were quite startling. And then someone knocked on the cabin door and Braun came out of his dream and slipped instantly into his old attitude of attentive deference.

"Come in," shouted Hornblower.

It was one of the midshipmen of the watch.

"Mr. Montgomery sent me with this signal from *Raven*, sir."

He held out the slate; it was scrawled with the words written on it by the signal officer:—

"Have met Swedish vessel desirous of speaking with commodore."

"I'll come on deck," said Hornblower. "Ask the captain if he'll be kind enough to come too."

"The cap'n's on deck, sir."

"Very good."

Bush and Montgomery and half a dozen officers had their glasses trained towards the topsails of the *Raven* at her station far out on the port beam as the squadron swept up the Baltic. There was still an hour of daylight left.

"Captain Bush," said Hornblower, "I'd be obliged if you would have the helm put up and run down towards her."

"Aye aye, sir."

"And signal for the squadron to take up night stations, if you please."

"Aye aye, sir."

Nonsuch heaved her ponderous self about, lying over as she took the wind abeam while the watch hauled aft on the starboard braces.

"There's a sail just astern of *Raven*, sir," said Montgomery. "Looks like a brig. A Swede from the cut of her tops'ls, sir. One of those Baltic traders you see in Leith Roads."

"Thank you," said Hornblower.

It would not be long before he heard what the news was. It might well be—it probably would be—something desperately unpleasant. Some new load of responsibility for his shoulders, for certain, even if it told of no actual disaster. He found himself envying Montgomery his simple duties of officer of the watch, with nothing more to do than simply obey orders and keep an eye on the weather, with the blessed obligation of having to refer all important decisions to a superior. Hornblower made himself stand still on the quarterdeck, his hands clasped behind him, as *Nonsuch* and the brig approached each other, as first the brig's courses and then her hull came up over the horizon. To the west the sky was a flaming crimson

112

but twilight lingered on as the brig came up into the wind.

"Captain Bush," said Hornblower, "will you heave-to, if you please? They are putting a boat overside."

He would not display vulgar curiosity by staring at the boat as it was launched, or by looking down into it as it came alongside; he paced peacefully up and down the quarterdeck in the lovely evening looking in every direction save towards the boat, while the rest of the officers and the men chattered and stared and speculated. Yet Hornblower, for all his air of sublime indifference, turned to face the entry port at the exact moment when the visitor was coming in over the side. The first thing Hornblower saw was a fore-and-aft cocked hat with a white plume that seemed familiar, and then under the hat appeared the heavy face and portly form of Baron Basse. He laid the hat across his chest to make his bow just as he had done before.

"Your servant, sir," said Hornblower, saluting stiffly. He was handicapped by the fact that although he could remember Basse very well, and could have described him to perfection, he did not remember his name. He turned to the midshipman of the watch. "Pass the word for Mr. Braun."

The Swedish gentleman was saying something, but what it was Hornblower could not imagine.

"I beg your pardon, sir," said Hornblower, and Basse repeated what he said, with no more success at conveying his meaning. He began once more laboriously, but cut himself short when he saw Hornblower distractedly looking away from him towards the entry port. Hornblower was doing his best to be polite, but he could see a bearskin headdress coming in at the entry port, and that was too intriguing a sight for him possibly to withstand its attraction. A big bearskin cap with a red plume, a bristling red moustache, a scarlet tunic, a red sash, a profusion of gold lace, blue pantaloons with a red stripe, high boots, a sword whose golden hilt glowed strangely in the fading light; that was the uniform of the Guards, surely. The wearer of the uniform was undersized for a Guardsman, but he certainly knew his ceremonial; his hand was at the salute to the quarterdeck as he came in through the entry port, and then he strode forward on short legs and brought his heels together in a smart Guards' salute to Hornblower.

"Good evening, sir," he said, "you are Captain Sir Horatio Hornblower?"

"Yes," said Hornblower.

"May I introduce myself? I am Colonel Lord Wychwood, of the First Guards."

"Good evening," said Hornblower coolly. As commodore he was decidedly senior to a colonel, and he could afford to be cool while waiting on events. He supposed that he would soon hear the explanation of this arrival of a colonel of the Grenadier Guards in full regimentals in the middle of the Baltic Sea.

"I have despatches," said Lord Wychwood, fumbling in the breast of his tunic, "from our ambassador at Stockholm for you, sir."

"Let us go to my cabin, sir," said Hornblower. He darted a glance at Basse.

"You have already made the acquaintance of Baron Basse, I understand? He has messages for you, too."

"Then perhaps the Baron will be kind enough to come below as well. If you gentlemen will allow me to precede you, I will show the way."

Braun interpreted ceremoniously as Hornblower headed the procession. In the darkened cabin Brown hastened to bring lamps and brought forward chairs; Wychwood lowered himself into his with all the caution demanded by his tight overalls.

"You've heard what Boney's done?" he began.

"I have heard nothing recently."

"He sent fifty thousand troops into Swedish Pomerania the moment he got the news of what you did off Stralsund."

"Indeed?"

114

"They acted in their usual style. Vandamme was in command. He began by fining the municipality of Stralsund a hundred thousand francs for not greeting his arrival with the ringing of the church bells. He interrupted the service at the Church of the Holy Ghost so as to lay hold of the communion plate. He seized the Governor-General and threw him into gaol. The troops were out of hand because the garrison of Rügen tried to oppose their crossing. There were looting and murder and rape all through Rügen. The Baron here escaped in a fishing boat. All the other officials and the troops are prisoners."

"So Boney is at war with Sweden now?"

Wychwood shrugged his shoulders; everyone in the Baltic seemed to shrug shoulders when it was a matter of having to make a downright statement regarding peace and war.

"The Baron here can tell you about that," said Wychwood. They turned their glances towards the Baron, who began a voluble explanation in Swedish; Braun standing against the bulkhead, translated.

"He says that the question of peace and war lies with the Crown Prince, His Royal Highness Charles John, who used to be known as Marshal Bernadotte. His Royal Highness is not in Sweden at the moment. He is visiting the Czar in Russia."

"I expect that's what these despatches I have for you are about, sir," said Wychwood. He produced a large canvas envelope, heavily sealed, and handed it over. Hornblower tore it open and read the contents.

EMBASSY OF HIS BRITANNIC MAJESTY
AT STOCKHOLM,
May 20, 1812.

Sir,

The bearer of this despatch, Colonel Lord Wychwood, First Guards, will inform you as to the political situation here. It is to be hoped that Bonaparte's invasion of Swedish Pomerania will

115

bring about a declaration of war on the part of the Swedish Government. It is therefore necessary that all possible aid should be given to Swedish officials who wish to communicate with H.R.H. the Crown Prince. You are therefore directed and required to use all diligence and despatch to escort or convey any such officials on their way to Russia. You are further directed and required to make all use of this opportunity to enable Lord Wychwood to open communication with the Russian Government so as to assure H.I.M. the Czar of the full support of His Majesty's forces by land and sea in the event of war between H.I.M. and the French Government. You will further make use of any opportunity which may present itself to you to further good relations between H.M. and H.I.M.

> Your obd't servant,
> H. L. MERRY, *H.B.M.'s Ambassador*
> *to the Court of Stockholm.*

CAPTAIN SIR HORATIO HORNBLOWER, K. B.,
Commodore Commanding the British Squadron in the Baltic.

Hornblower read the orders through twice, carefully. There was an important decision to be made. Merry had no business giving orders, and especially had no business to give orders in the explicit "directed and required" wording which was the cherished prerogative of his naval superiors. An ambassador was an important official—to a naval officer in foreign waters the most important official after the Lords of Admiralty—but he could only request and advise, not give orders. If Hornblower should follow Merry's instructions and the matter turn out ill he would have no excuse to plead to the Admiralty. Yet on the other hand Hornblower knew only too well that if he were to ignore Merry's letter there would be bitter complaints sent to London.

Hornblower recalled his Admiralty orders to himself; they gave him wide discretion as to how he should behave towards the northern powers. Merry's letter relieved him of no responsibility. He could allow Wychwood and Basse to proceed in the Swedish brig, or he could convey them himself; the point at issue was whether the news of Bonaparte's latest aggression should be conveyed by a British squadron or not. Bearers of bad tidings were always unpopular—a ridiculous detail to have to bear in mind, but an important one. The two potentates might feel exasperated at being reminded of the meddling British navy, bringing trouble to everyone. On the other hand, the presence of a British squadron far up the Baltic, at the very gates of St. Petersburg, might be a salutary reminder of the length of England's arm. Submission to Bonaparte on the part of Sweden and Russia must mean war, real actual war, with England this time; Bonaparte would be satisfied with nothing less. The sight of British topsails on the horizon, the knowledge that war would mean instant blockade, instant capture of every ship that ventured out, constant harassing of all their shores, might be a powerful argument at their councils. Bonaparte might be at their frontiers, but England would be at their doors. Hornblower made his decision.

"Gentlemen," he said, "I think it is my duty to convey you to Russia in this squadron. I can offer you the hospitality of this ship, if you would be kind enough to accept it."

Chapter XI

DESPITE the fact that he was a peer and a Guardsman, despite his little red moustache and his funny pop-eyes and his ludicrous appearance in uniform, Wychwood was a shrewd and experienced man

117

of the world. At thirty-five he had visited two thirds of the courts of Europe, he was familiar with their intrigues, knew their weaknesses and their strengths, the military power of which they could dispose, their prejudices and their traditions. He sat (at Hornblower's invitation) in Hornblower's cabin while a brisk westerly wind sent the squadron rolling and pitching up the Baltic. Basse was incapacitated in his berth with seasickness, so that they were not embarrassed by his presence—Wychwood's cheeks were a little pale as well, and his manner occasionally hinted at an inward preoccupation, but he controlled himself manfully.

"Boney's weakness," said Wychwood, "is that he thinks all the opposition in the world can be dissolved by force. Often he's right, of course; you have only to look back at his career to see that. But sometimes he is wrong. People would rather fight—would rather die—than be slaves to his will any longer."

"Spain showed that," said Hornblower.

"Yes. But with Russia it still may be different. Russia is the Czar, much more definitely than Spain was the Bourbon monarchy. If Alexander chooses to submit to Boney's threats, Russia will submit. Alexander's swallowed insults enough already."

"He's swallowed other things besides insults," said Hornblower dryly.

"Finland, you mean? That's perfectly true. And all the other Baltic provinces, Lithuania and Courland and so on. You know better than I do how much difference that makes to the security of St. Petersburg—I find it hard to blame him for it. At home, of course, his attack on Finland roused a good deal of feeling. I hope they forget it if he becomes our ally."

"And what are the chances of that?"

"God knows. If he can be sure of the Swedish alliance he may fight. And that depends on whether Bernadotte is willing to submit to having Pomerania taken away from him."

"Bonaparte made a false step there," said Hornblower.

"Yes, by God! The British colours are like a red rag to a bull to him. You have only to show them to get him to charge. The way you destroyed that ship—what was her name? The *Blanchefleur*—under his very nose must have driven him crazy. If anything makes the Swedish fight, it'll be that."

"Let's hope it does," said Hornblower, decidedly comforted.

He knew he had taken a bold step when he went in to destroy the *Blanchefleur;* if the subsequent political repercussions should be unfavourable he might well be called to account. His only justification would be the final event; a more cautious man would have held back and contented himself with keeping the privateer under observation. Probably that would have resulted in her slipping clean away the first foggy night, to resume her ravages among British shipping, but no man could be held responsible for fog. And if Sweden became an active enemy all England would clamour for the head of the officer they deemed responsible. Yet come what might he could not but feel that he had taken the best course in proving that England had the power to strike and would not hesitate to use it. There were few occasions in history when timidity was wise.

They were bringing further news to St. Petersburg, too. Wellington was on the offensive in Spain; in two desperate strokes he had cleared his front by storming Ciudad Rodrigo and Badajoz, and now was ready to strike into the heart of the Peninsula. The knowledge that a large part of Bonaparte's army was hotly engaged in the south might bring firmness to the councils of the north.

His brother-in-law was an earl now—another victory or two would make him a duke, reflected Hornblower. Barbara would be proud of him, and to Hornblower that was another reason to dread failure for himself—Barbara had a high standard of comparison. But she would understand. She would know how high were the stakes he was playing for in the Baltic—as high as those her brother was playing for in Spain; she would know what moral courage was needed to make the kind of decisions he had made. She would be considerate; and at that moment Hornblower told himself that he did not want his wife to have to be considerate on his account. The thought revolted him, drove him to make his excuses to Wychwood and plunge out on deck, into the pouring rain under the grey sky, to walk the quarter-deck while the other officers eyed him askance and kept well clear of him. There was not a soul in the squadron who had not heard that only fools crossed the commodore's hawse when he was walking the deck.

The brisk wind was chill, even in late May, here in the North Baltic; the squadron pitched and rolled over the short steep waves, leaden-hued under the leaden sky, as it drove ever northward towards the Gulf of Finland, towards Russia, where the destiny of the world hung in the balance. The night was hardly darker than the day, up here in the sixtieth degree of north latitude, when the sky cleared, for the sun was barely hidden below the horizon and the moon shone coldly in the pale twilight as they drove past Hogland and hove-to in sight of Lavansaari so as to approach Kronstadt after sunrise.

Braun was on deck early, leaning against the rail, craning over in fact; that faint grey smear on the horizon to the northward was his native land, the Finland of lake and forest which the Czar had just conquered and from which he was a homeless exile. Hornblower noted the dejection of the poor devil's pose and was sorry for him, even in the keen excitement of anticipation regarding the reception they might be accorded. Bush came bustling up, in all the glory of epaulettes and sword, darting eager glances

120

over the deck and aloft to make quite sure that everything in the ship was ready to bear the inspection of an unfriendly power.

"Captain Bush," said Hornblower, "I'd be obliged if you would square away for Kronstadt."

"Aye aye, sir."

Hornblower would have liked to ask if the arrangements for saluting were properly in train, but he forbore. He could trust Bush with any routine duty, and he had to be very careful not to interfere with the working of the ship. He was glad that so far he had never forgotten to make use of the polite forms of request when giving orders to Bush, who was his equal in substantive rank. "I'd be obliged" and "If you please" still came strangely enough to his lips as a preface to an order.

He turned his back on the dawn and trained his glass aft on the squadron; they were squaring away and taking up their stations astern in succession, the two sloops, and then the two bomb-vessels, and the cutter last.

"General signal," he snapped: "'Keep better station.'"

He wanted his squadron to come up the difficult channel in exact, regular order, like beads on a string. Out of tail of his eye he saw Basse and Wychwood come on deck, and he ignored them.

"Make the signal again," he rasped, "with *Harvey's* number."

Harvey was yawing slightly from her course; young Mound had better keep a sharp eye on his helmsman, or he would be in trouble. To starboard, where the wide shoals extended from the Oranienbaum shore, there were buoys to mark the limits of the channel, which serpentined back and forth in unpredictable fashion. If ever he had to penetrate this channel as an enemy he would find it a tricky business. There were the low fortifications of Kronstadt on the port bow; a turn in the channel sent the *Nonsuch* heading directly for them, so that in the event of fighting the fire of the guns there would enfilade the whole line. Then the channel swung back again, and then it straightened out so that all ships would be forced to pass close under the guns of Kronstadt. Through his glass Hornblower made out the blue and white flag of imperial Russia flying above the grey walls.

"Make the signal 'Anchor,'" said Hornblower to the signal midshipman, and then he darted a meaning glance at Bush, who nodded. He had everything ready. The ship crept forward, closer and closer under the guns.

"Haul down," said Hornblower, and the signal to anchor came down in a flash, putting the order into force at that moment. Six cables roared through six hawseholes. In the six ships a thousand men poured aloft, and the canvas vanished as though by magic as the ships swung round to their cables.

"Pretty fair," said Hornblower to himself, realising, with an inward smile at his own weakness, that no evolution could ever be carried out to his perfect satisfaction. Forward the saluting gun began to crash out its marks of respect for the Russian flag; Hornblower saw a puff of smoke from the fortress and then the sound of the first gun of the return salute reached his ears. Eleven guns; they recognised his broad pendant, then, and knew what compliments were due to a commodore. Here came the doctor's boat to give them *pratique;* the doctor was a man with a large black beard who spoke limping French. His visit was a good opportunity to test Braun's ability to speak Russian—Braun translated with facility Hornblower's declaration that there was no infectious disease on board. Everyone in the ship was a little excited at this visit to Russia, and they crowded the side to look down at the Russian boat's crew, seated in their boat with the bowman hooking onto the chains, but they appeared no different from any other boat's crew—much the same kind of coloured shirts and ragged trousers and

122

bare feet, and they handled their craft capably enough. It was Bush who drove the *Nonsuch's* crew from the side; he was hotly indignant about their blatant curiosity and the noise they made.

"Chattering like a herd of monkeys," said Bush indignantly to the first lieutenant. "Making more noise than a treeful of jackdaws. What'll these Russians think of us? Set the men to work and keep 'em at it."

In these conditions of doubtful neutrality it would be best for the first contact with the shore to be made by Basse. At least ostensibly the squadron had come to Kronstadt merely to bring him with his news to the Swedish Crown Prince. Hornblower had his barge hoisted out and sent Basse away in it, and the boat returned without him but with no other information. Basse had landed at the jetty and the barge, in accordance with Hornblower's orders, had immediately returned. Apart from the salute and the doctor's visit the Russian Empire chose to ignore the British squadron's existence.

"What sort of people do they think we are?" grumbled Bush, fretting, as usual, at inaction. Bush knew as well as Hornblower that in all matters of diplomacy it was best to display no eagerness at all, but he could not force himself to appear calm as Hornblower could. He gave a meaning glance at Hornblower's full uniform and ribbon and star, donned so as to be ready for any official occasion whatever; he wanted Hornblower to proceed on shore to call on the local governor and put the whole situation to the test, but Hornblower was obstinate. He was waiting for an invitation. England had survived the storm in Europe so far without a Russian alliance, and future relations would be simplified if Russia were to make the first advances now—provided she did make them. His squadron was present merely to bring Basse to report to Bernadotte; if the Russian government chose to take advantage of his presence

123

to approach him well and good. Otherwise he would have to devise some other plan.

"The telegraph hasn't ceased working since Basse reached shore," commented Bush, glass to eye. The three gaunt black arms of the semaphore on the top of the fortress were whirling busily round transmitting messages to the next station higher up the bay. Otherwise there was almost nothing to be seen; across the low land of the island were visible a few masts to mark the site of the naval dockyard; two or three merchant ships swung at anchor in that direction, and a few fishing boats plied their trade.

"There goes a boat!" said Montgomery suddenly.

A smart pinnace was shooting out from the direction of the dockyard heading across the channel almost directly away from *Nonsuch*.

"Russian Imperial colours," said Bush. "Can anyone see who's on board?"

But the pinnace was too far away for any details to be visible by telescope.

"I think I can see gold lace," said Carlin, doubtfully.

"Much good that is," said Bush; "a blind man would guess there was gold lace in a Russian navy pinnace at Kronstadt."

The pinnace passed away into the distance, quartering across the broad channel until her white sail dwindled to a speck.

"Call me if anything happens, if you please, Captain Bush," said Hornblower.

He went off below to his cabin; Brown relieved him of his heavy full-dress coat with the epaulettes, and, once more alone, he began to fidget about the cabin. He opened the case of pistols which Barbara had given him, read the card inside it—the last words he had received from her—and shut the case again. He stepped out into the stern gallery and returned to the cabin. The realisation that he was worried annoyed him; he took down Archdeacon Coxe's travels from

124

the bookshelf and set himself seriously to read the Archdeacon's intensely wearisome remarks about the condition of Russia, in the endeavour to inform himself more fully about the northern powers. But the words made sheer nonsense to him; he took up the slim volume of "Childe Harold" instead.

"Bombast and fustian," he said to himself, flipping through the pages.

He heard six bells strike; it was still no later than eleven in the morning, and he could not possibly dine before two. He got up from his chair and made himself lie on his cot, shut his eyes and grimly clenched his hands and tried to force himself to doze. He could not possibly go up on deck again and walk up and down, as he wanted to—that would be a public admission that he was restless and nervous. The minutes passed on leaden feet; he felt he had never been as caged and unhappy before in his life.

Eight bells went, and he heard the watch relieved; it was like an eternity before he heard the bustle on the half-deck outside and someone knocked on the door. Hornblower settled himself in an attitude of complete relaxation on his cot.

"Come in!" he called, and he blinked and peered at the midshipman as if he had just awakened from a sound sleep.

"Boat heading towards us, sir," said the midshipman.

"I'll come up," said Hornblower. "Pass the word for my cox'n."

Brown helped him into his dress coat, and he reached the deck while the boat was still some distance off.

"The same pinnace that we saw before, sir," commented Hurst.

The pinnace came into the wind, and took in her mainsail while the bowman hailed the ship in Russian.

"Where's Mr. Braun?" said Hornblower.

The hail was repeated, and Braun translated.

"He is asking permission to hook onto us, sir. And he says he has a message for you."

"Tell him to come alongside," said Hornblower. This dependence upon an interpreter always irritated him.

The boat's crew was smart, dressed in something like a uniform with blue shirts and white trousers, and in the sternsheets, ready to mount the side, was an officer in military uniform, frogged across the breast in Hussar fashion. The Hussar came clumsily up the side, and glanced round, saluting the mass of gold lace which awaited him. Then he produced a letter, which he offered with a further explanation in Russian.

"From His Imperial Majesty the Czar," translated Braun with a catch in his voice.

Hornblower took the letter; it was addressed in French:—

M. le Chef d'Escadre le Capitaine Sir Hornblower,
Vaisseau Britannique Noonsuch.

Apparently the Czar's secretary, however competent he might be in other ways, was shaky regarding both British titles and spelling. The letter within was written in French as well—it was pleasant to be able to translate without Braun's assistance.

THE IMPERIAL PALACE OF PETERHOF,
GRAND MARSHALATE OF THE IMPERIAL COURT.
May 30, 1812.

Sir,

I am commanded by His Imperial Majesty the Emperor of All the Russias to express to you His Imperial Majesty's pleasure at hearing of your arrival in His Imperial Majesty's waters. His Imperial Majesty and His Royal Highness the Prince of Sweden further command you to dinner

126

at this palace today at four o'clock accompanied by your staff. His Excellency the Minister of Marine has put at your disposal a boat which will convey you and your party direct to the quay, and the officer who conveys this letter to you will serve as your guide.

Accept, sir, the assurances of my highest consideration,

KOCHUBEY, *Grand Marshal of the Court.*

"I am invited to dinner with the Czar and Bernadotte," said Hornblower to Bush; he handed over the letter, and Bush looked at it wisely with his head on one side as if he could read French.

"You're going, I suppose, sir?"

"Yes."

It would hardly be tactful to begin his first encounter with the Russian and Swedish authorities by refusing an imperial and a royal command.

Hornblower suddenly glanced round to find half the officers of the ship hanging on his words. This public discussion of his affairs was not in the least dignified, and detracted vastly from the pomp and mystery which should surround a commodore. He had fallen sadly away from his old standards.

"Have none of you anything better to do than stand about and gape?" he bellowed, rounding on the herd. "I can find mastheads even for senior officers if necessary."

They began to slink away in gratifying fright, each one doing his best to avoid catching Hornblower's eye as he glowered round him. That was a very desirable result. Then he became aware that the Hussar had yet another letter in his hand. He took it from him and glanced at the superscription.

"Here, Colonel, this is for you," he said, handing it to Wychwood before turning back to Bush. "The Czar and Bernadotte are at Peterhof—the palace is marked

127

on the chart, on the Oranienbaum shore over there. You will be in command in my absence, of course."

Bush's face reflected a complexity of emotions; Hornblower knew that he was remembering other occasions when Hornblower had left him in command, to go on shore to beard a mad tyrant on the coast of Central America, or to undertake some hare-brained adventure on the coast of France.

"Aye aye, sir," said Bush.

"I have to take my staff," said Hornblower. "Who do you think would care to dine with the Czar?"

He could afford to be jocose with Bush, who held the same substantive rank as himself—especially after his recent assertion of his dignity.

"You'll need Braun, I suppose, sir?"

"I suppose so."

Dinner with the Czar would be a notable experience for any young officer, something he would be able to yarn about for the rest of his life. Good service could be rewarded by an invitation; and at the same time some future admiral might gain invaluable experience.

"I'll take Hurst," decided Hornblower; there were not the makings of an admiral in the first lieutenant, but discipline demanded that he be included in the party. "And young Mound, if you'll signal for him. And a midshipman. Who do you suggest?"

"Somers is the brightest, sir."

"The fat one? Very good, I'll take him. Have you been invited too, Colonel?"

"I have, sir," answered Wychwood.

"We must be there at four. How long will it take to arrive?"

He looked at the Hussar, who did not understand him, and then looked round for Braun, who had left the deck, which was perfectly infuriating. When Hornblower had turned on the idling crowd he had not meant Braun to go, of course. It was just like Braun with his mock humble pose to take his chief

128

literally. Hornblower angrily ordered the word to be
passed for him, and fumed until he came up again;
yet when he came there was small satisfaction to be
derived from his services, for when Hornblower's
question was translated to the Hussar the latter
merely raised his eyes to the sky and shrugged his
shoulders before offering the information—translated
by Braun—that it might be two hours and it might be
four. As a soldier the Hussar would make no estimate
of the time necessary for a journey by boat.

"We mustn't be late for a royal command, damn it,"
said Hornblower. "We'll leave in half an hour."

Hornblower came punctually to the ship's side to
find the others awaiting him, young Somers' plump
cheeks empurpled with the constriction of his stock,
Hurst and Mound uncomfortable in their full dress,
Braun stiffly uniformed.

"Carry on," said Hornblower.

Young Somers went first in accordance with the
age-old rule of the junior getting first into a boat, and
Braun followed him. Braun's lifted arm, as he went
over the side, pulled up his tight coat for a moment,
and his waistcoat with it. Something flashed momentarily into view at his waistband; something black—
Hornblower's eyes were resting on it at that moment.
It must have been the butt of a pistol, the barrel of it
pushed into the waistband of his breeches, round by
his hip where the bulge would be least noticeable. The
fellow was wearing his sword, of course. Hornblower
began to wonder why he should take a pistol. But
Mound and Hurst had followed him down by this time,
and Wychwood was heaving himself over, in his scarlet
tunic and bearskin. The Hussar should go next, so
that the commodore should descend last, but he was
hanging back with misplaced politeness, bowing and
making way for the commodore.

"After you, sir," said Hornblower to his deaf ears.

Hornblower had positively to stamp his foot to
compel the ignorant soldier to precede him, and then

129

he swung himself over to the shrilling of the pipes of the boatswain's mates and the rigid salutes of the ship's officers. He dropped into the sternsheets, encumbered with his boat cloak. There was a tiny cabin forward, where he joined Wychwood and Hurst. Mound and the warrant officers and the Hussar kept themselves discreetly in the stern. The coxswain yelled some strange order and the boat cast off, the lugsail was hoisted, and they headed over to the Oranienbaum shore.

From where he sat Hornblower could see Braun sitting stiffly in the sternsheets. That business of the pistol was rather curious. Presumably he had fears of attack or arrest on shore as a recent rebel, and wished to have the means to defend himself. But not even the Russians would lay hands on an English officer, in a British uniform. That was a big pistol butt; a black one, too. Hornblower suddenly moved uneasily on his locker, uncrossed his knees and recrossed them. That was one of the pistols Barbara had given him the butt of which he had seen in Braun's waistband. He remembered the shape of the ebony butt too well to be mistaken about it.

The presence of a thief on board a ship was always upsetting and disturbing; theft was so easy and suspicion could be spread so wide, although that was not true in this case. It would still be a nasty business accusing Braun of the crime and punishing him for it. An English-made rifled pistol with percussion caps—presumably the very first of its kind to reach Russia—would command a fabulous price at the Russian court. Braun could reasonably expect to obtain two or three hundred guineas for it. And yet even with all his prejudice against him he could not believe Braun capable of petty theft.

The coxswain suddenly shouted a new order, and the pinnace came about on the other tack; the dipping lug with which she was equipped had to be taken in and reset when she tacked, and Hornblower watched the evolution with professional intent. The Russian sailors were smart and handy enough, but that was to be expected of the crew of the pinnace specially attached to the service of the Russian Admiralty. The *Nonsuch* was already far astern, hull down. A buoy made its appearance close alongside, and passed away astern, the rapidity of its passage proof of the speed the pinnace was making through the water.

"We're heading sou'west now, sir," commented Hurst; "we're out of the fairway."

He climbed out of the little cabin and peered ahead.

"Land right ahead, sir," he reported, "but no sign of any palace."

"I know nothing about the Peterhof," remarked Wychwood. "I was in Czarskoe Selo and the old Winter Palace as a subaltern on Wilson's staff before Tilsit. The Peterhof's one of the lesser palaces; I expect they chose it for this meeting so that Bernadotte could arrive direct by sea."

It was quite futile to debate what would be the result of this evening's meeting, and yet the temptation was overwhelming. The minutes slipped by until the coxswain shouted a new order. The lugsail came down, and the piles of a jetty came into sight beside the pinnace as she rounded-to. Lines were thrown out and the pinnace drew in beside a broad companionway running down into the water from the top of the jetty. This time the Russian officer's politeness was not misplaced. First out of a boat and last in, in order of seniority, was the etiquette of the navy; Hornblower ducked out of the little cabin, stepped onto the companionway and began to walk up, hurriedly making sure that his cocked hat was on straight and his sword properly slung. As he reached the top someone shouted an order; there was a guard of twenty soldiers drawn up there, grenadiers in bearskins and blue coats. They put their left arms across

131

their breasts as they presented arms in a fashion that appeared back-handed to a man accustomed to receiving salutes from the Royal Marines. Yet the uniforms and the pose seemed strangely familiar; Hornblower realised that he was being reminded of the wooden soldiers that young Richard had been playing with—a box of German soldiers smuggled out of the continental blockade and presented to him by one of Barbara's diplomatic friends. Of course the Russian army was organised on the German model, and German uniforms had been introduced by Peter III. Hornblower stiffly returned the salute of the officer of the guard, standing at attention long enough for the rest of the party to catch him up; the Hussars spoke rapidly to Braun in Russian.

"There are carriages waiting for us, sir," Braun interpreted.

Hornblower could see them at the end of the jetty, two big open landaus, with fine horses to each; in the drivers' seats sat coachmen pigtailed and powdered wearing red coats—not the scarlet of the British army or of the British royal liveries, but a softer, strawberry red. Footmen similarly dressed stood at the horses' heads and at the carriage doors.

"Senior officers go in the first carriage," explained Braun.

Hornblower climbed in, with Wychwood and Hurst after him; with an apologetic smile the Hussar followed them and sat with his back to the horses. The door shut. One footman leaped up beside the coachman and the other sprang up behind, and the horses dashed forward. The road wound through a vast park, alternate sweeps of grass and groves of trees; here and there fountains threw lofty jets of water at the sky, and marble naiads posed by marble basins. Occasional turns in the road opened up beautiful vistas down the terraced lawns; there were long flights of marble steps and beautiful little marble pavilions, but also, at every turning, beside every fountain and every pavilion, there were sentries on guard, stiffly presenting arms as the carriages whirled by.

"Every Czar for the last three generations has been murdered," remarked Wychwood. "It's only the women who die in their beds. Alexander is taking precautions."

The carriage turned sharply again and came out on a broad gravelled parade ground; on the farther side Hornblower just had time to see the palace, a rambling rococo building of pink and grey stone with a dome at either end, before the carriage drew up at the entrance to the salute of a further guard, and white-powdered footmen opened the doors. With a few polite words in Russian the Hussar led the party forward up a flight of pink marble steps and into a lofty ante-room. A swarm of servants came forward to take their boat cloaks; Hornblower remembered to put his cocked hat under his arm and the others followed his example. The folding doors beyond were thrown open, and they went towards them, to be received by a dignified official whose coat was of the same imperial red where the colour was visible through the gold lace. He wore powder and carried in his hand a gold-tipped ebony stave.

"Kochubey," he said, speaking fair French, "Grand Marshal of the Palace. Commodore Hornblower? Lord Wychwood?"

They bowed to him, and Hornblower presented the others; he saw the Grand Marshal run an all-embracing eye over their uniforms to make sure that nothing unworthy of the court of the Czar would penetrate farther into the palace. Then he turned back to Hornblower and Wychwood.

"His Excellency the Minister of Marine would be honoured if Commodore Hornblower would grant him time for a short interview."

"I am at His Excellency's service," said Hornblower,

133

"but I am here at the command of His Imperial Majesty."

"That is very good of you, sir. There will be time before His Imperial Majesty appears. And His Excellency the Minister of Foreign Affairs would be honoured by Lord Wychwood's attention for a few minutes in a similar way."

"I am at His Excellency's service," said Wychwood. For a man of his experience his French was remarkably poor.

"Thank you," said Kochubey.

He turned, and three more officers of the court approached at his gesture. They wore less gold lace than Kochubey, and from the gold keys embroidered on their lapels Hornblower knew them to be chamberlains. There were further introductions, more bows.

"Now if you have the kindness to accompany me, sir—" said Kochubey to Hornblower.

Two chamberlains took charge of the junior officers, one took charge of Wychwood, and Kochubey led Hornblower away. Hornblower gave one last glance at his party. Even the stolid Hurst, even the deliberately languid Mound, wore rather scared expressions at being abandoned by their captain like this in an imperial palace. Hornblower was reminded of children being handed over by their parents to a strange nurse. But Braun's expression was different. His green eyes were glowing with excitement, and there was a new tenseness about his features, and he was casting glances about him like a man preparing himself for some decisive action. Hornblower felt a wave of misgiving break over him; during the excitement of setting foot in Russia he had forgotten about Braun, about the stolen pistol, about everything connected with him. He wanted time to think, and yet Kochubey was hurrying him away and allowing him no time. They walked through a magnificent room—Hornblower was only just conscious of its fur-

134

niture, pictures, and statuary—and through folding doors beyond, which were opened for them by two of the footmen who seemed to be present in hundreds. The corridor was wide and lofty, more like a picture gallery than a corridor, but Kochubey only went a few yards along it. He stopped abruptly at an inconspicuous door, from before which two more footmen stepped with alacrity at his approach. The door opened straight upon a steep winding stairway; halfway up there was another door, this one guarded by four burly soldiers in pink uniforms with high boots and baggy breeches whom Hornblower recognised as the first Cossacks he had ever seen in the flesh. They nearly jammed the narrow stairway as they drew back against the wall to make way; Hornblower had to push past them. Kochubey scratched upon the door and instantly opened it, immediately drawing Hornblower after him with a gesture as though he were a conspirator.

"Sir Hornblower," he announced, having shut the door. The big man in the vaguely naval uniform, with epaulettes and a string of orders across his breast, must be the Minister of Marine; he came forward cordially, speaking fair French and with a courtly apology for not speaking English. But in the far corner of the room was another figure, tall and slender, in a beautiful light blue uniform. He was strikingly handsome, but as though he came from another world; the ivory pallor of his cheeks, accentuated by his short black side-whiskers, was more unnatural than unhealthy. He made no move as he sat stiffly upright in the dark corner, his finger tips resting on a low table before him, and neither of the Russian officials gave any overt sign of acknowledging his presence, but Hornblower knew that it was the Czar; thinking quickly, he realised that if the Czar's own officials pretended the Czar was not there, then he could do no less. He kept his eyes on the Minister of Marine's.

"I trust," said the latter, "that I see you in good health?"

"Thank you," said Hornblower. "I am in the best of health."

"And your squadron?"

"That is in the best of health too, Your Excellency."

"Does it need anything?"

Hornblower had to think quickly again. On the one hand was the desire to appear utterly independent, but on the other there was the nagging knowledge that water would soon be running short. Every commanding officer, whether of ships or squadron, carried always at the back of his mind the vital, urgent need for renewing his ship's drinking water. And a Minister of Marine—even a Russian one—must be aware of that.

"Fire-wood and water, as always," said Hornblower, "would be of the greatest convenience."

"I shall inquire if it is convenient to send a water boat to your squadron tomorrow morning," said the minister.

"I thank Your Excellency," said Hornblower, wondering what he would be asked to do in exchange.

"You have been informed, sir," said the minister, changing the subject so obviously that Hornblower could only attribute it to nervousness at having the Czar listening to the conversation, "of Bonaparte's occupation of Swedish Pomerania?"

"Yes, Your Excellency."

"And what is your opinion of that transaction?"

Hornblower delayed his answer while he sorted out his thoughts and worked out the French phrases.

"Typical Bonapartism," he said. "He tolerates neutrality on the part of weak powers only while he can profit by it. The moment he finds it inconveniences him, he treacherously sends forward his army, and on the heels of the army march all the plagues of Bonapartism, terror and famine and misery; the gaol, the firing party, and the secret police. The bankers

136

and the merchants are stripped of all they possess. The men are thrust into the ranks of his army, and the women—all the world knows what happens to the women."

"But you do not believe his object was merely plunder?"

"No, Your Excellency—although plunder is always useful to Bonaparte's top-heavy finances. He overran Pomerania the moment it was apparent that its usefulness as a neutral base for his privateers had ceased with the appearance of my squadron."

Inspiration came to Hornblower at that moment; his expression must have changed, for as he hesitated the minister prompted him with obvious interest.

"Monsieur was going to say—?"

"Bonaparte controls the whole Baltic coast now as far as the frontiers of His Imperial Majesty's dominions. That would be most convenient to him in one particular event, Your Excellency. In the event of his deciding to launch an attack on Russia." Hornblower threw into those words all the power of speech he could muster, and the minister nodded—Hornblower did not dare, much as he wanted to, to throw a glance at the Czar to see what effect his words might have had on him.

"Bonaparte would never feel easy in his mind regarding his communications while Pomerania was Swedish as long as there was a British fleet in the Baltic. It could be too good a base for an attack on his rear, convoyed by my squadron. He has eliminated that danger now—he can march an army against St. Petersburg, should he attack Russia, without fear of its being cut off. It is one more threat to His Imperial Majesty's dominions."

"And how serious do you consider his threats to be regarding Russia, sir?"

"Bonaparte's threats are always serious. You know his methods, Your Excellency. A demand for concessions, and when the concessions are granted then new demands, each one more weakening than the one before, until the object of his attentions is either too weak to oppose him further or is at least so weakened as to make armed resistance fatal. He will not rest until all his demands are granted; and what he demands is nothing short of the dominion of the world, until every nation is in bondage to him."

"Monsieur is very eloquent."

"I am eloquent because I speak from the heart, Your Excellency. For nineteen years, since my boyhood, I have served my country against the monstrous power which overshadows Europe."

"And with what effect has your country fought?"

"My country is still free. In the history of the world that counts for much. And now it counts for more. England is striking back. Portugal, Sicily, are free too, thanks to England. Her armies are marching into Spain even while I am speaking to you here, Your Excellency. Soon Bonaparte will be defending the very frontiers of his boasted empire against them. We have found the weak spot in the vast structure; we are probing into it, onto the very foundations, and soon the whole elaborate mass will crumble into ruin."

The little room must be very warm; Hornblower found himself sweating in his heavy uniform.

"And here in the Baltic?"

"Here England has penetrated too. Not one of Bonaparte's ships will move from today without my permission. England is ready with her support. She is ready to pour in money and arms to help any power that will withstand the tyrant. Bonaparte is ringed in from the south and the west and the north. There is only the east left to him. That is where he will strike, and that is where he must be opposed."

It was the handsome, pale young man in the dark corner of the room to whom these remarks were really addressed. The Minister of Marine had a far smaller stake on the board of international politics than did his master. Other kings in war risked a province or two, risked their dignity or their fame, but the Czar of Russia, the most powerful and autocratic of them all, risked his life, and there was no gainsaying that. A word from the Czar might send a nobleman to Siberia; another word might set half a million men on the move to war; but if either word were ill-judged the Czar would pay for it with his life. A military defeat, a momentary loss of control over his courtiers or his guards, and the Czar was doomed, first to dethronement and then to inevitable murder. That had been the fate of his father, of his grandfather, and of his great-grandfather. If he fought and was unsuccessful, if he did not fight and lost his prestige, there would be a silken scarf round his throat or a dozen swords between his ribs.

An ormolu clock on a bracket on the wall struck in silvery tones.

"The hour strikes, you see, Your Excellency," said Hornblower. He was shaking with the excitement that boiled within him. He felt weak and empty.

"The hour strikes indeed," answered the minister. He was clearly struggling desperately not to glance back at the Czar. "As regards to the clock, I regret it deeply, as it reminds me that if I detain you longer you will be late for the imperial reception."

"I must certainly not be late for that," said Hornblower.

"I must thank you for the clear way in which you have stated your views, Captain. I shall have the pleasure of meeting you at the reception. His Excellency the Grand Marshal will show you the way to the Tauride Hall."

Hornblower bowed, still keeping his eyes from wavering towards the Czar, but he contrived to back from the room without either turning his back on the Czar of making his precaution too obvious. They squeezed past the Cossacks on the stairs down to the ground floor again.

"This way, if you please, sir."

Chapter XII

FOOTMEN opened two more huge doors, and they entered a vast room, the lofty ceiling soaring into a dome far above their heads. The walls were a mass of marble and gold, and grouped in the hall was a crowd of people, the men in uniforms of all the colours of the rainbow, the women in court dresses with plumes and trains. Orders and jewels reflected the light of innumerable candles.

A group of men and women, laughing and joking in French, opened their ranks to admit Hornblower and the Grand Marshal.

"I have the honour to present—" began the latter. It was a prolonged introduction: the Countess of This, and the Baroness of That, and the Duchess of the Other—beautiful women, some of them bold-eyed and some of them languid. Hornblower bowed and bowed again, the star of the Bath thumping his chest each time he straightened up.

"You will partner the Countess Canerine at dinner, Captain," said the Grand Marshal, and Hornblower bowed again.

"Delighted," he said.

The Countess was the boldest-eyed and most beautiful of them all; under the arches of her brows her eyes were dark and liquid and yet with a consuming fire within them. Her face was a perfect oval, her complexion like rose petals, her magnificent bosom white as snow above the *décolletage* of her court dress.

"As a distinguished stranger," went on the Grand Marshal, "you will take precedence immediately after the ambassadors and ministers. Preceding you will be the Persian Ambassador, His Excellency Gorza Khan."

The Grand Marshal indicated an individual in turban and diamonds; it was a bit of blessed good fortune that he was the most easily identified person in the whole crowd, seeing that Hornblower would have to follow him. Everyone else in the group looked with even greater interest at this English captain who was being accorded such distinction; the Countess rolled a considering eye upon him, but the Grand Marshal interrupted the exchange of glances by continuing the introductions. The gentlemen returned Hornblower's bows.

"His Imperial Majesty," said the Grand Marshal, filling in the gap in the conversation when the introductions were completed, "will be wearing the uniform of the Simonouski Guards."

Hornblower caught sight of Wychwood across the room, his bearskin under his arm and Basse at his side, being introduced to another group. They exchanged nods, and Hornblower returned, a little distractedly, to the conversation of his own group. The Countess was asking him about his ship, and he tried to tell her about *Nonsuch*. Through the far doors there was filing a double line of soldiers, tall young men in breast-plates that shone like silver—that probably were silver—with silver helmets with waving white plumes.

"The Chevalier Guard," explained the Countess, "all young men of noble birth."

She looked at them with distinct approval; they were forming against the walls at intervals of two or three yards, each standing like a silver statue as soon as he reached his post. The crowd was moving slowly away from the centre of the room, leaving it clear. Hornblower wondered where the rest of his officers were; he looked round, and realised that there was a further crowd of uniformed individuals in the gallery which ran at first-floor level three quarters of the way round the dome over his head. That would be where the lesser people could look down on the doings of the great. He saw Hurst and Mound leaning against the balustrade. Behind them young Somers, his low-crowned hat in his hand, was talking with elaborate pantomime to a trio of pretty girls, who were holding weakly onto each other as they laughed. Heaven only knew what language Somers was trying to talk, but he was evidently making himself agreeable.

It was Braun that Hornblower was worried about; yet what with the violence of his reaction after his speechmaking, and the chatter and glitter around him, and the sultry glances of the Countess, it was hard to think. Hornblower had to drive himself to keep his mind on his subject. The pistol in Braun's waistband—the fierce intensity of Braun's expression—that gallery up there. He could fit the pieces of the puzzle together if only he were left undistracted for a moment.

"The Prince of Sweden will make his entry with His Imperial Majesty," the Countess was saying.

The Prince of Sweden! Bernadotte, the initiator of a new dynasty, the supplanter of Gustavus, for whom Braun had risked life and fortune. Alexander had conquered Finland; Bernadotte had abandoned it to him. The two men whom Braun had most reason to hate in the whole world were probably Alexander and Bernadotte. And Braun was armed with a double-barrelled pistol, a rifled pistol with percussion caps that never missed fire and which carried true for fifty yards. Hornblower swept the gallery with his eyes. There he was, at the far end, standing unobtrusively between two pillars. Something must be done at once. The Grand Marshal was chattering affably with a couple of courtiers, and Hornblower turned to him, abandoning the Countess and breaking rudely into the conversation with the only excuse that he could think of.

"Impossible!" said the Grand Marshal, glancing at

the clock. "His Imperial Majesty and His Royal Highness enter in three and a half minutes."

"I'm sorry," said Hornblower, "I regret it deeply, but I must—it is absolutely necessary—it is urgent—"

Hornblower fairly danced with anxiety, and the gesture reinforced the argument he had already advanced. The Grand Marshal stood weighing the relative undesirability of interrupting a court ceremony and offending someone who, as the recent interview showed, might have the ear of the Czar.

"Go on through that door, then, sir," he said reluctantly at length, pointing, "and please, sir, come back without calling attention to yourself."

Hornblower fled, sidling rapidly but as unobtrusively as possible through the groups of people to the door; he slipped through it and glanced round desperately. The broad staircase to the left must lead up to the gallery. He grasped the scabbard of his sword to keep it from tripping him up and ran up the stairs two at a time; the one or two footmen whom he passed hardly spared him a glance. The gallery was crowded, although the dresses were not as beautiful nor the uniforms as brilliant. Hornblower hurried along towards the end where he had seen Braun; he took long strides while doing his best to look like a nonchalant stroller. Mound caught his eye—Hornblower could not spare the time to say anything, dared not risk saying a word, but he put all the meaning into his glance that he could, hoping that Mound would follow him. Down below he heard the sound of doors being thrown open, and the babble of conversation stopped abruptly. A loud harsh voice announced: *"L'Empereur! L'Impératrice! Le Prince Royal de Suède!"*

Braun stood there between the two pillars, glancing down. His hand was at his waist; he was drawing the pistol. There was only one silent way to stop him. Hornblower whipped out his sword—the hundred-guinea gold-hilted sword, the gift of the Patriotic

143

Fund, with an edge like a razor—and he slashed at the wrist of the hand that held the pistol. With the tendons severed the fingers opened nervelessly and the pistol fell heavily on the carpeted floor while Braun turned in gaping surprise, looking first at the blood spouting from his wrist and then at Hornblower's face. Hornblower put the point of the blade at his breast; he could lunge and kill him on the instant, and every line in his expression must have attested the genuineness of his determination to do so if necessary, for Braun uttered no sound, made no movement. Somebody loomed up at Hornblower's shoulder; it was Mound, thank God.

"Look after him," whispered Hornblower. "Tie that wrist up! Get him out of here somehow."

He glanced over the railing. A little crowd of royalty was advancing through the huge doors opposite and below him—Alexander in his light blue uniform; a tall swarthy man with a huge nose who must be Bernadotte; a number of women, two with crowns, who must be the Empress and Empress-Mother, and the rest in plumes. Braun would have had the easiest shot heart could desire. All round the vast room the court was making obeisance, the men bowing low and the women curtseying; as Hornblower looked they rose all together, plumes and uniforms like a breaking wave of flowers. Hornblower tore his eyes from the spectacle, sheathed his sword, and picked up the pistol from the floor, stuffing it down into his waistband. Mound, his eternal nonchalance replaced by swift catlike movements, had his long arms round Braun, who was leaning against him. Hornblower snatched out his handkerchief and put it in Mound's hand, but there was not time to do more. He turned away and hastened back along the gallery. The lesser courtiers up here had straightened up from their bows and their curtseys and were beginning to look around them again and resume their conversation. It was lucky that at the moment of crisis they had had no eyes or ears for anything save the royal party. Hurst and Somers were about to start talking to the women again when Hornblower caught their eyes.

"Go back there to Mound," he said. "He needs your help."

Then he walked quickly down the stairs again, found the door into the audience hall, and pushed past the footman on guard there. A glance showed him the position of the group he had left, and he sidled round to it and took up his position at the Countess's side. The royal party was making the circle of the room, making the usual conventional remarks to distinguished individuals, and it was only a matter of a few minutes before they reached Hornblower. The Grand Marshal presented him, and Hornblower, his head swimming with his recent excitement so that he felt as if he were in a nightmare, bowed to each crowned head in turn and to Bernadotte.

"It is a pleasure to meet Commodore Hornblower," said Alexander pleasantly. "We have all of us heard of his exploits."

"Your Majesty is too kind," gulped Hornblower.

Then the royal group passed on, and Hornblower turned to meet the Countess's glance again. The fact that the Czar had addressed a few words to him personally evidently confirmed her suspicions that he was a man of potential influence, and there was a considering look in her eyes.

"Will you be making a long stay in Russia?" she asked.

It was very hard, during this period of intense reaction, to keep his mind on anything. All he wanted to do was to sit down and rest quietly. He flogged his mind into making a polite rejoinder, and when the men of the party began to ply him with questions about the British navy and about maritime affairs in general he tried to answer sensibly, but it was a forlorn hope.

Footmen were rolling in long buffet tables, glittering with gold and silver; Hornblower forced himself to watch keenly, so as to commit no breach of etiquette. To one side the royal party had taken their seats, Empresses and Czar in armchairs and the princes and princesses in upright chairs, and everyone had to be careful always to face in that direction so as not to commit the heinous crime of letting royalty see a human back. People were beginning to take food from the buffets, and, try as he would, Hornblower could see no sign at all of any attention to precedence. But there was the Persian Ambassador munching something from a gold plate, so that he was justified in making a move in the same direction. Yet all the same this was the most curious dinner he had ever attended, with everyone standing up except royalty; and royalty, he could see, were eating nothing at all.

"May I offer you my arm, Countess?" he said, as the group began to drift towards a buffet.

The courtiers by dint of long practice had seemingly mastered the art of eating while standing up and while holding their hats under their arms, but it was not easy. His dangling sword was liable to trip him, too, and that infernal pistol in his waistband was digging uncomfortably into his side. The footmen serving at the buffets understood no French and the Countess came to Hornblower's rescue with an order.

"That is caviare," she explained to him, "and this is vodka, the drink of the people, but I think you will find that the two are admirably suited to each other."

The Countess was right. The grey, unappetizing-looking stuff was perfectly delicious. Hornblower sipped cautiously at the vodka, and in his present highly strung condition hardly noticed the fierce bite of the liquor; but there was no doubt that vodka and caviare blended together exquisitely. He felt the warm glow of the alcohol inside him, and realised that he was desperately hungry. The buffet was covered with foods of all kinds, some being kept warm in chafing dishes, some cold; under the tutelage of the Countess Hornblower went a fair way towards tackling them all. There was a dish apparently of stewed mushrooms that was excellent; slices of smoked fish; an unidentifiable salad; some varieties of cheese; eggs both hot and cold; a sort of ragout of pork. There were other liquors as well, and Hornblower ate and drank with his spirits rising momentarily, playing his part in the conversation and feeling more and more warmly grateful to the Countess. It might be a queer way to have dinner, but Hornblower thought he had never tasted such delicious food. His head began to whirl with the liquor; he knew the danger signal of old, although this time he did not resent it quite as bitterly as usual, and he checked himself in the midst of a laugh in time not to be too unrestrained. Laughter, chatter, and bright lights; this was one of the jolliest parties he had ever attended— he felt as if it had been someone else who had slashed Braun's wrist open with a sword an hour ago. Hornblower replaced his lovely porcelain plate on the buffet, among the gold dishes, and wiped his mouth with one of the silken napkins that lay there. He was comfortably replete, with the gratifying sensation of having eaten just too much and drunk just enough; he supposed coffee would be served soon, and a cup of coffee was all he needed to complete his internal gratification.

"I have dined extremely well," he said to the Countess.

The most remarkable expression passed over the Countess's face. Her eyebrows rose, and she opened her mouth to say something and then shut it again. She was smiling and puzzled and distressed all at the same time. She again started to speak but her words were cut short by the ceremonial opening of yet another pair of doors from which twenty or thirty footmen emerged to form an avenue leading into the next room. Hornblower became conscious that the royal party had risen from their chairs and were falling into formation, and the complete cessation of conversation told Hornblower that some specially solemn moment had arrived. Couples were moving about the room like ships jockeying for position. The Countess laid her hand on his arm with a gentle pressure as if to lead him. By George, a procession was forming behind the royal party! There went the Persian Ambassador, a smiling girl on his arm. Hornblower just had time to lead his own partner forward to join the procession next, and after two or three more couples had joined behind him the procession began to move forward, its tail being steadily lengthened as it went. Hornblower kept his eyes on the Persian Ambassador before him; they passed down the avenue of footmen, and entered the next room.

The procession was breaking off to left and to right in alternate couples as though in a country dance; the Persian Ambassador went to the left, and Hornblower was ready to go to the right without the prompting of the gesture of the Grand Marshal, who was standing there ready to direct anyone in doubt. It was another enormous room, lit by what seemed to be hundreds of cut-glass chandeliers dangling from the roof, and all down the length of it ran a vast table—miles long, it seemed, to Hornblower's disordered imagination—covered with gold plate and crystal and embanked with flowers. The table was shaped like a T with a very small cross-piece, and the royal party had already taken their seats at the head; behind every chair all the way down stood a white-wigged footman. It dawned upon Hornblower that dinner was about to begin; the food and drink which had been served in the domed hall had been something extra and introductory. Hornblower was ready to laugh at himself for his idiotic lack of comprehension at the same time as he was ready to groan with despair at the thought of having to eat his way through an imperial dinner in his present distended condition.

Save for royalty, the men were standing at their chairs while the ladies sat; across the table the Persian Ambassador was bending affably over the young woman he had brought in, and the aigrette in his turban nodded and his diamonds flashed. The last woman took her seat, and then the men sat down together—not quite simultaneously as marines presenting arms, but almost so. A babble of conversation began immediately, and almost immediately a golden soup plate was put under Hornblower's nose and a golden soup tureen full of pink soup was offered to him for him to help himself from. He could not help glancing down the table; everyone had been given soup at the same moment—there must be two hundred footmen at least waiting at table.

"That is Monsieur de Narbonne, the French Ambassador," said the Countess, indicating with a glance a handsome young man across the table two places higher than the Persian Ambassador. "Of course the Grand Marshal did not present you to him. And that is the Austrian Ambassador, and the Saxon Minister, and the Danish Minister, all your enemies officially. The Spanish Ambassador comes from Joseph Bonaparte, not from the Spanish partisan government which you recognise, so you could hardly be presented to him either. I don't believe there's a soul here except us Russians to whom it would be proper to present you."

There was a cool, pleasant yellow wine in a tall glass before Hornblower, and he sipped it.

"My experience today," he said, "is that Russians are the most delightful people in the world, and Russian women the most charming and most beautiful."

The Countess flashed a glance at him from her sultry eyes, and, it seemed to Hornblower, set his brains creeping about inside his skull. The golden soup plate was whisked away and replaced by a golden dinner

149

plate. Another wine was poured into another glass before him—champagne. It effervesced just as his thoughts appeared to him to be doing. His footman spoke to him in Russian, apparently offering him a choice, and the Countess settled the problem without referring to him.

"As this is your first visit to Russia," she explained, "I could be sure that you have not yet tasted our Volga River trout."

She was helping herself to one as she spoke, from a golden dish; Hornblower's footman was presenting another golden dish.

"A gold service looks very well," said the Countess sadly, "but it allows the food to grow unfortunately cold. I never use mine in my house save when I entertain His Imperial Majesty. As that is the case in most houses I doubt if His Imperial Majesty ever has a hot meal."

The gold knife and fork with which Hornblower dissected his fish were heavy in his hands, and scraped oddly against the gold plate.

"You have a kind heart, Madame," he said.

"Yes," said the Countess, with deep significance.

Hornblower's head whirled again; the champagne, so cold, so delicate, seemed perfectly adapted to put this right, and he drank of it thirstily.

A couple of fat little birds on toast followed the trout; they melted delicately in the mouth; some other wine followed the champagne. And there was a venison stew, and a cut of some roast which might be mutton but which was borne on Pegasus-wings of garlic beyond mundane speculation. Somewhere in the procession of food appeared a pink water ice, only the third or fourth which Hornblower had ever tasted.

"Foreign kickshaws," said Hornblower to himself, but he enjoyed the food and had no prejudice against foreign cookery. Perhaps he said "foreign kickshaws" to himself because that was what Bush would have

150

said had he been eating the dinner. Or perhaps it was because he was a little drunk—Hornblower's persistent self-examination brought him to this startling conclusion with a shock, comparable with that received by a man walking into a stanchion in the dark. He must certainly not get drunk while he was representing his country, and he would be a fool to get drunk while in the imminent personal danger which surrounded him. He personally had brought an assassin to the palace, and if the fact ever leaked out it would go hard with him, especially if the Czar should become aware that the assassin was armed with a rifled pistol which was Hornblower's private property. Hornblower sobered still further when it came to him that he had forgotten all about his junior officers—he had left them trying to dispose of the wounded assassin, and what they would do with him was more than he could guess.

The Countess beside him was pressing his foot under the table, and a little electric thrill ran through him and his steadiness vanished once more. He smiled at her beatifically. She gave him a long look with lowered lids and then turned away to address a remark to her neighbour on her other side, a tactful hint for Hornblower to pay a little attention to the Baroness, to whom he had hardly spoken a word. Hornblower plunged feverishly into conversation, and the general in the outlandish dragoon uniform on the far side of the Baroness joined in with a question about Admiral Keats, whose acquaintance he had made in 1807. The footman was offering a new dish; his hairy wrist was exposed between his cuff and his white glove, and that wrist was spotted with flea-bites. Hornblower remembered having read in one of the books he had been studying about the northern powers that the farther east one travelled the worse the vermin became—the Polish flea was bad but the Russian flea was unbearable. If it was any worse than the Spanish flea, with which Hornblower had an intimate ac-

151

quaintance, it must be a remarkably well-developed flea.

There must be hundreds—there must actually be thousands—of servants in this palace, and Hornblower could guess how closely they must be herded together. Having waged a ceaseless war against body vermin for twenty years in crowded ships Hornblower was well aware of the difficulty of extermination. But while one part of his mind was discussing with the dragoon general the principles of seniority and selection in the British navy another part was telling himself that he would greatly prefer not to be served by a flea-bitten footman. The conversation languished, and Hornblower turned back to the Countess.

"Do pictures interest Monsieur very much?" she asked.

"Of course," said Hornblower politely.

"The picture gallery in this palace is very fine. You have not seen it yet?"

"I have not yet had that pleasure."

"This evening, after the royal party has retired, I could show it to you. Unless you would rather join one of the card tables?"

"I would much prefer to see pictures," said Hornblower. His laugh rang a little loud even in his own ears.

"Then if, after the royal party has withdrawn, you are by the door on the far side of the room, I shall show you the way."

"That will be delightful, Madame."

They were drinking toasts at the head of the table, for the first everyone had to stand while they drank the health of the Prince of Sweden, and after that conversation perforce became disjointed with other toasts to be drunk, announced by a gigantic official with a colossal voice—Stentor with Hercules' frame, said Hornblower to himself, pleased with the classical touch—who stood behind the Czar's chair. Between

152

toasts there was music; not orchestral music, but vocal music from an unaccompanied male choir, seemingly of hundreds of voices which filled the vast room with their din. Hornblower heard it with the faint but growing irritation of the completely tone-deaf. It was a relief when the music ceased and everyone stood once more while the royal party withdrew through a doorway near the head of the table, and no sooner had the door closed after them than the women went out too, ushered through the far door by Madame Kochubey.

"*A bientôt,*" smiled the Countess, as she left him.

The men began to gather in groups along the table while footmen hastened in with coffee and cordials; Wychwood, his bearskin still under his arm, made his way round to Hornblower. His face was redder than ever; his eyes, if it were possible, stuck out even farther from his head.

"The Swedes'll fight if Russia will," said Wychwood, in a grating whisper. "I have that direct from Basse, who was with Bernadotte all day."

Then he passed on and Hornblower heard his remarkable French being practised on a uniformed group higher up the table. The room was unbearably hot, presumably because of the infinity of candles alight in it; some of the men were already beginning to drift away through the door where the women had preceded them. Hornblower drank his coffee and rose to his feet, transferring his cocked hat once more from his knees to under his arm. The room he entered must have been the counterpart of the one in which the royal reception had been held, for it was domed too, and of similar proportions; Hornblower remembered the two domes he had seen when his carriage drew up to the palace. It was dotted with chairs and sofas and tables, round one of which a group of dowagers were already playing cards, and an elderly couple were playing backgammon at another. At the far end his eye instantly discerned the Countess, seated on a

153

couch with her train spread beside her and her coffee cup and saucer in her hands, while she chatted with another woman; every line of the Countess's attitude proclaimed girlish innocence.

From the number of people already assembled it was clear that this was the meeting place of the whole court; presumably the hundreds of people who had perforce witnessed the royal reception from the gallery were permitted to descend and mingle with their betters after dining less elaborately. Young Mound was lounging towards him, his lean gangling body looking like an overgrown colt's.

"We have him in a side room aloft, sir," he reported. "He fainted with the loss of blood—we had to put a tourniquet on his arm to stop the bleeding. We bandaged him with half of Somers' shirt, and Somers and Mr. Hurst are keeping guard over him."

"Does anyone know about it?"

"No, sir. We got him into the room without anyone seeing us. I poured a glass of liquor over his coat and from the stink of him anyone'll think he's drunk."

Mound was obviously a capable man in an emergency, as Hornblower had already suspected.

"Very good."

"The sooner we get him away the better, sir," said Mound, with a diffidence to be expected of a junior officer making suggestions to a senior.

"You're quite right," said Hornblower, "except that—"

Hornblower was still having to think quickly. It would hardly be possible in any case to leave at once, the moment dinner was over. It would not be polite. And there was the Countess over there, presumably watching them. If they were to leave now, immediately after conferring together—and breaking an engagement with her—she would be full of suspicion, as well as of the fury of a woman scorned. They simply could not leave immediately.

"We shall have to stay another hour at least," he

said. "The conventions demand it. Go back and hold the fort for that time."

"Aye aye, sir."

Mound restrained himself in the nick of time from coming to attention as with the habit of years he had grown accustomed to do when uttering those words—further proof of the clearness of his head. He nodded and wandered off as if they had been merely discussing the weather, and Hornblower allowed his slow legs to carry him over towards the Countess.

She smiled at his approach.

"Princess," she said, "you have not met Commodore Hornblower? The Princess de Stolp."

Hornblower bowed; the Princess was an elderly woman with a good deal left of what must have been marvellous beauty.

"The commodore," went on the Countess, "has expressed a desire to see the picture gallery. Would you care to come with us, Princess?"

"No, thank you," said the Princess. "I fear I am too old for picture galleries. But go, my children, without me."

"I would not like to leave you alone, here," protested the Countess.

"Even at my age, I can boast that I am still never left long alone, Countess. Leave me, I beg you. Enjoy yourselves, children."

Hornblower bowed again, and the Countess took his arm, and they walked slowly out. She pressed his arm, while footmen stood aside to allow them passage.

"The Italian pictures of the cinquecento are in the far gallery," said the Countess as they came into the broad corridor. "Would you care to see the more modern ones first?"

"As Madame wishes," said Hornblower.

Once through a door, once out of the ceremonial part of the palace, it was like a rabbit warren—narrow passages, innumerable staircases, an infinity of rooms. The apartment to which she led him was on the first floor; a sleepy maid who was awaiting her coming vanished into the room beyond as they came into the luxurious sitting room. It was into the room beyond that the Countess called him, five minutes later.

Chapter XIII

HORNBLOWER turned over in his cot with a groan; the effort of turning brought back the pain into his temples, although he moved very cautiously. He was a fool to have drunk so much—it was the first time he had had this sort of headache for half a dozen years. Yet it had been hard to avoid, just as everything else had been hard to avoid; he did not know what else he could have done, once events had him in their grip. He raised his voice and shouted for Brown—it hurt his head again to shout, and his voice was a hoarse croak. He heard the voice of the sentry at the door passing on the word, and with an infinity of effort he sat up and put his legs out of bed, determined that Brown should not find him prostrate.

"Bring me some coffee," he said when Brown came in.

"Aye aye, sir."

Hornblower continued to sit on the edge of his cot. Overhead he heard the raucous voice of Hurst blaring through the skylight, apparently addressing a delinquent midshipman.

"A fine young flibbertigibbet *you* are," said Hurst. "Look at that brass-work! D'you call that bright? Where d'you keep your eyes? What's your division been doing this last hour? God, what's the navy coming to, when warrants are given to young jacka-napes who couldn't keep their noses clear with a marlin-spike! You call yourself a King's officer? You're more like a winter's day, short, dark, and dirty!"

Hornblower took the coffee Brown brought in.

"My compliments to Mr. Hurst," he croaked, "and ask him kindly not to make so much noise over my skylight."

"Aye aye, sir."

The first satisfaction that day was to hear Hurst cut his tirade abruptly short. Hornblower sipped at the scalding coffee with some degree of pleasure. It was not surprising that Hurst should be in a bad temper today. He had been through a harassing evening the night before; Hornblower remembered Hurst and Mound carrying Braun, unconscious and reeking with spirits, into the carriage at the palace door. Hurst had been strictly sober, but apparently the mental strain of keeping guard over a secret assassin in the Czar's palace had been too much for his nerves. Hornblower handed his cup back to Brown to be refilled when Brown reappeared, and pulled his nightshirt over his head as he waited. Something caught his eye as he laid his nightshirt on his cot; it was a flea, leaping high out of the sleeve. In a wave of disgust he looked down at himself; his smooth round belly was pockmarked with flea-bites. That was a striking commentary on the difference between an imperial palace and one of His Britannic Majesty's ships of the line. When Brown returned with his second cup of coffee Hornblower was still cursing fiercely both at imperial uncleanness and at the dreary prospect of the nuisance of having to rid himself of vermin to which he was peculiarly susceptible.

"Take that grin off your face!" snapped Hornblower. "Or I'll send you to the grating to see if you grin there."

Brown was not grinning; all that could be said about his expression was that he was too obviously not grinning. What irritated Hornblower was the knowledge that Brown was enjoying the superior and

157

paternal state of mind of one who has not a headache while the man who is with him has.

His shower-bath restored some of Hornblower's peace of mind, and he put on clean linen, gave Brown orders for the disinfection of his clothes, and went up on deck, where the first person on whom he laid eyes was Wychwood, bleary-eyed and obviously with a far worse headache than he had himself. Yet the keen air of the Russian morning was invigorating and refreshing. The normal early morning ship's routine, the sight of the rows of men holystoning the decks, the pleasant swish of the water over the planking, were comforting and restorative as well.

"Boat coming off to us, sir," reported a midshipman to the officer of the watch.

It was the same pinnace as had taken them ashore yesterday, and it brought a naval officer with a letter in French:—

His Excellency the Minister of the Imperial Marine presents his compliments to Commodore Sir Hornblower. His Excellency has given orders for a water boat to be alongside the *Nonsuch* at eleven o'clock this morning.

A distinguished nobleman, M. le Comte du Nord, having expressed a desire to see one of His Britannic Majesty's ships, His Excellency proposes to trespass upon Sir Hornblower's hospitality by visiting the *Nonsuch* at ten o'clock in company with the Comte du Nord.

Hornblower showed the letter to Wychwood, who confirmed his suspicions.

"That's Alexander," he said. "He used the title of Comte du Nord when he was travelling on the continent as Czarevitch. He'll be coming incognito, so that there'll be no need for royal honours."

"Yes," said Hornblower dryly, a little nettled at this soldier giving him advice beyond what he was asked for. "But an Imperial Minister of Marine must rank with a First Lord of the Admiralty. That'll mean nineteen guns and all the other honours. Midshipman of the watch! My compliments to the captain, and I shall be very obliged if he will be good enough to come on deck."

Bush heard the news with a low whistle, and instantly turned to sweep decks and rigging with his glance, anxious that his ship should be in the perfection of condition for this imperial visit.

"How can we take in water," asked Bush piteously, "and be in a fit state for the Czar to come on board, sir? What will he think of us? Unless we water the flotilla first?"

"The Czar's a man of sense," said Hornblower, briskly. "Let's show him the hands at work. He doesn't know the difference between the mizzen stay and the flying jib-boom, but he'll recognize efficient work if we show it to him. Start watering while he's on board."

"And the food?" asked Bush. "We'll have to offer him something, sir."

Hornblower grinned at his anxiety.

"Yes, we'll offer him something."

It was typical of Hornblower's contrary temperament that the more difficulties other people foresaw the more cheerful he became; the only person really capable of depressing Hornblower was Hornblower himself. His headache had left him completely, and he was positively smiling now at the thought of a busy morning. He ate his breakfast with appetite, and put on his full-dress uniform once more and came on deck to find Bush still fussing round the ship, with the crew all in clean white frocks and duck trousers, the accommodation ladder rigged, with hand ropes as white as snow, the marines all pipe-clayed and polished, the hammocks stowed in mathematical tiers. It was only when the midshipman of the watch reported a cutter approaching that he felt a little twinge of nervousness, a sudden catch in his breath, at the thought that the next few hours might have a decided bearing on the history of the world for years to come.

The calls of the boatswain's mates shrilled through the ship, and the ship's company fell in by divisions, officers to the front with epaulettes and swords, while Hornblower at the quarterdeck rail looked down at the assembly. British seamen on parade could not possibly rival the Prussian Guard in exactitude and uniformity, and to drill them into any approach to it would be likely to expel from them the very qualities that made them the valuable men they were; but any thinking man, looking down the lines of intelligent, self-reliant faces, could not fail to be impressed.

"Man the yards!" ordered Bush.

Another squeal from the pipes, and the topmen poured up the rigging in an orderly upward torrent, without a break in their speed as they hung back-downward from the futtock shrouds, going hand over hand up the top-gallant shrouds like the trained gymnasts they were, running out along the yards like tight-rope walkers, each man taking up his position on the foot-ropes the moment he reached it.

Various emotions warred in Hornblower's breast as he watched. There was a momentary feeling of resentment that these men of his, the cream of the service, should be put through their paces like performing bears to gratify an Oriental monarch. Yet as the evolution was completed, when each man reached his place, as though by some magic a gust of wind had whirled a heap of dead leaves into the air and left them suspended in a pattern of exquisite symmetry, his resentment was swamped by artistic satisfaction. He hoped that Alexander, looking on, would have the sense to realise that these men could be relied upon to perform the same feat in any conditions —in a black night with a howling gale blowing, on a raging sea with the bowsprit stabbing at the invisible sky and the yard-arms dipping towards the invisible sea.

The boatswain, looking with one eye over the starboard rail, gave an infinitesimal jerk of his head. A little procession of officers was coming up the accommodation ladder. The boatswain's mates put their calls to their lips. The sergeant-drummer of marines contrived to snap his fingers beside the seams of his trousers as he stood at attention, and the six sidedrums roared out in a bold ruffle.

"Present arms!" bellowed Captain Norman, and the fifty muskets with fixed bayonets of the marines left the fifty scarlet shoulders and came down vertically in front of fifty rows of gleaming buttons, while the swords of the three marine officers swept in the graceful arc of the military salute.

Alexander, followed by two aides-de-camp, came slowly on board, side by side with the Minister of Marine to whom nominally all this ceremony was dedicated. He put his hand to his hat brim while the pipes died away in a final squeal, the drums completed their fourth ruffle, the first gun of the salute banged out forward, and the fifes and drums of the marine band burst into "Hearts of Oak." Hornblower walked forward and saluted.

"Good morning, Commodore," said the Minister of Marine. "Permit me to present you to the Comte du Nord."

Hornblower saluted again, his face as expressionless as he could manage it even while he fought down a smile at Alexander's queer liking to be incognito.

"Good morning, Commodore," said Alexander; with a shock Hornblower realised that he was speaking English of a sort. "I hope our little visit does not discommode you too much?"

"Not in any way to compare with the honour done to the ship, sir," said Hornblower, wondering as he said it whether "sir" was the right way to address a Czar incognito. Apparently it sufficed.

161

"You may present your officers," said Alexander.

Hornblower brought them up one by one, and they saluted and bowed with the uneasy stiffness to be expected of junior officers in the presence of a Czar of All the Russias, and an incognito one at that.

"I think you can give orders to prepare the ship for watering now, Captain," said Hornblower to Bush, and then he turned back to Alexander. "Would you care to see more of the ship, sir?"

"I would indeed," said Alexander.

He lingered on the quarterdeck to watch the preparations begin. The topmen came pouring down from aloft; Alexander blinked in the sunlight with admiration as half a dozen hands came sliding down the mizzen backstays and the mizzen-topsail halliards to land on their feet on the quarterdeck beside him. Under the petty officers' urging the men ran hither and thither about their tasks; it was a scene of activity like a disturbed ants' nest, but far more orderly and purposeful. The hatches were whipped off, the pumps made ready, tackles rigged at the yard-arms, fenders dropped over the port side. Alexander stared at the sight of a half-company of marines tailing onto a fall and walking away with it in flat-footed rhythm.

"Soldiers and sailors too, sir," explained Hornblower, deprecatingly, as he led the way below.

Alexander was a very tall man, an inch or two taller than Hornblower, and he bent himself nearly double as he crouched under the low deck beams below decks and peered about with short-sighted eyes. Hornblower took him forward along the lower gun deck, where the head clearance was no more than five feet six inches; he showed him the midshipmen's berth, and the warrant officers' mess—all the unlovely details of the life of a sailor. He called away a group of seamen, had them unstow and sling their hammocks, and get into them, so that Alexander could see more clearly what twenty-two inches per man really meant, and he gave a graphic description of a whole deckful of hammocks swinging together in a storm, with the men packed in a solid mass. The grins of the men who made the demonstration were proof enough to Alexander not merely of the truth of what Hornblower was saying, but also of the high spirits of the men, far different from the patient uneducated peasants whom he was accustomed to see in the ranks of his army.

They peered down through the hatchway to see the working party down there breaking out the water casks and preparing the tiers for refilling, and a whiff of the stench of the orlop came up to them—bilgewater and cheese and humanity intermingled.

"You are an officer of long service, I believe, Commodore?" said Alexander.

"Nineteen years, sir," said Hornblower.

"And how much of that time have you spent at sea?"

"Sixteen years, sir. For nine months I was a prisoner in Spain, and for six months in France."

"I know of your escape from France. You went through much peril to return to this life."

Alexander's handsome forehead was wrinkled as he puzzled over the fact that a man could spend sixteen years of his life living in these conditions and still be sane and healthy.

"How long have you held your present rank?"

"As commodore, sir, only two months. But I have nine years' seniority as captain."

"And before that?"

"I was six years lieutenant, and four years midshipman."

"Four years? You lived four years in a place like the midshipmen's berth you showed me?"

"Not quite as comfortable as that, sir. I was in a frigate nearly all the time, under Sir Edward Pellew. A battleship is not quite as crowded as a frigate, sir."

Hornblower, watching Alexander closely, could see that he was impressed, and he could guess at the line of thought Alexander was following. The Czar was not so much struck by the miserable conditions of life on board ship—if he knew anything about his people at all he must be aware that nearly all of them lived in conditions a good deal worse—as by the fact that those conditions could train an officer of ability.

"I suppose it is necessary," sighed Alexander, revealing for a moment the humane and emotional side of his nature which rumour had long hinted that he possessed.

By the time they came on deck again the water boat was already alongside. Some of the *Nonsuch's* hands were down on her decks, mingling with the Russians to help with the work. Working parties were swinging away lustily at the pumps, and the long snake-like canvas hoses pulsated at each stroke. Forward they were swaying up bundles of fire-wood, the men chanting as they hauled.

"Thanks to your generosity, sir," said Hornblower, "we will be able to keep the sea for four months if necessary without entering port."

Luncheon was served in Hornblower's cabin to a party of eight—Hornblower, Bush, the two senior lieutenants, and the four Russians. Bush was sweating with nervousness at the sight of the inhospitable table; at the last moment he had drawn Hornblower aside and pleaded unavailingly for him to change his mind and serve some of his remaining cabin delicacies as well as the plain ship's fare. Bush could not get out of his mind the obsession that it was necessary to feed the Czar well; any junior officer entertaining an admiral would blast all his hopes of future promotion if he put the men's ration beef on the table, and Bush could only think in terms of entertaining admirals.

The Czar looked with interest at the battered pewter tureen which Brown set before Hornblower.

"Pea soup, sir," explained Hornblower. "One of the great delicacies of shipboard life."

Carlin, of long habit, began to rap his biscuit on the table, stopped when he realised what he was doing, and then started rapping again, guiltily. He remembered the orders Hornblower had given, that everyone should behave as if no distinguished company was present; Hornblower had backed up those orders with the direst threats of punishment should they be forgotten, and Carlin knew that Hornblower did not threaten in that way without every intention of doing what he promised. Alexander looked at Carlin and then inquiringly at Bush beside him.

"Mr. Carlin is knocking out the weevils, sir," explained Bush, almost overcome with self-consciousness. "If you tap gently they come out of their own accord, this way, you see, sir."

"Very interesting," said Alexander, but he ate no bread; one of his aides-de-camp repeated the experiment, peered down at the fat white weevils with black heads that emerged, and exploded into what must have been a string of Russian oaths—almost the first words he had said since boarding the ship.

The visitors, after this inauspicious beginning, gingerly tasted the soup. But in the British navy pea soup, as Hornblower had remarked, was the best dish served; the aide-de-camp who had sworn at the weevils exclaimed with surprised gratification when he had tasted it, speedily consumed his plateful, and accepted another. There were only three dishes served as the next course—boiled salt ribs of beef, boiled salt beef tongue, and boiled salt pork, with pickled cabbage to accompany the meat. Alexander studied the three dishes, and wisely accepted the tongue; the Minister of Marine and the aides-de-camp, at Hornblower's suggestion, took a mixed plateful, carved for them by Hornblower and Bush and Hurst. The once silent but now talkative aide-de-camp set himself to chew on the salt beef with a truly Russian appetite and found it a long hard struggle.

Brown was now serving rum.

"The life-blood of the navy, sir," said Hornblower, as Alexander studied his tumbler. "May I offer you gentlemen a toast which we can all drink with the heartiest good will? The Emperor of All the Russians! *Vive l'Empereur!*"

All rose except Alexander to drink the toast, and they were hardly seated before Alexander was on his feet in turn.

"The King of Great Britain."

The aide-de-camp's French broke down again when he tried to explain how deep an impression navy rum made on him at this, his first encounter with it. Eventually he gave the clearest proof of his appreciation by draining his tumbler and holding it out for Brown to refill. As the table was cleared Alexander was ready with another toast.

"Commodore Sir Horatio Hornblower, and the British Royal Navy."

As the glasses were drained Hornblower, looking round him, saw that he was expected to reply in form.

"The Navy," he said, "the guardian of the liberties of the world. The unswerving friend, the unremitting enemy. When the tyrant of Europe looks about him, seeking by fair means or foul to extend his dominion, it is the Navy that he finds in his path. It is the Navy which is slowly strangling that tyrant. It is the Navy which has baulked him at every turn, which is draining the life-blood from his boasted empire and which will bring him down in ruin at the end. The tyrant may boast of unbroken victory on land, but he can only deplore unbroken defeat at sea. It is because of the Navy that every victory only leaves him weaker than before, forced, like Sisyphus, to roll his rock once more up towards an unattainable summit. And one day that rock will crush him. May it be sooner rather than later!"

Hornblower ended his speech amid a little fierce

murmur from the others at the table. He was in an exalted mood again; this present occasion for making a speech had taken him a little by surprise, but he had hoped when he had first heard of the intended visit of the Czar to have an opportunity sometime during the day of calling his attention once more to the aid which the British alliance could afford him. Alexander was young and impressionable. It was necessary to appeal to his emotions as well as to his intellect. Hornblower stole a glance at the Czar to see if he had attained his end; Alexander was sitting rapt in thought, his eyes looking down at the table. He raised them to meet Hornblower's with a smile, and Hornblower felt a wave of exultation, of sublime confidence that his plan had succeeded. He had had plain fare served at luncheon of set purpose; he had shown Alexander exactly how the navy lived and slept and worked. The Czar could not be ignorant of the British navy's glory, and Hornblower's intuitive mind told him that proof of the hardship of naval life would be a subtle appeal to the Czar's emotions; it would be hard to explain exactly how it would appeal, but Hornblower was sure of it. Alexander both would be moved to help men who won glory at such a cost and also would desire to have such tough fighters on his side.

Alexander was making a move to leave; the aide-de-camp hurriedly drained his fifth tumbler of rum, and it and its predecessors so worked upon him as to make him put his arm round Bush's shoulders as they came up on the quarterdeck and pat him on the back with whole-hearted affection, while the long row of medals and orders on his chest jingled and clinked like tinkers working on pots and kettles. Bush, keenly aware of the eyes of the ship's company upon him, tried to writhe away from the embrace, but unavailingly. He was red in the face as he bawled the order for the manning of the yards, and sighed with evident relief as Alexander's departure down the accommodation ladder made it necessary for the aide-de-camp to follow him.

Chapter XIV

An easterly wind was not to be wasted. *Nonsuch* and the flotilla were heading back down the Gulf of Finland with all sail set, and the commodore was walking the quarterdeck, turning over in his mind all the problems which beset a commander-in-chief. The problem of drinking water at least was settled; it would be two months easily, four months if necessary, before he had to worry about that. The mere fact that he had refilled his water casks would be some sort of justification for his having had dealings with the court of St. Petersburg should Downing Street or Whitehall take exception to his recent activities—Hornblower ran through in his mind the wording of his report, which had laid as much stress on the advantage gained in this fashion as on the desirability of having made contact with the Russian government. He had a good case to plead. But—

Hornblower turned and looked back at the squadron.

"Make a signal to *Lotus*," he ordered: "'Why are you out of station?'"

The flags soared up the halliards, and Hornblower saw the sloop hurriedly correct her position.

"*Lotus* acknowledges the signal, sir," reported the midshipman.

"Then make 'Why do you not reply to my question?'" said Hornblower, harshly.

It was some seconds before any reply was visible.

"*Lotus* signals 'Inattention on the part of the officer of the watch,' sir."

"Acknowledge," said Hornblower.

He had stirred up trouble there; Vickery would be raging at this public censure, and the officer of the watch in question would be regretting his inattention at this very moment. There would be no harm done and probably some good. But Hornblower was perfectly aware that he had only launched the censure because he wanted an excuse to postpone thinking about the next unpleasant matter on which he had to decide. He wondered to himself how many of the other reprimands he had seen dealt out—which he himself had received as a junior officer, for that matter—had been administered by harassed admirals as a distraction from more unpleasant thoughts. He himself had to think about the case of Braun.

The low shore of Finland was just visible to the northward; down on the main deck Carlin had a division of guns at exercise, the men going through the drill of loading and running out. With the wind almost dead astern and studding sails set *Nonsuch* was making good speed through the water—if the sea were to get up any more she would have to shorten sail so as to allow the bomb-ketches to keep up. A boatswain's mate forward was starting one of the hands with the fore topsail clew-line, something altogether too thick to be used for that purpose. Hornblower was on the point, reluctantly, of interfering with the internal working of the ship when he saw a lieutenant intervene and save him the trouble. Some knowledge of his prejudices and desires had evidently filtered down through Bush to the junior officers. Hornblower watched the trio separate again about their business until there was absolutely no excuse for watching them any longer.

He simply had to think about Braun. The man had attempted to commit murder, and by laws of England and the Articles of War he should die. But being the holder of a Navy Board warrant, it would call for a court of five post-captains to pass a death sentence on him, and there were not five post-captains within a hundred miles. Bush and Hornblower were the only ones, Vickery and Cole being merely commanders. By law, then, Braun should be kept under arrest until a competent court could be assembled to try him, unless—and here he had discretion—the good of the service, the safety of the ship, or the welfare of England demanded immediate action. In that case he could summon a court composed of whatever senior officers were available, try him, and hang him on the spot. The evidence would be overwhelming; his own and Mound's would suffice to hang Braun ten times over.

The need for summary action was not so apparent, however. Braun, languishing in the sick bay with a right hand he would never use again, and half dead with loss of blood, was certainly not going to start a mutiny among the hands, or set fire to the ship, or seduce the officers from their duty. But there must be the wildest tales flying round the lower deck already. Hornblower could not imagine how the hands would try to account for Braun's being brought back from the Czar's palace badly wounded. There would be talk and gossip which sooner or later would reach the ears of Bonaparte's agents, and Hornblower knew Bonaparte's methods too well to doubt that he would make the utmost use of an opportunity to sow dissension between his enemies. Alexander would never forgive a country which had brought him within a hair's-breadth of assassination. When the authorities at home should come to know of the incident they would be furious, and it was he, Hornblower, who would be the object of their fury. Hornblower thought of the report locked in his desk, marked "Most Secret and Confidential," in which he had put down the facts. He could imagine that report being put in as evidence against him at a court-martial, and he could imagine what view his brother captains who would be his judges would take of it.

For a moment Hornblower toyed with the idea of concealing the incident altogether, making no report about it at all, but he put the notion aside as impractical. Someone would talk. On the other hand, there was the clause in his orders which bound him to make the freest use of Braun's experience; that might cover him, and besides, the insertion of that clause implied that Braun had friends in authority who would be interested possibly in protecting him and certainly in protecting themselves, and who in consequence would not wish too public a scandal to be made. It was all very complex.

"Mr. Montgomery," said Hornblower, harshly, "what sort of course do your quartermasters keep? Have 'em steer smaller than that, or I shall want an explanation from you."

"Aye aye, sir," said Montgomery.

At least he had done his part towards dragging Russia into war with Bonaparte—the last word he had received from Wychwood before leaving Kronstadt had been to the effect that Alexander had sent a defiant reply to Bonaparte's latest demands. Should war result, Bonaparte's main strength would have to be employed in the east for this summer, giving Wellington the opportunity to strike a blow in the south. But how much chance had Russia of withstanding the attack Bonaparte could launch against her? Every year for a dozen years had seen a great victory won by Bonaparte, one nation or another overthrown in a few weeks' campaign. Next winter might well see Russia beaten and as subservient to Bonaparte as Austria and Prussia were already; and Downing Street, faced by Russian hostility, would remember her previous dubious neutrality with regret, especially as Bonaparte would undoubtedly take advantage of a Russian defeat to overrun Sweden. So then the whole of Europe, from North Cape to the Dardanelles, would be

171

leagued against England; she would be driven from her meagre foothold in Spain, and left to face the alternatives of continuing a struggle in which there was no prospect of any relief, or making a still more dangerous peace with a tyrant whose malignant ill will could never be appeased. In that case it would not be to any man's credit that he had contributed to the catastrophe of Russia's entry into the war.

Bush had come on deck, clearly sent for by Montgomery as officer of the watch. He was reading the deck log which Montgomery had inscribed on the slate, and he was studying the traverse board. Now he came stumping over to the starboard side of the quarterdeck to touch his hat to Hornblower.

"Reval—Tallinn as those Swedish charts call it, sir—bears southeast twenty-five miles by my reckoning, sir. That point of land to port is the north cape of Naissaar Island, however it's pronounced."

"Thank you, Captain Bush."

Hornblower even felt the temptation to vent his ill temper on Bush; he could imagine keenly enough how Bush would wilt and the hurt look that would come into his face at a sarcastic gibe at his mispronunciation of foreign names and his self-consciousness regarding it. Bush was always an easy target, and a satisfactory one from the point of view of readily apparent results. Hornblower dallied with the temptation while Bush stood before him awaiting orders. It was even amusing to keep him waiting like this; Hornblower suspected that Bush was nervously wondering what devilment he had in mind. Then in a wave of reaction Hornblower felt contempt for himself. It was bad enough that Vickery's unknown officer of the watch should at this moment be in trouble because his commodore was worried about what to do with Braun; it was far worse that the faithful, capable Bush should be suffering mental unhappiness for the same reason.

"Lay a course for Königsberg, Captain Bush, if you please."

"Aye aye, sir."

So far did the reaction go that Hornblower went on to explain the motives that guided him in reaching this decision.

"Danzig and Königsberg and East Prussia are Bonaparte's base of operations. The army he has gathered in Poland is supplied by river and canal from there—by the Vistula and the Pregel and the Memel. We're going to see if we can put a spoke in Bonaparte's wheel."

"Aye aye, sir."

"I'll put the squadron through general evolutions this morning."

"Aye aye, sir."

Bush was simply beaming at this remarkable unbending of his unpredictable chief. He was a long-suffering individual; as second in command he would be justified in looking upon it as his right to be admitted to the commodore's secrets. After all, a stray bullet, a falling spar, a stroke of disease might easily put him in command of the whole force. Yet he remained grateful for any scraps of information which Hornblower condescended to throw to him.

Nonsuch came round on the port tack as Bush and the sailing master decided on what course to steer. She lay over under her pyramids of canvas, the taut weather rigging harping sharply to the wind, and Hornblower moved over from the starboard side to port, the windward side, as was his right. He looked back at the rest of the squadron, each vessel bracing sharp up in succession, following in the leader's wake, *Lotus* and *Raven*, *Moth* and *Harvey*. *Clam* was not with them—she had been kept at Kronstadt to follow with any news Wychwood might be able to pick up—but five vessels were quite enough to exercise at manœuvres.

"Bring me the signal book," ordered Hornblower.

Flags raced up the halliards, each signal a chain of black balls, like beads on a string, until it was broken out, but in the other ships keen eyes were watching through telescopes, reading the flags even before they were broken out, and anxious officers were ordering the replies to be bent on ready to hoist without a moment's delay. The squadron tacked in succession, wore together on a line of bearing, came to the wind again in succession into line ahead. They reduced sail in conformity with the leader—every ship sending every possible hand aloft to get in courses or topgallants the moment Hornblower's intentions became clear— and they made sail again. They reefed topsails, double-reefed them, shook them out again. They hove-to, hoisted out their boats manned with armed boarding parties, and hoisted the boats in again. Resuming their course they opened their posts, ran out their guns, secured them again, and then ran them out and secured them again. A fresh signal mounted *Nonsuch's* halliards, headed by *Raven's* number:—

"Commodore to captain. Why did you not obey my order?"

Hornblower's glass had detected that *Raven* had not fully secured her guns—she had left her gunports unbolted so as to open them more quickly if the order should come, but Hornblower could see the ports opening slightly with the roll of the ship; moreover, judging by the little of the action of the guns' crews that he could see she had not uncoupled and stowed her train-tackles, giving her a clear five seconds' start over the other ships. It was foolish of Cole to try an old trick like that, and one so easily detected; it was right that *Raven's* shame should be proclaimed to the rest of the squadron. Half the object of manœuvres was to sharpen the captains' wits; it they could manage to outguess the commodore, well and good, for there could be more likelihood of their outguessing a Frenchman should they meet one.

Raven hastily secured gunports and train-tackles; to

rub the lesson in Hornblower waited until he was sure the order had just been passed on her decks and then sent up the signal for running out the guns. The counter-order following so quickly upon the order caught *Raven* unready—Hornblower could imagine the cursing officers on her main deck—and she was seven full seconds behind any other ship in hoisting the "Evolution completed" signal. There was no need to comment on the fact, however—everybody in the *Raven* would be aware of what had happened and a further reprimand might weaken Cole's authority over his ship's company.

It was an active busy morning for all hands in the squadron, and Hornblower, looking back to the time when he was a midshipman, could well imagine the sigh of relief that must have gone round when at noon he signalled for the order of sailing and gave the men a chance to get their dinners. He watched the *Nonsuch's* crew form up to receive their ration of spirits; the eager, skylarking hands each carrying his wooden piggin; the guard over the grog tub—the latter with its painted inscription "The King, God bless him"; Montgomery and two master's mates watching the issue. Hornblower saw one hand come up to the tub and be indignantly hustled away; evidently he was a defaulter who had been sentenced to lose his ration and who had nevertheless tried to obtain it. Such an attempt would earn a man at least two dozen lashes in some ships, but, judging by Montgomery's actions, it would mean no more than a further deprivation or a spell at the pumps or perhaps a turn at cleaning out the heads.

The liveliness and high spirits of everyone were reassuring. He could rely on these men to fight as desperately as any occasion could demand; equally important, he could rely on them to endure the long tedious days of beating about at sea, the wearisome monotony of life in a ship of the line, without more complaint than one need expect. But he must drop a hint to Bush to see that this happy condition endured. A horn-pipe competition—theatricals—something of that sort would be necessary soon, unless there should happen to be enough action to keep the men's minds busy. And with that decision he turned and went below, having managed, as a result of this morning's activity, to drive out of his own mind any worry about what to do with Braun when the latter should recover from his wound. After all, he might yet die.

Besides, there were the charts of the Frisches Haff and the approaches to Königsberg to study, and plans to be made for assailing Bonaparte's communications in the neighbourhood, should that be possible. If this fair wind should persist he had no more than three days in which to think out some method of attack there. He had the charts got out for him and he pored over them, irritably calling for lamps to light his dim cabin so as to make it possible to read the little figures scattered over them. The soundings were fantastically complex, and the problem of studying them was not made easier by the fact that he had three different charts to study—a Swedish one with the soundings marked in Swedish feet, a new French one with the soundings in metres, and only a sketchy English one in fathoms. It was a toilsome business comparing them, and perfectly unsatisfactory in the end, seeing that they did not agree.

Yet the desirability of striking a blow there was perfectly obvious. In roadless Poland and East Prussia the only way of distributing provisions and munitions to Bonaparte's swelling armies was by water. His main advanced base was Danzig, whence the troops in central Poland could be supplied by the Vistula. But the large forces in East Prussia and in eastern Poland were dependent on the other river systems, radiating from Königsberg and Elbing on the Frisches Haff. This Frisches Haff, a long narrow lagoon almost cut off from the Baltic by a long sandspit, would quite obviously be the scene of extensive barge traffic from Elbing to Königsberg. Fifty miles long, a dozen miles wide, shallow—three or four fathoms at most—with the narrow entrance guarded by the guns of the fortress of Pillau, from the French point of view it would be a perfectly safe route for water-borne supplies, sheltered both from storms and from the English. Danzig was the best objective, of course, for a stroke anywhere along this Baltic coast, but Danzig was safe, several miles from the sea up the Vistula, and heavily fortified to boot. If it took Bonaparte and a hundred thousand men three months to capture Danzig, Hornblower was not likely to effect anything against the place with a couple of hundred marines. Danzig was impregnable to him. For that matter, so were Königsberg and Elbing. But it was the communications between them that he wanted to break; no more than that need be done. The wind was fair, too—a Roman would look on that as a good omen.

Chapter XV

THIS was an ideal night in which to reconnoitre the entrance to the Frisches Haff. Overcast, so that not much light came from the summer sky, with the sun only just below the horizon, and a strong breeze blowing—the sloop Hornblower had just quitted had single-reefed her topsails earlier in the evening. A strong breeze and a choppy sea meant that there would be far less chance of guard-boats—guard-boats manned by landsmen—rowing a close watch over this boom that Hornblower was setting out to investigate.

But at the same time Hornblower was suffering considerable personal inconvenience from the choppy sea. The cutter in whose stern-sheets he sat was rear-ing and plunging, standing first on her bows and then on her stern, with the spray flying across her in a continuous sheet, so that a couple of hands had to bale all the time. The spray was finding its way remorselessly through the interstices of his boat cloak, so that he was wet and cold, and the cold and the violent motion inevitably turned his mind towards seasickness. His stomach felt as uneasy as his body felt uncomfortable. In the darkness he could not see Vickery, beside him at the tiller, nor Brown tending the sheet, and he felt a poor sort of relief at the thought that his pallor and uneasiness were not apparent to them. Unlike some victims he had met he could never be seasick un-self-consciously, he told himself bitterly, and then with his usual rasping self-analysis he told himself that that should not surprise him, seeing that he was never un-self-conscious at all.

He shifted his position in the stern of the cutter, and clutched his cloak more tightly round him. The Germans and Frenchmen guarding Pillau had as yet no knowledge that an English squadron was so close to them; it was less than an hour ago that he had come up in the darkness with the two sloops, leaving *Nonsuch* and the bomb-vessels over the horizon. A soft-hearted senior officer in Königsberg might easily hesitate before giving orders that a guard-boat should toilsomely row guard up and down the boom on such a blustery night, and even if the orders were given there was every chance that the petty officer in charge of the boat might shirk his duty—especially as there could not be much love lost between French who would occupy the higher ranks and the Germans who would fill the lower ones.

A low warning cry came from the lookout in the bows, and Vickery put down his tiller a trifle, bringing the cutter closer to the wind. She rose over a crest, and then as she came down in the trough a dark object appeared close overside dimly visible in the darkness in a flurry of foam.

178

"A cable, sir," reported Vickery. "An' there's the boom, right ahead."

On the heaving surface of the sea just ahead could be seen a faint hint of blackness.

"Lay me alongside it," said Hornblower, and Vickery turned up into the wind, and at his shouted order the lugsail came down and the cutter ranged herself against the boom. The wind was blowing not quite along it, so that there was a tiny lee on their side of the boom; on the far side the steep waves broke against it with a roar, but on this side the surface for a narrow space was smooth although covered with foam that reflected what little light made its way from the dark sky. The bowmen had hooked onto the cable just where it was secured to the boom.

Hornblower put off his cloak and left himself exposed to the spray which hurtled at him, poised himself for a leap, and sprang for the boom. As he landed on it a wave broke across it, sousing him to the skin, and he had to clutch desperately with fingers and toes to save himself from being washed off. He was riding an enormous tree trunk, floating on the surface with very little of itself exposed above the surface. With the best timber country in Europe to draw upon, and easy water transport available, it was of course certain that the French would select the heaviest trees possible to guard the entrance to the port. He clawed his way on all fours along the log, balancing in nightmare fashion on his pitching and rolling mount. An active topman, or Vickery for that matter, would probably walk upright, but then Hornblower wanted the evidence of his own senses regarding the boom, not a report at second hand. The cable, when he reached it, was the largest he had ever seen in his life—a thirty-inch cable at least; the largest cable *Nonsuch* carried was only nineteen inches. He felt about the log with inquiring fingers while the icy water soused him to the ears, and found what he was expecting to find, one of the chain cables that attached this log to the next. It was a two-inch chain cable with a breaking strain of a hundred tons or so, heavily stapled down to the log, and further search immediately revealed another one. Presumably there were others below the surface, making four or five altogether. Even a ship of the line, charging down full tilt before the wind, would be hardly likely to break that boom, but would only cause herself desperate underwater damage. Peering through the spray, he could see the end of the next log and its cable; the gap was some ten feet only. The wind, blowing almost lengthwise along the boom, had pushed it down to leeward as far as the cables would allow, boom and cables making a herringbone with the cables as taut as could be.

Hornblower clawed his way back down the trunk, poised himself, and leaped for the boat. In the darkness, with the irregular motion of boom and boat in the choppy sea, it was hard to time the moment to jump, and he landed awkwardly across the gunwale with one leg in the sea, and Vickery hauled him into the boat without much dignity left him.

"Let her drop down to leeward," ordered Hornblower. "I want soundings taken at every log."

Vickery handled the boat well. He kept her bows to the wind after shoving off, and with a couple of oars pulling steadily he manœuvred her past each cable as the boat drifted to leeward. Brown stood amidships balancing himself against the boat's extravagant plunges, while he took soundings with the awkward thirty-foot sounding pole. It called for a powerful man to handle that thing in this wind, but properly used it was quicker and far less noisy than a hand lead. Four fathoms—three and a half—four—the boom was laid right across the fairway, as was only to be expected. At the windward end it was not more than a couple of hundred yards—a cable's length—from the beach at Pillau, and Hornblower, staring into the night, more than suspected a supplementary boom from that shore which, overlapping this one, would compel any vessel entering to go about so as to make the turn. That meant that any ship trying to enter with hostile intentions would be sunk or set afire for certain by the heavy guns in Pillau.

They reached the leeward end of the boom; a stretch of clear water extended from here towards the sandspit—the *Nehrung*, to use the curious German word for it—which divided the Haff from the Baltic for nearly twenty miles. The open stretch must be a quarter of a mile wide, but it was useless for navigation. Brown's pole recorded a depth of ten feet for a couple of soundings, and then the water shallowed to no more than six or eight.

Vickery suddenly put his hand on Hornblower's arm and pointed to the land. There was a nucleus of greater darkness there—a guard-boat beating out through the shallows to keep watch over the boom.

"Out oars," said Hornblower. "Get out to sea."

There were thrum mats round the looms of the oars to muffle the noise they made against the thole-pins; the men put their backs into their work, and the cutter crept out to sea as the guard-boat continued its course. When the two boats were far enough apart for the sail to be invisible Hornblower gave orders for the lug to be set and they began to beat back to *Lotus*, with Hornblower shivering uncontrollably in his wet clothes, bitterly ashamed though he was that Vickery should be aware that his commodore should shiver on account of a mere wet jacket which any tough seaman would think nothing of. It was irritating, though it was no more than was to be expected, that the first attempt to find *Lotus* in the darkness should be unsuccessful, and the cutter had to go about and reach to windward on the other tack before at last they picked up the loom of her in the night. When her hail reached their ears Brown made a speaking-trumpet of his hands.

"Commodore!" he shouted, and Vickery turned the

cutter into the *Lotus'* lee, and Hornblower went up the sloop's low side as the two came together. On the quarterdeck Vickery turned to him for orders.

"Haul up and make an offing, Mr. Vickery," said Hornblower. "Make sure *Raven* follows us. We must be out of sight of land by dawn."

Down in Vickery's tiny cabin, stripping off his wet clothes, with Brown hovering round him, Hornblower tried to make his dulled mind work on the problem before him. Brown produced a towel and Hornblower rubbed a little life into his chilled limbs. Vickery knocked and entered, coming, as soon as he had seen his ship on her proper course, to see that his commodore had all that he needed. Hornblower straightened up after towelling his legs and hit his head with a crash against the deck beams; in this small sloop there was hardly more than five feet clearance. Hornblower let out an oath.

"There's another foot of head room under the skylight, sir," said Vickery, diplomatically.

The skylight was three feet by two, and standing directly beneath it Hornblower could just stand upright, and even then his hair brushed the skylight. And the lamp swung from a hook in a deck beam beside the aperture; an incautious movement on Hornblower's part brought his bare shoulder against it so that warm stinking oil ran out of the receiver onto his collar-bone. Hornblower swore again.

"There's hot coffee being brought to you, sir," said Vickery.

The coffee when it came was a type which Hornblower had not tasted for years—a decoction of burnt bread with the merest flavouring of coffee—but at least it was warming. Hornblower sipped it and handed back the cup to Brown, and then took his dry shirt from the breech of the twelve-pounder beside him and struggled into it.

"Any further orders, sir?" asked Vickery.

"No," replied Hornblower heavily, his head poked

forward to make sure it did not hit the deck beams again. He tried to keep the disappointment and the bad temper out of his voice, but he feared he had not succeeded. It irked him to have to admit that there was no chance of any successful attempt against the Frisches Haff, and yet prudence, commonsense, his whole instinct dictated such a decision. There was no breaking that boom, and there was no going round it, not in any of the vessels under his command. He remembered bitterly his unnecessary words to Bush about the desirability of raiding this area from the sea. If ever he needed a lesson in keeping his mouth shut he was receiving one now. The whole flotilla was expecting action, and he was going to disappoint them, sail away without doing anything at all. In future he would double-lock his jaws, treble-curb his unruly tongue, for if he had not talked so lightheartedly to Bush there would not be nearly so much harm done; Bush, in the absence of orders to the contrary, would naturally have discussed the future with his officers, and hope would be running high—everyone was expecting great things of the bold Hornblower (said he to himself with a sneer) whose reputation for ingenious daring was so tremendous.

Unhappy, he went back again over the data. At the sandspit end of the boom there was water enough for a flotilla of ship's boats to pass. He could send in three or four launches, with four-pounders mounted in the bows and with a hundred and fifty men on board. There was not much doubt that at night they could run past the boom, and, taking everyone in the lagoon by surprise, could work swift havoc on the coasting trade. Very likely they could destroy thousands of tons of shipping. But they would never get out again; the exit would be watched far too carefully. The batteries would be manned day and night; gunboats would swarm round the end of the boom, and even gunboats manned by landsmen, if there were enough of them, would destroy the flotilla.

183

His squadron could ill afford to lose a hundred and fifty trained seamen—one tenth of the total ships' complements—and yet a smaller force might well be completely wasted.

No; no destruction of coasters would be worth a hundred and fifty seamen. He must abandon the idea; as if symbolically of that decision he began to pull on the dry trousers Vickery had provided for him. And then, with one leg in and one leg out the idea suddenly came to him and he checked himself, standing in his shirt with his left leg bare and his right leg covered only from ankle to knee.

"Mr. Vickery," he said, "let's have those charts out again."

"Aye aye, sir," said Vickery.

There was eagerness and excitement in his voice at once, echoing the emotion which must have been obvious in Hornblower's tone—Hornblower took notice of it, and as he buckled his waistband he reaffirmed his resolution to be more careful how he spoke, for he must regain his reputation as a silent hero. He stared down at the charts which Vickery spread for him—he knew that Vickery was studying his face, and he took great care to show no sign whatever of reaching a decision one way or the other. When his mind was made up he said "Thank you" in the flattest tone he could contrive, and then, suddenly remembering his most noncommittal exclamation, he cleared his throat.

"Ha—h'm," he said, without any expression at all, and, pleased with the result, he repeated it and drew it out longer still, "Ha—a—a—a—h'm."

The bewildered look in Vickery's face was a great delight to him.

Next morning, back in his own cabin in *Nonsuch*, he took a mild revenge in watching the faces of his assembled captains as he laid the scheme before them. One and all, they thirsted for the command, hotly eager to risk life and liberty on a mission which might at first seem utterly hare-brained. The two commanders yearned for the chance of promotion to post rank; the lieutenants hoped they might become commanders.

"Mr. Vickery will be in command," said Hornblower, and had further opportunity of watching the play of emotion over the faces of his audience. But as in this case everyone present had a right to know why he had been passed over, he gave a few words of explanation.

"The two captains of the bomb-vessels are irreplaceable; there are no other lieutenants with us who can use their infernal machines as well as they can. I don't have to explain to you why Captain Bush is irreplaceable. It was Mr. Vickery who happened to go with me to investigate the boom, and so he happens to know more about the situation than Mr. Cole, who's the other obvious candidate for the command."

There was no harm in soothing Cole's feelings with an excuse like that, for no good end would be served by letting people guess that he would not trust Cole with any command out of his sight—poor old Cole, grey-haired and bowed, almost too old for his work, hoping against hope for promotion to captain. Hornblower had an uneasy feeling that Cole saw through the excuse, and had to comfort himself with the trite thought that no war can be fought without someone's feelings being hurt. He passed hurriedly to the next point.

"Having settled that question, gentlemen, I would welcome your views on who else should go as Mr. Vickery's subordinates. Mr. Vickery first, as he is most concerned."

When those details were settled the next step was to prepare the four boats for the expedition—*Nonsuch's* launch and cutter, and the cutters from *Lotus* and *Raven*. A four-pounder in the eyes of the launch, a three-pounder in the eyes of each of the cutters; food, water, ammunition, combustibles for setting captures on fire. The crews that had been told off for the expedition were paraded and inspected, the seamen with pistols and cutlasses, the marines with muskets and bayonets. At the end of the day Vickery came back on board *Nonsuch* for a final confirmation of the future rendezvous.

"Good luck," said Hornblower.

"Thank you, sir," said Vickery.

He looked frankly into Hornblower's eyes.

"I have so much to thank you for, sir," he added.

"Don't thank me, thank yourself," said Hornblower testily.

He found it particularly irksome to be thanked for risking young Vickery's life. He calculated to himself that if he had married as a midshipman he might now be the father of a son just Vickery's age.

At nightfall the squadron stood in towards the land. The wind was backing northerly a little, but it was still blowing a strong breeze, and although the night was not quite as overcast as the preceding one, there was every chance that the boats would slip through unobserved. Hornblower watched them go, just as two bells struck in the middle watch, and as they vanished into the greyness he turned away. Now he would have to wait. It interested him to discover once more that he would genuinely and sincerely have preferred to be in action himself, that he would rather be risking life and limb and liberty there in the Frisches Haff than be here safe at sea with nothing to do but await results. He looked on himself as a coward; he dreaded mutilation and he disliked the thought of death only less than that, so that it was a matter of peculiar interest to find that there were some things he disliked even more than danger. When a long enough time had elapsed for the boats to have passed the boom—or for them to have fallen into the hands of the enemy—Hornblower went below to rest for the brief interval before dawn, but could only pretend to sleep, he could only hold himself down in his cot and prevent himself by sheer mental effort from tossing and turning. It was a positive relief to go out on the half-deck again when the sky began to grow lighter, to souse himself under the head pump, and then to go up on the quarterdeck and drink coffee there, glancing the while over the starboard quarter where (with the ship hove-to on the port tack) lay Pillau and the entrance to the Haff.

The growing daylight revealed it all through Hornblower's glass. At random cannon shot lay the yellow and green headland on which Pillau was set; the twin church steeples were clearly visible. The line of the boom showed up, lying across the entrance, marked by breaking waves and occasionally a glimpse of dark timber. Those dark mounds above the water's edge must be the batteries thrown up there to defend the entrance. On the other side lay the long line of the *Nehrung*, a yellowish green line of sand-hills, rising and falling with minute variations of altitude as far as the eye could see, and beyond. But through the entrance there was nothing to see at all, nothing except grey water, flecked here and there with white where the shoals dotted the lagoon. The opposite shore of the Haff was too distant to be visible from the deck.

"Captain Bush," ordered Hornblower, "would you please be good enough to send an officer with good eyes to the masthead with a glass?"

"Aye aye, sir."

Hornblower watched the young lieutenant dashing up the rigging, moving as fast as he could with his commodore's eye on him, hanging back-downward as he scaled the futtock shrouds, going hand over hand up the topgallant shrouds. Hornblower knew that in his present condition he could not do that without resting in the maintop for a space, and he also knew that his eyes were not as good as they were—not as good as the lieutenant's. He watched the lieutenant settle himself at the topgallant masthead, adjust his glass, and sweep the horizon, and he waited impatiently for a report. Unable to wait longer he grabbed his speaking-trumpet.

"Masthead, there! What do you see of the shore inside?"

"Nothing, sir. It's too hazy to see plain. But I can see no sails, sir."

Maybe the garrison was laughing up their sleeves at him. Maybe the boats had fallen straight into their hands, and now they were amusing themselves watching the squadron beginning an endless wait for any further sight of the lost boats and seamen. Hornblower refused to allow himself to be pessimistic. He set himself to picture the state of affairs in the batteries and in the town, when the dawn revealed a British squadron lying-to just out of range. How the drums would beat and trumpets peal, as the troops were hurriedly turned out to guard against a possible landing. That was what must be going on at this very moment. The garrison, the French governor, must be still unaware as yet that wolves had slipped into their sheepfold, that British boat crews had penetrated into the waters of the Haff where no enemy had been seen since Danzig fell to the French five years back. Hornblower tried to comfort himself with thought of all the additional bustle that would develop as soon as the situation disclosed itself to the enemy: the messengers that would gallop with warnings, the gunboats that would be hastily warned, the coasters and barges which would seek the shelter of the nearest batteries—if batteries there were; Hornblower was willing to bet that there was none between Elbing and Königsberg, for none had been necessary so far.

"Masthead! Can't you see anything inshore?"

"No, sir—yes, sir. There's gunboats putting out from the town."

Hornblower could see those himself, a flotilla of small two-masted vessels, rigged with the sprit mainsails usual to small Baltic craft, putting out from

Elbing. They were a little like Norfolk wherries. Presumably they each carried one heavy gun, a twenty-four-pounder possibly, mounted right up in the eyes of the boat. They anchored at intervals in the shoal water, obviously as a further protection to the boom in case of an attempt upon it. Four of them moved right across and anchored to guard the shallows between the boom and the *Nehrung*—not exactly locking the stable door after the horse had been stolen, decided Hornblower, rejecting the simile after it came to his mind; they were locking the stable door to prevent the thief getting out, if they knew as yet (which was highly doubtful) that there was a thief inside. The haziness was fast clearing; overhead the sky was almost blue and a watery sun was showing through.

"Deck, there! If you please, sir, there's a bit of smoke in sight now, right up the bay. Can't see more than that, sir, but it's black smoke and might be from a burning ship."

Bush, measuring with his eyes the dwindling distance between the ship and the boom, was giving orders to brace up and work a trifle farther out to sea again, and the two sloops conformed to the *Nonsuch's* movements. Hornblower wondered whether or not he had put too much trust in young Mound with the bomb-ketches. Mound had an important rendezvous for next morning; with the *Moth* and the *Harvey* he was out of sight below the horizon. So far the garrison of Elbing had seen only the three British ships, and did not know of the existence of the ketches. That was well—as long as Mound carried out his orders correctly. Or a gale might blow up, or a shift of the wind might raise too much of a surf for the project Hornblower had in mind. Hornblower felt anxiety surge upon him. He had to force himself to relax, to appear composed. He permitted himself to walk the deck, but slowed down his nervous strides to a casual saunter.

"Deck, there! There's more smoke inshore, sir. I can see two lots of it, as if there were two ships on fire now."

Bush had just given orders to back the main topsail again, and as the ship hove-to he came across to Hornblower.

"It looks as if Vickery had caught something, doesn't it, sir?" he said, smiling.

"Let's hope so," answered Hornblower.

There was no sign of any anxiety in Bush's expression; his craggy face denoted nothing more than fierce satisfaction at the thought of Vickery loose amid the coasting trade. His sublime confidence began to reassure Hornblower until the latter suddenly realised that Bush was not really paying consideration to circumstances. Bush knew that Hornblower had planned this attack, and that was enough for him. In that case he could imagine no possibility of failure, and Hornblower found it profoundly irritating that this should be the case.

"Deck, there! There's two small sail heading across the bay close-hauled for the town. And I can't be sure yet, sir, but I think the second one is our cutter."

"Our cutter it is, sir!" yelled another voice. Every idle hand in the ship was perched by now at the mastheads.

"That'll be Montgomery," said Bush. He had fitted the toe of his wooden leg into the ringbolt of the aftermost carronade tackle so that he could stand without effort on the gently heaving deck.

"She's caught her, sir!" yelled the voice from the masthead. "Our cutter's caught her!"

"That's one lot of beef and bread that Boney won't get," said Bush.

Very heavy destruction of the coastal shipping in the Haff might be some compensation for the loss of a hundred and fifty prime seamen. But it would be hard to convince Their Lordships of the Admiralty of

190

that, if there was no certain evidence of the destruction.

"Deck, there! The two sail are parting company. Our cutter's going off before the wind. The other has her mains'l brailed up, I think, sir. Looks to me as if—"

The lieutenant's report terminated abruptly in mid-sentence.

"There she goes!" yelled another voice, and at the same moment there came a cheer from everyone aloft.

"She's blown up!" shouted the lieutenant, forgetting in his excitement even to add "sir" to his words when addressing his commodore. "There's a pillar of smoke as high as a mountain! You can see it from the deck, I think."

They certainly could—a mushroom-topped pillar of smoke, black and heavy, apparent as it reached above the horizon. It lasted a perceptible time before the wind blew it into strange ragged shapes and then dispersed it utterly.

"That wasn't beef and bread, by God!" said Bush, pounding his left palm with his right fist. "That was powder! A barge load of powder! Fifty tons of powder, by God!"

"Masthead! What of the cutter?"

"She's all right, sir. Doesn't look as if the explosion harmed her. She's hull-down from here already, sir."

"Off after another one, please God," said Bush.

The destruction of a powder barge was the clearest possible proof that Bonaparte was using the inland water route for the transport of military stores. Hornblower felt he had achieved something, even though Whitehall might not be fully convinced, and he found himself smiling with pleasure. He suppressed the smile as soon as he was aware of it, for his dignity demanded that triumph should leave him as unmoved as uncertainty.

"It only remains to get Vickery and the men out tonight, sir," said Bush.

191

"Yes, that is all," said Hornblower, as woodenly as he could manage.

The blowing up of the powder barge was the only sure proof they had that day in the *Nonsuch* of success in the Haff, although more than once the lookouts hesitatingly reported smoke on the horizon inside. As evening came on another string of gunboats made their appearance, from Königsberg presumably, and took up their stations along the boom. A column of troops could be seen for a space, too, the horizontal lines of blue coats and white breeches clearly visible even from the deck as they marched in to strengthen the defences of Pillau. The entrance into the Haff was going to be stoutly defended, obviously, if the British should attempt a *coup de main*.

In the evening Hornblower came up from below, where he had been making pretence at eating his dinner, and looked round him again, although his senses had been so alert in his cabin that his glance told him nothing he did not know already. The wind was moderating with the dying of the day; the sun was on the point of setting, although there would be daylight for a couple of hours more at least.

"Captain Bush, I'd be obliged if you would send your best gun pointers to the lower gun-deck starboard-side guns."

"Aye aye, sir."

"Have the guns cleared away and run out, if you please. Then I would like it if you would allow the ship to drop down within range of the batteries there. I want to draw their fire."

"Aye aye, sir."

Pipes twittered round the ship; bosun and bosun's mates roared out orders, and the hands ran to their stations. A long earthquake tremor shook the ship as the massive twenty-four-pounders of the lower gun deck ran thunderously out.

"Please see that the gun captains are certain what their target is," said Hornblower.

He knew how limited was the view afforded a man on the lower deck, looking through a gunport only a yard or so above the water's edge, and he did not want the enemy to jump to the conclusion that the feint he was about to make was no more than a feint. The hands at the main-topsail lee brace, walking smartly down the deck, swung the big sail round and *Nonsuch* came to the wind and slowly gathered way.

"Port a little," said Bush to the helmsman. "Let her fall off. Meet her there! Steady as you go!"

"Steady as you go, sir," echoed the helmsman, and then by a neat feat of facial gymnastics transferred his quid from his cheek to his mouth, and a moment later spat accurately into the spit kid beside the wheel without transferring any of his attention from the leech of the main topsail and the compass in the binnacle.

Nonsuch edged down steadily towards the entrance and the batteries. This was a ticklish business, coming down to be shot at. There was smoke as from a fire visible not far from the batteries; maybe it was merely rising from the cooking stoves of the garrison, but it might well be smoke from the furnaces for heating red-hot shot. But Bush was aware of that possibility when in action against coastal batteries, and had needed no warning. Every available man was standing by with fire buckets, and every pump and hose was rigged. Now he was measuring the range with his eye.

"A little closer, if you please, Captain Bush," said Hornblower to prompt him, for to Hornblower it was obvious that they were still out of range. A fountain of water was visible for a moment on the surface of the choppy sea, two cables' lengths from the starboard bow.

"Not near enough yet, Captain Bush," said Hornblower.

In tense silence the ship moved on. A whole cluster of fountains sprang suddenly into existence close under the starboard quarter, one so close indeed that a hatful of water, flung by some freak of wave and wind, hit Bush full in the face.

"God damn it to hell," spluttered Bush, wiping his eyes.

That battery had no business to have come as close as that with that salvo. And there was no smoke near it either. Hornblower traversed his glass round, and gulped. It was another battery altogether which had fired, one farther to the left, and moreover one whose existence he had not suspected until that moment. Apparently the grass had grown over the parapets sufficiently to conceal it from quite close inspection; but it had unmasked itself a trifle too soon. If the officer commanding there had been patient for another ten minutes *Nonsuch* might have found herself in a difficult situation.

"That will do, Captain Bush," said Hornblower.

"Full and by," said Bush to the helmsman and then raised his voice, "Lee braces, there!"

Nonsuch swung round, turning her starboard broadside towards the batteries, and, close-hauled, was now edging towards them far less rapidly. Hornblower pointed out the exact situation of the newly revealed battery to the midshipman on the watch, and then sent him flying below to carry the information to the guns.

"Keep your luff!" growled Bush to the helmsman.

"Keep your luff, sir."

For a moment or two there were waterspouts leaping from the surface of the sea all round, and the loud noise of cannonballs passing through the air assaulted their ears. It was remarkable that they were not hit; at least, it was remarkable until Hornblower, glancing up, saw two elliptical holes in the mizzen topsail. The shooting was poor, for there were at least twenty heavy guns firing at them, as Hornblower calculated from the smoke appearing on shore. He

194

took careful note of the sites of the batteries—one never knew when such intelligence might be useful.

"Open fire, Captain, if you please," said Hornblower, and before the polite ending of the sentence had passed his lips Bush had raised his speaking-trumpet and was repeating the order at the top of his lungs. The gunner's mate posted at the main hatchway relayed the message to the lower gun deck. There was a brief pause which Hornblower noted with pleasure, because it showed that the gun captains were taking pains to train their guns on the target, and not merely jerking the lanyards the moment the word reached them. Then came a ragged crash; the ship trembled, and the smoke surged up and blew away to leeward. Through his glass Hornblower could see sand flying all round the masked battery. The seventeen twenty-four-pounders roared out again and again, the deck vibrating under Hornblower's feet with the concussion and with the rumble of the gun trucks.

"Thank you, Captain Bush," said Hornblower, "you can put the ship about, now."

Bush blinked at him momentarily, his fighting blood roused so that he had to stop and think before dealing with the new order.

"Aye aye, sir." He raised his trumpet. "Cease fire! Stand by to go about!"

The order was relayed to the guns, and the din died down abruptly, so that Bush's "Hard-a-lee" to the helmsman sounded unnecessarily loud.

"Mainsail haul!" bellowed Bush.

As *Nonsuch* went ponderously about, rising to an even keel with her canvas slatting, a further cluster of waterspouts grouped closely together for the first time, rose from the surface of the sea on the starboard bow. If she had not made the sudden turn the shots might well have hit her. Hornblower might be a mutilated corpse lying on the quarterdeck with his guts strung out beside him at this moment.

Nonsuch had passed the wind, and the after sails were filling.

"Let go and haul!" yelled Bush. The forward sails filled as the hands came aft with the lee braces, and *Nonsuch* settled down on the new tack.

"Any further orders, sir?" asked Bush.

"That will do for the present."

Close-hauled on the starboard tack the ship was drawing away fast from the land, beating out to where the two sloops were backing and filling while waiting for her. The people on shore must be exulting over having driven off a serious attack; probably some garrulous gunner was swearing that he had seen with his own eyes damaging hits striking home on the British intruder. They must be encouraged in the belief that something desperate was still being meditated in this neighbourhood.

"Midshipman!" said Hornblower.

Strings of coloured flags soared up *Nonsuch's* halliards; it was good practice for the signal midshipman to try to spell out "The curfew tolls the knell of parting day" with the fewest possible number of flag hoists. With his telescope pointed the midshipman read off *Raven's* reply.

"The—" he read, "l—o—w—must be 'blowing.' No, it's 'lowing,' whatever he means by that. H—e—r—d. Herd. Two—five. That's 'wind,' and 's.' That's 'winds.' S—l—o—"

So Cole in the *Raven* was at least familiar with Gray's "Elegy," and whoever was responsible for the flag hoists on board her was ingenious enough to use the code hoist for "winds." As Hornblower expected, he used the code hoist "lee" for "lea" as well, thereby saving one signal flag.

"The lowing herd winds slowly or the lee, sir," reported the puzzled midshipman.

"Very good. Acknowledge."

All these innumerable signals between battleships and sloops must be visible from the shore and exciting their interest. Hornblower sent up another signal under *Lotus'* number—"The ploughman homeward plods his weary way"—only to receive the puzzled reply, "Signal not understood." Purvis, the first lieutenant of the *Lotus,* at present in command, was obviously not very bright, or perhaps not very well read. What in the world, at that rate, he was making of all this was beyond even Hornblower's imagination, although the thought of it brought a smile to his lips.

"Cancel the signal, then," he ordered, "and substitute, 'Report immediately number of red-haired married men on board.'"

Hornblower waited until the reply came; he could have wished that Purvis had not been so literal-minded and had been able to think up an answer which should combine the almost incompatible qualities of deference and wit, instead of merely sending the bald reply "Five." Then he turned to business.

"Signal to both sloops," he ordered. "'Advance on boom in threatening manner avoiding action.'"

In the dwindling daylight he watched the two vessels move down as though to attack. They wheeled, edged into the wind, and fell away again. Twice Hornblower saw a puff of smoke and heard, echoing over the water, the dull flat boom of a twenty-four-pounder as a gunboat tried the range. Then, while there was just light enough for the signal to be read, he hoisted: "Discontinue the action after half an hour." He had done all he could to attract the enemy's attention to this end of the bay, the only exit. The garrison ought to be quite certain now that the raiding boats would attempt to escape by this route. Probably the garrison would anticipate a rush in the first light of dawn, assisted by an attack by the big ships from outside. He had done all he could, and it only remained now to go to bed and spend the rest of the night in tranquillity if that were possible.

Naturally, it was impossible, with the fate of a

hundred and fifty seamen at stake, with his own reputation for good fortune and ingenuity at stake. Half an hour after he had got into bed Hornblower found himself wishing that he had ordered three junior officers to join him in a game of whist until dawn. He dallied with the idea of getting up and doing so now, but put it aside in the certainty that if he should do so now everyone would know that he had tried to go to sleep and had failed. He could only turn over stoically and force himself to stay in bed until dawn came to release him.

When he came on deck the pearly mist of the Baltic morning was making the vague outline of visible objects vaguer yet. There was every promise of a fine day, wind moderate, backing a little. Bush was already on deck—Hornblower knew that, before he went up, because he had heard Bush's wooden leg thumping over his head—and at first sight of him Hornblower hoped that his own face did not show the same signs of sleeplessness and anxiety. They had at least the effect of bracing him up to conceal his own anxiety as he returned Bush's salute.

"I hope Vickery's all right, sir," said Bush.

The mere fact that Bush ventured to address Hornblower at this time in the morning after so many years of service under him was the best possible proof of his anxiety.

"Oh yes," said Hornblower, bluffly. "I'll trust Vickery to get out of any scrape."

That was a statement made in all sincerity; it occurred to Hornblower as he made it—what he had often thought before—that worry and anxiety were not really connected with the facts of the case. He had done everything possible. He remembered his profound study of the charts, his careful reading of the barometer, his painstaking—and now clearly successful—attempts to predict the weather. If he were compelled to bet, he would bet that Vickery was safe, and moreover he would judge the odds to be at least

198

three to one. But that did not save him from being anxious, all the same. What did save him was the sight of Bush's nervousness.

"With this breeze there can't have been much surf, sir," said Bush.

"Of course not."

He had thought of that fifty times during the night, and he tried to look as if it had not been more than once. The mist was thin enough now to make the land just visible; the gunboats were still stationed along the boom, and he could see a belated guard-boat rowing along it.

"The wind's fair for the bomb-ketches, sir," said Bush. "They ought to have picked Vickery up by now and be on their way towards us."

"Yes."

Bush turned a searching eye aloft to make sure that the lookouts were at their posts and awake. It was twelve miles down the *Nehrung*, the long spit of sand that divided the Haff from the Baltic, that Mound with the bomb-ketches was going to pick up Vickery and his men. Vickery was going to land in the darkness on the *Nehrung*, abandon his boats, cross the sandspit, and rendezvous with Mound an hour before dawn. With their shallow draft the ketches would be safe among the shoals, so that they could send in their boats and bring Vickery off. Vickery's four ships' boats would all be lost, but that was a small price to pay for the destruction he must have caused, and Hornblower hoped that, what with the distraction of his own demonstrations off Pillau, and what with the fact that the possibility of Vickery's abandoning his boats might easily never occur to the enemy's mind, Vickery would find no opposition on the *Nehrung*. Even if there were, the *Nehrung* was fifteen miles long and Vickery with a hundred and fifty determined men could be relied upon to break through any thin cordon of sentries or customs officials.

Yet if all had gone well the bomb-ketches ought to

199

be in sight very soon. The next few minutes would be decisive.

"We couldn't have heard gunfire in the bay yesterday, sir," said Bush, "the wind being where it was. They may have met with any sort of armed vessel in the bay."

"So they may," said Hornblower.

"Sail ho!" yelled the masthead lookout. "Two sail on the port beam! It's the bomb-ketches, sir."

They might possibly be coming back having been unable to pick up Vickery, but it was unlikely that in that case they would have returned so promptly. Bush was grinning broadly, with all his doubts at an end.

"I think, Captain," said Hornblower, "you might put the helm down and go to meet them."

It would not be consonant with the dignity of a commodore to hang out a signal of inquiry as the vessels closed to visual range, for it to be read the moment a telescope in the *Harvey* could distinguish the flags. But *Nonsuch* was making a good five knots, with the water lapping cheerfully under her bows, and *Harvey* was doing the same, so that it was only a matter of waiting a few more minutes.

"*Harvey's* signalling, sir," reported the midshipman. He read the flags and hurriedly referred to the code book: " 'Seamen on board,' sir."

"Very good. Make: 'Commodore to Captain. Come on board with Mr. Vickery to make your report.' "

There was not much longer to wait. As the two vessels came within hail they rounded-to, and *Harvey's* gig dropped into the water and came bobbing across to *Nonsuch*. It was a weary Vickery who came up the side with Mound beside him; his face was grey, and below his eyes were marks like new scars as proof that he had not slept for three successive nights. He sat down gratefully when Hornblower gave him permission to do so as soon as they were in his cabin.

"Well?" said Hornblower. "I'll hear you first, Vickery."

"It went off very well, sir." Vickery dragged a scrap of paper out of his pocket on which apparently he had kept notes. "There was no trouble going past the boom on the night of the fifteenth. We saw nothing of the enemy. At dawn on the sixteenth we were off the mouth of the Königsberg River. There we took and destroyed the—the *Fried Rich*, coaster, of Elbing, about two hundred tons, seven of a crew, with a cargo of rye and live pigs. We burned her, and sent the crew ashore in their own boat. Then we caught the—the—*Blitzer*, also of Elbing, about one hundred tons, laden with grain. We burned her, too. Then the *Charlotte*, of Danzig. She was ship-rigged, four hundred tons, twenty five crew, laden with general cargo of military stores—tents, stretchers, horseshoes, ten thousand stand of small arms; we burned her. Then the *Ritter Horse*, powder barge, about seventy tons. We blew her up."

"We saw that, I think," said Hornblower. "That was *Nonsuch's* cutter."

"Yes, sir. That was all at this end of the bay. Then we bore down to the westward. We caught the *Weece Ross* of Kolberg, two hundred tons. She carried four six-pounders and showed fight, but Montgomery boarded her over the bows and they threw down their arms. We had two men wounded. We burned her. Then there was—"

"How many altogether?"

"One ship, sir. Eleven sail of coasting vessels. Twenty four barges. All destroyed."

"Excellent," said Hornblower. "And then?"

"By then it was nigh on dark, sir. I anchored on the north side of the bay until midnight. Then I ran over to the sandspit. We found two soldiers there, and made 'em prisoners. 'Twas easy enough crossing the spit, sir. We burned a blue light and made contact with the *Harvey*. They started taking us aboard at two A.M., and I was aboard at three, by the first light.

I went back and burned the boats before I embarked, sir."

"Better still."

The enemy, then, had not even the sorry compensation of the capture of four ships' boats in exchange for the frightful destruction Vickery had wrought. He turned to Mound.

"I have nothing particular to report, sir. Those waters are shoal, without a doubt, sir. But I had no difficulty making my way to the rendezvous. After taking Mr. Vickery's party on board we touched bottom, sir. We had nearly a hundred extra hands on board an' must have been drawing nigh on a foot more water. But we got off all right. I had the men run from side to side to rock the vessel, an' I threw all aback an' she came off."

"I understand."

Hornblower looked at Mound's expressionless face and smiled inwardly at his studied languid manner. Picking the way in the dark through the shoals to the rendezvous must have been something of an epic achievement. Hornblower could estimate the seamanship it called for, but it was not in the tradition to lay stress on difficulties surmounted. And a less reliable officer might have tried to suppress the fact that his ship had touched ground once. It was to Mound's credit that he had not done so.

"I shall call attention of the Admiralty," said Hornblower, trying his best to combat the pomposity which persisted in making itself heard in his voice, "to the conduct of both of you officers. I consider it excellent. I shall of course require reports from you immediately in writing."

"Aye aye, sir."

Now that he was a commodore, Hornblower felt more sympathy towards senior officers who had been pompous to him; he was pompous himself—it was one way in which could be concealed the fact that he had been anxious.

202

Chapter XVI

Hornblower was dining by himself. He had Gibbon securely wedged against the cheese crock on the table before him, and his legs stretched out at ease under it. Today he was indulging himself extraordinarily with a half bottle of wine, and the sea pie from which he was about to help himself smelt most appetising. It was one of those days when there was nothing wrong with the world at all, when he could allow himself to sway with the rhythm of the ship without any further thought, when food tasted good and wine delicious. He dug a spoon into the sea pie just at the moment when there was a knock on the door and a midshipman entered.

"*Clam* in sight to wind'ard, sir," he said.

"Very good."

Hornblower proceeded to transfer the sea pie from the dish to his plate, and as he spread out his helping to allow it to cool, his mind began to rouse itself. *Clam* would be bringing news; she had been left at St. Petersburg for the very purpose of waiting for news. Maybe Russia was at war with Bonaparte now. Or maybe Alexander had made the abject surrender which would be the only thing that could save him from war. Or maybe Alexander was dead, murdered by his officers as his father had been. It would be by no means the first time that a change in Russian policy had been ushered in by a palace revolution. Maybe—maybe anything, but the sea pie was growing cold. He applied himself to it, just as the midshipman knocked at the door again.

"*Clam* signals 'Have despatches for commodore,' sir."

"How far off is she?"

"Hull up to wind'ard, sir. We're running down to her."

"Make: 'Commodore to *Clam*. Send despatches on board as soon as practicable.'"

"Aye aye, sir."

There was nothing surprising about *Clam's* message; the surprise would have been if she carried no despatches. Hornblower found himself shovelling sea pie into his mouth as if the faster he ate it the faster the despatches would come. He checked himself and took a sip of his wine, but neither wine nor food had any attraction for him. Brown came in and served him with cheese, and he munched and told himself he had dined well. Cocking his ear to the noises on the deck overhead he could guess there was a boat coming alongside, and directly afterwards one more knock on the door heralded the arrival of Lord Wychwood. Hornblower rose for him, offered him a chair, offered him dinner, took over the bulky canvas-wrapped despatch which Wychwood handed him, and signed a receipt for it. He sat with it on his knee for a moment.

"Well," said Wychwood, "it's war."

Hornblower could not allow himself to ask "War with whom?" He made himself wait.

"Alexander's done it, or rather Boney has. Boney crossed the Niemen with fifteen army corps ten days back. No declaration of war, of course. That's not the sort of courtesy one would expect of two potentates who have been blackguarding each other in every sheet in every language in Europe. War was inevitable the moment Alexander sent his answer a month ago—the day before you left us. Now we'll see."

"Who's going to win?"

Wychwood shrugged.

"I can't imagine Boney being beaten. And from what I've heard the Russian army did not show to advantage last year in Finland despite their reorganisation. And Boney has half a million men marching on Moscow."

Half a million men; the largest army the world had seen since Xerxes crossed the Hellespont.

"At least," went on Wychwood, "it will keep Boney busy all this summer. Next year we'll see—maybe he'll lose so many men his people will bear it no longer."

"Let's hope so," said Hornblower.

He took out his penknife and ripped open his despatch.

BRITISH EMBASSY,
ST. PETERSBURG, *June 24th,* 1812.

Sir,

The bearer of this despatch, Colonel Lord Wychwood, will inform you of affairs in this country and of the state of war which now exists between His Imperial Majesty the Czar and Bonaparte. You will, of course, take all necessary steps to render all the assistance in your power to our new ally. I am informed, and have reason to believe, that while the main body of Bonaparte's army is marching on Moscow, a very considerable detachment, believed to consist of the Prussian army corps and a French *corps d'armée,* the whole under the orders of Marshal Macdonald, Duke of Tarentum, altogether some 60,000 men, has been directed on the northern route toward St. Petersburg. It is highly desirable that this army should be prevented from reaching its goal, and at the request of the Russian Imperial Staff I must call your attention to the possibility that your squadron may be able to give assistance at Riga, which the French must capture before continuing their march on St. Petersburg. I wish to add my own advice to that of the Russian staff, and to press upon you as urgently as possible that you should give assistance at Riga for as long as may be compatible with your original orders.

In virtue of the powers granted me under the terms of my instructions, I must inform you that I consider it important to the national safety that the cutter *Clam*, at present under your command, shall be despatched to England in order to carry with the utmost rapidity the news of the outbreak of war. I trust and hope that you will raise no objection.

I have the honour to be, sir,

Etc., etc.,

CATHCART, *His Britannic Majesty's Minister-Plenipotentiary and Ambassador Extraordinary to H.I.M.*

"Cathcart's a good man," commented Wychwood, observing that Hornblower had completed his reading. "Both as a soldier and as a diplomat he's worth two of Merry at Stockholm. I'm glad Wellesley sent him out."

Certainly this despatch was better worded than the last Hornblower had received, nor did Cathcart presume to give orders to the commodore.

"You will be going on in *Clam* to England," said Hornblower. "I must ask you to wait while I complete my own despatches for the Admiralty."

"Naturally," said Wychwood.

"It will only be a matter of minutes," said Hornblower. "Perhaps Captain Bush will entertain you while you are waiting. Doubtless there are many letters awaiting carriage to England. Meanwhile, I am sending my secretary back to England in *Clam* too. I shall put in your charge the papers relative to his case."

Alone in his cabin, Hornblower opened his desk and found himself pen and ink. There was little enough to add to his official despatch. He read the last words—"I wish most strongly to call Their Lordship's attention to the conduct and professional ability of Commander William Vickery and Lieutenant Percival Mound." Then he began a new paragraph. "I am taking the opportunity of the departure of *Clam* to England to forward this letter to you. In accordance with the recommendation of His Excellency Lord Cathcart, I shall proceed at once with the rest of my squadron to render all the assistance in my power to the Russian forces at Riga." He thought for a moment of adding some conventional expression such as "I trust this course of action will meet with Their Lorship's approval," and then put the notion aside. It meant nothing, was merely waste verbiage. He dipped his pen again and merely wrote, "I have the honour to be, Your obed't servant, Horatio Hornblower, Captain and Commodore."

He closed the letter, shouting for Brown as he did so. While he wrote the address—"Edward Nepean, Esq., Secretary to the Lords Commissioners of the Admiralty"—Brown brought him a candle and sealing wax, and he sealed the letter and laid it on one side. Then he took another sheet and began to write again.

H.M.S. *Nonsuch*, IN THE BALTIC.

My dear wife,

The cutter waits for me to complete my correspondence for England, and I have only time to write these few lines to add to the other letters which have been awaiting an opportunity to make the voyage. I am in the best of health, and the progress of the campaign remains satisfactory. The great news of the outbreak of war between Bonaparte and Russia has just reached me. I hope that the event will prove this to be Bonaparte's worst mistake, but I can only anticipate long and costly fighting, with small possibility of my returning to your dear presence, at least until the freezing of the harbours makes further operations in these waters impracticable.

I trust most sincerely that you are well and happy, and that the rigours of the London season have not proved too trying for you. I like to think of the good air of Smallbridge restoring the roses to your cheeks, so that the vagaries of costumiers and milliners will not exact too excessive a toll on your health and peace of mind.

Also I trust that Richard is comporting himself towards you with the duty and obedience you expect, and that his teeth have continued to make their appearance with as little disturbance as possible. It would be a great delight to me if he were old enough to write to me himself, especially if that would give me further news of you; only a letter from you yourself could give me greater pleasure. It is my hope that soon letters will reach me from England, and that it will be my happiness to hear that all is well with you.

When next you see your brother, Lord Wellesley, I trust you will give him my duty and respects. For you I reserve my whole love.

Your affectionate husband,
HORATIO.

Wychwood took the letters Hornblower gave him, and wrote out a receipt on Bush's desk with Bush's pen. Then he held out his hand.

"Good-bye, sir," he said, and hesitated; then, with a rush, he added, "God knows how this war will turn out. I expect the Russians'll be beaten. But you have done more than any one man to bring the war about. You've done your whole duty, sir."

"Thank you," said Hornblower.

He was in a disturbed and unsettled mood; he stood on the quarterdeck of the *Nonsuch* while over his head the ensign was dipped in a parting salute to the *Clam*, and he watched the cutter sail off towards England. He watched her until she was out of sight, while *Nonsuch* put up her helm and bore away for

Riga and whatever new adventures awaited him there. He knew quite well what was the matter with him; he was homesick, plunged into a storm of emotional disturbance as he always was when he wrote home, and, oddly enough, Wychwood's last words added to his disturbance. They had reminded him of the terrible load of responsibility that he bore. The future of the world and the survival of his country would be profoundly affected by his doings. Should this Russian adventure end in defeat and disaster everyone anxious to shuffle off responsibility would blame him. He would be condemned as inept and short-sighted. He even found himself envying Braun, now on his way back to London under arrest and awaiting probable trial and possible execution, and he remembered with longing his petty troubles at Smallbridge; he smiled at himself when he recalled that his heaviest burden there had been to receive a deputation of welcome from the village. He thought of Barbara's ready sympathy, of the intense pleasure he had known when it first dawned upon him that Richard loved him, and enjoyed and looked forward to his company. Here he had to be content with Bush's unthinking loyalty and the precarious admiration of the young officers.

Recalling himself to reality, he forced himself to remember with what a bubble of excitement he had received his orders back to active service, the light heart with which he had left his child, the feeling of—there was no blinking the matter—emancipation with which he had parted from his wife. The prospect of once more being entirely his own master, of not having to defer to Barbara's wishes, of not being discommoded by Richard's teeth, had seemed most attractive then. And here he was complaining to himself about the burden of responsibility, when responsibility was the inevitable price one had to pay for independence; irresponsibility was something which, in the very nature of things, could not co-exist with independence.

This was all very well and logical, but there was no blinking the fact that he wished he were home; he could conjure up in imagination so vividly the touch of Barbara's hand on his own that it was an acute disappointment to realise that it was only an imagination. He wanted to have Richard on his knee again, shrieking with laughter over the colossal joke of having his nose pinched. And he did not want to imperil his reputation, his liberty, and his life in combined operations with these unpredictable Russians in a God-forsaken corner of the world like Riga. Yet then and there—his interest rousing itself spontaneously—he decided that he had better go below and reread the Sailing Directions for Riga; and a close study of the chart of Riga Bay might be desirable, too.

Chapter XVII

T HE northern continental summer had come speedily, as ever. Last week at Pillau there had still been a decided touch of winter in the air. Today, with Riga just over the horizon, it was full summer. This blazing heat would have done credit to the doldrums were it not for an invigorating quality which the tropics never knew. A brassy sun shone down from a cloudless sky, although there was just enough mist to leave the distant horizon undefined. There was a gentle two-knot breeze blowing from the southwest, just enough wind to give *Nonsuch* bare steerage way with all her canvas set, studding sails on both sides to the royals. The squadron was making the best speed it could, with *Lotus* hull-down on the starboard bow, *Raven* close astern, and the two bomb-ketches trailing far behind; even the clumsy *Nonsuch* could outsail them in the prevailing conditions.

Everything was very peaceful. Forward a party of seamen under the sail-maker's supervision were overhauling a mainsail for repair. In the waist another party was dragging a "bear" up and down the deck—a huge coir mat weighted down with sand which could scrub the planking more effectively than holystones could do. On the quarterdeck the sailing-master was holding a class in navigation, his mates and the midshipmen standing round him in a semicircle, their sextants in their hands. Hornblower walked near enough to hear one of the midshipmen, a mere child whose voice had not broken, piping up a reply to the question just shot at him.

"The parallax of an object is measured by an arc of a vertical circle intercepted between a line extended from the centre of the earth and a line—and a line—a line—"

The midshipman suddenly became conscious of the awful proximity of the commodore. His voice quavered and died away. So far he had been quoting Norie's *Epitome of Navigation* with word-perfect exactitude. It was young Gerard, nephew of the second lieutenant of the *Sutherland*, whom Bush had taken into his ship for the sake of his uncle, still languishing in a French prison. The sailing-master's brows drew together in a frown.

"Come, come, Mr. Gerard," he said.

Hornblower had a sudden mental picture of young Gerard bent over the breech of a gun while a lithe cane taught him at least the necessity of knowing Norie's *Epitome* by heart. He intervened in hurried pity.

" 'Between a line extended from the centre of the earth,' he said, over Gerard's shoulder, 'and a line extended from the eye of the observer, through the centre of the object.' Is that correct, Mr. Tooth?"

"Quite correct, sir," said the sailing-master.

"I think Mr. Gerard knew it all the time. Didn't you, youngster?"

"Y—yes, sir."

"I thought so. I was just your age when I learned that same passage."

Hornblower resumed his walk, hoping that he had saved Gerard's skinny posterior from punishment. A sudden scurrying by the midshipman of the watch to grab slate and pencil told him that one of the squadron was making a signal, and two minutes later the midshipman saluted him, message in hand.

"*Lotus* to commodore. Land in sight bearing south."

That would be Pitraga Cape, the southern headland of the entrance to the Gulf of Riga.

"Reply 'Heave-to and await commodore,'" said Hornblower.

If the weather were not so thick the island of Oesel ought to be just in sight to the northward from the masthead. They were just passing the threshold of a new adventure. Some seventy miles ahead, at the bottom of the gulf, lay Riga, presumably even now being assailed by the armies of Bonaparte. With this mere pretence of a wind it would be a couple of days before he reached there. The fact that they were entering Russian waters again was making not the least ripple on the placid surface of the ship's life. Everything was progressing as before, yet Hornblower felt in his bones that many of the men now entering the Gulf Riga would never come out from it, if any should. Even with this hot sun blazing down upon him, under this radiant sky, Hornblower felt a sudden chill of foreboding which it was hard to throw off. He himself—it was curious to think that his dead body might be buried in Russia, of all places.

Someone—the Russians, or the Swedes, or the Finns—had buoyed effectively the channel that wound its way through the treacherous shallows of the Gulf of Finland. Even though the squadron had to anchor for the night a slight freshening and veering of the wind enabled them to ascent the whole gulf by the evening of the next day. They picked up a pilot at noon, a bearded individual who wore sea boots and a heavy jacket even on this blazing day. He proved to be an Englishman, Carker by name, who had not set eyes on his native land for twenty-four years. He blinked at Hornblower like an owl when the latter began to fire questions at him regarding the progress of the war. Yes, some cavalry patrols of French and Prussians had shown themselves advancing towards Riga. The last news of the main campaign was of desperate fighting round Smolensk, and everyone was expecting Bonaparte to be beaten there. Riga was preparing itself for a siege, he believed—at least, there were plenty of soldiers there when he had left in his cutter yesterday, and there had been proclamations calling on the people to fight to the last, but no one could imagine the French making a serious attack on the place.

Hornblower turned away from him impatiently in the end, as a typical example of the uninformed civilian, with no real knowledge of affairs or appreciation of the seriousness of the situation. Livonia, having been for centuries the cockpit of northern Europe, had not seen an enemy during the last three generations, and had forgotten even the traditions of invasion. Hornblower had no intention at all of taking his squadron into the Dwina River (queer names these Russians used!) if there was a chance of his retreat being cut off, and he stared out through his glass at the low green shore when it came in sight at last from the deck. Almost right astern of the squadron the sun was lying on the horizon in a fiery bed of cloud, but there were two hours more of daylight left, and *Nonsuch* crept steadily closer to Riga. Bush came up to him and touched his hat.

"Pardon, sir, but do you hear anything? Gunfire, maybe?"

Hornblower strained his attention.

"Yes, gunfire, by God," he said.

It was the lowest, faintest muttering, coming up-wind from the distant shore.

"The Frogs have got there before us, sir," said Bush.

"Be ready to anchor," said Hornblower.

Nonsuch crept steadily on, gliding at three or four knots towards the land; the water around her was greyish yellow with the mud borne down by a great river. The mouth of the Dwina was only a mile or two ahead, and with the spring rains and the melting of the snows the river must be in full flood. The buoys of a middle ground shoal enabled Hornblower to make sure of his position; he was coming within long cannon shot of those flat green shores. As though standing in the yellow water there was a church visible on the starboard bow, with an onion-shaped dome surmounted by a cross which reflected back to him, even at that distance, the red glare of the sunset. That must be the village of Daugavgriva, on the left bank; if it were in French hands, entrance to the river would be dangerous, perhaps impossible, as soon as they had big guns mounted there. Maybe they already had.

"Captain Bush," said Hornblower, "I'd be obliged if you would anchor."

The cable roared out through the hawsehole, and *Nonsuch* swung round to the wind as the hands, pouring aloft, took in the sails. The rest of the squadron came up and prepared to anchor just when Hornblower was beginning to feel he had been too precipitate, or at least when he was regretting bitterly that night had come upon him before he could open communication with the shore.

"Call away my barge," he ordered. "Captain Bush, I am shifting to *Harvey*. You will assume command of the squadron during my absence."

Mound was at the side to welcome him as he swung himself up over *Harvey's* low freeboard.

"Square away, Mr. Mound. We'll close the shore in the direction of that church. Set a good hand at work with the lead."

The bomb-ketch, with anchor catted and ready to let go, stole forward over the still water. There was still plenty of light from the sky, for here in 57° North, within a few days of the solstice, the sun was not very far below the horizon.

"Moon rises in an hour's time, sir," said Mound, "three quarters full."

It was a marvellous evening, cool and invigorating. There was only the tiniest whisper of water round the bows of the ketch as she glided over the silvery surface; Hornblower felt that they only needed a few pretty women on board and someone strumming a guitar to make a yachting expedition of it. Something on shore attracted his attention, and he whipped his glass to his eye at the very moment when Mound beside him did the same.

"Lights on shore," said Mound.

"Those are bivouac fires," said Hornblower.

He had seen bivouac fires before—the fires of El Supremo's army in Central America, the fires of the landing force at Rosas. They sparkled ruddily in the twilight, in roughly regular lines. Traversing his glass round, Hornblower picked up further groups of lights; there was a dark space between one mass and the other, which Hornblower pointed out to Mound.

"That's no man's land between the two forces, I fancy," he said. "The Russians must be holding the village as an outwork on the left bank of the river."

"Couldn't all those fires be French fires, sir?" asked Mound. "Or Russian fires?"

"No," said Hornblower. "Soldiers don't bivouac if they can billet in villages with roofs over their heads. If two armies weren't in presence they'd all be comfortably asleep in the cottagers' beds and barns."

There was a long pause while Mound digested this.

215

"Two fathoms, sir," he said, at length. "I'd like to bear up, if I may."

"Very good. Carry on. Keep as close inshore as you think proper."

The *Harvey* came round with the wind abeam, half a dozen hands hauling lustily on the main sheet. There was the moon, rising round and red over the land; the dome of the church was silhouetted against it. A sharp cry came from the forward lookout.

"Boat ahead! Fine on the port bow, sir. Pulling oars."

"Catch that boat if you can, Mr. Mound," said Hornblower.

"Aye aye, sir. Starboard two points! Clear away the gig. Boat's crew stand by!"

They could see the dim shape of the boat not far ahead; they could even see the splashes of the oars. It occurred to Hornblower that the rowers could not be men of much skill, and whoever was in charge was not very quick in the uptake if he wanted to avoid capture; he should have healed instantly for shoal water if he wanted to avoid capture, while as it was he tried to pit oars against sails—a hopeless endeavour even with that light breeze blowing. It was several minutes before they turned for the shore, and during that time their lead was greatly reduced.

"Hard-a-lee!" roared Mound. "Away, gig!"

Harvey came into the wind, and as she lost her way the gig dropped into the water with the boat's crew falling into it.

"I want prisoners!" roared Hornblower at the departing boat.

"Aye aye, sir," came the reply as the oars tore the water.

Under the impulse of the skilled oarsmen the gig rapidly was overtaking the strange boat; they could see the distance narrowing as the two boats disappeared in the faint light. Then they saw the orange-red flashes of half a dozen pistol shots, and the faint reports reached them over the water directly after.

"Let's hope they're not Russians, sir," said Mound.

The possibility had occurred to Hornblower as well, and he was nervous and uncomfortable, but he spoke bluffly:—

"Russians wouldn't run away. They wouldn't expect to find Frenchmen at sea."

Soon the two boats, rowing slowly, emerged from the gloom.

"We've got 'em all, sir," said a voice in reply to Mound's hail.

Five prisoners were thrust up onto the deck of the *Harvey*, one of them groaning with a pistol bullet through his arm. Someone produced a lantern and shone it on them, and Hornblower heaved a sigh of relief when he saw that the star which glittered on the breast of the leader was the Legion of Honour.

"I would like to know Monsieur's name and rank," he said, politely, in French.

"*Jussey, Chef de Bataillon du corps du Génie des Armées de l'Empereur.*"

A major of engineers; quite an important capture. Hornblower bowed and presented himself, his mind working rapidly on the problem of how to induce the major to say all he knew.

"I regret very much the necessity of taking *M. le Chef de Bataillon* prisoner," he said, "especially at the beginning of such a promising campaign. But good fortune may allow me the opportunity of arranging a cartel of exchange at an early date. I presume *M. le Chef de Bataillon* has friends in the French army whom he would like informed of what has happened to him? I will take the opportunity of the first flag of truce to do so."

"The Marshal Duke of Tarentum would be glad to hear," said Jussey, brightening a little. "I am on his staff."

The Marshal Duke of Tarentum was Macdonald,

the local French commander-in-chief—son of a Scottish exile who had fled after the Young Pretender's rebellion—so that it seemed likely that Jussey was the chief engineer, a bigger catch than Hornblower had hoped for.

"It was extremely bad fortune for you to fall into our hands," said Hornblower. "You had no reason to suspect the presence of a British squadron operating in the bay."

"Indeed I had none. Our information was to the contrary. These Livonians—"

So the French staff was obtaining information from Livonian traitors; Hornblower might have guessed it, but it was as well to be sure.

"Of course they are useless, like all Russians," said Hornblower, soothingly. "I suppose your Emperor has met with little opposition?"

"Smolensk is ours, and the Emperor marches on Moscow. It is our mission to occupy St. Petersburg."

"But perhaps passing the Dwina will be difficult?"

Jussey shrugged in the lamplight.

"I do not expect so. A bold push across the mouth or the river and the Russians will retreat the moment their flank is turned."

So that was what Jussey was doing; reconnoitring for a suitable place to land a French force on the Russian side of the river mouth.

"A daring move, sir, worthy of all the great traditions of the French army. But no doubt you have ample craft to transport your force?"

"Some dozens of barges. We seized them at Mitau before the Russians could destroy them."

Jussey checked himself abruptly, clearly disturbed at realising how much he had said.

"Russians are always incompetent," said Hornblower, in a tone of complete agreement. "A prompt attack on your part, giving them no chance of steadying themselves, is of course your best plan of

218

operations. But will you pardon me, sir, while I attend to my duties?"

There was no chance of wheedling anything more out of Jussey at the moment. But he had at least yielded up the vital information that the French had laid hands on a fleet of barges which the Russians had neglected, or been unable, to destroy, and that they planned a direct attack across the river mouth. By feigning entire indifference Hornblower felt that Jussey might be inveigled later into talking freely again. Jussey bowed, and Hornblower turned to Mound.

"We'll return to the squadron," he said.

Mound gave the orders which laid the *Harvey* close-hauled on the starboard tack—the French prisoners ducked hastily as the big mainsail boom swung over their heads, and the seamen bumped into them as they ran to the sheet. While Jussey and Hornblower had been talking two of the prisoners had cut off the sleeve of the wounded man and bandaged his arm; now they all squatted in the scuppers out of the way, while the *Harvey* crept back to where the *Nonsuch* lay at anchor.

Chapter XVIII

O ARS," said Brown, and the barge's crew ceased to pull. "In bows."

The bow oarsman brought his oar into the boat and grabbed for the boathook, and Brown laid the barge neatly alongside the quay while the rushing Dwina River eddied about it. An interested crowd of the people of Riga watched the operation, and stared stolidly at Hornblower as he ran up the stone steps to road level, epaulettes, star, and sword all a-glitter in the scorching sunshine. Beyond the line of ware-houses along the quay he was vaguely aware of a wide square surrounded by mediaeval stone buildings with high pitched roofs, but he had no attention to spare for this his first close sight of Riga. There was the usual guard of honour to salute, the usual officer at its head, and beside it the burly figure of the governor, General Essen.

"Welcome to the city, sir," said Essen. He was a Baltic German, a descendant of those Knights of the Sword who had conquered Livonia from the heathen centuries before, and the French which he spoke had some of the explosive quality of the French spoken by an Alsatian.

An open carriage, to which were harnessed two spirited horses who pawed restlessly at the ground, awaited them, and the governor handed Hornblower in and followed him.

"It is only the shortest distance to go," he said, "but we shall take this opportunity of letting the people see us."

The carriage lurched and bounced frightfully over the cobbled streets; Hornblower had twice to straighten his cocked hat which was jerked sideways on his head, but he endeavoured to sit up straight and unconcerned as they dashed along narrow streets full of people who eyed them with interest. There was no harm in allowing the inhabitants of a beleaguered city the opportunity of seeing a British naval officer in full uniform—his presence would be a pledge that Riga was not alone in her hour of trial.

"The Ritterhaus," explained Essen, as the coachman pulled up his horse outside a handsome old building with a line of sentries posted before it.

The reception awaited them, officers in uniform, a few civilians in black, and many, many women in gala dresses. Several of the officers Hornblower had already met at the conference that morning at Dwina

Munde; Essen proceeded to present the more important of the rest of the company.

"His Excellency the Intendant of Livonia," said Essen, "and the Countess—"

"It has already been my great pleasure to meet the Countess," interposed Hornblower.

"The commodore was my partner at dinner at the Peterhof," said the Countess.

She was as beautiful and as vivacious as ever; maybe, as she stood there with her hand on her husband's arm, her glance was not as sultry. She bowed to Hornblower with a polite indifference. Her husband was tall, bony, and elderly, with a thin moustache that drooped from his lip, and short-sighted eyes that he assisted with a quizzing-glass. Hornblower bowed to him, endeavouring to behave as though this were only one more ordinary meeting. It was ridiculous to feel embarrassed at this encounter, yet he was, and had to struggle to conceal it. But the beaky-nosed Intendant of Livonia eyed him with even more indifference than did his wife; most of the others who were presented to Hornblower were obviously delighted to meet the English naval officer, but the Indendant made no effort to hide the fact that to him, the direct representative of the Czar and an habitué of imperial palaces, this provincial reception was tedious and uninteresting and the guest of honour nobody of importance.

Hornblower had learned his lesson regarding the etiquette of a Russian formal dinner; the tables of hors-d'œuvres he knew now to be mere preliminaries. He tasted caviare and vodka once again, and the very pleasant combination of flavours called up a sudden host of memories. Without being able to prevent himself he glanced across at the Countess, and caught her eye as she stood chattering with half a dozen grave men in uniform. It was only for a moment, but that was long enough. Her glance seemed to tell him that she, too, was haunted by the same memories. Hornblower's head whirled a little, and he made a prompt resolve to drink nothing more that night. He turned and plunged hastily into conversation with the governor.

"How delightfully complementary to each other are vodka and caviare," he said. "They are worthy to rank with those other combinations of food discovered by the pioneers of the gastronomic art. Eggs and bacon, partridge and Burgundy, spinach and—and—"

He fumbled for a French word for "gammon," and the governor supplied it, his little pig's eyes lighting up with interest in the midst of his big red face.

"You are a gastronome, sir?" he said.

The rest of the time before dinner passed easily enough then, with Hornblower well exercised in having to discuss food with someone to whom food was clearly a matter of deep interest. Hornblower drew a little on his imagination to describe the delicacies of the West Indies and of Central America; fortunately during his last period of leave he had moved in wealthy London circles with his wife and had eaten at several renowned tables, including that of the Mansion House, which gave him a solid basis of European experience with which to supplement his imagination. The governor had taken advantage of the campaigns in which he had served to study the foods of the different countries. Vienna and Prague had fed him during the Austerlitz campaign; he had drunk resinated wine in the Seven Islands; he rolled up his eyes in ecstasy at the memory of *frutti di mare* consumed in Leghorn when he had served in Italy under Suvaroff. Bavarian beer, Swedish *schnapps*, Danzig *Goldwasser*—he had drunk of them all, just as he had eaten Westphalian ham and Italian *beccaficoes* and Turkish *rahat lakoum*. He listened with rapt attention when Hornblower spoke of grilled flying fish and Trinidad pepperpot, and it was with the deepest regret that he parted from Hornblower to take his place at the head of the dinner table; even then he persisted in calling Hornblower's attention to the dishes being served, leaning forward to address him across two ladies and the Intendant of Livonia, and when dinner was ended he apologised to Hornblower for the abrupt termination of the meal, complaining bitterly of the fact that he had to gulp his final glass of brandy because they were already nearly an hour late for the gala performance of the ballet where they were next due to go.

He walked heavily up the stone stairs of the theatre, his spurs ringing and his sword clattering as it trailed beside him. Two ushers led the way, and behind Hornblower and Essen walked the others of the inner circle, the Countess and her husband and two other officials and their wives. The ushers held open the door of the box, and Hornblower waited on the threshold for the ladies to enter.

"The commodore will go first," said Essen, and Hornblower plunged in. The theatre was brightly lighted, and parterre and gallery were crowded; Hornblower's entrance drew a storm of applause, which smote upon his ears and momentarily paralysed him as he stood there. A fortunate instinct prompted him to bow, first to one side and then to the other, as if he were an actor, as he said to himself. Then someone thrust a chair behind him and he sat down, with the rest of the party round him. Throughout the auditorium ushers immediately began to turn down the lamps, and the orchestra broke into the overture. The curtain rose to reveal a woodland scene, and the ballet began.

"A lively thing, this Madame Nicolas," said the governor in a penetrating whisper. "Tell me if you like her. I can send for her after the performance if you desire."

"Thank you," whispered Hornblower in reply, feeling ridiculously embarrassed. The Countess was close on his other side and he was too conscious of her warmth to feel comfortable.

The music hurried on, and in the golden glow of

the footlights the ballet went through its dazzling maze, skirts flying and feet twinkling. It was incorrect to say that music meant nothing to Hornblower; the monotonous beat of its rhythm, when he was compelled to listen to it for long, stirred something in the depths of him even while its guessed-at sweetness tormented his ear like a Chinese water torture. Five minutes of music left him dull and unmoved; fifteen minutes made him restless; an hour was sheer agony. He forced himself to sit still during the long ordeal, even though he felt he would gladly exchange his chair in the box for the quarterdeck of a ship in the hottest and most hopeless battle ever fought. He tried to shut his ears to the persistent insidious noise, to distract himself by concentrating his attention on the dancers—on Madame Nicolas as she pirouetted across the stage in her shimmering white, on the others as, chin on finger and the other hand supporting the elbow, they came down the stage a-tiptoe in alluring line. Yet it was of no avail, and his misery increased from minute to minute.

The Countess at his side was stirring too. He knew, telepathically, what she was thinking about. The literature of all ages, from the *Ars amatoria to Liaisons Dangereux,* told him theoretically of the effect of music and spectacles upon the feminine mind, and in violent revulsion he hated the Countess as much as he hated music. The only movement he made, as he sat there stoically enduring the tortures of the demand for the sake of duty, was to shift his foot away out of reach of hers—he knew in his bones that she would endeavor to touch him soon, while her beaky-nosed husband with his quizzing-glass sat just behind them. The *entr'acte* was only a poor respite; the music at least ceased, and he was able to stand, blinking a little as the thrown-open door of the box admitted a stream of light, and he bowed politely when the governor presented a few late-comers who came to pay their respects to the British visitor. But in no time at all, it seemed, he was forced to seat himself again, while the orchestra resumed its maddening scraping, and the curtain rose on a new scene.

Then a distraction came. Hornblower was not sure when he first heard it; he might have missed the first premonitory shots in his determined effort to shut himself inside himself. He came out of his nightmare conscious of a new tension in the people round him; the boom of heavy artillery was very noticeable now—it even seemed as if the theatre itself were vibrating gently to the heavy concussions. He kept his head and neck still, and stole a glance out of the corner of his eye at the governor beside him, but the governor seemed to be still entirely engrossed in watching Madame Nicolas. Yet the firing was very heavy. Somewhere not very far away big guns were being fired rapidly and in large numbers. His first thought was for his ships, but he knew them to be safe, anchored at the mouth of the Dwina, and if the wind was still in the direction it was blowing when he entered the theatre Bush could get them out of harm's way whatever happened, even if Riga were taken by storm that very hour.

The audience was taking its cue from the governor, and as he refused to allow the gunfire to distract him everyone made a brave attempt to appear unconcerned. But everyone in the box, at least, felt tightened nerves when rapid steps outside in the stone-flagged corridor, to the accompaniment of the ringing spurs, heralded the entrance of an orderly officer, who came in and whispered hurriedly to the governor. Essen dismissed him with a few words, and only when he had gone, and after a minute's interval which seemed like a hour, leaned over to Hornblower with the news.

"The French have tried to take Daugavgriva by a *coup de main*," he explained. "There is no chance of their succeeding."

That was the village on the left bank of the Dwina,

in the angle between the sea and the river, the natural first objective for a besieging force that was desirous of cutting off the town from all hope of relief by sea. It was nearly an island, with the Gulf of Riga covering one flank, and the mile-wide Dwina River covering the rear, while the rest was girt by marshes and ditches and protected by breastworks thrown up by the peasant labour called in from miles round. The French would be likely to try a direct assault upon the place, because success would save them weeks of tedious siege operations, and they had no knowledge as yet of whether or not the Russians were able or willing to offer effective resistance. This was the first time Macdonald had encountered any serious opposition since he had begun his advance across Lithuania—the main Russian armies were contesting the road to Moscow in the neighbourhood of Smolensk. Hornblower had inspected the works that very morning, had observed the strength of the place and the steady appearance of the Russian grenadiers who garrisoned it, and had formed the conclusion that it was safe against anything except systematic siege. Yet he wished he could be as sublimely confident about it as the governor was.

On the other hand, everything possible had already been done. If the village fell, it fell, and nothing more serious had happened than the loss of an outwork. If the attack were beaten off there could be no question of following up the success, not while Macdonald disposed of sixty thousand men and the Russians of fifteen thousand at most. Of course Macdonald was bound to attempt a *coup de main* upon Daugavgriva. It was interesting to speculate what would be his next move should the assault fail. He might march up the river and endeavour to force a passage above the town, although that meant plunging into a roadless tangle of marsh and attempting a crossing at a place where he would find no boats. Or he might try the other plan and use the boats which had fallen into his hands at Mitau to pass a force across the mouth of the river, leaving Daugavgriva untaken while he compelled the Russians in Riga to choose between coming out and fighting the landing party, or retreating towards St. Petersburg, or being shut in completely in the town. It was hard to guess what he would decide on. Certainly Macdonald had sent out Jussey to reconnoitre the river mouth, and although he had lost his chief engineer in doing so, he might still be tempted by the prospect of being able to continue immediately his advance on St. Petersburg.

Hornblower came back to himself, delighted to find that he had missed in his abstraction some substantial amount of the ballet. He did not know how long his absent-mindedness had endured, but it must be, he thought, for some considerable time. The gunfire had ceased; either the assault had failed or had been completely successful.

At that very moment the door opened to admit another orderly officer with a whispered message for the governor.

"The attack has been beaten off," said Essen to Hornblower. "Yakoulev reports his men have hardly suffered at all, and the front of the place is covered with French and German dead."

That was to be expected, granted the failure of the attack. The losses would be dreadful in an unsuccessful assault. Macdonald had gambled, risking a couple of thousand lives against a speedy end to the siege, and he had lost. Yet an imperial army would be exasperated rather than depressed by such a preliminary reverse. The defence could expect further vigorous attacks at any moment.

It was wonderful to discover that he had managed to sit through another whole ballet without noticing it. Here was another *entr'acte*, with the light shining into the box, and the opportunity to stand and stretch one's legs; it was even delightful to exchange polite banalities in French tinged with half the accents of

Europe. When the *entr'acte* ended Hornblower was quite reconciled to reseating himself and bracing himself to endure one more ballet; yet the curtain had only just risen when he felt himself heavily nudged in the thigh by Essen, who rose and made his way out of the box with Hornblower at his heels.

"We may as well go and see," said Essen, the moment they stood outside the closed door of the box. "It would not have been well to get up and go when the firing began. But the people will not know now that we left in haste."

Outside the theatre a troop of Hussars sat their horses, while two grooms stood at the heads of two more horses, and Hornblower realised that he was committed to riding in his full-dress uniform. It was not the serious business it used to be, though; Hornblower thought with pleasure of his dozen reserve pairs of silk stockings stored away in *Nonsuch*. Essen climbed onto his horse, and Hornblower followed his example. The bright full moon filled the square with light, as, with the escort following, they trotted clattering over the cobbles. Two turns and a moderate descent brought them to the big floating bridge that spanned the Dwina; the roadway over the pontoons drummed hollow beneath the horses' hoofs. Across the river a road ran on the top of a high levee beside the water; on the far side the land was cut and seamed with ditches and ponds, around which twinkled innumerable campfires, and here Essen halted and gave an order which sent the Hussar officer and half the escort riding ahead of them.

"I have no desire to be shot by my own men," explained Essen. "Sentries will be nervous, and riding into a village that has just suffered a night attack will be as dangerous as storming a battery."

Hornblower was too preoccupied to appreciate the point very much. His sword and his ribbon and star and his cocked hat added to his usual difficulty of retaining his seat on horseback, and he bumped ungracefully in his saddle, sweating profusely in the cold night, and grabbing spasmodically at items of his equipment whenever he could spare a hand from his reins. They were challenged repeatedly as they rode along, but despite Essen's gloomy prognostication no jumpy sentry fired at them. Finally they drew up in reply to another challenge at a point where the dome of the church of Daugavgriva stood up black against the pale sky. With the cessation of the noise of the horses' hoofs a fresh sound claimed Hornblower's attention—a wailing, clamour coloured by high agonised screams, a whole chorus of groans and cries. The sentry passed them through, and they rode forward into the village, and as they did so the groans and screams were explained, for they passed on their left the torch-lit field where the wounded were being treated—Hornblower had a glimpse of a naked writhing body being held down on a table while the surgeons bent over it in the glare of the torches like the familiars of the Inquisition, while the whole field was carpeted with writhing and groaning wounded. And this had been a mere outpost skirmish, a trifling matter of a few hundred casualties on either side.

They dismounted at the door of the church and Essen led the way in, returning the salute of the bearded grenadiers at the door. Candles within made a bright pool of light in the midst of the surrounding gloom, and at a table there sat a group of officers drinking tea from a samovar which hissed beside them. They rose as the governor entered, and Essen made the introductions.

"General Diebitsch, Colonel von Clausewitz—Commodore Sir Hornblower."

Diebitsch was a Pole, Clausewitz a German—the Prussian renegade Hornblower had heard about previously, an intellectual soldier who had decided that true patriotism lay in fighting Bonaparte regardless of which side his country nominally assisted. They made their report in French; the enemy had attempted at moonrise to storm the village without preparation, and had been bloodily repulsed. Prisoners had been taken; some had captured an outlying cottage and had been cut off in the counterattack, and there were other isolated prisoners from various units who had fallen into Russian hands at other points of the perimeter of the village.

"They have already been questioned, sir," said Diebitsch. Hornblower had the feeling that it would be an unpleasant experience to be a prisoner submitted to questioning at the hands of General Diebitsch.

"Their statements were useful, sir," added Clausewitz, producing a sheet of notes. Each prisoner had been asked what was his battalion, how many men there were in it, how many battalions in his regiment, what was his brigade and division and army corps. Clausewitz was in a fair way by now to reconstituting the whole organisation of the French part of the attacking army and to estimating its numbers fairly accurately.

"We know already the strength of the Prussian corps," said Essen, and there was a moment's awkwardness while everyone avoided meeting Clausewitz' eye, for he had brought in that information.

"It is only half an hour before dawn, sir," interposed Diebitsch with more tact than could have been expected of a man of his countenance. "Would you care to climb to the dome and see for yourself?"

The sky was brighter still by the time they had climbed the narrow stone stair in the thickness of the wall of the church and emerged into the open gallery that encircled it. The whole of the flat marshy countryside was revealed for their inspection, the ditches and the lakes, and the little Mitau River winding its way down from the far distance, through the village almost under the side of the church, to lose itself at the very angle where the vast Dwina entered the bay. The line of breastworks and abattis thrown up by the garrison to defend the left bank of the

Dwina was plainly traced, and beyond them could be seen the scanty works which were all that the invaders had bothered to construct up to the moment. The smoke of a thousand cooking fires drifted over the country.

"In my opinion, sir," said Clausewitz deferentially, "if the enemy should decide to proceed by regular siege that is where he will begin. He will tract his first parallel *there*, between the river and that pinewood, and sap forward against the village, establishing his batteries on that neck of land *there*. After three weeks' work he could expect to bring his batteries forward onto the glacis and deliver a regular assault. He must effect the reduction of this village before proceeding to the attack on the town."

"Perhaps," said Essen.

Hornblower could not imagine a Napoleonic army of sixty thousand men in full march for St. Petersburg condescending to spend three weeks in siege operations against an outwork without trying first every extemporary method, like the brusque assault, of last night. He borrowed a telescope from one of the staff, and devoted his time to examining the maze of waterways and marshes that stretched before him, and then, walking round the dome along the gallery, he turned his attention to the view of Riga, with its spires, beyond the huge river. Far off, well down the channel, he could just see the masts of his own squadron, where it swung at anchor at the point where the river blended with the gulf. Tiny specks of ships, minute in their present surroundings and yet of such vast importance in the history of the world.

Chapter XIX

Hornblower was asleep in his cabin in the *Nonsuch* when the alarm was given. Even while he was asleep—or perhaps it may be granted that he woke occasionally without knowing it—his subconscious mind had been taking note of conditions. At least, when he woke fully, he was already vaguely aware of the changes that had occurred during the night. His sleeping or half-awakened mind had noted the veering of the wind that had swung *Nonsuch* round to her anchor, and the brief sharp rain squalls that had pelted down on the deck. Certainly he had awakened to the sharp cry of the watch on deck, and had heard the footsteps overhead of the midshipman of the watch running to him with the news. He was fully awake by the time the midshipman pounded on the door and burst in.

"Rocket from *Raven,* sir."

"Very good," said Hornblower, swinging his legs out of his cot.

Brown, the good servant, was already in the cabin—God only knew how he had picked up the warning—with a lighted lantern to hang on the deck beam above, and he had trousers and coat ready for Hornblower to pull over his nightshirt. Hornblower rushed up to the dark quarterdeck, cannoning into another hurrying figure as he did so.

"Damn your eyes!" said the figure, in Bush's voice, and then, "I beg your pardon, sir."

The ship was alive with the twittering of the pipes as the hands were summoned from their hammocks, and the main deck resounded with the drumming of bare feet. Montgomery, officer of the watch, was at the starboard rail.

"*Raven* sent up a rocket, sir, two minutes back. Bearin' sou' by east."

"Wind's west by north," decided Bush, looking down into the tiny light of the binnacle.

A westerly wind and a dark blustery night; ideal conditions for Macdonald to try and push a force across the river mouth. He had twenty big river barges, into which he could cram five thousand men and a few guns; if he once managed to push a force of that size across the river the Russian position would be hopelessly turned. On the other hand, if he were to lose a force of that size—five thousand men killed or drowned or prisoners—it would be a staggering blow which might well give him pause and so gain time for the Russians. A fortified position, in the final analysis, was only a means of gaining time. Hornblower hoped most passionately that the French flotilla had been allowed to thrust its head well into the noose before Cole in the *Raven* gave the alarm.

A shout from the masthead claimed his attention.

"Gunfire to loo'ard, sir!"

From the deck they could just see a pinpoint of flame stab the darkness far to the westward, and then another one.

"That's too far to the wes'ard," said Hornblower to Bush.

"I'm afraid it is, sir."

At anchor on the very edge of the shoals in that direction was the *Raven*; it was her light draught that had dictated her position there. Vickery in *Lotus* guarded the other bank of the river, while *Nonsuch* perforce still lay anchored in the fairway. All the armed boats of the squadron were rowing guard in the mouth of the river—a navy cutter with a three-pounder could be counted on to deal with a river barge, even if the latter did carry three hundred soldiers. But from the direction of the gunfire it looked as if Cole had given the alarm prematurely. Another gun flashed to leeward; the wind prevented them from hearing the sound of it.

"Call my barge," ordered Hornblower. He felt he could not stay here in useless suspense.

The boat pushed off from the *Nonsuch*, the men tugging at the oars to move the boat in the teeth of the wind. Brown, in the darkness beside Hornblower, felt his captain's restlessness and anxiety.

"Pull, you bastards!" he shouted at the rowers. The boat crawled forward over the tossing water, with Brown standing in the sternsheets with his hand on the tiller.

"'Nother gun, sir. Right ahead," he reported to Hornblower.

"Very good."

A tedious quarter of an hour followed, while the boat lurched and pitched over the steep little waves, and the hands slaved away at the oars. The wash of the seas overside and the groaning of the oars against the thole-pins made a monotonous accompaniment to Hornblower's racing thoughts.

"There's a whole lot o' guns firin' now, sir," reported Brown.

"I can see them," replied Hornblower.

The darkness was pierced by shot after shot; it was evident that the guard-boats were all clustered round a single victim.

"There's *Raven*, sir. Shall I make for her?"

"No. Steer for the firing."

The dark shape of the sloop was just visible ahead; Brown put his helm over a little to lay the barge on a course that would take her past the sloop at a cable's length's distance, heading for the gunfire. They had drawn up abeam of the sloop when there came a flash and a roar from her side, and a shot howled close overhead.

"Jesus!" said Brown. "Ain't the fools got eyes in their heads?"

Presumably the sloop had hailed the passing boat, and, receiving no reply—the hail being carried away by the wind—had incontinently fired. Another shot came from the *Raven,* and someone in the barge squawked with dismay. It was demoralising to be fired upon by one's own side.

"Turn towards her," ordered Hornblower. "Burn a blue light."

At any moment the sloop might fire a full broadside, with every chance of blowing the barge out of the water. Hornblower took the tiller while Brown wrestled, cursing under his breath, with flint and steel and tinder. The hand pulling at the stroke oar said something to try to quicken his movements.

"Shut your mouth!" snapped Hornblower.

Everything was in a muddle, and the men knew it. Brown caught a spark on the tinder, jabbed the fuse of the blue light upon it, and then blew the fuse into a glow. A moment later the firework burst into an unearthly glare, lighting up the boat and the water round it, and Hornblower stood up so that his features and his uniform should be visible to the sloop. It was poor revenge to think of the consternation in the *Raven* when they saw that they had been firing on their own commodore. Hornblower went up the sloop's side in a state of cold fury. Cole was there to receive him, of course.

"Well, Mr. Cole?"

"Sorry I fired on you, sir, but you didn't answer my hail."

"Did it occur to you that with this wind blowing I could not hear you?"

"Yes, sir. But we know the French are out. The boats fired on them an hour back, and half my crew is away in the boats. Supposing I were boarded by two hundred French soldiers? I couldn't take chances, sir."

It was no use arguing with a man as jumpy and as nervous as Cole evidently was.

"You sent up the alarm rocket?"

"Yes, sir. I had to inform you that the barges were at sea."

"You did that the first moment you knew?"

"Yes, sir. Of course, sir."

"Did it occur to you that you would alarm the French as well?"

"I thought that was what you wanted, sir."

Hornblower turned away in disgust. The man in his excitement had clean forgotten every order given him.

"Boat approaching from to wind'ard, sir," reported someone, his white shirt just visible in the gathering dawn. Cole ran forward excitedly, with Hornblower striding after him, catching up to him as he stood at the knightheads staring at the boat.

"Boat ahoy!" yelled Cole through his speaking-trumpet.

"Aye, aye," came the answering hail down-wind. That was the correct reply for an approaching boat with officers on board. She was a ship's cutter under a dipping lugsail; as Hornblower watched she took in the sail with considerable clumsiness and came dropping down to the sloop under oars. Level with the bow she turned, clumsily again, and headed in to lie alongside the sloop. Hornblower could see she was crammed with men.

"Soldiers!" suddenly exclaimed Cole, pointing at the boat with an excited forefinger. "Stand to your guns, men! Sheer off, there!"

Hornblower could see shakos and cross-belts; it must be just the kind of vision Cole's imagination had been toying with all through the night. A reassuring English voice came back to them from overside.

"Avast, there! This is *Lotus'* cutter with prisoners."

It was Purvis' voice without a doubt. Hornblower walked to the waist and looked down. There was Purvis in the stern, and British seamen in check shirts at the oars, but every inch of space was filled with soldiers, sitting in attitudes of apprehension or dejection. Right up in the eyes of the boat, round the

236

boat's gun, four red-coated marines held their muskets at the ready; that was the way Purvis had prepared to deal with any attempt by the prisoners to regain their freedom.

"Let 'em come up," said Hornblower.

They climbed the side, greeted by the grinning seamen as they reached the deck, and stared round in the growing light. Purvis swung himself up and touched his hat to Hornblower.

"They're all Dutchmen, I think, sir. Not Frogs. We got 'em off the barge we caught. Had to fire into 'em a long time—just shot the barge to pieces, us an' the other boats. They're following us, sir, with the other prisoners."

"You only caught one barge?"

"Yes, sir. The others ran for home the moment the rocket went up. But we got two hundred prisoners, I should think, an' we had to kill nigh on a hundred more."

One single barge taken, with two hundred men, when Hornblower had hoped for a dozen barges at least and three thousand men! But Purvis in his innocence was obviously delighted with his capture.

"Here's one of their officers, sir."

Hornblower turned on the blue-coated man who was wearily climbing over the side.

"Who are you, sir?" he asked in French, and after a moment's hesitation the officer replied haltingly in the same language.

"Lieutenant von Bülow, of the Fifty-first Regiment of Infantry."

"French infantry?"

"Of the King of Prussia," said the officer, sternly, with a Teutonic explosiveness in the word *Prusse* which indicated his annoyance at the suggestion that he would be a Frenchman.

So Macdonald had not risked French lives in this highly dangerous venture; that was to be expected, of course. Bonaparte had made war largely at the expense of his allies for the last ten years.

"I will see that you are given refreshment," said Hornblower, politely. "Please order your men to sit down against the rail there."

The officer barked the order. It was significant how at the first warning *Achtung* the dispirited soldiers came instantly to attention, standing stiff and straight. Most of them were wet and bedraggled, apparently having been in the water before surrendering. Hornblower gave orders for them to be fed, at the same time as the other boats came back down-wind, each with its quota of prisoners. On the cramped decks of the *Raven* the two hundred prisoners made a fine show; Cole had the two foremost chase guns run inboard and trained round upon them, a round of canister in each gun, and the gun captains posted with lighted matches ready to fire into them. Seamen, still grinning, went along their ranks handing out bread and beer.

"See how they eat, sir!" said Purvis. "Look at that one, layin' into his biscuit like a wolf with a bone. God damme, it's gone a'ready. It's true what they say, sir, about Boney never feedin' his men."

An imperial army was wont to gather its food from the countryside as it marched; Macdonald's sixty thousand had been stationary now for over two weeks, and in a thinly populated country. They must be on short commons. Every day the siege of Riga could be prolonged would cost lives in plenty to Bonaparte, and although he was ever prodigal with lives there must come a time at last when he would have no more to spare, not even Prussian ones or Italian ones. The greater the pity, then, that the whole division that had tried to pass the river had not been wiped out. Hornblower told himself that was his fault; he should not have entrusted any vital part of the operation to a nervous old woman like Cole. He ought instead to have stayed on board *Raven* himself.

Yet it was hard to be sure of that; the other end of the line, which he had entrusted to Vickery in *Lotus*, was just as important, and it was desirable that he should be in the centre in *Nonsuch* to co-ordinate the activities of his two wings. If Vickery and Cole had had their positions interchanged—as would have to be done—although Vickery could have been relied upon not to spring the trap too soon, could Cole have been relied upon to keep it closed? There might be five thousand Prussians on the farther bank of the Dwina at this moment if it had been up to Cole to head them off. Hornblower found himself wishing that he had known exactly which night Macdonald would make the attempt; he might as well have wished for the moon.

"Mr. Cole," said Hornblower, "make a signal to *Nonsuch*: 'Commodore to captain. Am proceeding to Riga with prisoners.' Then the guard-boats can return to their respective ships, and if you will kindly up anchor we'll start."

Chapter XX

HORNBLOWER was once more up in the gallery that encircled the dome of the church of Daugavgriva.

"You see what I was telling you about, sir," said Clausewitz, pointing.

Out beyond the Russian works stretched a long line, brown against the green, the parapet of the trench the French had thrown up during the night. Macdonald must be a general with energy, for he had had this work done at the same time as he had sent the Prussians on their risky endeavour to cross the river, so that while one attempt had failed he had made a solid gain, profiting by the dark and rainy night to throw up this entrenchment far forward unobserved.

"That is his first parallel, sir, and in the centre of it is the battery he is constructing. And see there, sir? That is where he is sapping forward."

Hornblower stared through his telescope. At a point towards the end of the face of the first parallel he could see something that looked like a wall constructed of bundles of timber. The guns in the Russian works far below him were firing at it; he could see earth flying as the shots struck around it. At the end of the wall of timber was something that looked strange—a sort of shield on wheels. He was studying it when he saw it moved out suddenly, leaving a narrow gap between it and the end of the timber wall, in which for a fleeting moment he saw a couple of men in blue uniforms. It was only a fleeting moment, for immediately the gap was filled with a new bundle of timber. Above the new bundle he could see the blades of spades rising and then disappearing; apparently the bundle of timber was hollow, barrel-shaped, and as soon as it was in position the men sheltering behind it set to work to fill it up with earth dug from behind it. Hornblower realised that he was witnessing the classic method of sapping towards an enemy's position with gabion and fascine. That big timber basket was a gabion, now being filled with earth. Farther back, under cover of the line of filled gabions, the besiegers were revetting their breastwork with fascines, six-foot bundles of wood, and farther back still they were building the whole thing solid with earth dug from a trench behind the breastwork. As he watched, the shield was suddenly pushed forward another yard, and another gabion was put in position; the French were three feet nearer the earthworks which guarded Daugavgriva. No, not a yard, a little less, because the sap was not pointing straight at its objective, but out at its flank so that it could not be enfiladed. Soon it would change its direction, and point towards the other flank, approaching the fortress in zigzag fashion, ruthlessly, and remorselessly. Of all operations of war a scientific siege was the most certain if relief did not arrive from the outside.

"See there, sir!" said Clausewitz suddenly.

From behind a high embankment had suddenly emerged a long string of horses, looking like ants at that distance, but the white breeches of the men who led them showed up clearly in the sunshine. The horses were dragging a cannon, a big piece of artillery when its apparent size was compared with that of the horses. It crawled towards the battery in the centre of the first parallel, myriad white-breeched specks attending it. The high breastwork of the first parallel screened the operation from the sight of the Russian gunners and shielded it from their fire. When the guns had all been brought into the battery, Hornblower knew, openings—embrasures—would be made in the breastwork through which the guns would open fire on the village, silencing the return fire of the defence, and then hammering a breach; meanwhile the sap would be expanded into a wide trench, the second parallel, from which, or if necessary from a third parallel, the stormers would rush out to carry the breach.

"They will have that battery armed by tomorrow," said Clausewitz. "And look! There is another gabion put in place."

Siege operations had the remorseless cold inevitability of the advance of a snake on a paralysed bird.

"Why do your guns not stop the work on the sap?" asked Hornblower.

"They are trying, as you see. But a single gabion is not an easy target to hit at this range, and it is only the end one which is vulnerable. And by the time the sap approaches within easy range their battery fire will be silencing our guns."

Another siege gun had made its appearance from

241

behind the high embankment, and was crawling towards the battery; its predecessor was at that moment being thrust finally onto its position at the breastwork.

"Can you not bring your ships up, sir?" asked Clausewitz. "See how the water comes close to their works there. You could shoot them to pieces with your big guns."

Hornblower shook his head; the same idea had already occurred to him, for the long glittering arm of the Gulf of Riga which reached into the land there was very tempting. But there was less than a fathom of water in it, and even his shallow bomb-ketches drew nine feet—seven at least if he emptied them of all their stores save those necessary for the action.

"I would do so if I could," said Hornblower, "but at the present moment I can see no means of getting my guns into range."

Clausewitz looked at him coldly, and Hornblower was conscious that goodwill between allies was a frail thing. Earlier that morning British and Russians had been the best of friends; Essen and Clausewitz had been thoroughly elated at the turning back of Macdonald's attempt to cross the river, and—like the unthinking junior officers in the squadron—had thought the annihilation of a half battalion of Prussians a notable success, not knowing of the much more far-reaching plan which Hornblower had made and which Cole's nervousness had brought to almost naught. When affairs went well, allies were the best of friends, but in adversity each naturally tended to blame the other. Now that the French approaches were moving towards Daugavgriva he was asking why the Russian artillery did not stop them, and the Russians were asking why his ships' guns did not do the same.

Hornblower made his explanation as fully as he could, but Clausewitz turned an unsympathetic ear, and so did Essen when the matter came up for discussion as Hornblower was saying good-bye to him. It was a poor showing for a navy whose boast was that nothing was impossible; Hornblower was irritable and snappy when he returned that afternoon to the *Non-such,* and he had no word for Bush who came hastily to greet him as he came up the side. His cabin was unfriendly and inhospitable to his jaundiced eye when he entered it, and it was "make and mend" day on board, with the hands skylarking noisily on the deck, so that he knew that if he went up to walk the quarterdeck his train of thought would be continually interrupted. He toyed for a moment with the idea of ordering Bush to cancel his order to make and mend and instead to put the hands to some quiet labour. Everyone would know that it was because the commodore wanted to walk the deck in peace, and might be properly impressed with his importance, but there was never a chance of his acting on the notion. He would not deprive the men of their holiday, and the thought of swelling his importance in their eyes acted as a positive deterrent.

Instead, he went out into the quarter-gallery, and, bowed below the overhanging cove above, he tried to stride up and down its twelve-foot length. It was indeed a pity that he could not bring his ships' guns to bear on the siege works. Heavy guns at close range would play havoc with the French breastworks. And behind the high dyke from which he had seen the guns being dragged must lie the French park and train—a few shells from the bomb-vessels would wreak havoc there, and if only he could get the ketches up the bay it would be easy to drop shells over the dyke. But over most of the bay there was only three or four feet of water, and nowhere more than seven. The thing was impossible, and the best he could do was to forget about it. To distract himself he stepped over the rail into the other quarter-gallery, and peeped through the stern window into Bush's cabin. Bush was asleep on his cot, flat on his back with his mouth open, his hands spread wide at his sides and his wooden leg hanging in a becket against the bulkhead. Hornblower felt a twinge of annoyance that his captain should be sleeping so peacefully while he himself had so many cares on his shoulders. For two pins he would send a message in to Bush and wreck his nap for him. But he knew he would never do that, either. He could never bring himself to a wanton abuse of power.

He stepped back into his own quarter-gallery, and as he did, as he stood with one leg suspended and with the rudder gudgeons creaking a little in their pintles in the stream below him, the idea came to him, so that he stood stock-still for a space, with one leg in mid air. Then he brought his leg over and walked into his cabin and shouted for a messenger.

"My compliments to the officer of the watch, and will he please signal to *Harvey* for Mr. Mound to come on board at once."

Mound came down into his cabin, young and expectant, and yet with his eagerness thinly overlaid with assumed nonchalance. It suddenly dawned upon Hornblower as he greeted him that that careless lackadaisical air of Mound's was assumed in imitation of himself. Hornblower realised that he was something of a hero—more than that, very much of a hero—to this young lieutenant who was paying him the sincerest flattery of imitation. It made him grin wryly to himself even while he motioned Mound to a chair, and then it was forgotten as he plunged into the vital discussion.

"Mr. Mound, do you know of the progress of the French siege works?"

"No, sir."

"Then look at this chart with me. They have a line of trenches here, with a battery here. Their main flank and stores are behind a dyke, here. If we could bring the bomb-vessels up the bay we could shell them out of both places."

"Shoal water, sir," said Mound regretfully.

"Yes," said Hornblower, and for the life of him he could not stop himself from making a dramatic pause before uttering the crucial word. "But with camels we could reduce the draught."

"Camels!" exclaimed Mound, and as he realised all the implications his face lit up. "By George, sir, you're right."

Camels are a means of reducing the draught of a ship—loaded vessels lashed tightly one on each side and then emptied, so as to raise the centre ship farther out of the water. Mound was already grappling with the details.

"There are lighters and barges in Riga, sir. They'll give us some, sure as a gun. Plenty of sand to ballast 'em, or we can fill 'em with water and pump 'em out. With two big lighters I could lessen *Harvey's* draught by five feet easy—lift her clear out of the water for that matter. Those lighters are two hundred tons burden an' don't draw more than a couple of feet empty."

A difficulty had occurred to Hornblower while Mound was speaking, one which he had not thought of before.

"How are you going to steer 'em all?" he demanded. "They'll be unmanageable."

"Rig a Danube rudder, sir," replied Mound instantly. "Make it big enough and you could steer anything with one."

"Give me a fulcrum and I will move the world," quoted Hornblower.

"Exactly, sir. An' I'll pierce the lighters for sweeps. There'll be no beatin' to wind'ard any more than in a raft. I could put the men to work at once if you'll give the order, sir."

Mound might have been a boy of ten instead of one of twenty from the eagerness of his voice. The languid calm was quite forgotten.

"I'll send a note to the governor," said Hornblower, "asking for the loan of four lighters. I'll make it six, in case of accidents. Have your plans ready in an hour's time. You can draw upon this ship and the sloops for the materials and men you'll need."

"Aye aye, sir."

There was need for haste, for that very evening there came sullenly booming across the bay the sound of heavy guns firing, not the higher-pitched incisive growl of the field pieces they had heard before, but the deep-toned roar of siege artillery; the enemy was trying a few shots with the first of the big guns dragged up into their battery. And the next morning, just as Hornblower came out on the quarterdeck, there was a sudden loud crash ashore, like a peal of thunder, to herald the opening salvo of the enemy. Its echoes had not died away before a more ragged salvo succeeded it, and then another more ragged still, and so on until the air was ceaselessly tormented by the loud reports, like a continuous thunderstorm from which the ear waited continually for relief that was not granted it. The masthead lookout reported a long smear of smoke drifted by the breeze across the countryside from the enemy's battery.

"Call away my barge," said Hornblower.

At *Nonsuch's* boat booms there already lay an assortment of the boats of the squadron, piled high with the stores which had been taken out of the two bomb-ketches. The barge danced over the water in the sparkling dawn to where the bomb-ketches lay anchored, each with a lighter on either side. Duncan, captain of the *Moth*, was being rowed round the group in a jolly-boat. He touched his hat as the barge approached.

"Morning, sir," he said, and then instantly turned back to the work in hand, raising his speaking-trumpet to his lips. "Too much by the bows! Take up the for'ard cable another pawl!"

Hornblower had himself rowed on to the *Harvey*, and leaped from his barge to the lighter on her starboard side—not much of a leap, because she was

246

laden down with ballast—without bothering officers or men for compliments. Mound was standing on his tiny quarterdeck, testing with his foot the tension of the big cable—one of *Nonsuch's*—which was frapped round his own ship and both lighters, two turns round each, forward and aft.

"Carry on, port side!" he yelled.

In each of the lighters a large working party was stationed, the men equipped with shovels for the most part extemporised out of wood. At Mound's order the men in the port-side lighter recommenced lustily shovelling the sand over the side. Clouds of it drifted astern on the faint wind. Mound tested the tension again.

"Carry on, starboard side!" he yelled again, and then, perceiving his commodore approaching, he came to the salute.

"Good morning, Mr. Mound," said Hornblower.

"Good morning, sir. We have to do this part of it step by step, you see, sir. I have the old ketch so light she'll roll over in the cables if I give her the chance."

"I understand, Mr. Mound."

"The Russians were prompt enough sending out the lighters to us, sir."

"Can you wonder?" replied Hornblower. "D'you hear the French battery at work?"

Mound listened and apparently heard it for the first time. He had been engrossed too deeply in his work to pay any attention to it before; his face was unshaven and grey with fatigue, for his activity had not ceased since Hornblower had summoned him the afternoon before. In that time both ketches had been emptied of their stores, the cables roused out and got across to them, the lighters received and laid alongside in the dark, and each group of three vessels bound into a single mass with the cables hauled taut by the capstans.

"Excuse me, sir," said Mound, and ran forward to examine the forward cable.

With the shovelling out of the sand, hove overside by a hundred lusty pairs of arms, the lighters were rising in the water, lifting the ketch between them, cables and timber all a-creaking, and it was necessary to keep the cables taut as the rising of the lighters relieved the strain upon them. Hornblower turned aft to see what another working party were doing there. A large barrel half filled with water had been streamed out astern with a line to either quarter of the ketch, conducted in each case through a fair-lead to an extemporised windlass fixed to the deck. Paying out or heaving in on the lines would regulate the pull of the barrel, were the ketch under weigh, to one side or the other, exerting a powerful leverage. The barrel then was intended to undertake the duties of the rudder, which was already sufficiently high out of the water to be almost useless.

"It's only a contraption, sir," said Mound, who had returned from forward. "I had intended, as I told you, sir, to rig a Danube rudder. It was Wilson here who suggested this—I'd like to call your attention to him, sir. It'll be much more effective, I'm sure."

Wilson looked up from his work with a gap-toothed grin.

"What's your rating?" asked Hornblower.

"Carpenter's mate, sir."

"As good a one as I've known, sir," interpolated Mound.

"What service?"

"Two commissions in the old *Superb*, sir. Once in *Arethusa*, an' now this one, sir."

"I'll make out an acting warrant for you as carpenter," said Hornblower.

"Thankee, sir, thankee."

Mound could easily have taken the whole credit for devising this jury rudder to himself if he had wished. Hornblower liked him all the more for not having done so. It was good for discipline and for the spirits of the men to reward good work promptly.

"Very good, Mr. Mound. Carry on."

Hornblower went back to his barge and rowed over to the *Moth*. The work here was a stage more advanced; so much sand had been shovelled out of the lighters that it was only with slow effort that the working parties could heave their shovelfuls over the side, shoulder high. A wide streak of the *Moth's* copper was already visible, so high was she riding.

"Watch your trim, Mr. Duncan," said Hornblower. "She's canting a little to port."

"Aye aye, sir."

It called for some complicated adjustment of the cables, veering out and hauling in, to set *Moth* on an even keel again.

"She won't draw more'n two feet by the time we're finished with her, sir," said Duncan exultantly.

"Excellent," said Hornblower.

Duncan addressed himself to putting more men to work in the lighters, shovelling sand across from the inboard to the outboard sides, to ease the work of those actually heaving the sand over.

"Two hours more an' they'll be clear, sir," reported Duncan. "Then we'll only have to pierce the sides for sweeps."

He glanced over at the sun, still not far above the horizon.

"We'll be ready for action half an hour before noon, sir," he added.

"Put the carpenters to work piercing the sides now," said Hornblower. "So that you can rest your men and give them a chance to have breakfast. Then when they start again they can shovel through the ports and work quicker."

"Aye aye, sir."

Half an hour before noon seemed to be a more likely sort of estimate with that improvement in the programme, yet even if the completion of the work were delayed by two hours there would still be long hours of daylight left in which the blow could be

249

struck. While the sides of the lighters were being pierced Hornblower called Duncan and Mound to him and went over their final orders with them.

"I'll be up in the church with the signalling party," he said in conclusion. "I'll see that you're properly supported. So good luck."

"Thank you, sir," they answered in unison. Excitement and anticipation masked their weariness.

So Hornblower had himself rowed over to the village, where a tiny jetty saved him and the signallers from splashing through the shallows; the roar of the bombardment and the counter-bombardment grew steadily louder as they approached. Diebitsch and Clausewitz came to meet them as they mounted the jetty, and led the way towards the church. As they skirted the foot of the earthworks which ringed the village on its landward side Hornblower looked up and saw the Russian artillerymen working their guns, bearded soldiers, naked to the waist in the hot sun. An officer walked from gun to gun in the battery, pointing each piece in succession.

"There are few men in our artillery who can be trusted to lay a gun," explained Clausewitz.

The village was already badly knocked about, great holes showing in the walls and roofs of the flimsy cottages of which it was composed. As they neared the church a ricochetting ball struck the church wall, sending a cloud of chips flying, and remaining embedded in the brickwork like a plum in a cake. A moment later Hornblower swung round to a sudden unusual noise to see his two midshipmen standing staring at the headless corpse of a seaman who a moment before had been walking at their heels. A ball flying over the earthworks had shattered his head to atoms and flung his body against them. Somers was eyeing with disgust the blood and brains which had spattered his white trousers.

"Come along," said Hornblower.

In the gallery under the dome they could look

down upon the siege. The zigzag approach trench was almost half-way towards the defences, the head of it almost obscured by flying earth as the Russians fired furiously upon it. But the central redoubt which covered the entrance to the village was in bad shape, its parapets battered into nothing more than mounds, a gun lying half-buried beside its shattered carriage, although the other one was still being worked by a devoted little group. The whole of the French works were obscured by the thin pall of smoke which spread from the breaching battery, but the smoke was not so thick as to hide a column of infantry marching down towards the first parallel from the rear.

They relieve the guard of the trenches at noon," explained Clausewitz. "Where are these boats of yours, sir?"

"Here they come," said Hornblower.

They were creeping over the silvery water, fantastic in appearance, the ketches with their sails furled and the ugly bulks of the lighters beside them. The long clumsy sweeps, a dozen on each side, looked like the legs of a water boatman on a pond, but far slower in movement as the toiling seamen who manned them tugged them through each successive endless stroke.

"Somers! Gerard!" said Hornblower, sharply. "How are your signalling arrangements working out? Lash those blocks to the cornice up there. Come along, you haven't all day to get ready in."

The midshipmen and seamen addressed themselves to the business of making a signalling station up on the gallery. The blocks were lashed to the cornice and the halliards rove through them, the Russian staff watching the operation with interest. Meanwhile the bomb-ketches came crawling up the bay, painfully slowly under their sweeps, heading crabwise on account of the gentle breeze on their bow, before which they sagged away to leeward quite perceptibly to Hornblower's eye above them. No one among the enemy seemed to be paying them the least attention;

Bonaparte's armies, lords of Europe from Madrid to Smolensk, had had few opportunities of becoming acquainted with bomb-ketches. The firing from the big battery went on steadily, pounding at the crumbling Russian earthworks below, with the Russians returning the fire with desperate energy.

The *Harvey* and the *Moth* came creeping in until they were quite close to shore; Hornblower through his glass could see minute figures moving in their bows, and knew they were dropping their anchors. The sweeps worked spasmodically, first on one side and then on the other—Hornblower up in the gallery, his heart beating fast, could well picture Mound and Duncan on their quarterdecks shouting their orders to the rowers as they manœuvred themselves about like beetles pinned to a card. They were placing themselves in position to drop other anchors at the stern, so that by veering and hauling in on their cables they could swing themselves so as to be able to point their mortars anywhere along a wide arc. Clausewitz and the staff looked on uncomprehending, having no notion of the meaning of these manœuvres. Hornblower saw the stern anchors let go, and could see little groups of men bending to work at the capstans; the bomb-ketches turned almost imperceptibly first this way and then that as their captains trained them round by the aid of the leading marks on the shore.

"There's the 'Ready' flag going up in *Harvey*," said Hornblower, the glass at his eye.

The sheave in the block above his head shrilled noisily as the halliard ran over it, bearing the acknowledgment. A big puff of smoke suddenly spurted upwards from the *Harvey's* bows; Hornblower at that distance could see nothing of the shell in its flight, and he waited nervously, compelling himself to search the whole area round about the battery to make sure of seeing the burst. And he saw nothing, nothing at all. Reluctantly he ordered hoisted the black cone for "Unobserved," and *Harvey* fired again. This time he could see the burst, a little volcano of smoke and fragments just beyond the battery.

"That was over, sir," said Somers.

"Yes. Make that to *Harvey*."

Duncan had anchored *Moth* by now, and was flying the signal of readiness. *Harvey's* next shell fell square in the center of the battery, and immediately afterwards *Moth's* first shell did the same. At once the two ketches began a systematic bombardment of the battery, dropping shells into it in constant succession, so that there was not a moment when a fountain of smoke and earth was not apparent within its earthworks. It was a plain rectangular structure, without traverses or internal subdivisions, and there was no shelter for the men within it now that their enemy had found means to circumvent their earthworks. They only maintained their fire for a few seconds, and then Hornblower could see them running from their guns; the interior of the battery looked like a disturbed ants' nest. One of the big thirteen-inch shells landed full on the parapet, and the smoke, clearing away, revealed the breastwork blown flat, opening the interior of the battery to view from ground level in the village, and through the gap was visible the muzzle of a dismounted siege gun, pointed skyward and helpless—a cheering sight for the defence. That was only the beginning. Gap after gap was blown in the earthworks; the whole interior was plastered with shells. At one moment there was a much bigger explosion than usual, and Hornblower guessed that an "expense magazine"—the small store of gunpowder kept in the battery and continually replenished from the rear—had blown up. Down below him the defence had taken new heart, and every gun along the menaced front had reopened fire; it was a shot from the village, apparently, which hit the muzzle of the dismounted gun and flung it back upon the ground.

"Signal 'Cease fire,'" said Hornblower.

Thirteen-inch shells were not munitions of war that could be readily obtained in the Baltic, and there was no purpose in wasting them upon a target which was silenced and at least made temporarily useless. And then came the counter-move on the part of the attack, as he had expected. A battery of field artillery was coming over the distant slope, six guns, minute at that distance, jolting and swaying after their limbers. The country was still marshy, for the summer was not yet old enough to have dried up the fields, and the artillery, hock- and axle-deep in the mire, made only slow progress.

"Signal for the target to change," ordered Hornblower.

There was no means of observing the fall of the shells on the new target, for the bomb-ketches were dropping them just over the high dyke. It was a matter of chance should they do any destruction, but Hornblower could guess that the park and depots of an army of sixty thousand men conducting a first-class siege were likely to be both extensive and crowded; a few shells dropped there might do good. The first field battery was approaching the water's edge, the horses wheeling round to leave the guns pointing at the bomb-ketches at neat geometrical intervals.

"*Harvey* signals she's shifting target, sir," reported Gerard.

"Very good."

Harvey was firing at the field battery; it took her a little while to get the range, and field guns, spaced far apart in a long thin line, were not a good target for mortars, even though the fall of the shells was now under direct observation. And a second battery was coming up on the flank of the first and—Hornblower's telescope could easily make them out across the narrow extremity of the bay—there were more guns coming into action to put the bomb-vessels under a cross-fire. One of *Harvey's* shells burst close beside one of the guns, presumably killing every man serving it, but by chance leaving the gun itself still on its wheels. The other guns had opened fire, the smoke creeping lazily from their muzzles. Across the bay the other field batteries were coming into action, although at very long range for field artillery. There was no purpose in continuing to expose the bomb-ketches to the fire of the shore; Macdonald had two hundred field guns, and there were only two bomb-ketches.

"Signal 'Discontinue the action,'" ordered Hornblower.

Now that he had given the word it seemed to him that he had waited over-long. It seemed ages before the bomb-ketches got their anchors hoisted, and Hornblower could see, as he waited anxiously, the splashes thrown up all round them by the shots from the shore. He saw the sweeps thrust out from the sides of the lighters take a grip on the water, swinging the vessels round, and then the white sails mounted the masts, and the queer craft sailed away out of range, making vast leeway which caused them to head crabwise aslant of their course. Hornblower turned away with relief to meet the eyes of the governor, who had been standing silently watching the whole operation through a vast telescope which he had mounted upon the shoulder of a patient orderly whose back must have ached with the crouching.

"Excellent, sir," said the governor. "I thank you, in the name of the Czar. Russia is grateful to you, sir, and so is the city of Riga."

"Thank you, Your Excellency," said Hornblower.

Diebitsch and Clausewitz were awaiting his attention. They were eager to discuss future operations with him, and he had to listen to them. He dismissed his midshipmen and signalling party, hoping that Somers would have the sense to interpret the glance he threw him as a warning not to let his men get hold of any Lettish spirits while they were ashore. Then he resumed the conversation, which was continually interrupted by the coming and going of orderlies with messages, and hasty orders given in languages that he could not understand. But the results of those orders were soon apparent; two regiments of infantry came filing up through the village with bayonets fixed, lined the earthworks, and then dashed out on the glacis with a yell. The heavy guns in the battery which should have been torn to pieces with grape-shot were all silent; Hornblower watched the sortie reach the approach trench almost without opposition; the men burst into it over the parapets, and hurriedly began to tear down the sandbags and gabions with which it was constructed, while down into the ruined battery came a French infantry force too late to stop them, even if they had been able to do so under the artillery fire of the besieged. In an hour the work was done, the approach trench levelled over large sections, the tools taken, spare gabions heaped together and set on fire.

"Thanks to you, sir," said Clausewitz, "the progress of the siege has been delayed by four days."

Four days; and the French had all the rest of the year to continue pounding the defences. It was his duty, and the Russians', to maintain them as long as might be. There was something a little depressing about the prospect of trying to maintain this outwork while Bonaparte was marching, irresistibly, into the heart of Russia. Yet the game had to be played out to the end. He parted from his hosts feeling weary and disconsolate, a dark shadow overhanging any elation he might feel regarding the success—the success that had won four days—of his attack on the French. The pipes squealed as he came over the side of the *Nonsuch;* Captain Bush and the first lieutenant and the officer of the watch were on the quarterdeck to receive him.

"Good evening, Captain Bush. Would you be kind enough to hand out a signal for Mr. Duncan and Mr. Mound to repair on board here immediately?"

"Yes, sir." Bush did not speak again for a second or

two, but he did not turn away to obey. "Yes, sir. Mound was killed."

"What's that you say?"

"One of the last shots from the beach cut him in two, sir."

Bush was trying to keep his expression harsh as usual, but it was obvious that he was deeply moved. Yet he had not grown as fond of Mound as had Hornblower. And in that one moment there came flooding over Hornblower all the torrent of regrets and doubts which he was to know for so long to come. If only he had ordered the bomb-ketches out of action earlier! He had been wantonly reckless of human life in keeping them in action after the field batteries began to return fire? Mound had been one of the best young officers he had ever been fortunate enough to command. England had suffered a severe loss in his death, and so had he. But his feeling of personal loss was more acute still, and the thought of the finality of death oppressed him. The wave of torment was still breaking over him when Bush spoke again.

"Shall I signal for Duncan and *Harvey's* first lieutenant, sir?"

"Yes, do that, if you please, Captain Bush."

Chapter XXI

HORNBLOWER was endeavouring to write a note in French to the governor—a weary exercise. Sometimes it was words and sometimes it was phrases which were beyond his power to express in French, and each hitch meant retracing his steps and beginning the sentence again.

"Despatches received at this moment from England"—he was trying to say—"inform me that the armies of His Majesty the King of Great Britain and Ireland have been successful in a great battle fought on the 14th of last month at Salamanca in Spain. Marshal Marmont, Duke of Ragusa, was wounded, and some ten thousand prisoners were captured. The British general, the Marquess of Wellington, is, according to the advices I have received, in full march for Madrid, which is certain to fall for him. The consequences of this battle cannot be estimated too highly."

Hornblower swore a little to himself; it was not for him to recommend to the governor what action he should take regarding this news. But the fact that one of Bonaparte's armies had been thoroughly beaten, in a battle fought between equal numbers on a large scale, was the highest importance. If he were governor he would fire salutes, post proclamations, do all that he could to revive the spirits of soldiers and civilians in their weary task of holding Riga against the French. And what it would mean to the main Russian army, now drawing together in the south to defend Moscow in one last desperate battle, it was impossible to estimate.

He signed and sealed the note, shouted for Brown, and handed it over to him for immediate despatch ashore. Beside him in addition to the official despatches just received lay a pile of fifteen letters all addressed to him in Barbara's handwriting; Barbara had written to him every week since his departure, and the letters had piled up in the Admiralty Office awaiting the time when *Clam* should return with despatches, and he had opened only the last one to assure himself that all was well at home, and picked it up again to reread it.

My beloved husband,

This week the domestic news is quite overshadowed by the great news from Spain. Arthur has beaten Marmont and the whole usurping government in that country is in ruin. Arthur is to be made a Marquess. Was it in my first letter or in my second that I told you he had been made an Earl? Let us hope that soon I shall be writing to you that he has been made a Duke, not because I wish my brother to be a Duke, but because that will mean another victory. All England is talking of Arthur this week, just as two weeks back all England was talking of Commodore Hornblower and his exploits in the Baltic.

The household here at Smallbridge is so much agog with all this news that our most important event bade fair to pass unnoticed. I refer to the breeching of Richard Arthur. He is in small-clothes now, and his petticoats are put away for ever. He is young for such a transformation, and Ramsbottom melted into tears at the passing of her baby; but if you could see him I think you would agree that he looks vastly well in his new clothes, at least until he can escape from supervision and indulge himself in his favourite recreation of digging holes in the ground in the shrubbery. He exhibits both physically and morally a partiality for the soil which appears odd in the son of such a distinguished sailor. When I have completed this letter I shall ring and send for him so that he can affix his mark, and I daresay he will add such grubby finger-prints as will further identify his signature.

Hornblower turned the page, and the grubby fin-gerprints were there, sure enough, along with the shaky X that Richard Arthur had scrawled under his stepmother's signature. Hornblower felt a desperate longing to see his son at that moment, happily muddy and spading away at his hole in the shrubbery, all-engrossed in the business of the moment with baby-hood's sublime concentration of purpose. Above the X were the last few lines Barbara had written.

As always, it is my constant dream that my dear husband shall soon return victorious, when I shall be able to exert myself to increase his happiness in place of merely praying for it as I do now.

Hornblower refused to allow himself to grow sentimental, brutally strangling any emotion which he experienced. So now he had two brothers-in-law who were marquesses, and one of them was a full general, while he himself was no more than a Knight of the Bath and—unless there should be an unusual casualty rate among his seniors—it would still be eight years before he became even a rear admiral, even if he should live so long and his career were not cut short by disciplinary action. He reached for the despatch which had been the first one he had opened, and read once more the passage which had the greatest bearing on the present moment.

Their Lordships desire me to call your particular notice to the fact that the Government attaches the greatest importance to maintaining the defence of Riga as long as it is possible. They instruct me that they consider the safety of the squadron under your command as secondary compared with the prolongation of the siege and they charge you, on your peril, to do everything in your power to prevent the enemy from continuing his march on St. Petersburg.

In other words, thought Hornblower, Riga must be defended to the last man—and ship—and they would shoot him if they thought he had not done his utmost. He shouted for his barge, locked his desk, seized his hat, and after a moment's hesitation, his pistols, and had himself rowed once more to Daugavgriva.

The village was now a mere mass of ruins, save for the church, whose solid walls had withstood the

260

flames that had swept the place and the continual storm of ricochetting shots which came over from the bombardment of the ramparts. The place stank of death, for the dead were many and the earth over them scanty. Trenches had been driven from cellar to cellar of the ruined houses to permit of safe passage through the village, and it was by way of these that he made his way to the church. From the gallery there the view was ominous. The besiegers' second parallel was completed, no more than two hundred yards from the defences, and the approaches were continuing their remorseless progress towards the ditch. The fire from the big battery was ceaseless, and there was but small reply from the ramparts; too many gunners had been killed and too many guns knocked to pieces, and guns and artillerymen were scarce, so that it was better to try to preserve the remainder to beat off the assault when it should come. Down at the water's edge on the besiegers' side a well-constructed battery displayed the guns that were ready to sweep the area where the bomb-ketches had anchored; there was no chance of repeating the surprise bombardment of the breaching battery which had prolonged the siege for four days at the cost of Mound's life.

Clausewitz commented coolly on the situation to Hornblower as they looked at all this through their glasses. To a doctrinaire soldier a siege was an intellectual exercise. It was mathematically possible to calculate the rate of progress of the approaches and the destructive effect of the batteries, to predict every move and counter-move in advance, and to foretell within an hour the moment of the final assault. The time had come, now that it was impossible to maintain fire upon the head of the sap, to attempt to delay the progress of the besiegers by a sortie.

"But," expostulated Hornblower, "if the French know that a sortie is due, will not they make preparations for it?"

261

"Yes," said Clausewitz, his cold grey eyes expressionless.

"Would it not be better to surprise them?"

"Yes. But in a siege how is that to be done?"

"We surprised them with the bomb-vessels."

"Yes. But now—"

Clausewitz indicated the battery which denied the end of the bay to them.

"But still—" began Hornblower, and then bit off the sentence. There was no purpose in being critical without having a helpful suggestion to make at the same time. He turned his attention once more to the siege works, looking for inspiration, while the guns roared out below him. They roared from farther up the river as well, where the French had opened another front of attack on the Mitau suburb directly across the river from Riga. The resources of the defence were being stretched very thin, and Macdonald had locked his teeth, bulldog fashion, into the siege and it would be hard to shake his hold. All the resources of Prussia were being drawn upon to supply his army with stores for the siege, and he had already proved that nothing would distract him from it, not even the fact that the Lettish and Livonian and Lithuanian peasantry had risen in revolt in his rear and had set all the country behind him in a turmoil.

"The dead are beginning to come down the river," said Clausewitz. He had big yellow teeth that revealed themselves at the least provocation. Hornblower looked at him without comprehension.

"From the fighting two weeks ago," explained Clausewitz. "At Vitebsk and Smolensk two hundred miles to the south of us. Some of the corpses have succeeded in making the journey. Russian corpses, many of them. But French corpses too, and Bavarian corpses, and Westphalian corpses, and Italian corpses—many Italians. It must have been a big battle."

"Very interesting," said Hornblower, scanning the

262

siege works again. In the centre of the second parallel was a new battery, the fire from whose guns would cut up any force attacking frontally in the hope of destroying the works. It would be asking much of any sallying force to cross two hundred yards of naked glacis in the teeth of such a fire and then storm ditch and parapet. The flanks were secure, too, one guarded by the little river and the other trending back towards the bay. The bay! The French batteries might be able to sweep the bay sufficiently effectively to prevent bomb-vessels anchoring there in daylight, but they would not be able to stop an infantry attack launched from boats at night. Then the parallel could be rushed at dawn from the flank. Hornblower turned to Clausewitz with the suggestion, and Clausewitz adopted it instantly. These continental soldiers were always likely to forget about the sea when making their plans, but Clausewitz, Prussian though he was, was a man of sufficient elasticity of mind still to be able to see the merits of a plan based on command of the sea.

There was no time to be lost if the assault upon Daugavgriva were to be anticipated. The plan had to be given form instantly; time-tables worked out, signals agreed upon, troops allocated for the landing and marched to the point where Hornblower could have boats' crews ready to man the river barges which were to carry the troops to the point selected for landing. Hornblower had to detail crews and officers, issue his orders, and make sure they were understood. Montgomery and Duncan, Purvis and Carlin, had to be sent for, brought up to the dome and shown the objectives to be aimed at—Hornblower fretted himself weary walking round the gallery while waiting for them to come ashore after he had sent for them. Mounted messengers, riding in hot haste, brought back a trio of Russian colonels to the gallery; it was their regiments which were detailed to make the landing. Hornblower explained to them in French, and then explained to his officers in English. Then he had the job of interpreting the questions which everyone wanted to ask. Half a dozen Russian subalterns, squatting on the floor of the gallery nursing pieces of board on which sheets of paper were pinned, wrote out the orders which Clausewitz dictated to them. Essen arrived in the midst of all the bustle; he had given his verbal consent at once to the proposed attack, and when, on his arrival, he found the preparation so far advanced, like a sensible man he left the elaboration of the details to the men who had devised the scheme. All this went on with the steady roar of the bombardment supplying a loud undertone to every conversation, while the Russian ramparts crumbled steadily under the hail of shot, and while the approach trenches crept steadily nearer.

It was before noon that Hornblower had made the suggestion to Clausewitz; it was eight in the evening, and the sun had set, before everything was completed, before Hornblower had had himself rowed to the Dwina mouth to inspect the boats which had been provided, and to watch the Russian grenadiers marching down to be herded into them.

"You understand your orders, Duncan?" asked Hornblower.

"Yes, sir."

"Let's see your watch. Set it by mine."

"Aye aye, sir."

"Mr. Montgomery. Mr. Purvis. Remember what I said about keeping the landing force together. You must strike all at once—no landing in driblets. Make sure the soldiers know the direction in which to advance when they land."

"Aye aye, sir."

"Good luck, then."

"Thank you, sir."

It was quite dark by the time Hornblower set foot again on the little jetty at Daugavgriva; dark, and there was a chilly breath in the air. So far had the year advanced since he had first cast anchor in Riga Bay. Midsummer had gone and autumn was at hand. He had to feel his way along the trenches and up to the church, and his legs felt hardly strong enough to carry him up the interminable dark stairs to the gallery. He had hardly sat down since the morning, and he had eaten nothing, and his head was swimming with fatigue and hunger. Clausewitz was still on duty, up in the gallery where the stars shone bravely down upon him, giving a light which seemed bright compared with the pitchy darkness of the stairs Hornblower had just climbed.

"The French seem unusually active tonight," was Clausewitz' greeting to him. "At dusk they changed the guard of their trenches."

A string of bright orange flames suddenly lit up the French lines, and the roar of a salvo reached their ears.

"They are periodically spraying the ditch with grape," explained Clausewitz, "to hinder our repair parties. It is what is always done, but after half a dozen rounds they lose direction and range."

If siege warfare was such a mechanical art, if every step was obvious and would be foreseen, there was always the chance of an original-minded general breaking the rules. In two days the breaches and approaches would be ripe for an assault—what was to prevent an assailant from making his attack a little prematurely and catching the defender off his guard? Hornblower made the suggestion to Clausewitz.

"It is always possible," said Clausewitz, pontifically. "But our trench guards are unusually strong tonight because of the sortie at dawn."

Hornblower felt round in the gloom, and found one of the trusses of straw which had been carried up to the gallery in an endeavour to make this advanced headquarters more comfortable. He sat down gratefully, for his legs were actually trembling with fatigue. He wrapped his cloak closer round him against the chill of the night, and the thought of sleep became inexpressibly alluring. He stretched himself out on the crackling straw, and then heaved himself up on his elbow again to pinch up a wad of straw as a pillow.

"I shall rest awhile," he announced, and lay back and closed his eyes.

There was something more than mere fatigue about this desire for sleep. Asleep, he would be quit of this siege, of its stinks and perils and bitterness; he would be free of his responsibilities; he would not be plagued with the endless reports of Bonaparte's steady advance into the heart of Russia; he would no longer be tormented with the feeling of fighting a desperate and hopeless battle against an enemy who was bound, because of his colossal might, to prevail in the end. Oblivion awaited him if he could only sleep—oblivion, *nepenthe,* forgetfulness. Tonight he yearned to sink into sleep as a man might yearn to sink into the arms of his mistress. His nerves were curiously steady, despite the strain of the last few weeks—perhaps (such was his contrary nature) because of it. He settled himself down in the straw, and even the tumultuous dreams that assailed him were (as he was somehow aware) not nearly as serious as the thoughts from which he would have suffered had he been awake.

He awoke to Clausewitz' arm on his shoulder, and pieced himself back into the Hornblower who was aiding in the defence of Riga like a man fitting together a jigsaw puzzle.

"An hour before dawn," said Clausewitz, still only a vague shadow in the brooding darkness.

Hornblower sat up; he was stiff, and had grown cold under the inadequate cover of his cloak. The landing force, if all had gone well, must be creeping up the bay now. It was too dark to see anything as he peered over the parapet of the gallery. Another shadow loomed up at his elbow and thrust something

266

scalding hot into his hand—a glass of tea. He sipped it gratefully, feeling its warmth penetrate into his inner recesses. The faint report of a single musket shot reached his ears, and Clausewitz began a remark to him which was cut short by a violent outburst of firing down in no man's land between the trench systems. The darkness was spangled with points of flame.

"Possibly patrols with a fit of nerves," said Clausewitz, but the firing showed no signs of dying down. Instead, it grew in violence. There was a great spearhead of flame down below, pointing towards an irregular mass of flashes, where apparently a column was meeting a line. The flashes flared up and died away with the ragged volleys; soon cannons were contributing their orange flames, and immediately afterwards there was more fire as blazing combustibles—carcasses—were flung by attackers and defenders from the parapets to illuminate their enemies. From the bay arose a curving streak of yellow fire, soaring upwards towards the sky, and then bursting into scarlet stars.

"Thank God for that!" said Hornblower, but he kept the words to himself.

The landing party had reached their station a little ahead of their time, and somebody, English or Russian, had sensibly decided to launch the flank attack immediately upon seeing the firing ashore. Clausewitz turned and rapped out an order which sent an aide-de-camp hurrying down the stairs. At almost the same moment a messenger came running up, gabbling Russian so rapidly that Clausewitz, with his limited command of the language, had to make him repeat his words more slowly. When the message was delivered he turned to Hornblower.

"The enemy is in strong force, apparently intending to make a surprise attack. He might save two days if it were successful."

A fresh tumult broke out down below; the landing

party had encountered their first opposition, and the invisible landscape towards the shore was spangled with a new pattern of flashes. There was a desperate battle going on, where attackers and counter-attackers and the flank attack drove together; there was a faint light beginning to show now, enough to reveal Clausewitz, unshaven, and with his uniform covered with bits of straw, in direct contrast with his usual spruce appearance. But still nothing could be seen of the fighting, save for vague smoke clouds drifting in the semidarkness. Hornblower was reminded of Campbell's lines in "Hohenlinden" about the level sun at morn being unable to pierce the dun war clouds. The clatter of musketry and the crash of artillery told of the bitter struggle, and once Hornblower heard a deep shout from many throats answered by a wild yell. That was when some attack met a counter-attack, presumably. Steadily the landscape grew brighter, and the messengers began to pour in.

"Shevstoff has stormed the battery guarding the shore," said Clausewitz, exultantly.

Shevstoff was the general commanding the landing party. If he had stormed the battery the boats' crews would be able to effect an unmolested retreat, while the arrival of a messenger here in Daugavgriva from him meant that he was in full touch with the defenders, and presumably his force had executed its orders and fallen on the flank of the French position. The firing seemed to be dying away, even though the smoke still blended with the low ground mist of autumn and kept everything concealed.

"Kladoff is in the approaches," went on Clausewitz. "His workmen are breaking down the parapets."

The firing increased again, although now there was so much light that no flashes were visible. A frightful death struggle was apparently going on, so desperate that the arrival of the governor in the gallery attracted little attention from the group straining to see through the fog and smoke.

Essen gathered the details with a few quick questions to Clausewitz, and then he turned to Hornblower.

"I would have been here an hour ago," he said, "but I was detained by the arrival of despatches."

Essen's massive countenance was gloomy; he took Hornblower's arm and drew him out of earshot of the junior staff officers.

"Bad news?" asked Hornblower.

"Yes. The worst. We have been beaten in a great battle outside Moscow, and Bonaparte is in the city."

That was the worst news indeed. Hornblower could foresee a future time when he supposed that battle would rank along with Marengo and Austerlitz and Jena, as a smashing victory which laid a nation low, and the entry into Moscow would rank with the occupation of Vienna and Berlin. A week or two more and Russia would sue for peace—if she had not begun to do so already—and England would be left alone, with the whole world in arms against her. Was there anything in the world that could stand against Bonaparte's craft and power? Even the British navy? Hornblower forced himself to take the blow impassively, forced his face to bear no hint of his dismay.

"We shall fight it out here all the same," he said.

"Yes," said Essen, "my men will fight to the last. So will my officers."

There was almost a grin on his face as he jerked his head towards Clausewitz; that was a man who had his neck in a noose if ever a man had, fighting against his own country. Hornblower remembered Wellesley's hint to him that his squadron might well serve as a refuge for the Russian court. His ships would be jammed with refugees fleeing from this, the last continental country in arms against Bonaparte.

The mist and smoke were thinning, and patches of the field of battle were visible now, and Hornblower and Essen turned their attention to the work in hand as if with relief from contemplating the future.

"Ha!" said Essen, pointing.

Portions of the approaches were in plain view, and here and there were jagged gaps in the parapets.

"Kladoff has carried out his orders, sir," said Clausewitz.

Until those gaps were repaired, one by one, starting with the gap nearest the first parallel, no one would be able to reach the head of the sap, and certainly no strong force could use the approaches. Another two days had been won, decided Hornblower, gauging the amount of destruction with his eye—experience had brought him facility already in appreciating siege operations. There was still heavy firing going on as the rear-guard covered the retreat of the sallying forces to the ramparts. Essen balanced his huge telescope on the shoulder of his aide-de-camp and pointed it down at the scene. Hornblower was looking through his own glass; the big barges which had brought the landing party were lying deserted on the beach, and the boats which were conveying back his crews which had manned them were already safely out of range. Essen's hand on his shoulder swung him round.

"See there, Commodore!" said Essen.

Hornblower's glass revealed to him in a flash the thing to which Essen had wanted to call his attention. Isolated infantrymen from the besiegers were ranging over no man's land on their way back to their own trenches and—Hornblower saw it done—they bayoneted the Russian wounded who lay heaped in their path. Perhaps it was only to be expected, in this long and bloody siege, that bitterness and ferocity should be engendered on this scale, especially among Bonaparte's hordes who had wandered over Europe for years now, since boyhood, living on what they could gather from the countryside, with the musket and bayonet as the only court of appeal. Essen was white with anger, and Hornblower tried to share his rage, but he found it difficult. That kind of atrocity was what he had come to expect. He was perfectly prepared to go on killing Bonaparte's soldiers and sailors, but he would not flatter himself that he was executing justice by killing one man because some other man had murdered his wounded allies.

Down in the shattered remains of the village, as he walked along the trenches, those of the wounded who had been fortunate enough to drag themselves back were receiving treatment. Shuddering, Hornblower told himself that perhaps those who had been bayoneted in no man's land were the lucky ones. He pushed past ranks of smoke-blackened and ragged Russian soldiers, talking with the noisy abandon of men who have just emerged from a hard-won victory.

Chapter XXII

AMONG the mass of long-delayed mail from England were great packets of printed pamphlets, in French and in German, a few even in Dutch and in Danish. They were appeals to Bonaparte's forces to desert his standard—not suggestions for mass desertions, but intended for the individual soldier, telling him that he could be sure of a welcome if he were to come over. They denied the statement that Bonaparte was continually making in his proclamations, to the effect that England confined her prisoners in floating hells of hulks, and that deserters were forced by ill treatment to take service in England's mercenary regiments. They offered a life of ease and security, with the honourable alternative, only if requested, of enlistment in British forces, to those who wished to strike a blow against the tyrant. The French pamphlet was certainly well written, and presumably the others were too; maybe Canning, or that fellow—what was his name, now?—Hookham Frere—had had a hand in composing them.

The letter that accompanied the pamphlets, charging him to do his utmost to get them into the hands of Bonaparte's forces, had an interesting enclosure—a copy of a letter from Bonaparte to Marmont, intercepted presumably somewhere in Spain, in which the Emperor raged against this new evidence of British falseness and perfidy. He had seen some of the first pamphlets, apparently, and they had touched him on a sore spot. Judging by the wording of his letter, he was driven quite frantic at this attempt to seduce his men from their allegiance. If the violence of the imperial reaction was any guide, then this method of warfare was likely to be effective. The usually well-fed and well-cared-for Prussians under Macdonald's command were on meagre rations now that the country round had been stripped bare by foragers; an offer of a life of well-fed ease combined with an appeal to their patriotism might bring in deserters in plenty. Hornblower mapped out in his mind a formal letter to the governor in which he would suggest that a few pedlars be sent into the French camp ostensibly to sell luxuries but really to distribute these pamphlets. Here where Bonaparte's men were suffering real hardship and meeting with small success the appeal might carry more weight than with Bonaparte's main army in Moscow; Hornblower was inclined to distrust the flamboyant Russian bulletin about the burning of Moscow, and Alexander's fervent public declaration that he would never make peace while a Frenchman was on Russian soil. In Hornblower's opinion French morale was likely to be still high enough, and Bonaparte's strength still great enough, to force peace at the bayonet's point from Russia in the Russian capital, be the destruction of Moscow never so great—even as great as Moscow said it was.

Someone knocked at the door.

"Come in," bellowed Hornblower, irritated at the

interruption, for he had intended to spend all day catching up on his arrears of paper work.

"A letter from the beach, sir," said the midshipman of the watch.

It was a brief note from the governor with its point compressed into a single sentence:—

I have some new arrivals in the city who I think will interest you if you can spare the time for a visit.

Hornblower sighed; his report to London would never be finished apparently, but he could not ignore this invitation.

"Call away my barge," he said to the midshipman, and turned to lock his desk.

God knew who these "new arrivals" would be. The Russians were sometimes so portentously mysterious about trifles. It might be a fool's errand, but on the other hand he must find out what this new development was before sending off his despatch to England. As his barge danced across the water he looked over at the siege lines; the battering guns were still volleying away—he had grown so used to the noise that he only noticed it when his attention was called to it—and the usual long pall of smoke lay over the flat country there.

Then the boat entered the mouth of the river and Daugavgriva's ruins were hidden from view save for the dome of the church where he had so often stood. Riga came steadily nearer and nearer, and they had to keep close to the bank to avoid the worst of the Dwina's rapid current, until at last the oars ceased and the barge slid against the steps of the river wall. At the head of them waited the governor with his staff and a spare horse for Hornblower.

"It is only a short ride," said Essen, "and one I think you will consider worth the making."

Hornblower climbed onto his horse, with a nod of

273

thanks to the groom who held its head, and then they all wheeled and dashed away through the clattering streets. A postern was opened for them in the eastern fortifications—so far no enemy had shown his face to this bank of the Dwina—and they rode out over a drawbridge spanning the ditch. On the glacis beyond the ditch was a large force of soldiers, squatting and lying in rank; as soon as the cavalcade appeared they came hastily to their feet, dressed their lines, and then, in obedience to a shrill chorus of bugles, presented arms, their regimental colours fluttering in the little breeze. Essen reined up, returning the salute.

"Well, what do you think of them, sir?" he asked Hornblower with a chuckle.

They were ragged soldiers—bare skin showed frequently in the ranks through holes in the blue or dirty grey uniforms. They were shambling, unsoldierly soldiers, too; any troops who had seen hard service might be ragged, but Hornblower, looking along the ranks, had the impression of voluntary dirt and disorder. Essen was still chuckling, and Hornblower looked the harder to find the reason for this mirth. Essen would not have brought him out here just to see ragged soldiers—Hornblower had seen enough of those in the past three months to last him the rest of his life. There were several thousand men, a strong brigade or a weak division; Hornblower glanced at the regimental standards to ascertain the number of units present, and then he nearly lost his precarious seat with surprise. Those flags were red and yellow, the national colours of Spain, and the moment this dawned upon him he realised that the ragged uniforms were the remains of the Bourbon white and blue he had come so much to hate ten years ago during his captivity at Ferrol. Not only that, but on the left of the line there was a single standard of silver and blue—the Portuguese flag, held aloft before a single shrunken battalion of scarecrows.

"I thought you would be surprised, sir," said Essen, still chuckling.

"Who are these men?" asked Hornblower.

"Some of Bonaparte's willing allies," explained Essen, ironically. "They were in St. Cyr's corps at Polotsk. One day they found themselves on the very fringe of the outpost line, and fought their way down the river to join us. Come and meet their general."

He urged his horse forward, and he and Hornblower cantered up to where a ragged officer sat a bony white horse at the head of an even worse-mounted staff.

"I have the honour to present," said Essen, formally, "His Excellency the Conde de los Altos—His Excellency Commodore Sir Horatio Hornblower."

The Conde saluted; it took Hornblower a few moments to make himself think in Spanish—the last time he had used that language was during the abortive attack on Rosas, two years ago.

"It is highly gratifying to meet Your Excellency," he said.

The Conde's expression revealed his startled pleasure at being addressed in his own tongue, and he replied rapidly.

"You are the English admiral, sir?"

Hornblower did not see fit to enter into explanations regarding the difference between an admiral and a commodore. He merely nodded.

"I have asked that my men and the Portuguese be returned by sea to Spain, there to fight against Bonaparte on our own soil. They tell me that as this can only be done by sea your consent must be secured. You will grant it, of course, sir?"

That was asking a good deal. Five thousand men at four tons a man meant twenty thousand tons of shipping—a large convoy; it would be straining his powers for him to pledge his government to provide twenty thousand tons of shipping to carry the Spaniards from Riga to Spain. There never were enough ships. And there was also the question of the moral effect on the garrison of Riga if they were to see this seasonable reinforcement which had dropped from the clouds, so to speak, shipped away again as soon as it arrived. Yet on the other hand there was a chance that Russia might make peace with Bonaparte, and in that case the sooner these Spaniards were beyond the clutches of either country the better. Five thousand men would make a considerable army in Spain—where the Spaniards were likely to do their best—while it was only a trifling force in this continental war of millions. But none of this was of nearly as much importance as the moral side. What would be the effect on the other unwilling allies of Bonaparte, the Prussians and the Austrians, the Bavarians and the Italians, when they heard that a national contingent not merely had fought its way to join the allies, but had been received with open arms, feted and made much of, and finally shipped back to their native land with the least possible delay? Hornblower expected a tremendous revulsion of feeling among Bonaparte's satellites, especially if the Russians executed their determination to keep on fighting through the winter. This might be the beginning of the crumbling of Bonaparte's empire.

"I shall be very happy to send you and your men to Spain as quickly as it can be arranged," he said. "I will issue orders today for shipping to be collected."

The Conde was profuse in his thanks, but Hornblower had something to add.

"There is one thing I ask in return," he said, and the Conde's countenance fell a little.

"What is it, sir?" he asked. The embittered suspicion resulting from years of being a victim of international double-dealing, of lies and deception and threats—from Godoy's pitiful subterfuges to Bonaparte's mailed-fisted bullying—showed instantly in his face.

"Your signature to a proclamation, that is all. I shall endeavour to circulate among Bonaparte's other forced allies the news of your joining the cause of liberty, and I would like you to attest its truth."

The Conde darted one more keen look at Hornblower before he agreed.

"I will sign it," he said.

That immediate consent was a pretty compliment, first to Hornblower's obvious honesty of purpose, and second to the reputation the navy had acquired of always fulfilling its engagements.

"There is nothing more to be done, then," said Hornblower, "save to draw up the proclamation and to find ships for your forces."

Essen was fidgeting in his saddle beside them while this conversation was going on in Spanish; he clearly knew no word of that language and was restless in consequence—Hornblower found it gratifying, for during the past few months he had had to be an uncomprehending listener to so many conversations in Russian and German. This was some slight revenge.

"Has he told you about conditions in Bonaparte's army?" asked Essen. "Have you heard about the hunger and the disease?"

"Not yet," said Hornblower.

The story came out rapidly, staccato, drawn from the Conde's lips by explosive promptings from Essen. Bonaparte's army had been dying on its feet long before it reached Moscow; hunger and disease had thinned its ranks as Bonaparte hurried it by forced marches across the desolated plains.

"The horses are nearly all dead already. There was only green rye to give them," said the Conde.

If the horses were dead it would be impossible to drag supplies in to the main body of the army; it would have to scatter or starve, and as long as the Russians had any sort of army in existence it would be impossible for the main body to scatter. As long as Alexander's nerve held, as long as he maintained the struggle, there was still hope. It began to seem certain that Bonaparte's army in Moscow had spent its strength, and the only way in which the French could bring fresh pressure upon Alexander would be by advancing upon St. Petersburg with the army here before Riga. That made it more imperative still to hold on here. Hornblower felt considerable doubt as to Alexander's constancy if he were to lose both his capitals.

The wretched Spanish infantry had been standing presenting arms during all this long conversation, and Hornblower felt uncomfortable about them. He let his attention wander to them obviously, recalling the Conde to a sense of his duty. The Conde gave an order to his staff, and the colonels repeated it; the regiments ordered arms awkwardly and then stood easy.

"His Excellency tells me," said the Conde, "that you have recently served in Spain, sir. What is the news of my country?"

It was not easy to give a thumbnail sketch of the complicated history of the Peninsula for the last four years, to a Spaniard who had been cut off from all news during that time. Hornblower did his best, glossing over the innumerable Spanish defeats, laying stress on the devotion and efficiency of the *guerrilleros,* and ending on a hopeful note as he told of Wellington's recent capture of Madrid. The Spanish staff pressed more and more closely around him as he spoke. For four long years, ever since the Spanish people had declared their will, ceasing to be subservient allies and becoming the most bitter enemies of the Empire, Bonaparte had seen to it that these Spanish troops of his, three thousand miles from home, had received not a single word which might tell them of the real situation in Spain. They had had only the lying imperial bulletins on which to base their vague theories. It was a strange experience to talk to these exiles; Hornblower felt a curious sensation, as if there were an actual movement inside his brain, as he remembered the conditions in which he himself had learned of the Spanish change of front. That had been on the deck of the *Lydia,* in the uncharted tropical

Pacific. For a few seconds his brain was a battle-ground of memories. The blue and gold of the Pacific, the heat and the storms and the fighting there, El Supremo and the Governor of Panama—he had to tear himself away from them to bring himself back to this parade ground on the shores of the Baltic.

An orderly officer was galloping madly towards them, the dust flying from beneath the ringing hoofs of his charger. He reined up before Essen with a perfunctory salute, the words of his message pouring from his lips before his hands had left his forehead. A word from the governor sent him flying back whence he came, and Essen turned to Hornblower.

"The enemy is massing in his trenches," he said. "They are about to assault Daugavgriva."

Essen began blaring orders to his staff; horses wheeled and pranced as spurs were struck into their sides and the cruel bits dragged their heads round. In a moment half a dozen officers were galloping in different directions with the messages flung at them.

"I'm going there," said Essen.

"I shall come too," said Hornblower.

Hornblower found it hard to stay in the saddle as his excited horse swung round beside the governor's; he had to resettle himself, his hand on the pommel, and regain his lost stirrup as they clattered along. Essen turned his head with another order shouted to one of the few remaining orderlies accompanying them, and then spurred his horse yet again; as the brute sprung forward with increased speed the low muttering of the bombardment increased in intensity. They clattered through the streets of Riga, and the timber road bed of the boat bridge roared under their horses' hoofs. The sweat was running from Hornblower's face in the clear autumn sunshine, his sword leaped against his thigh, and time and again his cocked hat rode precariously up his forehead and was only saved by a hurried grab at the last moment. Hornblower was conscious of the swirling water of the Dwina as they crossed the bridge, and then on his right land as they galloped along the quays. The roar of the bombardment grew louder and louder, and then suddenly died away.

"It is the moment of the assault!" bellowed Essen, bending his clumsy body forward in an effort to get more speed out of his labouring horse.

Now they were in the village itself, among the ruins of the cottages, and here they met broken troops, stumbling back pell-mell, blue uniforms grey with dust, with cursing officers trying to rally them, and beating the stupefied men with the flats of their swords. Essen's voice blared out again, like a tuneless trumpet; he was waving his sword over his head and spurring forward into the press. At the sight of him the men began to rally, turning back to face the enemy, and instinctively closing together into line.

Down through the ruins came a disordered column of the enemy—it must have come up over the breach like a whirlwind. By now it was more of a mob than a column, officers capering at the head of their men, waving their hats and swords. A standard waved over them. The appearance of a formed line caused a momentary hesitation, and ragged firing broke out on both sides; Hornblower saw one of the capering officers fall dead as he called to his men to come on. He looked over at Essen, but he was still towering high in the smoke. Hornblower wheeled his horse towards the flank; his mind was working with the ecstatic speed of excitement, bullets were singing by him, and he knew that this was the crisis of the assault. Halt an attacking column for one moment, and then any trifle might turn the scale, and it would go back as fast as it had advanced. He reached the door of the church just as a flood of men came pouring out of it—the garrison of the building hastening to make good their retreat before they should be cut off and isolated. Hornblower tore his sword from his sheath, miraculously retaining his seat in the saddle.

"Come on!" he yelled, waving the weapon.

They did not understand his words, as they blinked at this vision in blue and gold before them, but anyone could understand his gestures. At the back of the group Hornblower caught a momentary glimpse of Clausewitz and Diebitsch, who should have taken command here, but there was no time for argument, and racing through Hornblower's brain went the conviction at the same time that although they might be scientific soldiers they would be useless in a physical rough-and-tumble like this.

"Come on!" yelled Hornblower again, pointing with his sword at the flank of the assaulting column.

The men turned to follow him—no one could have resisted the inspiration of his example and gestures. Column and line were still exchanging ragged volleys, the column still moving forward little by little, the line wavering and falling back.

"Form line!" yelled Hornblower, turning in his saddle, his spread arms and gesticulating fists telling the Russians what he wanted them to do. "Load your muskets!"

They formed their line, marching up after him, hands busy with their ramrods—a couple of hundred men at most, jostling each other as they stumbled over the ruins of the cottages. Now they were right on the flank of the column; Hornblower saw faces turn towards them. He was even near enough to see surprise and dismay in the attitudes of the men who suddenly realised that a new force was about to assail their flank.

"Fire!" yelled Hornblower, and some sort of volley crashed out from the ragged line he led.

He saw two ramrods sail forward in soaring arcs, fired out of their muskets by excited men who had been caught in the act of loading by his order, and who had incontinently put their weapons to their shoulders and pulled their triggers. One ramrod buried itself like an arrow in the body of a French soldier. The column wavered and staggered—not one man in a hundred there had expected this attack on the flank; all their attention had been taken up by Essen's line in front of them.

"Charge!" yelled Hornblower, waving his sword and urging his horse forward.

The Russians followed him with a cheer; the whole column of the enemy, Hornblower saw, was wavering and melting away, the disordered ranks crumbling. They were turning their backs, and the memory streaked through his excited mind of a saying he had heard somewhere to the effect that the knapsacks of the enemy were the most cheering sight a soldier could behold. Then he saw one of the enemy swing back again and level his musket at him. As the smoke gushed from the barrel his horse gave a convulsive leap and then put his nose to the ground and somer-saulted; for a moment Hornblower felt himself flying through the air; he was too excited and exalted to feel any fear, so that the crash with which he hit the earth came as a startling surprise to him. But even though the breath was dashed from his body and the jar shook every bone in it, his fantastic mind still thought clearly, and he heard and felt the flank attack which he had led sweep cheering over him. Only when he rose to his feet did he come to the sudden realisation that he was bruised and weak, so that it was hard to balance on his legs—they nearly gave way under him as he hobbled forward to pick up his sword which lay shining on the dusty earth between two dead men.

He felt suddenly alone, but the feeling had hardly time to take hold of him when he was engulfed in a wave of humanity, Essen and his staff roaring with exaltation and delight. He stood there, bruised and torn, his sword dangling from his hand, as they over-whelmed him with incomprehensible congratulations. One of the officers leaped down from his horse, and Hornblower was hauled and pushed up into the saddle, and they cantered forward, the horses picking their way delicately over the dead and wounded, over the tortured ground, towards the ramparts. The last remnants of the assaulting forces were being driven back through the breach to the accompaniment of a straggling musketry fire. As they neared the fortifications the guns of the foiled besiegers reopened fire, and a shot or two came howling overhead. Essen reined up, like a sensible man, and then walked his horse out of the line of fire.

"That was a moment to remember," he said, looking round at the area where the clash had occurred.

Hornblower's head was still clear. He realised what a bitter blow this reverse must be to the besiegers. After all the fierce preliminary fighting they had sapped up to the ramparts, made their breach, and launched the assault which should have captured the place, only to be flung back when the breach was in their hands. He knew that Macdonald would have the greatest difficulty in inducing his men to assault again—a bloody failure like this would make them sulky and grudging of their lives. Certainly Macdonald would have to allow a considerable time to elapse, and would have to continue his battering for several more days, and multiply his approaches and parallels, before he could risk another assault. Maybe the town would hold. Maybe that attack would be the last. Hornblower felt prophetic, inspired. He remembered how he had heard the news of Masséna's retreat from before Lisbon—that had been the first of the ebb of the Empire in the south, and now Wellington was in Madrid and threatening France. Maybe Riga would mark the limits of the Empire in the north. Maybe that penetration through the breach would be remembered as the farthest north Bonaparte's men would ever attain. At that rate— Hornblower's pulse beat quicker—the flank attack he had led, the unforeseen charge of a couple of hundred men hurriedly gathered up in the tumult, had been the blow which had thwarted Bonaparte's schemes to conquer the world. That was what he had done. And it would look extraordinarily well in *The Times* that "Commodore Sir Horatio Hornblower, K.B., had his horse killed under him while leading a charge." Barbara would be pleased.

Exultation and inspiration ended abruptly, and Hornblower felt suddenly weak and ill. He knew that if he did not dismount quickly he would fall from his saddle. He took hold of the pommel and kicked his right foot clear of the stirrup, swung his leg over, and then as his feet touched ground the ground came up to meet him. He only recovered some indefinite number of minutes later, to find himself seated on the ground, his stock unbuckled, and his face clammy with cold sweat. Essen was bending anxiously over him, and someone, apparently a surgeon, was kneeling at his side. His sleeve was rolled up above the elbow, and the surgeon, lancet in hand, was about to open a vein to bleed him. Hornblower withdrew his arm abruptly, for he did not want to be touched by that thing, nor by those hands which were black with other men's blood.

The assembled staff raised their voices in protest, but Hornblower disregarded them with the sublime abstraction of a sick man. Then Brown appeared, cutlass at his side and pistols in his belt, followed by other members of the barge's crew. Apparently he had seen his captain ride over the bridge, and, like the good subordinate he was, had brought the boat across after him. Brown's face was contorted with anxiety, and he threw himself, too, on his knees beside Hornblower.

"Wounded, sir? Where is it? Can I—"

"No no no," said Hornblower pettishly, pushing Brown away and getting to his feet, swaying. "It's nothing."

It was extraordinarily maddening to see a look of admiration come over Brown's face. Anyone would think he was being heroic instead of merely sensible. Not far away—at the foot of the beach, apparently—a trumpet was pealing, high challenging notes, and this served to distract the crowd from their solicitude. Everyone looked in the direction of the sound, and presently a group of Russian officers approached them, leading a blindfold figure dressed in the blue trimmed with grey astrakhan of the French imperial staff. A word from Essen removed the bandage, and the officer—he wore a grey Hussar moustache—saluted with dignity.

"The *Chef d'Escadron* Verrier," he said, "aide-de-camp to Marshal the Duke of Tarentum. I am ordered by the Marshal to suggest a suspension of hostilities for two hours. The breach is covered with the wounded of both sides, and it would be only humane to remove them. Each side can remove its own."

"There are more French and German wounded than Russian, I am sure," said Essen, in his horrible French.

"French or Russian, sir," said the *parlementaire*, "they will die unless they receive speedy aid."

Hornblower's mind was beginning to work again. Ideas were leaping to the surface like wreckage from a sunken ship. He caught Essen's eye and nodded meaningly, and Essen, like a good diplomatist, gave no sign of having received the hint as he shifted his glance back to Verrier.

"The request is granted, sir," he said, "in the name of humanity."

"I thank Your Excellency, in the name of humanity," said Verrier, saluting, and then looking round for someone to blindfold him again and lead him through the breach.

The moment he was gone Hornblower turned.

"Take the barge back to the ship," he ordered Brown. "Hurry. My compliments to Captain Bush, and I would like you to bring back Lieutenant von Bülow to me. One of the lieutenants of equal rank will have to accompany him. Hurry!"

"Aye aye, sir."

That was all that was necessary with Brown or with Bush, thank God. A simple order brought simple yet intelligent obedience. Hornblower saluted Essen.

"Would it be possible, Your Excellency," he asked, "to bring the Spanish troops over to this side of the river? I have a German prisoner whom I am going to return to the enemy, and I should like him to see the Spaniards with his own eyes first."

Essen grinned with blubber lips.

"I do my best not merely to comply with every one of your wishes, sir, but even to anticipate them. The last order I gave on the other side of the river was for the Spaniards to be brought over—they were the nearest formed troops and I intended to use them as garrison for the warehouses on the quay. I have no doubt they are there already. You would like them marched in this direction?"

"If you would be so kind, sir."

Hornblower was casually waiting for nothing in particular at the jetty when the boat touched at it, and Lieutenant von Bülow, of the Fifty First Regiment of Prussian Infantry, stepped ashore under the escort of Mr. Tooth and Brown and his men.

"Ah, Lieutenant," said Hornblower.

Bülow saluted him stiffly, clearly puzzled at this new development, which had snatched him from his confinement aboard ship and dumped him at a moment's notice in the ruined village.

"There is an armistice at the moment," explained Hornblower, "between your army and ours. No, it is not peace—merely to clear the wounded from the breach. But I was going to take this opportunity of returning you to your friends."

Bülow looked questions at him.

"It will save much formality with cartels and flags of truce," explained Hornblower. "At this moment you have merely to walk down the breach and join the men of your own army. Naturally, you have not been properly exchanged, but you can, if you wish, give me your word that you will not serve against His Britannic Majesty nor against His Imperial Russian Majesty until an exchange has been effected."

"I give you my word," said Bülow, after a moment's thought.

"Excellent! Then perhaps I might give myself the pleasure of walking with you as far as the breach?"

As they left the jetty and began the brief walk through the ruins of the village Bülow was darting the quick glances of a professional soldier about him; he was perfectly entitled, under any military code, to take every advantage of carelessness on his enemy's part. His professional curiosity would have led him to stare about him in any case. Hornblower made polite conversation as they strolled.

"Your assault this morning—I daresay you heard the hubbub even on board?—was made by picked grenadiers, as far as I could judge by the uniforms. Most excellent troops—it is indeed a pity they suffered such loss of life. I trust that when you rejoin your friends you will convey to them my deepest condolences. But they had not a chance, of course." At the foot of the church tower there was a Spanish regiment, the men lying down in their ranks. At the sight of Hornblower the colonel called his men to their feet and saluted. Hornblower returned the salute, conscious as he did so that Bülow at his side had suddenly changed his gait; stealing a glance out of the tail of his eye he saw that Bülow was ponderously goose-stepping as long as the salutes were being exchanged. Yet it was very noticeable that even though Bülow's formal training forced him into a goose-step at a moment of military courtesy, he had not failed to notice the troops. His eyes were bulging with unasked questions.

"Spanish troops," said Hornblower, casually. "A division of Spaniards and Portuguese joined us from

Bonaparte's main army a little while ago. They fight well—in fact they were responsible for the final repulse of the last assault. It is interesting to notice how Bonaparte's dupes are falling away from him now that the hollowness of his power is revealed."

Bülow's astonished reply must either have been inarticulate or in German, for Hornblower could not understand it, but his tone conveyed his meaning well enough.

"It goes without saying," said Hornblower casually, "that I would like to see the magnificent Prussian army ranged among Bonaparte's enemies and England's allies, too. But naturally your King knows his own policy best—unless, of course, surrounded as he is by Bonaparte's men, he is not free to choose."

Bülow stared at him in amazement; Hornblower was putting forward a viewpoint which was quite new to him, but Hornblower still made himself talk with the utmost casualness, as if he were doing no more than making polite conversation.

"That's high politics," he said with a laugh and a wave of his hand. "But one day in the future we might look back on this conversation as prophetic. One cannot tell, can one? Sometime when we meet as plenipotentiaries I will be able to remind you of this talk. And here we are at the breach. It irks me to have to say good-bye, at the same moment as it gives me pleasure to restore you to your friends. My heartiest good wishes, sir, for you for the future."

Bülow saluted stiffly again, and then, as Hornblower held out his hand, shook hands with him. To the Prussian it was a remarkable occurrence, for a commodore to condescend to shake hands with a mere subaltern. He picked his way down the breach, over the tortured earth where the stretcher-bearers still swarmed like disturbed ants, gathering in the wounded. Hornblower watched him until he reached his own men, and then turned away. He was dreadfully tired, quite weak with fatigue, in fact, and he was angry at himself for his weakness. It was all he could do to walk back with dignity to the jetty, and he swayed as he sat in the sternsheets of his barge.

"Are you all right, sir?" asked Brown, solicitously.

"Of course I am," snapped Hornblower, amazed at the man's impertinence.

The question irritated him, and the irritation made him mount the ship side as fast as he could, and acknowledge merely coldly the salutes he received on the quarterdeck; down in his cabin his irritation persisted, and prevented him from obeying his first impulse to throw himself across his cot and relax. He paced about for a moment. For something to do he peered into the mirror. There was some excuse for Brown, after all, and his foolish questions. The face he looked at was grimy with dust caked upon sweat, and there was a smear of blood over one cheek-bone from a slight scratch. His uniform was filthy, with one epaulette awry. He looked like someone who had just emerged from the fury of a battle to the death.

He peered more closely. That face was lined and drawn, the eyes red-rimmed; with a sudden increase of attention he looked again, turning his head. On his temples his hair was quite white. Not merely did he look like someone fresh from battle; he looked like someone who had been under frightful strain for a long time. So he had, indeed, he realised, half wondering at himself. He had been bearing the burden of this horrible siege for months now. It had never occurred to him that his face, Hornblower's face, would tell tales about him as other men's faces told tales about them. He had striven all his life to restrain his features from revealing his feelings. There was something ironic and interesting about the fact that he could not prevent his hair from greying, nor the grim lines from deepening about his mouth.

The deck under his feet was swaying, as if the ship were in the open sea, and yet even his veteran sea legs had difficulty in keeping him upright, so that he had to hold onto the bracket before him. Only with extreme care could he let go his hold and pick his way to his cot, and fall across it, face downward.

Chapter XXIII

THE new problem which Hornblower was debating as he walked his quarterdeck, while H.M.S. *Nonsuch* swung at anchor in Riga Bay, was one which he had long foreseen, but which lost none of its urgency for all that. Here was winter coming; there had been heavy frosts at night for as far back as he could remember, and the last two days had brought flurries of snow, which had temporarily whitened the landscape and had left a few drifts which even now showed as white streaks on the nothern faces of the dykes. The days were growing short and the nights long, and the brackish water of Riga Bay was covered with a thin scum of ice. If he stayed much longer his ships would be frozen in. Essen had assured him that for at least two more weeks he would be able to make his exit along a channel sawn in the ice by labourers whom Essen would supply, but Hornblower was not so sure. A northerly gale—and one might arise at any moment—could keep him wind-bound while at the same time it would freeze everything up and jam the narrow exit to the bay, between Oesel and the mainland, with piled-up drift ice that neither saws nor even explosives could pierce. A squadron frozen in was a squadron immobilised until next spring; and a squadron frozen in was one which was certain prey to the French if Riga should fall. Twenty years ago a Dutch squadron at Amsterdam had been captured by French Hussars charging over the ice. What a thundering bulletin of triumph Bonaparte would make of it if a British squadron, under the notorious Commodore Hornblower, should fall into his hands in the same way! Hornblower turned in his stride a yard before he had reached the limit of his walk. Prudence dictated an immediate withdrawal.

The breechings of that carronade were frayed. When Bush noticed it someone was in for a bad quarter of an hour. And yet he could not withdraw. When he had mentioned the possibility Essen had shown positive dismay. If his men were to see the British ships go away they would be quite sure the place was doomed. They would lose heart completely. The British naval officer who had led the final charge at Daugavgriva had grown into a legendary figure in their minds, a mascot, a symbol of good luck. If he were to leave them that would be a proof, in the men's minds, that he had lost hope. He could not possibly withdraw. He might compromise; he might send most of the squadron out and retain only a sloop and a gunboat; he might send everything out and remain himself, but to separate himself from his command was in direct violation of the Articles of War.

Here was a fool of a midshipman in his way, dodging about in front of him as though bent on distracting him from his train of thought. It would be the masthead for him; God knew the commission had lasted long enough for every single person on board to have learned that the commodore must not be distracted when he was walking the deck.

"What the hell?—?" he bellowed at the blenching midshipman.

"B—b—boat approaching, sir," stammered the youth. "M—Mr. Hurst told me to tell you. He thinks the governor's on board."

"Why wasn't I told before?" said Hornblower. "Have you sent for Captain Bush, Mr. Hurst? Call the guard!"

"Aye aye, sir!" said Hurst, and Hornblower saw Bush appear on the quarterdeck as the words left

291

Hurst's lips, and the marine guard was already forming up abaft the mizzenmast.

Of course Hurst had done all these things without waiting for orders; roused abruptly from his reverie Hornblower had not had the sense to realise it. He strode to the side. The governor was approaching in a big pulling boat, which was steering towards them along the clear channel through the thin ice which the last eddies of the Dwina, never still, kept clear before they lost themselves in the bay. As the governor caught sight of him he sprang up into the stern-sheets waving his cocked hat; he even tried to dance, precariously, both arms extended over his head, at imminent risk of falling overboard.

"Something's up, sir," said Bush at Hornblower's side.

"That looks like good news," said Hornblower.

The governor arrived on the quarterdeck, hat still in hand. He flung his arms round Hornblower and hugged him, swinging his lean body up into the air so that his feet left the deck. Hornblower could imagine the grins that were being exchanged around him, as he kicked in the air like a baby. The governor put him down, clapped his hat on his head, and then seized first Hornblower's hand and then Bush's, and tried to dance a sort of ring-a-ring-of-roses with the two Englishmen. There was no more controlling him than one could control a bear.

"What is the news, Your Excellency?" asked Hornblower; Essen's grip on his hand was painful.

"Oh," said Essen, flinging the Englishmen's hands away so as to spread his arms again. "Bonaparte has started to retreat."

"Has he, by God!" said Hornblower.

"What does he say, sir?" asked Bush, quite incapable of understanding Essen's French, but Hornblower had no time for Bush, because the governor was pouring out his news in a torrent of gutturals, drawing upon the vocabularies of half Europe for his words so that even Hornblower could hardly understand what he was saying.

"He left Moscow five days back," roared Essen. "We beat him at Malo-Yaroslavets. Beat him in a pitched battle, and now he's running as hard as he can for Smolensk and Warsaw. And he won't get there before the snows! He'll be lucky if he gets there at all! Chichagov is marching hard to cut off his retreat at the Berezina. He's ruined. They're dying in thousands every night already! Nothing to eat, and winter's here!"

Essen stamped grotesquely about the deck, more like a dancing bear than ever.

"Please, sir, *please*. What does he say?" asked Bush pathetically.

Hornblower translated to the best of his ability, the other quarterdeck officers eavesdropping shamelessly. As the wonderful nature of the good news dawned upon them, they began to cheer; down on the main deck they caught the infection, and all through the ship men were cheering and tossing their hats in the air, even though they hardly knew what they were cheering about, save for the hurried words that flew from lip to lip—"Boney's beaten!"

"We can get out of this bay before the ice comes, by God!" said Bush, snapping his fingers; it was obvious that if he had not a wooden leg he would be dancing too.

Hornblower looked across at the mainland.

"Macdonald's shown no sign of retreating yet," he said. "If he had the governor would have mentioned it."

"But don't you think he'll have to, sir?" Bush's expressive face showed anxiety now instead of joy. A moment before anything delightful had been possible—escape from Riga Bay, possibly even escape from this landlocked Baltic altogether, maybe even a return to England, but now Bush was back again to the cold reality that the siege of Riga was still going on.

"He may have to retreat," said Hornblower, "but until then we stay here, unless I receive orders to the contrary."

Essen caught sight of their sober faces and turned on them again. He slapped Bush on the back so that he staggered with the force of the blow; he snapped his fingers under Hornblower's nose, and pirouetted with the grace of a performing seal. It was absurd that with all this going on, with Bush asking questions regarding the future, with Essen acting like a lunatic, and with the whole ship forgetting discipline in a mad outburst of cheering, Hornblower's brain should be planning and thinking still, with that swift clarity and that fevered rapidity which he knew by now portended some new development. Bonaparte in retreat, Bonaparte beaten, meant a tremendous revulsion of feeling throughout Europe. All the world knew that Wellington was threatening France from the south; and now the Empire was in peril from the east. It would hardly be possible for Bonaparte's shattered army to hold onto Poland once it had begun its retreat; the next campaign would see the allies on the frontiers of Prussia and Austria, and it was likely that both Prussia and Austria would in that case be glad to change sides. The King of Prussia was practically a prisoner in French hands, but the Prussian army—the greater part of the force now besieging Riga—could act as a free agent if it wished. The desertion of the Spaniards had shown them the way, and the pamphlets which he had had printed in Riga and distributed among the besiegers by Russian pedlars would not let them forget the lesson. Bülow would be able to bear witness to the truth of his assertions—Hornblower was glad he had set him free.

"I am sending Diebitsch out to beat up the besiegers' lines with a sally," Essen was saying. "I must see how *they* take this news. Would you care to accompany me, sir?"

"Of course," said Hornblower, coming out abruptly from his dreaming. What with fatigue—he was always weary now—and rapid thinking and excitement he was still a little "mazy," as they said of fuddled men in the village when he was a boy. He announced his departure to Bush.

"You're worn-out, sir," protested Bush. "You're no more than a shadow. Send someone else, sir. Send me. Send Duncan. You've done all that's necessary, sir."

"I haven't yet," said Hornblower, but he stooped so far as to risk delay by offering Essen refreshment, with the suggestion that they should drink a toast to celebrate this glorious news.

"Thank you, no," said Essen, to Hornblower's relief. "Diebitsch will attack at dusk, and the days are short now."

"You'll take your barge, sir, won't you?" persisted Bush. "Take Brown."

Bush was like a fussy parent with a venturesome child—like a hen with one chick. He was always nervous about entrusting his precious Hornblower to these unpredictable Russians; Hornblower grinned at Bush's solicitude.

"Anything to keep you happy," he said.

Hornblower's barge followed the governor's pulling boat along the channel through the ice; Hornblower sat with the governor in the stern of the Russian boat. There was a chill wind blowing, and the skies were grey.

"We shall have more snow," said Essen, looking up at the clouds. "God help the French."

In the absence of any sunshine there was a mortal chill in the air. Hornblower thought of the French marching over the desolate plains of Russia, and was sorry for them. And the snow came indeed, that afternoon, sweeping over river and village, making white innocuous mounds of the battered parapets and the

295

shattered guns and the graves which were scattered through the village. It was already prematurely dark when the ever-patient Russian grenadiers lined the trenches and then sallied forth upon the enemy's lines. They were not more than half-way across no man's land before the guns began to fire upon them, stabbing the falling snow with their bright orange flashes.

"No sign of any retreat there," was Clausewitz' comment as he watched the fierce struggle from the gallery of the church, beside Essen and Hornblower.

And if confirmation was needed the attacking party could supply it when it came drifting back in the darkness, decimated. The besiegers had met their sally with spirit; they had had patrols out in no man's land, and the trenches were adequately guarded. In retaliation, the besiegers opened fire with their breaching batteries; the ground shook to the rumble of the discharges, and the black night was stabbed again by the flames of the guns. It was impossible to maintain good aim or elevation in the darkness; it was only a short time before the shots were flying wild, all over the village, so that the defenders as far back as the Dwina River had to keep low in their trenches. Shells were coming over, too, curving in high arcs from the mortar batteries which the besiegers had established in their second parallel. They fell and burst here, there, and everywhere, one every two or three minutes, in fountains of fragments and flame, save when chance guided them into deeper snow which extinguished the fuses.

"They have plenty of ammunition to waste," grumbled Essen, shivering in his cloak.

"Perhaps they plan a counter-assault in the darkness," said Clausewitz. "I have kept the trenches fully manned in case they try it."

Immediately under Hornblower's gaze there was a battery of four heavy pieces, firing regular salvos at short intervals. He noted the four bursts of flame over and over again, so that when there was a longer interval he was surprised first by the absence of sound and then by its unexpected coming. The flashes endured their brief moment, to be succeeded again by night, but Hornblower found himself wondering what difference there had been between this salvo and the last, apart from the longer interval which had preceded it. One flash—the right-hand one—had not been as distinct as the other three, longer and yet intense. Some error in loading, perhaps. Then came the next salvo, and only three flashes; the right-hand gun had not fired. Maybe it had "unbushed" itself—blown out its vent fitting, as guns sometimes did. Another long interval, and then another salvo—two sharp flashes, and one longer one. The next salvo only two guns fired, and Hornblower realised what had been going on. He plucked at Essen's sleeve.

"They were destroying their guns over there," he said. "They are firing some shots at us while at each salvo they fire a shot against the trunnions of one of the guns. There were four guns over there, Your Excellency. Now—see—there are only two."

"Possibly," admitted Essen, staring into the darkness.

"The firing is dying away," agreed Clausewitz, "but perhaps they are only growing tired of wasting ammunition."

There was only one flash from the battery next time, and there was something clearly odd about it.

"The last gun in the battery," commented Essen. "Probably they have burst it by overloading."

He trained his telescope in the darkness.

"Look over there at their main camps," he added. "Watch those fires. They seem to be burning brightly, but—"

Hornblower directed his gaze to the distant rows of campfires, sparkling very dimly in the thick night. He looked backwards and forwards along one of the rows, trying to keep track of them all. He thought he saw one fire wink and go out, but he could not be sure. His eyes were watering with the cold and with the strain, and as he rubbed them Essen shut his telescope with a snap.

"They are dying down," he said. "I'm sure of it, and no troops would allow their camp-fires to die down on a night like this. Clausewitz, get your men ready to attack again. Diebitsch—"

The governor began rapping out orders. Hornblower had a momentary feeling of pity for the Russian soldiers, huddled in their freezing trenches, dispirited by their recent repulse and losses, now ordered to go out again to what would seem to them to be certain disaster in the night. The wind suddenly shrieked down upon them, piercing him to the bone, despite the cloak he clutched round himself.

"'Ere you are, sir," said Brown's voice unexpectedly in his ear. "I've brought you up a blanket. Let's put it round you under your cloak. And 'ere's your gloves, sir."

Deftly in the darkness Brown draped the blanket over him, so that his cloak held it down over his shoulders. It would look fantastic in the daylight, but fortunately it was still dark. Hornblower was shivering, and he stamped his frozen feet in an endeavour to warm them.

"Aren't those men of yours *ever* going to attack, Clausewitz?" grumbled Essen. "What's the time? One o'clock? Send down to your brigadier and tell him I'll have him cashiered if he does not pull his men together for an immediate advance."

There was a long freezing interval, before the darkness in front of them was pricked by a few little pin points of flame—musket shots in the second parallel.

"Ha!" said Essen.

There was another long wait before the message came back. The sortie had found the advanced trenches abandoned save for a few posts. They were pushing forward now through the snow and the darkness towards the main camp.

"They're going, then," said Essen. "Have the cavalry paraded two hours before dawn. I'll catch their rear-guard at daylight. I want all troops across the river then. And now a glass of tea, for the love of God."

Warming himself at the fire burning on the flagged floor of the church, drinking hot tea through his chattering teeth, Hornblower looked round at these men of iron who showed no sign of fatigue and hardly any of cold. He himself was too chilled, and, oddly, too fatigued, to gain much benefit from the chance of resting for a couple of hours on the trusses of straw laid out beside the high altar, but Essen snored volcanically until the moment when his aide-de-camp shook him awake. Outside it was still dark, and colder than ever, when the horses were brought up to the church door for them to mount.

"I better come with you, sir," said Brown. "I got myself a 'orse."

How Brown had done that Hornblower could not imagine, seeing the difficulties of language. Hornblower supposed Brown had learned to ride in those incredibly distant days at Smallbridge. The cavalcade moved slowly in the darkness towards the Mitau suburb, the horses slipping and stumbling in the snow; Hornblower found himself wishing he had been able to retain his blanket when he mounted, for it was colder than ever in the faint grey light. Suddenly from far ahead of them came a sullen flat thud, and another, and another—field guns firing a long way off.

"Diebitsch is up to their rear-guard," said Essen. "Good!"

There was enough light now to reveal the desolation of their surroundings as they approached the deserted siege works. They could look down into the littered trenches; there were the batteries, with the

299

shattered siege guns standing drunkenly at the embrasures, and here was a dead horse, lying on its back, its belly shrouded with snow, out of which its legs pointed stiffly at the grey sky. And here was the main camp, rows and rows of little huts, mostly only two or three feet high, with the dead remains of camp-fires already buried in snow. Outside one hut, larger than the others, lay a soldier swathed in the grey capote of the French Army. He was face downwards and not dead, for they saw his feet move.

"Have they been fighting here?" conjectured Essen, puzzled; there was no sign of blood.

Someone dismounted and turned him over; his face was mottled with mulberry-coloured marks, and his eyes, though open, were unseeing.

"Keep away!" shouted one of the aides-de-camp suddenly. "That is the plague!"

Everyone drew away from the dying man, and then they realised that the plague was all around them. One of the huts was full of dead, another was full of the dying. Essen shook his horse into a trot, and the party jingled away.

"It is in our ranks already," said Essen to Hornblower. "Kladoff had ten cases in his division two days ago."

This, the first march in retreat of the invading army, was already finding out the weaklings. There were dead men, sick men, dying men alongside the track they were following, despite the fact that no fighting had taken place along it—Diebitsch at the head of the pursuing force was on the Mitau road away on the left front, where the guns were still firing occasionally. When at last they reached the point where the track joined the high-road the signs of real fighting began—dead and wounded soldiers, Russian, French, and German, where the Russian advanced guard had clashed with the rear-guard. Then they caught up with the Russian columns plodding sturdily up the road, and trotted past their interminable length, one division and then another; the men were silent with the exertion of stepping out as fast as their legs would carry them under their heavy knapsacks, and this ten miles of fast marching had greatly modified the first jubilation of pursuit.

"Macdonald has made a good retreat," said Clausewitz, "at the cost of leaving his sick and his guns behind. I wonder how long he will be able to keep this pace up?"

Hornblower did not trouble to enter into the discussion. Saddle soreness was making him abstracted, apart from his fatigue and his general feeling of *malaise*. But he had to be able to report to his government that he had followed up the retreating army for at least one march on its way back to Germany; it would be better if it were two or three. And there was something else. He wanted to catch up with the Prussians, even if it were the last thing he did—and it was odd that he had this feeling that it was the last thing he was ever going to do. His head was whirling, and there was something comforting about the knowledge that Brown was just back there with the mounted orderlies.

A messenger brought back news from the advanced guard, and Hornblower heard Clausewitz' explanation as if in a dream.

"The Prussians are making a stand at the fork in the roads ahead," he said. "They are covering the retreat while the other two army corps get away by the two roads."

It was strange that this was just what he was expecting, as if it were a story he had already heard being retold.

"The Prussians!" he said, and without willing it he pressed his legs against his horse's sides to urge it to a faster pace, towards the flat reports of the guns which showed where the Prussians were holding back the advanced guard. The headquarters party was clear of the main body now, trotting along the deeply rutted road, hemmed in here by a dense wood of coniferous trees. Beyond the wood the desolate landscape opened up to reveal a low ridge up which the road mounted ahead of them. On either side of the road here a brigade of the Russian advance guard was halted, a battery of artillery was in action, and up on the ridge could be seen the Prussian infantry columns, black blocks against grey fields. Over on the right a grey-clad Russian column was plodding across country to turn the flank of the position, while between the two forces Russian horsemen—Cossacks—trotted in ones and twos on their shaggy ponies, their long lances vertical at their sides. A watery sun broke through the clouds at this moment, seeming merely to accentuate the gloominess of the landscape. A general came up to salute Essen, but Hornblower did not want to listen to what he had to say. He wanted to press forward towards the Prussians, and as the horses of the party followed the example of his own they moved steadily up the road, Essen half-unconscious of the movements of his horse as he listened to the general's report. He was only recalled to his surroundings by the howl of a cannon shot which pitched at the roadside near him, throwing snow and earth in all directions.

"What do we think we're doing?" he asked. "We'll be getting ourselves shot in a moment."

Hornblower was staring forward at the Prussian army, at the glitter of bayonets and the flags black against the snow.

"I want to go up to the Prussians," he said.

The discharge of the battery close at hand drowned the words Essen said in reply, but what he meant to say was plain enough.

"I am going," said Hornblower stubbornly. He looked round and caught Clausewitz' eye. "Are you coming too, Colonel?"

"Of course he cannot," expostulated Essen. "He cannot risk being taken."

302

As a renegade, a man fighting against his own country, Clausewitz was likely to be hanged if ever the Prussians laid hands on him.

"It would be better if he came," said Hornblower, woodenly. This was a strange feeling of simultaneous clairvoyance and illness.

"I'll go with the commodore," said Clausewitz suddenly, making what was probably the bravest decision of his life. Perhaps he was carried away by Hornblower's automation-like recklessness.

Essen shrugged his shoulders at this madness which had descended upon them.

"Go, then," he said. "Perhaps I may be able to capture enough generals to exchange for you."

They trotted forward up the road; Hornblower heard Essen bellow an order to the battery commander to cease fire. He looked back; Brown was trotting after them, a respectful five lengths behind. They passed close to some of the Cossack light horse, who looked at them curiously, and then they were in among Prussian skirmishers, who, from the shelter of bushes and inequalities in the ground, were taking long shots at the Cossacks. No one fired at them as they rode boldly through. A Prussian captain beside the road saluted them, and Clausewitz returned the salute. Just beyond the skirmishing line was the first formed infantry, a Prussian regiment in battalion columns of companies, two on one side of the road and one on the other. The colonel and his staff were standing in the road staring at the odd trio approaching them—the British naval officer in his blue and gold, Clausewitz in his Russian uniform with the row of medals, and the British seaman with cutlass and pistols at his belt. The colonel asked a question in a loud dry tone as they approached, and Clausewitz answered it, reining in.

"Tell them we must see the general," said Hornblower in French to Clausewitz.

There was a rapid exchange of dialogue between

Clausewitz and the colonel, ending in the latter's calling up two or three mounted officers—his adjutant and majors, perhaps—to accompany them up the road. Here they saw a larger infantry force formed up, and a line of guns, and here was a party on horseback, the feathers and braid and medals and mounted orderlies indicating the presence of a general's staff. This must be the general—Yorck, Hornblower remembered his name to be. He recognised Clausewitz at once, and addressed him abruptly in German. A few words on each side seemed only to add to the tension of the situation, and there was a short pause.

"He speaks French," said Clausewitz to Hornblower, and they both turned and waited for him to speak.

"General," said Hornblower; he was in a dream, but he made himself speak in his dream. "I represent the King of England, and Colonel Clausewitz represents the Emperor of Russia. We are fighting to free Europe from Bonaparte. Are you fighting to maintain him as a tyrant?"

It was a rhetorical question to which no answer was possible. Silent perforce, Yorck could only await the rest of what Hornblower had to say.

"Bonaparte is beaten. He is retreating from Moscow, and not ten thousand of his army will reach Germany. The Spaniards have deserted him, as you know. So have the Portuguese. All Europe is turning upon him, having found out how little his promises mean. You know of his treatment of Germany—I need not tell you about that. If you fight for him you may keep him on his tottering throne for a few days longer. You may drag out Germany's agony by that length of time. But your duty is to your enslaved country, to your King who is a prisoner. You can free them. You can end the useless pouring out of the blood of your men now, at this moment."

Yorck looked away from him, over the bleak country-side, at the Russian army slowly deploying, before he replied.

"What do you suggest?" he said.

That was all Hornblower wanted to hear. If Yorck was willing to ask questions, instead of immediately making prisoners of them, the matter was as good as settled. He could leave the discussion to Clausewitz, and sink back into the dream which was rising round him like a tide. He brought Clausewitz into the conversation with a glance.

"An armistice," said Clausewitz. "An immediate suspension of hostilities. The definitive terms can be settled easily enough at leisure."

Yorck still hesitated for a moment. Hornblower, despite his weariness and illness, could study him with a renewed flicker of interest—the hard face, sunburned to mahogany, the white hair and moustache in strange contrast. Yorck was on the edge of his fate. At present he was a loyal subject of the King of Prussia, a comparatively undistinguished general. He had only to say two words, and they would make him a traitor now and conceivably a historic figure in the future. Prussia's defection—at any rate, the defection of the Prussian army—would reveal the hollowness of the Napoleonic Empire in a way nothing else could do. It rested with Yorck.

"I agree," said Yorck.

That was all Hornblower wanted to hear. He could lapse into his dream—his nightmare—now, let the rest of the discussion take whatever course it would. When Clausewitz turned back down the road Hornblower's horse followed him without any guidance from Hornblower. Brown appeared, just his face; there was nothing else that Hornblower could see.

"Are you all right, sir?"

"Of course I am," said Hornblower automatically.

The earth that Hornblower found himself treading was soft, as though he were walking on feather beds or on a loosely stretched bit of sailcloth. It might be better to lie down. And Hornblower was suddenly conscious that there was something beautiful about music after all. He had gone all his life thinking that it was only an irritating muddle of noises, but revelation had come to him at last. It was lovely, ecstatic, this music that he heard, peals and peals of it, great soaring melodies. He had to raise up his voice to join in with it, to sing and sing and sing. And then the music ended in a final crashing chord, leaving a silence in which his voice sounded hoarse, like a crow's. He stopped, feeling rather embarrassed. It was as well that somebody else was available to take up the song. The boatman was singing as he pulled his sculls.

"Row, row, row you together to Hampton Court—"

A delightful tenor voice; on account of it Hornblower was ready to excuse the wherryman for such an impertinence as singing while he rowed up the river.

"Rowing in sunshiny weather—"

Barbara beside him was laughing deliciously. The sunshine was beautiful and so were the green lawns on the river-banks. He had to laugh too, laugh and laugh. And here was little Richard climbing over his knees. What the devil was Brown doing, staring at him like this?

Chapter XXIV

CHURCH BELLS were jangling and Hornblower lay and listened to them. It was not a noise that usually brought any gratification to his tone-deaf ear, but now he was content to lie and listen to it with vague satisfaction. He was not even sure at first that he was listening to church bells; he was not sure of anything. His mind, as he listened, filled with memories of other vague noises which he seemed to have heard lately, undercurrents of sound acting as accompaniments to some main motive which was not plain in his mind. He could remember the peal upon peal of guns, and then the monotonous beat of horses' hoofs, and then the interminable squeaking of wheels; but he was too comfortable and peaceful to try to sort these memories out. Brown's face kept appearing and disappearing through the mental pictures, and then other strange faces, and then horrible gloomy memories like thunderclouds on the horizon.

But those really were church bells to which he was listening, jangling away as if in a world at peace. At peace! That was something to think about. Church bells would never ring like that except in a place where there was no war. He must be somewhere on land far from any fighting. And this cool delightful thing under his chin was a linen sheet, and here under his head was a feather pillow in a linen pillowcase, and he stretched out his legs languorously and luxuriously in the dawning knowledge that he lay in a feather bed. His eyes began to focus; above him was the gilded canopy superbly carved, but the green silk curtains were not drawn and he could look out from his bed into the room. There were some impressive articles of furniture there, desks and tables and chairs and couches, all gilded and carved and inlaid with tortoise shell and brass. The walls were hung with a red and gold tapestry wherein horsemen in three-cornered hats sounded horns and followed a pack of hounds after a stag. It could hardly be less than a palace he was in, and although Hornblower, with an effort, realised that his last exact memory was of a bleak hillside patched with snow he was much too comfortable to attempt to explain the transition to himself. He shut his eyes on the buhl furniture and dozed off again.

Later he woke to a slight noise to find Brown standing hesitating by the bed with a tray in his hand, obviously in two minds about whether to disturb him or not. Similarly Hornblower was at first in two minds about whether to let him go or not, until he found himself to be so acutely hungry that there was nothing that he would have disliked more than to let that steaming tray disappear from his sight. He struggled to sit up while Brown put the tray down on the bedside table. Then Brown put a firm arm behind his back to support him while with the other hand he presented a spoonful of what seemed extraordinarily delicious broth to Hornblower's lips. Hornblower sucked it down thirstily, looked for more, and then, not satisfied with the slow rate of spoon feeding, reached out for the cup. Brown held it to his lips indulgently and the delicious life-giving stuff ran warmly down into Hornblower's interior. He remembered to be nonchalant as he looked about him and spoke.

"I suppose this is a palace?" he said—his voice sounded odd and childlike in his ears.

"Yes, sir," said Brown, "the King of Prussia's palace."

"Where?"

"Königsberg, sir."

There was a good deal to digest in that information. If he were a prisoner he would not be in a state bedroom. So the King of Prussia must have changed sides, following the example of his army. There was something else he must know at once, with the immediate instinctive reaction of the naval officer.

"Is the harbour frozen?" he asked.

"Not yet, sir. There's just a scum of ice."

Of course Königsberg would freeze a good deal later than Riga, which was both farther north and farther up the Baltic. That suggested the next question.

"Where's the squadron?"

"It sailed for home, sir, under Cap'n Bush's orders, after you was certified too ill to command. But *Clam's* just come in with despatches, sir."

"Has she, by God!"

All sense of languor and comfort disappeared; all his restless spirit reasserted itself. He made to throw off the bedclothes and climb out of bed.

"Easy, sir, easy," protested Brown, replacing the bedclothes, and somehow it seemed better to yield to him and sink back again. But he could still give orders.

"My compliments to the captain of the *Clam* and I'd like him to visit me at his earliest convenience."

"Aye aye, sir. And I'll have the doctor come in to you, sir."

"You'll do what you're told."

"Aye aye, sir."

Still delaying, Brown picked up and comb and a hand mirror; the latter he put into Hornblower's hand while he passed a comb through Hornblower's hair. Hornblower glanced into the mirror and recoiled with surprise.

"Good God!" he said, the exclamation torn from him despite his self-control.

A wildly hairy face gibbered at him from the glass, bristle-bearded to the eyes. The inch-long hairs seemed all to be sticking straight out from his face. He looked like a baboon. Curiosity overcame him sufficiently to make him look more closely. There were grey hairs among the brown, making him in his own eyes more obscene than ever. The lofty expanse of bare forehead added to this effect. He had no idea he could look so hideous.

"How long has this been going on?" he demanded.

"Nigh on four weeks, sir."

"Get me a barber at once, before Mr. Freeman comes in."

"Aye aye, sir. Mr. Freeman, a barber, and the doctor, sir."

There was no use arguing with Brown. The first person to come in was the doctor, whose sword and cocked hat indicated that he was a court official. He talked to Hornblower in barbarous French, hauled up his nightshirt with hands whose nails bore black semicircles, and laid his ear on Hornblower's chest. Hornblower caught a glimpse before the bedclothes were replaced of his prominent ribs, and belly fallen away to nothing. His thighs and legs were like sticks.

"What has been the matter with me?" asked Hornblower.

"The typhus," said the doctor.

The typhus. Gaol fever. The scourge of armies and fleets.

"You have lived through it," said the doctor; "others have died. Thousands. Tens of thousands."

From the doctor's lips Hornblower heard a little of the story of the contending armies on their frightful march from Moscow back across Poland; how hunger and cold and disease had slain the Grand Army—and the Russian army as well—until at this present moment only a few thousand Frenchmen out of the half million who had started were still on their feet plodding back towards Germany. All East Prussia, every part of Germany not held down by a Napoleonic garrison, was in a fever of revolt.

"Then my work is done here," said Hornblower. "I must return to England."

"In two months' time, perhaps," said the doctor.

"Tomorrow," said Hornblower.

The barber was both cleaner in his person and more efficient at his business than the doctor. He clipped off Hornblower's beard and then shaved him. The keen edge of the razor felt delightful against his cheeks. With a flourish the barber held the mirror for Hornblower to see. It was something like the old face that Hornblower remembered, but still very different. For the first time in twenty years the sunburn had disappeared, leaving him a prison pallor which combined with his sunken cheeks to throw his jaws and cheekbones into unwonted prominence. The last time he had looked he thought he looked like a baboon, but now he thought he looked like a death's-head.

Freeman came rolling in, short and square and swarthy, his long hair hanging in greasy curls over his collar.

"What are your orders?" demanded Hornblower, cutting short Freeman's anxious questionings.

"To sail for any home port for which the wind may serve, sir," was the reply. "I am to wait for despatches as long as I can without risking being frozen in, and then—Leith, Yarmouth, or Sheerness, sir."

"Will you have room for an invalid?"

"Of course, sir. But—"

Brown and the doctor had obviously warned Freeman that this was what Hornblower would ask. Hornblower swept aside Freeman's protests.

"You will take me back with you," he said. "Those are my orders, personally given, and you disobey them at your peril. Have you heard them?"

It was pleasant to give orders like that, even though it was not so pleasant, afterwards, to sink back on his pillow when he was alone again, and to find himself weak and almost lightheaded with the effort. He was still weak two days later when they put him on a stretcher, spread a great bearskin rug over him, and carried him down a tortuous staircase out into the courtyard and down to the quay. A wagon creaked and groaned past them on their way, its piled-up load concealed by a tarpaulin, but from under the tarpaulin, over the side of the wagon dangled a naked human arm. Brown, who was supervising the carrying of the stretcher, tried to interpose his burly figure between Hornblower's eyes and the wagon, but too late.

"The death cart, I suppose," said Hornblower;

despite the horror of the sight it was well to show Brown that he was not as clever as he wanted to be.

"That's so, sir," said Brown, "they're still dyin' in thousands."

Freeman had had the after hatch enlarged and the companion removed, and they lowered Hornblower, stretcher and all, down below with a whip rove through the main topping-lift block. It was a giddy moment as he swung up from the quay, and when he found himself safely in the cabin Hornblower was content to lie back and let the official farewells pass unregarded over his head. Excitement was exhausting, but he could not help feeling keenly pleasurable anticipation as he heard the bustle when *Clam* cast off and warped away from the quay. The southwesterly wind was not quite foul for Pillau and the open sea; lying in his cot Hornblower could feel each time the *Clam* went about as she made first a long board and then a short board, beating down the channel. The boom which had guarded the entrance to the Haff, on which he had climbed so long ago—in another existence it seemed—had been removed now that Prussia was England's ally, and *Clam* was able to pass the entrance before nightfall and start the long beat down the Baltic. Even though the wind stayed foul and they had to beat about off Malmo for two mortal days before they got a slant of wind to carry them down The Sound, Hornblower refused to allow himself to fret. Sweden was England's firm ally now, and there was no danger to be anticipated as they kept to the Swedish side. As they ran for The Skaw he had himself helped on deck and was able to sit in a chair, enveloped in the bearskin rug, in the bleak wintry day, smiling secretly at Freeman's nervousness at having to handle his ship under the eye of a commodore. Beyond The Skaw a northerly gale was waiting for them, blowing freezing from the Norwegian uplands, and sent them flying homeward triplereefed. Before it blew itself out they had to lie-to for half a day, and then it backed round westerly.

"We're bearing up for Sheerness, sir," reported Freeman.

"Very good," said Hornblower, and that was when the first great thrill of excitement surged up in his strengthening body. For all of the places in England which the *Clam* could have reached Sheerness was the nearest to Smallbridge. Smallbridge, where Barbara was waiting, and where Richard was making mud pies in the shrubbery. It was eight months since he had seen them last.

It was eight months since he had seen England; it seemed like a dream as he sat under his bearskin rug and saw the grey sands and then the low green hills of the Essex shore. It was logical, as in a dream, that a fortunate slant of wind should carry them up with the tides of Sheerness, and that in the nick of time, under the urging of Freeman, the hands were able to sweep her in round Garrison Point to the dockyard, where the smoke rose hazily from the chimneys of Blue Town. It was even logical that the admiral—Sir Dennis Clough, Vice Admiral of the Red—should come down to greet him the moment he heard of his presence on board, and should offer him hospitality for that night.

Sitting up at the admiral's big mahogany table was a little tiring, and while this feeling of being in a dream persisted it was not easy to pretend an interest in the admiral's professional conversation, even though it was directed to matters that most intimately concerned him. Clough was delicately complimentary about Hornblower's exploits in the Baltic; he spoke about the tide of war sweeping back across the continent, and discussed the chances of the allies being in Paris before midsummer.

"That fellow Braun they saddled you with turned out a pretty bad character," said Clough, lifting a white eyebrow at Hornblower across the table.

"Yes," said Hornblower noncommittally.

"If you'd come home two months ago you'd have seen the last of him as you came in. His bones only fell apart a few weeks back."

Hornblower looked a question.

"They hanged him on Execution Point," explained the admiral. "We had him there for a couple of months, and he'd have lasted longer than that if they'd tarred him properly."

"We were short of Stockholm tar at that time, until Hornblower brought Sweden in on our side," chuckled one of the captains lower down the table.

It was a harsh world, as Hornblower assured himself for the ten thousandth time in his life. He still thought it harsh in the bleak grey morning, despite the admiral's kindness in lending him his own barge to take him up to Rochester. The busy Medway was chill and grey, and even Brown's concealed excitement did not seem to affect Hornblower as they threaded their way through the lively shipping.

"Thirty miles from Smallbridge, sir," said Brown as they stepped on shore.

That was as it should be, something destiny had preordained. It was market day in the town, and the streets were crowded as they walked slowly to the Crown. Hornblower sat over the fire in the coffee room with the conversation of garrulous farmers surging round him while Brown was hiring the postchaise. Then they clattered out over the cobbles, up the great road between the wintry fields.

The lodge-keeper who opened the gates stood with gaping mouth at the sight of Hornblower, but his surprise was nothing compared with that of Wiggins when he threw open the door in answer to Brown's thundering upon it. He could not even say a word but stood yammering before he drew aside to admit his master. There was the sound of singing in the hall, which was gay with holly and bright with candles.

Apparently Barbara was entertaining the village carol singers.

"Glad ti—idings of com—fort and joy," sang the carolers.

There was a rush of feet, and here was Barbara, and Barbara's arms were about his neck and Barbara's lips were upon his. And here came Richard, his steps hesitating a little, big-eyed and solemn and shy at the sight of this strange father of his. Hornblower caught him up in his arms, and Richard continued to inspect him solemnly at close range.

"Glad tidings of comfort and joy," said Barbara, her hand on his arm.

THE END